D0379517

stargazey point

Also by Shelley Noble

Beach Colors

stargazey point

SHELLEY NOBLE

WILLIAM MORROW
An Imprint of HarperCollins*Publishers*

This book is a work of fiction. The characters, incidents, and dialogue are drawn from the author's imagination and are not to be construed as real. Any resemblance to actual events or persons, living or dead, is entirely coincidental.

STARGAZEY POINT. Copyright © 2013 by Shelley Freydont. All rights reserved. Printed in the United States of America. No part of this book may be used or reproduced in any manner whatsoever without written permission except in the case of brief quotations embodied in critical articles and reviews. For information address HarperCollins Publishers, 10 East 53rd Street, New York, NY 10022.

HarperCollins books may be purchased for educational, business, or sales promotional use. For information please write: Special Markets Department, HarperCollins Publishers, 10 East 53rd Street, New York, NY 10022.

FIRST EDITION

Designed by Diahann Sturge

Library of Congress Cataloging-in-Publication Data has been applied for.

ISBN 978-0-06-225834-2

13 14 15 16 17   OV/RRD   10 9 8 7 6 5 4 3

To my grandmothers, Minnie and Letty, strong Southern women with staunch opinions, steadfast loyalties, and zest for life

Acknowledgments

As always thanks to my agent, Kevan Lyon, and to my editor, Tessa Woodward, and to the HarperCollins art department for another wonderful cover.

I spent many happy and informative hours reading Deborah Lange's *Restoring the Glen Echo Park Carousel,* an inspiration for anyone who loves historic carousels and is interested in learning about the work that goes into keeping them "alive" for a new generation.

A special thanks to all those who came to our aid when Sandy gave us firsthand experience of the devastation left in the wake of a hurricane. Little did I know while writing *Stargazey Point* that we would soon have so much in common with my fictional little South Carolina town still rebuilding many years later.

And three cheers to the Floyd L. Moreland Dentzel/Looff Carousel in Seaside Heights, New Jersey. May you ride again.

stargazey
point

Prologue

Even when the carousel music slowly wobbled to silence, Cab could still hear it playing inside his head. Sometimes he heard it in his dreams, and he and Midnight Lady would gallop over the sand, wild like the wind—his uncle Ned had read that from a book once, *wild like the wind*.

His uncle locked up the carousel, stuck the cash box under his arm, and came to stand beside him. "Tired, son?"

"No, sir," Cab said, stifling a yawn.

"It's a mighty fine night, ain't it?"

Cab nodded. Stargazey Point was just about the best place in the world. Like living in a carnival.

Uncle Ned said good night to the women closing up the community store. They were going home for the night, but out on the pier people played the arcades and ate cotton candy and drank lemonade. If he listened real hard, Cab could hear music coming from the pavilion out at the end, where the grown-ups would be dancing to a real live band.

Ned put his arm around Cab's shoulders. "Time we were getting home. Have us some leftover barbecue and get to bed."

They walked away from the beach, the lights, and the sounds and into the night. They were halfway home when Uncle Ned stopped in the middle of the dark street. "Look up at the sky, Cab."

Cab did. The sky was black and there were more stars than you could ever count. He sighed. School would be starting soon, and he'd have to leave his uncle for another year. He didn't want to go; he didn't like boarding school, and everyone here was nice.

"I wish I could stay in Stargazey Point forever."

"Maybe you will one day. It's a magical place, sure enough. It can mend your heart, make you strong, and show you the way to follow your dream. You remember that, Cab. There's not a better place in the whole world than right here at the Point."

Chapter 1

Hate. How many times a day did that word come up in conversation. *I hate these shoes with this outfit. I hate Jell-O with fruit.* People laugh and say *I hate it when that happens.* Hate could be a joke. Or an all-consuming fire that singed your spirit before eating your soul.

Abbie Sinclair had seen it in all its forms. Okay, maybe not all, and for that she was thankful, but in too many forms to process, to turn a cold eye, to keep plugging away in spite of it all.

A sad commentary on someone who had just turned thirty. Somehow, Abbie thought that the big three-oh would set her free, leave the crushed, dispirited twenties behind. But as the therapist told her during her first session, she wouldn't be able to go forward until she came to terms with her past. She didn't go back—to the therapist or the past.

So here she was five thousand feet above Indiana, Kentucky, or some other state on her way from Chicago to South Carolina, thinking about hate instead of worrying about what to have for dessert instead of Jell-O or what shoes *would* go with this outfit.

Abbie knew she had to jettison her hate or it would destroy

her. But no matter how many times she'd written the word, torn the paper into little strips, shredded it, burned it, ran water over it until it disintegrated, stepped on it—no matter how many times she'd symbolically thrown it away, forced it out of her heart—there seemed to be just a little left, and it would grow back, like pus in an infected wound.

Pus? Really? Had she really just made that analogy? Abbie pressed her fingers to her temples. The absolute lowest. Purple prose. Bad writing and ineffective emotion, something her mentor and lover insisted had no place in cutting-edge documentaries. Something her post-flower-child mother insisted had no place anywhere in life. And something that her best friend, Celeste, said was just plain tacky.

Besides, it didn't come close to what she really felt.

Abbie had been full of fire when she started out. She'd planned to expose the evils of the world, do her part in righting injustice, make people understand and change. The Sinclairs' youngest daughter would finally join the ranks of her do-gooding family. Instead, that fire had turned inward and was destroying her. How arrogant and naive she had been. How easily she'd lost hope.

"Don't be so hard on yourself," Celeste said when Abbie showed up at her apartment with one jungle-rotted duffel bag and a bucketful of tears. "You can probably get your old job back. Want me to ask?"

Abbie just wanted to sleep, except with sleep came dreams peopled by the dead, asking why, why, why of the living.

They decided what she needed was a change of scene. At least that's what Celeste decided. Somewhere comfortable with people who were kind. Celeste knew just the place. With her relatives in a South Carolina beach town named Stargazey Point.

"You'll like it there," Celeste said. "And you'll love Aunt Marnie and Aunt Millie and Uncle Beau. They're really my

great or maybe it's my great-great . . . but they're sweethearts
and they'd love to have you."

It did sound good: quiet, peace, sun, and surf. "I'll go,"
Abbie said.

She was a basket case. She needed therapy. She went on vacation instead.

Celeste drove her to O'Hare. "You'll have to take a cab from
the airport. I don't think they drive anymore. It'll take about
forty minutes if there's no traffic and costs about sixty dollars.
Here." She thrust a handful of bills at Abbie then tried to take
her coat. "You won't need it there."

Abbie refused the money and clung to her coat; she didn't
need it. That burning emotion she couldn't kill was enough to
keep her warm on the coldest day.

There was a mini bottle of unopened chardonnay on the
tray table before her. She was still clutching her coat.

She wasn't ordinarily a slow learner. And she usually didn't
run. That had changed in a heartbeat. And that's when the hate
rushed in.

She hated the company whose arrogance had washed away
an entire schoolroom of children and the boy and his donkey,
hated the security people who had smashed their cameras,
hated those who stood by and watched or ran in terror, who
dragged her away when she was only trying to save someone,
anyone. Those who arrested Werner and threw him in a jail
where he met with an "unfortunate accident."

For that she hated them most of all. Selfish, but there it was.
They had killed Werner on top of everything else.

And there was not a damn thing she could do about it. There
was no footage, no Werner; she'd barely escaped before they
confiscated her visa. Others weren't so lucky.

The tears started, but she forced them back. How could she
allow herself tears when everyone else had suffered more?

She should be here any minute now, Sister, and you haven't gotten out the tea service. Do you think it's goin' to polish itself? And look how you're dressed."

Marnie Crispin glanced down at her dungarees and the old white T-shirt that Beau had put out for the veterans' box, then looked at her younger sister and sighed. Millie was dressed in a floral print shirtwaist that had to be twenty years old but was pressed like it had just come off the rack at Belks Department Store.

"I know how I'm dressed; the garden doesn't weed itself. I'm planning to change. And I'm not getting out the tea service."

"But, Sister."

"You don't want to scare the girl away, do you?"

"No," said Millie, patting at the white wisps of hair that framed her thin face. "But she's come all the way from Chicago, poor thing. And I want everything to be just perfect for her. Beau, you're droppin' shavings all over my carpet."

Their younger brother, who would turn seventy-nine in two months, was sitting in his favorite chintz-covered chair, the ubiquitous block of wood and his pocketknife in hand. He looked down at his feet and the curls of wood littered there.

"Oh." He attempted to push them under the chair with the side of his boot.

"How many times have I told you not to drop shavings on my carpet?"

Beau rocked forward and pushed himself to his feet.

"Where do you think you're going?"

Beau looked down at the carving in his hand, back at Millie. "Going to watch out for that taxicab from the front porch."

Millie pursed her lips, but there was no rancor in it. Beau was Beau and they loved him. "Just you mind you don't drop shavings all over my porch."

Beau shuffled out of the room.

"And tuck that shirttail in," Millie called after him.

Cabot Reynolds heard the car go by. They didn't get much sightseeing this time of year, a few fishermen, an occasional antiquer, a handful of die-hard sun worshippers, though most of them preferred the more upscale hotels of Myrtle Beach.

There were a few year-round residents and hearing a car wasn't all that unusual. In the year he'd lived here, he'd come to recognize the characteristic sound of just about every car, truck, and motorcycle in the area. And he didn't recognize the one that had just passed. Which could only mean one thing.

Wiping his hands on a well-used chamois, he climbed over the engine housing and looked out between the broken lattice of the window. Whoever it was had come and gone.

He tossed the chamois on his worktable, lifted his keys off the peg by the door, and stopped to look around as he did at the end of every workday. For a full minute he just stood and breathed in the faint odor of machine oil, mildew, and childhood memories.

He tried to imagine the time when he'd stop for the day, look up, and see all the work he'd put into the old derelict building gleaming back at him; the colored lights refracting off the restored mirrors bursting into fractured reds, blues, and yellows, while music swirled around his head and the smell of fresh sawdust curled in his nostrils.

So far he only saw a dark almost empty room, locked away from the world by a sagging plywood door. Right now he only saw how much more there was to do. But never once since he'd returned had he ever looked over the space and thought, *What the hell have I done?*

Cabot padlocked the door, then crossed the street to Hadley's, the local grocery store, bait shop, and gas station. He jogged up the wooden steps to the porch and was just pulling a Coke out of the old metal ice chest when Silas Cook came out the door, a string bag of crabs slung over his shoulder. He dropped the bag into a bucket of water and sat down on the steps. Cab sat down beside him and took a long swig from the bottle of Coke.

"You see that taxicab drive through town awhile back?" Silas asked.

"I heard it. Did you?"

"Sure did. Me and Hadley came right out here on the porch and watched it drive by."

"See the passenger?"

"A girl come all the way from Chicag-ah."

Cabot nodded. Like Chicago was the end of the earth.

"You goin' on over there?" asked Silas, nodding down the street toward the old Crispin House.

"After I get cleaned up. I finagled myself an invitation to dinner."

"Well, you in luck there, 'cause I just dropped off a dozen of the finest lady blue claws you'll see this season. Told Ervina she oughta just drop em in the pot but Miss Millie, she want crab bisque. So she make crab bisque."

Cabot leaned back and rested his elbows on the top step. "Fine dining and a chance to get a good, close look at the Crispins' guest. Find out just what she's up to."

"What do you think she's up to? She's a friend of their niece's, like they said, come on vacation."

"Maybe. But what do we know about their niece? They haven't seen her in years. Maybe she sees a gold mine waiting to be exploited."

Silas pushed to his feet and looked down at Cab. "Go on, Mr. Cab. You don't trust much of nobody, do you?"

Cabot was taken aback. "Why do you say that? I trust you, and Hadley, and Beau and . . ."

"I mean other people."

"Sure I do."

"You more protective of this town than folks who've lived here all their lives, and their daddies and granddaddies, too."

"You gotta protect what's yours, you should know that, Silas."

"Yessuh, I know it. And I learnt it the hard way. I just don't get why you know it. Well, I'd best be getting these gals in my own pot." Silas started down the steps; when he got to the bottom, he turned back to Cabot. "You tell Mr. Beau, I'm going out fishin' tomorrah if he wanna come."

"I will." Cabot gave the older man a quick salute and finished his Coke while he watched Silas walk down the street. Then he went inside to pay for his drink.

"One Co-cola," Hadley said, punching the keys of an ancient cash register. "You see Silas outside?"

"Yeah," Cab said. "I'm getting crab bisque at the Crispins' tonight."

"Did he also tell you we seen their visitor?"

"Yep."

"She was a pretty thing as far as I could see. Pale as a ghost though, even her hair, kinda whitelike. She looked out of the window just as she passed by and I swear it was like she looked right into me. It was kinda spooky."

"Spooky or speculative? Like someone planning to cheat the Crispins out of their house and land?"

"Don't know about that. Silas says they're expecting her. Friend of their great-niece's or some such."

"Maybe," Cabot agreed. "I'll keep an eye on her."

"Know you will, son. Know you will."

Cabot walked home, thinking about the Crispins and his uncle Ned, who was the reason he was here. Or at least the reason that brought him to Stargazey Point this last time. Ned had died and left Cabot everything.

He'd hardly seen his uncle since he'd graduated from high school over fifteen years ago. But before that, he'd spent every summer with Ned, working long hours at the now defunct boardwalk.

He'd driven over from Atlanta to settle Ned's estate. It wasn't much, the old octagonal building, a small tin-roofed cottage in the backside of town. And the contents of a shed situated inland and watched over by an ancient Gullah man named Abraham.

That discovery had sealed his fate. The memories of the magical summers he'd spent with Ned broke through the high-pressured, high-tech world he inhabited, and he knew he had to recapture that magic. He gave up his "promising" career as an industrial architect for an uncertain future. Traded his minimalist-designed, state-of-the-art apartment for a rotten porch, broken windows, and peeling paint.

According to his Atlanta colleagues, he'd lost his mind.

When he asked his fiancée, Bailey, to move to Stargazey Point with him, she accused him of playing Peter Pan. Just before she threw her two-karat engagement ring at his head.

Peter Pan or crazy, he didn't care. He was working longer hours than he had in Atlanta, but he fell into bed each night and slept like a baby until sunrise. Woke up each morning with a clear conscience and he felt alive.

Things had changed in the years since he'd visited here as a boy. People had been hit hard. Houses sat empty, where their owners had given up and sold out or just moved on. All around them, real estate was being gobbled up by investors.

Silas was right; he didn't trust people. Especially ones who came with big ideas on how to improve their little, mostly forgotten town—starting with selling all your property to them. He knew those people; hell, he'd been one of those people.

And now suddenly, out of the blue, a friend of the niece shows up, which was a stretch considering they hadn't seen their great-niece in years. He'd tried to convince the Crispins not to let her stay in the house. They knew nothing about her; she might have ulterior motives and he'd be damned if he'd let those three be taken advantage of. They were proud, old-fashioned, and close to penniless. Vulnerable to any scam.

Abbie Sinclair. Just the name sounded like pencil skirts and four-inch heels. A calfskin briefcase attached to a slender hand with perfectly manicured fingernails, talons just waiting to snatch away their home and way of life.

Abbie should have seen it coming once the taxi entered the tunnel of antebellum oak trees. One second she'd been looking at the ocean, the next the sun disappeared and they bounced along uneven ground beneath an archway of trees. The temperature dropped several degrees, and Abbie's eyes strained against the sudden darkness to see ahead. Another minute and they were spit out into the sunshine again.

And there was Crispin House.

It was more than a house, more like a Southern plantation. Not the kind with big white columns, but three-storied white wood and stucco, with wraparound porches on the upper two floors. The first floor was supported by a series of stone arches that made Abbie think of a monastery with dark robed monks going about their daily chores in the shadows. Italianate, if she remembered her architectural styles correctly.

The taxi stopped at the steps that led up to the front door. For a long minute Abbie just sat in the backseat of the cab and stared.

"Whooo." The driver whistled. "Somebody sure needs to give that lady a coat of paint."

He was right. The house had been sorely neglected. She just hoped the inside was in better shape.

She could see spots of peeling paint and a few unpainted balusters where someone had repaired the porch rail. There was a patch of uneven grass and one giant solitary oak that spread its branches over the wide front steps, casting the porch in shadow.

This was crazy. Celeste had merely said her relatives would love to have her stay with them, they had plenty of room. She hadn't said that they could have housed a large portion of the Confederate army. Well, she'd stay one night and if things didn't work out, she'd seen an inn in the little town they'd just driven through. It at least had a coat of paint.

She paid the driver, added a generous tip since it seemed that he wouldn't have any return fares, and prepared to meet the Crispin family.

There was movement on the porch, and Abbie realized that a man had been sitting on the rail watching her. He stood, fumbled in his pockets, brushed his palms together, and started down the stairs, lean and lanky and moving slow, his knees sticking out to the side with each downward step.

Abbie reached for the door handle, but the door opened and a face appeared in the opening. His skin was crinkled and deeply lined from the sun. A shock of thick white hair had escaped from his carefully groomed part and stuck up above his forehead. Bright blue eyes twinkled beneath bushy white eyebrows and managed to appear both fun loving and wise at the same time. Abbie suspected he'd been quite handsome as a young man. He still was.

"Miz Sinclair?"

"Yes," Abbie said, though it took her a second to recognize her own name. In its slow delivery, it sounded more like Sinclayuh. It was soft and melodious, like a song, and Abbie relaxed just a little. "You must be Mr. Crispin."

"Yes'm, that's me. But folks round here all call me Beau." He held out a large bony hand, the veins thick as ropes across the back, then he snatched it back, rubbed it vigorously on his pants leg, and presented it again.

Abbie smiled up at Beauregard Crispin, took his proffered hand, and got out of the car.

The driver carried her two bags up to the porch. "Y'all have a nice stay," he said, then nodded to Mr. Crispin, got back in the taxi, and drove away.

Abbie felt a moment of panic. She had a feeling there might not be another taxi for miles.

"After you."

She hesitated, just looking at Beau's outstretched hand, then she forced a smile and began to climb the wide wooden steps. She'd just reached the porch when the screen door opened and two women stepped out of the rectangle of darkness. They had to be Millie and Marnie. The Crispin sisters.

Here's the thing about my relatives, Celeste had told her. *They're sweet as pie, but they're old-fashioned. I mean really old-fashioned, like pre–Civil War old-fashioned.*

Abbie had laughed, well, her version of a laugh these days. *I get it, they're old-fashioned. No four-letter words, no politics, no religion. Not to worry, I have better sense than to talk politics to people who lost the wahr.*

The what?

The war. That was my attempt at a Southern accent. No good?

Celeste shook her head. *Not by a long shot.* She dropped into a speech pattern that she'd nearly erased through much practice and four years of studying communications. *The wahuh. Two syllables and soft. It's South Carolina, not Texas. We're refined. We've got Charleston.*

Abbie impulsively grabbed Celeste's hand. *Don't you want to go with me?*

I'd love to but I can't get away from the station.

When was the last time you had a vacation?

Can't remember. You know the media. Out of sight, out of— Go have a good time. Let them pamper you. They're experts.

Now, Abbie suddenly got it. She would have recognized them in a crowd. Millie, the younger sister, prim, petite, neatly dressed and hair coifed in a tidy little bun at the nape of her neck. And Marnie, taller, rawboned, dressed in a pair of dungarees and a tattered man's T-shirt smeared with dirt. Her white hair was thick and wild with curls. According to Celeste, Marnie had left the fold at sixteen only to return fifty years later, the intervening years unspoken of, what she had done or where she had been, a mystery.

Us kids used to make up stories about her. Once we were convinced she was a spy for the CIA, then we decided she traveled to Paris and became the mistress of a tortured painter and posed nude for him. We were very precocious.

She came for a visit once, but we weren't allowed to see her. She only stayed two days, and I heard Momma tell Daddy that she was drinking buttermilk the whole time she was there, 'cause it was the only thing she missed. And Daddy said, it was because it covered the smell of the scotch she poured into it.

They're teetotalers.

Not at all. Aunt Millie has a sherry every afternoon.

"My de-ah," Millie Crispin said, coming forward and holding out both hands. "Welcome to Crispin House. We're so glad to have you. Beau, get Abbie's luggage and bring it inside."

"Please, I can—" But that was as far as she got before she was swept across the threshold by the deceptively fragile-looking Millie.

"Now you just come inside and leave everything to Beau."

Abbie didn't want to think of Beau struggling with her suitcases, but she saw Marnie slip past them to give her brother a hand, just before Millie guided her through a wide oak door and into a high-ceilinged foyer.

"I thought you might like to see your room first and get settled in," Millie said in her soft drawl.

"Thank you." Abbie followed her up a curved staircase to the second floor, matching her steps to Millie's slower ones.

At the top of the stairs was a landing that overlooked the foyer. A portrait of a man in uniform hung above a side table and large Chinese vase. Three hallways led to the rest of the house.

Millie started down the center hall. "We've put you in the back guest suite. Celeste and her mama and daddy used to stay there when they visited." Millie sighed. "There's a lovely view." She chattered on while Abbie followed a footstep behind her and tried to decipher the pattern of the faded oriental runner.

They came to the end of the hall and Millie opened a door. "Here we are. I hope you like everything." They stepped inside to a large darkened room. A row of wooden shutters blocked the light from the windows and a set of French doors that Abbie hoped led to a balcony. Millie hurried over to the windows and opened the shutters. Slices of sunlight poured in, revealing an elegant but faded loveseat and several chairs.

"Over here is your bedroom," Millie said, guiding Abbie through another door to another room, this one fitted out with a high four-poster bed with the same shuttered door and windows. Millie bustled about the room opening the shutters and pointing out amenities. "The bath's through there . . ."

Millie's words buzzed about Abbie's ears. She appreciated her desire to be welcoming, but she wanted—needed—solitude, anonymity, not someone hovering solicitously over her every second. Coming here had been a big mistake.

"If you need anything, anything at all, you just pull that bell pull and Ervina will come see to you."

Ervina? Was there another sister Celeste hadn't told her about?

"You just make yourself at home. We generally have dinner at six, but come down any time you like."

Abbie followed her back into the sitting room and to the door. "Now you have a rest and then we'll have a nice visit." Millie finally stepped into the hallway.

Abbie shut the door on Millie's smile and leaned against it.

There was a tap behind her that made Abbie jump away from the door. *Be patient,* she told herself. *She's trying to be nice.* She opened the door.

Marnie was there with her suitcases. Abbie opened the door wider and Marnie lugged them in. She was followed by an even older African American woman carrying a tray.

"You shouldn't have carried my bags."

"No bother. We send the luggage up on a dumbwaiter. Ervina, put that tray over on the Hepplewhite."

Ervina wasn't a sister. She was the servant. And she was ancient.

Ervina shuffled into the room, carrying a tray laden with cups, saucers, and plates of food that looked heavier than the woman who carried it. Abbie felt a swell of outrage and fought not to take the load from the woman.

Marnie walked through the room turning on several lamps. "We'll leave you alone. Millie insisted on the tray. Don't over-eat because she's going to feed you again in a couple of hours. And don't worry that you'll be trapped in the house listening to two old broads talk your ear off. You just do however you

want. Come, Ervina, let's leave the poor girl alone." Marnie
headed for the door.

Ervina followed. She slanted a look at Abbie as she passed by,
nodded slowly as if Abbie had just met her expectations, then
she shuffled through the door and shut it without a backward
look.

Bemused, Abbie turned off the lamps Marnie had just turned
on. They had to be conserving electricity. Because from the
little she'd seen of Crispin House, shabby genteel wasn't just a
lifestyle, it was a necessity.

And then there was the elaborate tea tray, sterling silver,
filled with cakes and little sandwiches with the crusts cut off,
tea in a bone china pot and a pitcher of lemonade.

"Celeste, I could brain you. What the hell have you gotten
me into?"

Abbie took a cucumber sandwich and crossed to the French
doors. After fumbling one handed with the handle, she popped
the rest of the little sandwich in her mouth and used both hands
to pull the doors open.

She stepped out to the wraparound porch where several
white rocking chairs and wicker side tables were lined up
facing the ocean. The air was tangy with salt, and she breathed
deeply before crossing to the rail.

Below her a wide lawn slid into white dunes that dipped
and billowed before the old mansion like a crinoline. Delicate
tufts of greenery embroidered the way to the beach, wide and
white and ending in a point that stretched like a guiding finger
to the horizon.

And beyond that, water and sky. She'd come to the edge of
the world. Not a violent wave-crashing, jagged-rock edge that
you'd expect, but the Southern genteel version with fat lazy
waves rolling in, tumbling one over the other before spilling
into white foam on the sand.

Abbie filled her lungs with the spicy, clean air and slowly let it out. Part of her tension oozed away. She was tempted just to stay right there looking at the ocean forever, but they were expecting her for dinner.

She went inside to unpack. Her coat was lying across the chenille bedspread.

Her cell phone rang. She turned her back on the coat and checked caller ID.

"Perfect timing," she said, answering it.

"Did you just arrive?" Celeste's voice crackled at the other end of the call. Great. Lousy cell reception. Well, she wanted solitude.

"A few minutes ago. This place is incredible, kind of Southern gothic."

"Ugh. Is it in really bad shape? I've been meaning to get back, but I never seem to find the time."

"The outside more than the interior, though it looks like someone has started repairs. But everything is very comfortable, the sisters are a hoot, and Beau . . . I adore him already."

"Which room did they give you?"

"One with peach paint that opens onto the veranda and a view of the ocean. Why didn't you tell me about the beach?"

"I did."

"Oh, well, it's incredible. I haven't had a chance to go down yet, but I plan to spend tomorrow laying out. Thank you."

"No prob. Don't forget your sunscreen. It isn't hot yet, but the sun can burn. Especially with your skin."

"Thanks, Ma."

"Oh, hell, I know you know more about sunburn than I do, considering the sun hardly ever creeps into my office." Celeste sighed. "I'm kind of envious."

"Then why don't you try to get away? It's really quite wonderful," Abbie said. And her stay here would be easier to handle with Celeste to deflect some of the attention.

"I wish. I told you it was just what you needed. You have to promise to soak up some rays for me."

"I will, and you were right. Even if I had to fall apart to realize it."

"Don't think about that. You'll get back into it—when you're ready."

And nobody, not even Abbie, thought she would ever be ready. She knew she could never go back. Back had been torn away from her. Back was no longer an option.

"Hey, listen, I have a very important question for you."

"Yes?"

Abbie could hear the wariness in her friend's voice. "Am I expected to dress for dinner?"

Celeste laughed. It was a sound that made Abbie feel homesick.

"Well, I haven't been there in years, but it is Sunday dinner."

"I take that to mean yes. But how dressed?"

"You know, just nice, a dress, not too short, maybe some pearls."

"Got it. I'd better get hopping. I don't want to be late. And Celeste. Thanks. I take it back, all that stupid stuff I said. You were right. This is just what I needed."

Chapter 2

Abbie half expected a gong to announce dinner. But when it didn't ring at a quarter to six, she knew she couldn't hide in her room any longer. She'd dressed in her any-occasion black dress and softened it with a string of faux pearls and a short floral jacket that she'd picked up on the sale rack at Marshall Fields. She opted for sandals and prayed that the sisters wouldn't be waiting for her in chiffon hostess gowns.

She managed to find her way to the parlor where the Crispins were sipping amber liquid from small glasses. The sherry Celeste had told her about.

Millie, dressed in light green, sat on the edge of a delicate upholstered chair, her skirts spread about her like an octogenarian Scarlett O'Hara. Marnie was sitting on the couch, legs crossed. She'd changed into a pair a navy blue slacks and a silky blouse covered in a blue hyacinth pattern.

Beau, wearing a dark suit and looking uncomfortable, stood up when Abbie stepped through the archway. And so did another man.

"Abbie, come in and sit down over here," said Millie. "Beau, pour Abbie a little glass of sherry."

"She might prefer something else, Sister," Marnie said.

"Oh." Millie's hand flew to her chest. "Of course." She frowned at Abbie, more flustered than judgmental.

"Sherry's fine," Abbie said. She could swear Marnie snorted. Abbie took a closer look at Marnie's sherry glass and wondered if it might contain the infamous scotch.

The stranger had sat down and was lounging in a big club chair, one ankle crossed over his knee. He was drinking something dark in a tumbler. It matched his attitude and his looks, which were pretty okay even by Chicago standards. Dark hair, dark eyes, tanned, fit from what she could tell by the shirt front that showed through his unbuttoned sports jacket. He eyed her speculatively and not at all friendly.

Good. For a minute she'd been afraid the sisters were trying to set her up.

"My goodness, where are my manners," Millie said. "Cabot, this is our guest, Abbie Sinclair. Abbie, this is Cabot Reynolds . . . the third."

The third, right. Abbie fought not to roll her eyes; Marnie didn't bother.

"How do you do?" he said dryly.

"Nice to meet you," she said, matching his tone. The air between them could have chilled lemonade. Fine by Abbie.

"And how long are you staying, Miss Sinclair?"

Longer than you want me to, obviously, thought Abbie. And what was that all about? She thought Southern men were supposed to have impeccable manners. But maybe he wasn't totally Southern. His voice modulated from a soft Southern drawl to something with more bite. Probably educated at a stuffy private school, where Reynolds the first and second had attended.

At that moment a gong echoed from somewhere in the house.

Marnie shook her head and stood up. They walked across the hall to the dining room. Cabot the third escorted Millie; Beau offered an elbow first to Abbie, then Marnie.

Marnie leaned past her brother. "Don't get used to all this grandeur," she whispered. "Usually we just eat on trays in front of the television."

Abbie smiled. "Good to know." Whatever this trip would be, Abbie was getting the feeling it wouldn't be dull. The three siblings alone would make a great study. Gentility gone to seed, but struggling to survive. A way of life, fragile and soon to become extinct . . .

Abbie's step faltered as her mind automatically switched into documentary mode. Beau's hand tightened over hers, and he gave her an encouraging smile. She smiled back and with an effort pulled her mind back to dinner.

No more lapses like that, she warned herself. That life was over. She wouldn't go there again.

The dining room was a long rectangular room painted a pale yellow and surrounded by a white chair rail. At the far end, French doors opened onto a brick patio and overgrown shrubbery. The oval dining table was placed off center, which Abbie surmised was because several leaves had been taken out to accommodate only five diners. It was still huge and she was glad that the place settings had been clustered around one end with Millie at the head of the table, Beau and Marnie to her left, and Cabot and Abbie to her right.

Dinner was everything she had imagined a Southern dinner to be. Crystal wine and water glasses, the good china, and sterling flatware. The house itself might be slowly fading away, but they were still dining in style.

The first course arrived in a flowered gold-rimmed soup tureen carried by a young African American man dressed in a white coat and black trousers several inches too short. He held the tureen as if it contained nitroglycerin while Ervina ladled a rich crab bisque, pale pink with chunks of crabmeat, into their bowls.

"Thank you, Ervina," Marnie said. "How are you doing this evening, Jerome?"

Jerome grinned at her for a second before he lowered his head. "Fine, ma'am," he mumbled and sped back to the kitchen. Ervina followed at a slower pace.

The soup was thick and rich, and Abbie was stuffed by the time the first course arrived. She hadn't been eating very much lately. She looked apprehensively at the roasted chicken, the potatoes, greens of some variety, corn bread, and several other dishes. And she wondered how she could manage to eat enough not to appear rude.

"Why, Millie, this is a feast fit for a king." Cabot the third smiled charmingly at Millie then cut Abbie a sideways look.

"Delicious," she agreed, resenting the arrogant so-and-so who thought he had to prompt her on good manners.

Millie beamed back at the two of them.

Marnie looked across the table and said, "Only eat what you want. It's sometimes hard to eat at the end of a travel day." She aimed the last part of the sentence at Millie.

"Why, of course," said Millie. "And if you get hungry during the night, you just come down to the kitchen and make yourself at home. Ervina goes home at night so you'll have to fend for yourself."

"I'm sure I'll be fine."

"We are early risers and eat breakfast about seven o'clock, but you sleep in and we'll fix you something when you're good and ready."

"Thank you, really. But you don't have to feed me. I'm sure there are plenty of places in town. I'm just happy that you're letting me take advantage of your hospitality."

"Nonsense," Millie said. "We love takin' care of our young people. Though most of them seem to move away as soon as they can. It might be a little dull around here until the season begins, but I'm sure Cabot would love to show you around town."

"Thank you, but—"

"When you're rested up. You'd love to do that, wouldn't you, Cabot?"

Abbie doubted it. "I wouldn't want to take Mr. Reynolds away from . . ." *Whatever it is he does.*

"I'd be happy to." He smiled tightly at Abbie.

She smiled back just as tightly. She'd have to have a talk with the sisters tomorrow and gently, but firmly, tell them she was not interested. Not in Cabot "the third" or anyone else.

"But I can't until Tuesday. The community center's water heater's rusted out and I told Sarah I'd come over and help Otis install the new one. Then I have a job over in Plantersville in the afternoon."

So he worked. As a plumber? Before she could ask him, Jerome came back with individual crystal dishes of a thick yellow pudding filled with chunks of bananas and vanilla wafers.

Abbie managed to eat dessert, which was delicious, listening politely to the conversation without having to think of too much to say. Between the food, and the slow lyrical voices, exhaustion began to creep over her. Millie and Cabot did most of the talking, while Marnie occasionally put in a word or two. Beau just ate, answered when he was spoken to directly, but didn't volunteer any conversation of his own.

A block of partially carved wood sat by his plate, and several times Abbie saw his hand inch toward it only to draw away again at a mere glance from Millie. Abbie wished she had asked more about the family before coming. She knew anecdotal-over-a-martini details, like Marnie camouflaging the smell of scotch with buttermilk, and how Millie ruled the house even though it was really Beau's inheritance. But she hadn't heard any real history, and it was obvious there was some interesting history between the three.

As Abbie watched their interplay, she became more intrigued. She liked the siblings. What she didn't get was how Cabot Reynolds the third fit into it. Celeste hadn't mentioned him. He didn't seem to be a relative, and yet he obviously had free rein of the place. Maybe that's why she was picking up such unfriendliness from him. He was afraid she'd usurp his position as favored guest?

He might be a plumber, but Crispin House and the land that surrounded it must be worth a fortune. And Cabot the third might just be trying to parlay friendship into financial gain—for himself.

Don't get involved, she warned herself. She wasn't going to do that anymore. No more lost causes. No more exposés. No more long weeks of grueling work in hideous conditions just to have your film confiscated, your cameras destroyed, your . . .

"And we want you to stay just as long as you can. If you don't think it will be too dull."

Abbie realized that everyone was looking at her; there was concern on Marnie's face.

God, what had they been talking about? "I don't think it will be dull at all. Solitude is just what I came for."

"Well, you'll find plenty of that here," Marnie said under her breath.

"We won't bother you at all," added Millie. "Will we, Sister?"

"Not at all," Marnie said, attention focused on Abbie. "You just come and go as you like."

Abbie sneaked a peek at Cabot Reynolds. He was frowning at his water glass. He definitely didn't want her around.

Millie stood, and the others took their cue. Beau surreptitiously slipped the piece of wood in his pocket and edged toward the door.

"I'd best be taking off," Cabot announced as soon as they reached the archway to the parlor. "Your guest looks like she might nod off midsentence."

Abbie widened her eyes and suppressed a yawn.

"By the way, Beau, Silas said he was going fishing tomorrow if you were interested."

"Yes, thank you, Cabot, I think I am. I'll walk you back into town."

"Don't you stay out till all hours," Millie said.

"Haven't stayed out till all hours since I was in the merchant marines," Beau said and winked at Abbie.

"Thank you for dinner," Cab said. "You tell Ervina for me that that's the best crab bisque I had all season."

"I will. Beau, you keep that jacket on if you're going outside."

"G'night, Cab," Marnie said.

Abbie smiled and nodded; Cab nodded. The two men left.

"Well, we won't see him back anytime soon," Millie said with a sigh.

It took Abbie a couple of seconds to realize she was talking about Beau and not Cabot. Beau didn't say much, and he was definitely more comfortable with a piece of wood in his hand than sitting over a china bowl of bisque making polite conversation—something Abbie could relate to—but he seemed perfectly capable of taking care of himself.

"Would you like to go up to your room, dear? You're welcome to watch some television with Sister and me. We don't have cable, but we can pick up the Charleston and Myrtle Beach stations pretty good."

"I think I'll go up and read for a bit. It must be the salt air, but I'm tired. It was a lovely dinner. Thank you."

"Our pleasure. Good night, dear."

Abbie climbed the stairs to her room, dreading the idea of

going to sleep, but dreading the idea of having to watch the evening news with Marnie and Millie more.

She wondered how long she could stand Millie's solicitude. It was probably what Southern hostesses did. Abbie had visited a lot of countries, met all kinds of people, but she'd never met anyone like Millie. It was as if she belonged in another era, like one of those characters in the recent burst of Southern movies. Which, Abbie realized, were probably based on people like Millie.

"I always rely on the kindness of strangers," Abbie mumbled to herself in a pitiful rendition of a Southern accent. And realized she *was* actually relying on the kindness of strangers. And she was grateful.

That night she slept like the dead, and the dead came back to haunt her.

Beau and Cab walked back into town. It was a cool evening, growing cooler as the sun sank beneath the horizon, but Beau had shed his suit jacket the minute they were outside and left it hanging on the porch rail.

"You get that engine up and running yet?" Beau asked.

"Not yet, but I'm close," Cab said. "I got it tuned properly and it goes for a few seconds, then it gets hung up. I've scoured rust, oiled parts, refitted pieces, but it still gets hung up."

"I'll come over and take a look for you tomorrow."

"That would be great. Thanks."

Beau nodded. Reached into his pocket for his piece of wood.

"So," Cabot began. "Your visitor seems nice enough."

"Pretty girl," Beau said as he fumbled in his shirt pocket for his knife. "I was always partial to blue-eyed blondes."

Cab groaned inwardly. It wouldn't take much for Abbie Sinclair to have Beau wound around her little finger.

"She's a friend of your niece's?"

"Celeste."

"Right. What did Celeste tell you about her?"

Beau stopped and peered at Cabot. "You interested in her, son?"

"If you mean are we gonna have to fight over her, no."

Beau chuckled.

"She hardly said a word at dinner. I was just curious why she would choose Stargazey Point for a vacation. She looks like an Aruba kind of woman."

"Huh," Beau said. "Don't strike me that way. Something int'resting about her though."

"What?"

"Don't know. But you can feel it."

The only thing Cab felt was trepidation that this was another developer's ploy to cheat the Crispins out of their property. She wouldn't be the first. They'd been circling like buzzards since Cab had been back and probably before then. Silas and a handful of others had sold their property for way below what it was worth, but that was before Cab's return. These days, pretty much everybody came to him for advice. Most of the time he'd tell them not to sell.

It was selfish he knew. Many of them were barely getting by. Hell, he even had to take on some local design jobs, but most of the offers were way below the value of the property.

They reached the old pier and Beau stopped. "You're mighty quiet tonight, boy."

"Got a lot on my mind, I guess."

"Nothin' bad, I hope."

"No, nothing bad." He'd make sure it wasn't. It was a good thing after all that Millie had coerced him into taking Ms. Sinclair sightseeing. The best thing he could do was to trap her into giving herself away while he was showing her around on Tuesday. And if she did, he'd have her on her way to the airport before she could whistle "Dixie," if she even knew the tune.

"Well, I'll be seeing you tomorrow then." Beau wandered off toward the pier. Cabot watched him climb down the rotting pylons to sit on the cement seawall below. It was still just light enough to see the blade of his knife as it sliced into the unformed block of wood.

Cabot turned toward home thinking about Beau and what it must be like to live surrounded by those two strong-willed women. It would drive Cab mad, but Beau took everything in stride, wandering off to carve beautiful, mysterious forms. Mysterious because Cab had never seen a finished product, not even in all the summers he'd spent here. Maybe Beau never finished them, just carved and whittled until he carved the wood away.

Cab couldn't imagine the Point without Beau and his block of wood.

And he couldn't imagine himself anywhere else.

Instead of going home, he walked the half block to his reason for being in Stargazey. Riffled through his keys until he found the one that opened the padlock that secured the double plywood door. The original doors had been blown off in Hurricane Hugo in 1989, then again in '99 and '04. After the last time, Ned hadn't opened up again. Tourism was off, the beaches had eroded, and with the opening of the big theme parks, there wasn't much call for his kind of business.

Cab pulled at one side of the door. It scraped against the dirt as it arced outward. He'd have to put proper doors on soon— these were too unwieldy and probably not that safe—but he had some time still. He wanted new windows installed, the place painted, the electricity working. . . .

He stepped into the dark cavernous space, thinking he could smell the freshly laid sawdust, hear the distant echo of music, the whirl of lights and mirrors, the delighted squeals of children, the laughter of adults.

Peter Pan? Maybe. He just knew that even with a promising future, a beautiful fiancée, and a substantial stock portfolio, his life had been sterile and bleak. Until he'd come back to Stargazey Point to settle Ned's estate. He'd returned to Atlanta seemingly the same, but he had changed in the space of a few short days and the discovery of Ned's legacy.

He looked into the dark at the strange machinery and half-finished structures and felt happy. He'd given up everything for this, and he'd be damned if he'd let anyone, including Abbie Sinclair, take it away.

Abbie scrambles on her hands and knees. Past the donkey, eyes rolling in terror. She thrusts a rigid arm toward the small hand that stretches open-fingered from the mud. She can't reach it. The harder she tries, the farther it slides away. Only the donkey stays, his head thrashing in the mud. But she can't reach the boy. "I'm sorry, I'm sorry, I'm sorry."

Werner yells at her, she turns. His lips move, but she can't hear him. "What?" she screams. His eyes widen, his arms fly out as his body recoils and blood splatters the air. He falls, slowly, slowly to the ground, calling to her, but she can't hear.

Abbie thrashed against the covers. Sat up. Gasping for breath. It was a dream. The dream. She clutched the sheet as the bed began to shake, move across the floor, the tall posts wavering in the dark, until they disintegrated like ashes around her. She rolled off the bed and crawled toward the French doors across an undulating floor.

Not real, not awake, not real. She grabbed at the door handles, flung the doors wide, and stumbled onto the veranda. She pulled herself up to the balcony rail and peered out to sea. The wind hit her damp skin, and she shivered uncontrollably.

She was in South Carolina with Celeste's family. She was standing on firm wood.

It was dark. Only a lighter aura marked the northern shore where the lights from civilization broke through the night. But straight out to sea was black. And though the stars blinked erratically above her, their light didn't shine on the land.

Abbie crossed her arms over her chest. Closed her eyes and opened them again. She looked up and down the porch, making sure she hadn't wakened the others, not knowing if she'd talked or screamed or cried in her sleep. She heard nothing but the whisper of the waves touching the sand.

This had to stop. She might have awakened one of the Crispins, scared any of the three into a heart attack.

Something creaked in the dark. She whirled around and peered into the shadows. One of the rocking chairs moved slowly back and forth. Abbie backed against the balcony rail. The chair ceased rocking. Hopefully, it was over for tonight.

Just as she began to relax, the chair lurched forward and something clunked to the ground. She froze, felt something rub against her ankles. And then a low rumbling.

It seemed to take forever for her brain to kick into gear. Not a hallucination, not a nightmare. A cat was purring at her feet.

She exhaled so sharply she nearly fell backward.

She knelt down, and the cat bumped against her knee. He, or she, was big and seemed in no hurry to leave. She reached out her hand, and the cat stretched his neck to be stroked.

"Now where did you come from? You're not feral, you're too friendly to be a scavenger, so I'm guessing you're a resident, too."

The cat made a rusty sound that Abbie took as a meow, made a final pass under her hand, and turned to walk slowly and stately, tail twitching, down the veranda. He was swallowed by the darkness long before he reached the end.

Abbie shivered. Her nightshirt was clammy with sweat. She looked quickly around, assuring herself that she was indeed awake. She took a deep breath of salt air, a long last look at the dark, heaving waves, and went back to her room.

She hurried across the carpet and jumped onto the high four-poster, pulled the covers up to her neck. Okay. No one had seen or heard her. And she couldn't be too crazy; the cat liked her. But this couldn't go on. She had to pull herself together.

She'd done her best. She couldn't have done more. She knew that. And yet somehow that wasn't enough. *I'm sorry, I'm sorry, I'm sorry.*

Chapter 3

Marnie pushed stiffly to her feet and brushed the soil off her garden gloves.

"She's been sittin' out there half the morning," Millie said. "She's not even wearing a hat."

Marnie came to stand by her sister and looked out at the beach where Abbie sat on the sand, arms wrapped around her knees. "Maybe she's enjoying the weather. She just came from all that snow."

Marnie said this just to calm her sister. There was something definitely not happy about that girl. She recognized the deep, carefully hidden panic, not just fear, but gut-wrenching panic. She'd felt it herself, many years ago. Sometimes even now it came back to haunt her.

"Let's just leave her alone and see."

"I was hoping she and Cabot would hit it off, but he wasn't actin' like himself at all last night."

"Maybe he thought you were playing matchmaker."

Millie turned innocent eyes on her. "Sister, he comes almost every Sunday night."

"He comes," Marnie said, "about once a month, and he was here last week."

"He heard we were having crab bisque."

"And who did he hear that from?"

"Hmmph. I just happened to run into him yesterday down at the hardware store."

Marnie raised a disbelieving eyebrow.

"Well, I did. For all the good it did," Millie added under her breath. "And now look at that poor child alone out there on the beach." She pulled the yellow petals from a forsythia branch and let them drop to the ground. It catapulted Marnie back about sixty years, Millie upset over some mistreated dog, some unpopular student, and helpless to do anything but worry the forsythia leaves. But that was a long time ago, before Millie lost touch with the world.

Millie was a worrier. It drove Marnie crazy sometimes, but not today. She was a little worried herself about this young woman whom Celeste had sent to them with no more than, "She's my friend and she needs a safe haven for a while."

"Is she in any kind of trouble?" Marnie had asked. Not that it would make any difference, but sometimes it was best to know what you were dealing with ahead of time.

"Not legally or anything like that. She needs to regroup. I thought of Stargazey Point. I thought of you."

"Okay. Send her on. Millie will spoil her rotten, and I'll kill her with kindness."

"Just let Stargazey work its magic. And be there for her. Thank you. I love you bunches."

"Uh-huh. When are you coming for a visit?"

"Soon I hope. It's just so hard to get away from work."

Just as well, Marnie thought. She didn't want to worry Celeste with the state of affairs.

For now, Millie had something to do, someone to take care of beside Beau. Marnie just hoped her constant attention wouldn't drive Abbie away.

Not that Marnie had any illusions about them actually being able to help the girl beyond giving her a refuge from whatever was ailing her. She'd met Abbie in the kitchen earlier that morning, hollow eyed and pale, as if she hadn't slept well. Marnie managed to press a cup of coffee on her, but she refused any breakfast—girl was too damn thin, even for these times.

Abbie asked her if it would be okay to take her coffee to the beach.

Of course, Marnie told her. Before she could even offer her a beach towel, she'd disappeared wraithlike through the back door.

"Well?" Millie asked, interrupting her thoughts.

"Give her time, Millie. Let her have some solitude."

"Solitude. Hmmph. She has old age for solitude." Millie brushed her hands off and slowly went back into the house.

Ervina stood at the edge of the sand in the shadowed shelter of the trees. She'd been watchin' that girl for nigh on an hour. She hadn't moved. But the air around her was rollin' like the tide. The girl didn't know. But it was there. And so alive Ervina could almost hear it.

Change was comin'. She'd brought it with her, this pale girl with the ghost hair. It was comin'. Might be good. Might be bad. But it was comin'.

Abbie lifted her head to the sun. It was warm, and the slight breeze off the water kept the morning from being hot.

Ordinarily Abbie loved the beach. She always tried to spend a few days between jobs at some sunny vacation spot. Werner would never go. He was always in postproduction or preproduction or both at once.

Abbie used to kid him about being constitutionally unable to sit still. He'd just shrug, kiss her, and tell her to have a good time. He'd be there when she got back. He always was. But he wouldn't be there now. Not anymore.

Hell. He'd left a hole inside her that all the sand on earth couldn't fill. She knew he would never think twice about giving his life for what he believed in. But not like this. Not when their work was destroyed and witnesses silenced.

She was the coward. She'd let him down. Let herself down.

She looked up at the sky, knowing he wouldn't be there. Werner had always said he would never go to heaven, since all the interesting people would be in hell. "See you there," he'd quip, when she faltered. When she worried about him. When she was afraid. She hoped he was right. Hell wouldn't be such a bad place with Werner making stories about it.

She wished Celeste had been able to come with her. She'd said she wanted solitude, but solitude was too crowded. She wanted distraction. Something to keep her busy. Something that would point her to the future, prevent her from looking at the past.

Celeste could always make her laugh. Celeste loved the beach almost as much as Abbie, though they hardly ever got their vacations at the same time.

Once, years ago, they had gone to St. Bart's. Spent forty-eight hours flirting with skin cancer and hot young men before they were on the plane headed back, Celeste to her desk job as copyeditor for a local news channel, Abbie to another plane, another country, another story—to Werner.

Abbie knew she was going to have to go solo from now on. This was her new life. She'd accepted that. She'd known what to do before, and her life had been exciting and purposeful. But this new life was vague and unfocused, one that she had no experience in, no skills, no desire to explore.

She took a stinging breath, trying to ease the tightness in her chest. She couldn't just sit here. This was not the relaxation, decompression time before jumping back into the next project. There was no next project.

This was the end of the line—the edge of the world.

And she was being pathetic. She forced her unwilling body to her feet, brushed off the seat of her jeans, and looked up the long white beach. She could take a walk; there was plenty of unspoiled beach before she reached the town with its damaged pier and the row of stilted beach houses beyond.

She could probably keep walking for days along the shore that continued past the town and curved slightly before spreading at the feet of a line of condos that littered the horizon like sentinels guarding some hazy emerald city, close but out of reach. The image actually brought a half smile to her lips. The wizard had turned out to be a fake.

She turned her back on the mirage and walked to the point. On the far side was more beach, and more water. Not the waves of the ocean but an inlet where the water merely swelled and troughed, appearing between the row of trees that lined the lawn and filling the marshes on the far side, before draining out again.

Abbie walked up the sand to the lawn where she discovered to her surprise, a gazebo, or what was left of one.

It obviously wasn't being used. There was a hole in the roof. Several railings had rotted away and weeds grew up around it. She walked along the outside until she found two wooden steps that were covered in debris.

She tested the first step and when it held her weight, she stepped onto the other and onto the floor. The structure was larger than it looked from the outside. Big enough for a garden party, though it hadn't been used for anything for a very long time. Drifts of sand covered the floor and piled up under the benches that ran along the perimeter.

But the view of the sea was magnificent. A panorama of

ocean, dunes, marshes, lawn, and trees. Something for every-one. She wondered if anyone came down to sit and watch the sunrise or the sunset. It seemed a shame to let it fall into ruin.

A shame maybe, but not a high priority in the scheme of things she bet. And instead of wandering aimlessly, she should be helping with whatever she could up at the house. She was, after all, her mother's daughter. And that was what she was counting on to help her through this ordeal. Her mother knew about loss and how to keep going. Abbie could only hope that she'd inherited that gene, too.

A path led from the gazebo up the lawn to Crispin House. She'd noticed a brick-walled garden on her way to the beach that morning, and now she stopped to peer over the iron gate. A huge vegetable garden sprawled on the other side, rows upon rows marked out by weathered wooden stakes.

Marnie was kneeling by a row of fledgling plants covered with windows. She saw Abbie and waved.

Abbie lifted the latch and let herself in. She trod care-fully over the freshly turned soil until she was standing above Marnie.

"Can I help?"

"Wouldn't mind the company, but look inside the shed over there and get a hat, smock, and pair of gloves. The sun's decep-tive, and your nose is already pink."

Abbie made her way between the rows and across the enclo-sure to the little brick garden shed. Inside was dark and cool. The walls were thick. Herbs hung from the rafters, bushel bas-kets were stacked high in one corner, and a workbench and a piece of fiberboard with hooks and hanging tools took up most of the wall beneath a small square window. And on pegs by the door an old blue garden smock and straw hat hung next to a basket of well-used gardening gloves.

Abbie shook the smock, in case there were any resident spiders, then put it on, grabbed the hat and a pair of gloves, and went back outside.

She blinked against the sudden glare, then made her way to where Marnie knelt on a pad made from old newspapers.

Marnie glanced up at her, nodded brusquely, and handed her a three-toed hand tool. "Can you recognize a weed from a vegetable?"

"Usually. My family always had a garden." Even if they didn't stay long enough to see it yield. Gardening hadn't been Abbie's favorite chore, but she knew how to water and weed and pour beer into jar tops to draw the slugs away. And she'd tried to share what knowledge she had with women in the villages they'd filmed, helping them to get better production from the poor and sometimes arid soil. It astounded her now to think of how oblivious she'd been.

Marnie struggled to one knee. Abbie resisted the urge to help her. Just knowing Marnie for a few hours had told her that the older woman wouldn't like to admit she couldn't manage on her on. But Marnie fooled her. She reached up. "Help me up, please."

Marnie grabbed on to Abbie's arm and hauled herself up; she didn't let go when she'd gained her feet. "Thank you. Sometimes people can use a helping hand or shoulder to lean on. Nothing weak about asking for help when you need it. Now come on over, and I'll teach you how to tell a dandelion from a broccoli seedling."

They spent the next hour silently working in separate rows. Abbie had just finished her second row when a triangle sounded from the house.

Marnie stood up. Abbie noticed she didn't bother to ask for help. She decided not to analyze that too closely.

"That's the lunch bell. Keeps Millie from having to walk out here and yell. Let's get cleaned up."

They returned the gardening clothes and tools to the shed. Marnie picked up a basketful of dark green leaves she'd just picked and they headed for the house, where Millie waited with a worried look on her face.

"Have you been making Abbie work all morning, Sister?"

"I volunteered," Abbie said quickly.

"Besides, she needed something to do," Marnie said.

"Hmmph. Marnie's always gotta do, do, do, but you're supposed to take it easy and enjoy your vacation."

Marnie handed her the basket of greens. "Something you have never understood, Millie, there are some people who like to be busy."

"Busy is one thing," Millie said as Marnie hustled Abbie through a side entrance and into a crowded mudroom where they shed their shoes. "But workin' the poor girl to the bone is another."

"I'm fine, really. I enjoy gardening."

The kitchen table was set for three with dishes edged with roses and large, heavy glasses. Millie was bending into a refrigerator right out of a fifties sitcom. So things were more informal during the day. And hopefully during the rest of the weeknights.

Lunch consisted mainly of leftovers. The crab bisque was thinner—possibly to stretch it to feed them all—which made Abbie a little guilty to think that she was straining a budget that might already be strained. If she stayed, she'd have to find a way to contribute without offending them.

"Ervina is getting too old to do for us," Millie explained as she set a platter of cold chicken on the table. "So we just have her come every now and then. We wouldn't dare hurt her feelings by hiring someone to take her place."

Marnie raised her eyes to the ceiling, and Abbie bet anything that they'd pulled Ervina out of retirement just for that welcoming meal.

"Where is Beau today?" Abbie asked.

"Oh, he left at the crack of dawn," Millie said. "Gone fishing with Silas Cook. Didn't even have breakfast. Said he and Silas would grab some sausage biscuits from the Tackle Shack." Millie tsked, giving her opinion of breakfast at the Tackle Shack.

"All that cholesterol," Marnie explained to Abbie, mischief in her eyes. "Unlike the eggs, grits, bacon, and biscuits and gravy he would have had here."

Millie pursed her lips at her sister. "Won't you have a biscuit, Abbie? I made them just this morning."

Abbie took one, not daring to look at Marnie and risk bursting out laughing.

Millie passed the platter to Marnie. "I just hope they catch something worth eating."

The bisque might be thinner, but it was still delicious. And the salad was so fresh that Abbie knew the lettuce must have come straight from the garden.

The sisters refused to let Abbie help with the cleaning up. She noticed there was no dishwasher and she could only sympathize with Ervina having to wash all those pieces of china and silverware by hand the night before.

"You go on and enjoy yourself." Millie began folding a dish towel, a crease between her eyebrows. "I do wish Cabot was available today to show you around. So much more fun with someone your own age, though I expect he is a bit older than you, still . . . I suppose we could get out the car ourselves."

"No, really, I'm fine," Abbie said.

"Maybe Abbie would just like to explore a bit on her own," Marnie said. "We have a library full of old musty books if you'd like to drag one of the chaises out into the sun. Or take an umbrella down to the beach, equally musty I'm sure, since God knows when anyone has been down to the beach."

"I thought I might walk into town. Maybe pick up some writing supplies. Keep a journal while I'm here." Try to get rid of her damn anger and resident ghosts.

"Oh, but I'm sure we must have—" Millie began.

"The Stargazey Inn has a lovely gift shop," Marnie said. "Tell Bethanne you're staying with us and she'll give you the local rate. Or if you want something more utilitarian, Hadley's probably keeps some school supplies."

"Abbie doesn't want to go into Hadley's. He hasn't given that old shack a painting or a sweeping in decades."

"But he's convenient, and it'll give Abbie a bit of local color. Hadley's quite friendly, once you get past the missing tooth." Marnie grinned at Abbie.

Abbie smiled back. "I think I saw it on my way through town."

"I just don't know why they can't fix up this end of town like everyone else has."

Marnie closed her eyes, then looked at Abbie. Obviously a long and repeated complaint. "This end of town took the brunt of the last big hurricane. It ripped the beach out and devastated the pier and the surrounding buildings. It's taken them longer to recover than the people more inland."

Her interest piqued, Abbie said. "It looks like Crispin House survived. That was pretty lucky."

Marnie nodded slowly. "The old place lives a charmed life, that's for sure. We lost a bunch of outbuildings, had some minor damage to the porches and the roof, but we were a lot luckier than most." She paused, looking out the kitchen window.

"So far, anyway." She tapped the woodwork three times. Millie did the same.

Abbie let herself out the back door and walked to town. Beneath the tunnel of trees, the air was dense, heavy with humidity. Moss hung from the overhead branches, like Merlin's beard, shrouding the leaves and blocking out the sun. And the light at the far end seemed smaller than the light behind her. Abbie wondered if this is what Alice felt falling down the rabbit hole.

She didn't much like that image. She was supposed to be going forward not falling down. But as her mother often told the many schoolteachers who tried to reason with her about her children's educations, "It's a crime to stifle a creative mind." Which in consequence had given the Sinclair children license to think outside the box. Which for the most part, they did. It was a blessing and a curse. Instigator of bright ideas and irrational fears.

And Abbie would like to be free of it for just a few minutes today.

So spill. What does she look like? What's she doing here? Does she seem nice? How long is she going to stay?"

"The wrench?" Cabot stretched out his hand for the pipe wrench that Sarah Davis held just out of reach.

"Not until you give me the scoop." Sarah took a step back and wiggled the wrench at him.

"I thought you wanted me and Otis to put in the water heater for you."

"Not until you give me the lowdown on the mysterious visitor." Sarah flashed a smile at him. She was all of five feet two in heels. Today she was barefooted. She was swallowed by a pair of oversized overalls rolled up at the cuff to show athletic nut-brown calves. A batik headscarf was tied turban style around her head.

Hard to believe she had a PhD and lived on the Upper West Side of Manhattan.

"Hell, Sarah, I don't know. Blond, blue eyes, late twenties, early thirties, hard to tell. She looked tired." She'd looked haunted, he thought, dark hollows under her eyes, a marked contrast to a soft creamy complexion and that fine pale hair.

"She's not the only one lookin' tired this morning. You lose sleep dreaming about her blue eyes?"

"Oh, cut the crap," Cabot said. "I didn't give her a thought after I left Crispin House."

Which might or might not be the truth. He didn't actually think about Abbie Sinclair, not consciously anyway. But for the first time since moving to Stargazey, Cabot had not slept well, and he was afraid he might have the Crispins' new guest to thank for that.

Sarah raised one eyebrow and fisted both hands and the wrench on her nonexistent hips. "Cat got'cha tongue? Because, honey, if you don't start spilling the beans, I'm gonna get Ervina to put the hoodoo on you."

Cabot barked out a laugh. "What would your colleagues at Columbia think if they could hear you now?"

"Pots and kettles, Cabot Reynolds . . . the third," Sarah said, lapsing into her normal New York accent.

Cabot snorted. "That's how Millie introduced me to Ms. Sinclair last night. She was not impressed."

"Is she pretty?"

Cab sighed. "I guess. Yeah, she is. But kind of, I don't know, elusive. Or maybe she was just being reserved . . . or secretive, conniving, dishonest . . ."

"Okay, I get the picture. Here's your wrench. I'm obviously going to have to scope this out myself. Now come on outside. I think I just heard Otis drive up with the new water heater."

Cabot returned the wrench to the toolbox and followed Sarah through the three-room community center and onto the front porch. Otis Monroe was climbing out of a rusted Chevrolet. It had once been an Impala, but Otis had torched off the top, making it a rather suspect convertible. A huge cardboard box was strapped into the backseat.

Otis opened the back door and climbed in to loosen the

straps, then he and Cabot maneuvered it out of the car. With Sarah giving directions, they carried it back through the house to the storeroom.

"So what do you know about the visitor up at the house?" Otis asked.

"God," Cabot said, exasperated. "You'd think this town never saw a tourist before."

Otis snorted. "Haven't seen too many in the last few years. And especially not this time of the year. I saw Silas and Beau getting into the bateaux this morning. Both mentioned that you had been up to the house last night for dinner. Beau seems to think she's a pretty thing."

Which didn't make Cabot feel any better.

Otis gave him a cocky grin. That grin mixed with his red-orange hair and the freckles spread across his latte-colored skin always made Cab think of a Gullah Huck Finn.

"Maybe you're just keeping secrets."

"Hell, I don't know more than anybody else. She hardly said a word during dinner and I left afterward."

"You are some kind of somethin'." Otis turned to Sarah and confided, "For a man who doesn't know much and for a woman who don't say much, Cab here still managed to get himself a date for tomorrow."

"What?" Sarah stopped pulling tape off the water heater box and screwed up her face at him.

"Ooo-ee, you've gone and made Sarah jealous."

"Hush your mouth, boy. Cabot the third would give his eyeteeth to go out with me."

"Absolutely," Cab said and was only half kidding, not that he was about to go down that road. Ervina would put more than hoodoo on him if she found out he was messing with her great-granddaughter, no matter what kind of sophisticated New Yorker Sarah had become. "What are eyeteeth again?"

Sarah threw a wad of packing tape at him.

"Come on, you two. I ain't got all day."

"Lord, don't tell me you got a job."

"Aw hell, Sarah. It's not like I'm not looking. But I'm not gonna commute to no Myrtle Beach. If I wanted to drive a half hour to work and back each day, I'd move to Manhattan with you."

"Not with me, you won't." Sarah stepped aside so Cab could pull the box away.

He and Otis lifted the water heater and shimmied it over to stand next to the old one.

Cab gave the old one a shake. "Seems empty to me." He knelt down and loosened the rusted connection that had been soaking in WD-40 for the last hour. The three of them managed to roll the old water heater out the back door and to the side of the house.

"I'm not putting that dirty old thing in my car," Otis said.

"Well, I'm not going to let it sit here in the yard like some kind of white trash." Sarah's fists went back to her hips. Then she looked past them and her eyes widened.

"Well, well, I do believe that's the Crispins' mystery guest in the flesh. And she's gonna pass right by us."

Chapter 4

Abbie was glad when she stepped out into sunlight and a wide street lined with palmettos and shrubbery.

To her left she could see the openings of drives on the far side of the street. But on her side, there was unbroken shrubbery, which lent credence to her idea that the Crispins owned a whole lot of beachfront property.

She turned toward town. She'd hardly been aware of it as the taxi drove through yesterday. She had the impression of several blocks of colorful quaint shops petering out to the more derelict "this end of town" that Millie had talked about.

And this end of town was in pretty bad shape, she had to agree. She came to a stop in the middle of the tarmac where it widened to make a parking lot in front of the old pier she'd seen from the beach. Though it was hardly recognizable as a pier. It tilted, twisted, and folded in on itself until it terminated at a covered pavilion perched precariously against the tide.

She walked across the parking lot toward the octagonal building she'd seen on her ride through town. A closer look revealed broken latticework and a damaged cupola at the peak of the eight-sided roof. It could have been an old meeting hall or possibly a church, and it was a shame that it had been abandoned and left to fall.

Next to it was a whitewashed house with a sign above a blue door. COMMUNITY CENTER. A rusted car was parked in front of it, and three people were standing next to it, one of whom might be the man she'd met last night.

Abbie quickly looked away and crossed the street. She wasn't ready to meet the locals yet, and she was in no hurry to renew her acquaintance with Cabot Reynolds the third sooner than necessary.

She found herself standing in front of Hadley's, a clapboard store with one ancient gas pump and wooden steps that led up to a porch complete with barrels, an old chest-style drinks cooler, and a screen door that didn't close all the way.

She just needed a notebook. She could buy it here and return to Crispin House. But as she contemplated going inside, three men accompanied by a lumbering hound dog came out. All four stopped to stare at her. She kept walking.

She passed two abandoned buildings with their windows boarded over. The chimney of one had fallen, and the bricks still lay in a pile at the side. The other's porch had been removed, and the boarded door hovered three feet above the ground. The hurricane could have happened last week for all the rebuilding that had taken place.

After a gap the size of a small house, she came to a brick sidewalk. And like Dorothy, she stepped into a Technicolor world.

The town transformed into an assortment of pastel storefronts and clapboard businesses, big and small, tasteful and not so tasteful. Colorful and quaint as all get-out. A café, a real estate agent, a gift store, a tea shop, an art gallery, and some other businesses that were closed for the season. On the next block she came to the Stargazey Inn.

Sitting back from the street behind an ornamental iron

fence, the inn was a square, cream-colored building with the door and windows picked out in blue. There was no sign of it being open except for the white rocking chairs that sat unoccupied on the small porch. But the gate was unlatched, and from what Marnie had said, Abbie figured at least the gift store was open for business.

She climbed the steps, deliberated about ringing the bell or just walking in, and decided on the latter. She stepped into a charming foyer, decorated in chintz and wicker. A dark wooden registration desk curved against one pale green wall; next to it an archway led to the gift shop. It appeared to be open, but no one came to see who had entered the premises.

Abbie walked into the shop almost tiptoeing. The ambiance seemed to call for it. A glass display case was filled with jewelry and figurines. A floor-to-ceiling bookshelf held the latest fiction, cookbooks, books about the South and about Charleston, and a pamphlet on Stargazey Point.

Abbie picked it up and was just beginning to read when a woman about the same age as Abbie came into the room.

"Oh, I am sorry," she said in a soft drawl, "I was in back."

Abbie noticed that she had a purse slipped over one shoulder. "Are you open? I didn't see anyone so I just came in."

"Yes, I'm open. Can I help you with anything in particular?" The woman smiled. She was nice-looking, though not wearing makeup, with dark shoulder-length hair and dark eyes. As she reached to put her purse down, Abbie saw that her fingernails were bitten down to the quick.

"Actually I just came in to see if you sold writing materials."

"For writing letters or journaling?"

Did people still write letters? Or journaling. It's what people in the suburbs or in recovery called putting your thoughts on paper. Abbie couldn't bring herself to call it that. "A journal, if you have it, or any kind of a notebook."

"Sure. Just over here." She led Abbie to a rolltop desk that held stacks of colorful journals and beach-themed notepaper.

"You must be the guest the Crispins have been expecting."

"Yes." Abbie reached for a seashell fabric journal.

The woman was just trying to be helpful, and Abbie was being rude. She forced a smile and looked up. "I just got in yesterday."

"I know. I mean, I'm not usually so nosy. But you're all Millie has talked about for the last week. We've all been waiting for your arrival." She bit her lip. "They're just so sweet, all three of them. Beau comes in for my rhubarb pie sometimes." She looked thoughtful. "And to talk."

"Beau? He hasn't said much since I've been here."

"Oh, well, mainly I talk and he listens. It's nice to have someone listen."

Abbie smiled. "I'll take this one." She thrust the seashell-patterned journal into the woman's hands. "And two of these pens." She grabbed the first two she could reach and handed them over.

The woman flushed. Looked as if Abbie had slapped her, and Abbie chastised herself for being so abrupt. The woman was probably lonely. The town wasn't exactly crawling with tourists. But she hadn't thought it would be this hard—a simple conversation with a stranger. She'd been holed up with herself far too long.

"I'm Abbie Sinclair," she said.

"Hi. I'm Bethanne Bridges. I run the inn and the gift shop. Actually I own it; well, my husband and I did, but . . ." She shrugged, trailed off.

"It's lovely," Abbie said.

Bethanne rang up her purchase and Abbie paid cash. No reason to keep receipts for her taxes. She wasn't on location.

Bethanne returned her purchases in a neat white bag with a

picture of the inn marked out in blue. White and blue seemed to be a theme around here. She'd seen the blue door on the community center she'd passed by as well as on the real estate office and a tiny hole in the wall that she assumed was a post office.

"Thanks." Abbie started to leave. Bethanne grabbed her purse and caught up to her. "I was just going over to Flora's. They serve afternoon tea or coffee. It can be daunting in a new place where you don't know anyone. Would you like to join me?"

Abbie's first response was to decline, but she stopped herself. Bethanne was being friendly, and Abbie needed to start interacting with people again. "Sure. That would be . . . great." Abbie let Bethanne lead her out of the gift shop and through the front door.

She turned a sign over that said back in ten minutes. "Which hardly matters since I don't have a soul staying at the inn now. Come on, it's just right down the street."

They walked to Flora's Tea Shoppe, which was spelled with two *p*'s and an *e* at the end, though a sign in the window assured passersby that they made the best mocha cappuccinos in town, which wasn't hard to believe since they appeared to be the only coffee/tea shop in town.

Inside Flora's was everything you'd expect and more. Blue gingham half curtains finished in blue gingham ruffles. Polished wood-planked floors. A glass display case only partially filled with an array of pastries.

Bethanne led her to a table by the window.

"It's such a luxury to have all this space to ourselves. In season you can't buy a seat."

"That's good," Abbie said, wondering how any of them could do enough business to stay open; she hadn't seen a car except for the rusted-out Chevy since she'd come to town. There was no one staying at the inn, and none of the other tables in Flora's were occupied.

Flora turned out to be a middle-aged woman with springy reddish-blond curls, bright red lipstick, wearing jeans and a Vanderbilt sweatshirt.

"Before you ask," she said, addressing Abbie, "I'm Penny Farlowe, owner of Flora's. Flora died twenty-something years ago. I should put up a sign." Penny looked down at her with eyes a shade of blue green that Abbie had never seen. Contacts?

"This is Abbie Sinclair," Bethanne volunteered. "She's staying up at Crispin House."

"So she is," Penny said. She seemed to be perpetually bubbly, perhaps cultivated for the ambiance of the tea shop. "This calls for high tea." She leaned over the table and effervesced. "At least the Point's version of it."

"As long as it doesn't involve pastries with fish heads sticking out of it." Abbie had eaten a lot of weird things while out on a shoot, but fish heads . . . not so much.

Penny laughed. "I see you've heard of the famous Stargazey Pie. We tend not to push that delicacy here too much. We love our fish, especially of the shellfish variety, but summer people can get a bit squeamish."

Bethanne frowned at them. "What are y'all talking about? Did I miss something?"

"Just a kind of pie they make in Cornwall," Abbie said. "I only know about it because when I googled Stargazey Point, it was the first thing to come up."

"Is it something weird, Stargazey Pie?"

"It's fish pie, with their little heads sticking out of the pastry," Penny said.

"Ugh." Bethanne wrinkled her nose. "Sorry, but it sounds disgusting. Do people really eat it?"

"Beats me," Penny said. "Do you know?"

"I guess they must," said Abbie.

"I think we'll just have some of your cucumber and wa-
tercress sandwiches and your pimento cheese strips. Does that
sound okay, Abbie? And Penny makes a really good pecan
torte."

"I'll bring you the works. Coffee or tea?"

"Actually, I'd kill"—Abbie's voice caught on the word—
"for a double-shot latte."

"From your mouth to Penny's ears. Bethanne? The usual?"

"Constant Comment, please."

Penny bounced away . . . there was no other way to describe it.

"She's very . . . upbeat," Abbie said.

"She's a good person and a good friend."

Abbie heard the *whoosh* of the steamer, and her mouth automatically salivated. That was one of the things she'd missed
most when they were out on location. Good specialty coffee.
Guess she wouldn't be missing that anymore.

"Is something wrong?"

"What?" Abbie looked up to see Bethanne frowning at her.
"Oh no. Just thinking. It's nothing."

Bethanne nodded, and Penny reappeared with a three-tiered
plate loaded with enough food for several people.

"So sue me," she said when she saw Abbie's look of surprise.
"Gotta use these babies up while they're fresh."

She was gone and soon back again with a tray of tea and a
huge cup of coffee.

"It smells heavenly," Abbie said.

"That alone will get you the local rate." She placed the cups
and teapot down on the table. "Y'all just yell if you need anything else. I'll be in back making cheese straws for the Gentry-
Palmer wedding reception on Saturday. They want three
hundred. Hell, my arm might fall off before then."

Bethanne sighed. "They wanted to have the reception at the inn, but there just isn't enough room. At least most of our rooms are let for the weekend."

The front door opened.

"Well, look what the cat dragged in," Penny said.

"I smell caramel macchiato," said the newcomer, a young petite African American woman wearing overalls and a batiked turban.

"Hi, Sarah. Come join us." Bethanne scooted her chair over to make room. Then she stopped. "You don't mind, do you?"

"Me?" asked Abbie. "The more the merrier."

Sarah pulled up a chair from another table and sat down. "Okay, I confess. I saw y'all comin' over and I just wanted to say hello."

"And find out the scoop on the new girl," Penny said, placing another cup on the table.

"This is Sarah Davis," Bethanne said. "She's home taking care of her great-grandmother and running the after-school program at the community center."

"Oh, girl, you better not let Ervina hear you say she needs takin' care of."

"Ervina?" Abbie said. "I think I met her last night at the Crispins'."

Sarah rolled her eyes. "There was a time that woulda pissed me off plain and simple. But, hell, it's turned into a kind of bad dinner theater."

"Playing a role?" Abbie asked and took a sip of coffee and sighed.

"Oh yeah."

"I thought maybe they were playing a joke of some kind. They seemed more like old friends."

Sarah barked out a laugh. "They weren't friends unless it was on the sly. They grew up in the same town, around the same time. Ervina is a bit older, we think. She claims she doesn't remember how old she is.

"But they didn't grow up 'together.' Ervina lived over the way with, let's just say, folks of her kind. It was a long time ago, remember. Her mother worked for the Crispin family and then Ervina after her."

"A long history."

"Yeah, for all the good it's doing me."

Bethanne leaned forward. "Sarah's having the kids put together an oral history of their families."

"Was. The whole project was a bust," Sarah said, and slumped against the chair back.

"What happened?"

"I thought I could accomplish two things at once. Preserve a culture while keeping the kids engaged. But none of the parents cooperated. The kids got bored. The equipment is ancient. I guess we'll just have to limp along until I can come up with something else to keep them out of trouble all summer long."

"How old are the kids?" Abbie asked.

"Five to fourteen, mostly. A few older."

"Wow. Maybe a more focused project?"

Sarah dipped her chin and looked up at Abbie. "You got any suggestions?"

Abbie nearly bolted out of her seat. "Me? No. Why would I?"

Sarah shrugged. "Don't know. Just asking."

Abbie peered at her, trying to read her expression and wondering how much she knew. Jeez, she was getting paranoid. Sarah had more to worry about than googling some tourist. She let out the breath that had stuck in her lungs.

"Heard you also met Cabot, the third, last night."

Abbie grinned. "Millie introduced him as the third. Do people really go by that here?"

"No," said Bethanne, swatting Sarah with her napkin.

"Well, maybe Miss Millie when she's having one of her spells, but just Sarah when she wants to annoy him."

"Why? Because he acts like he owns the place?"

"Was he doin' that?" asked Sarah in round-eyed mock surprise.

"A bit. I got the feeling he didn't like me being there."

"That's Cab all right, like a mangy dog with a bone."

Bethanne giggled. "Sarah. You're awful."

"Well, he is sometimes."

"Does the Reynolds family own property around here? I'm guessing he isn't a plumber though he said he was helping you with your new hot water heater."

Sarah threw back her head and laughed. "He's no plumber."

"No, he's—" Bethanne began.

"He owns horses," Sarah said, interrupting.

Bethanne smiled. Abbie noticed that one cheek had a dimple.

"Oh. I didn't see any horse farms on my way in. Of course, I wasn't looking. Racing stock?"

"Something of the sort."

Bethanne reached for a sandwich, which conveniently kept her from having to look at either Sarah or Abbie. What weren't they telling her?

"He doesn't play polo, does he?"

Sarah snorted and pressed a napkin to her mouth. "Lord, polo. I can just see ole Cab in one of those funny helmets."

"Okay, not polo," Abbie said. "Breeding stock?" Not that she really cared what he did.

Sarah shook her head. "Somewhere in between. You get him to tell you on your date tomorrow."

Coffee sloshed out of her cup, and she quickly set it down on the table. "It's not a date." To Abbie's horror her eyes filled up. She blinked rapidly, cursing herself for letting herself be caught off guard. "Millie coerced him into offering to show me the sights. That's all it is."

"The sights? Honey, if you walked into town, you've seen 'em."

"It is pretty small," Abbie said. "Maybe I should let him off—"

"A date." A sob broke from Bethanne. Abbie looked up to see tears spilling over her cheeks. "Bethanne?"

"Excuse me, I have to talk to Penny about something." She pushed her chair back and ran toward the kitchen.

"Oh, my God. Is it something I said?" Abbie asked. "Are she and Cab . . . ?"

Sarah leaned on her elbows across the table. "It wasn't you. And she and Cab aren't."

"Then what?"

"She and her husband, Jim, moved into town a few years back, fixed up the old hotel, and made it into a real showplace. They were pretty successful, too, considering . . . Well, you've seen the town. Tourism is off, which is tying a ribbon around it.

"Then one day Jim comes down with a virus; it turned to pneumonia, and before they got him to the hospital, he was dead. Just about killed her, too. Did kill the baby. Bethanne miscarried the next week." Sarah shook her head. "Now you know her business."

"That's awful." Abbie's head began to pound. She ripped out the elastic that held her ponytail and rubbed her scalp.

Sarah narrowed her eyes at Abbie. "But it seems to me, Bethanne wasn't the only one tearing up at this table. You got any business, Abbie Sinclair?"

No way was she going to talk about her personal life to Sarah, not to anyone.

"Actually I do, and I'd better get going or I'll be late," Abbie said, purposely misunderstanding Sarah's question. She stood up, shoved her hand into her jeans pocket, pulled out a twenty-dollar bill, and placed it on the table. "Nice to have met you. Thank Bethanne for me."

She grabbed her gift shop bag and went out the door without looking back. Once out on the sidewalk, she hesitated. A braver woman would go back, thank Bethanne for the tea, maybe even tell her they had something in common.

But Abbie wasn't brave. If she were, she might have saved something from their last story, even though she couldn't save Werner. She didn't think she could be any help to Bethanne, and she knew for certain no one could help her.

Chapter 5

Abbie was nearly to the Crispin driveway when she saw Beau and another man walking down the middle of the street, coming her way. Beau was carrying fishing poles and a thermos. His companion held a large red-and-white cooler in each hand.

Her first inclination was to pretend she hadn't seen them. She was still a little rattled from the Bethanne breakdown. But they saw her, so she waited at the driveway entrance until they reached her.

"Abbie, my dear. This is Silas Cook. My old friend and fishing buddy."

"Ma'am." Silas dipped his chin at her. He was an older African American man, much smaller than Beau, wiry with grizzled white hair and an easy smile.

"Nice to meet you, Silas. Did you guys catch anything today?"

"We might be able to eke a bite or two out of them," said Beau. "If we're lucky."

Great, thought Abbie. Millie was hoping he'd catch enough for dinner. He hadn't caught enough for the three of them much less an extra mouth to feed. Maybe she should get a room at the inn. They were too polite to say so, but she had to be a strain on the Crispin budget.

"You go on now, Beau," Silas said. "These here coolers are full up." He raised the two coolers to demonstrate their weight. He put one of them on the ground at Beau's feet.

"Just about did catch our limit." Beau handed the fishing poles off to Silas.

"Nice to meet you, ma'am. See you tomorrah, Beau." Silas hoisted his fishing gear and cooler and cut across the street to a dirt path that led through the trees.

Beau picked up the cooler Silas had left. "Shall we?"

They walked up the drive, cool and dark beneath the trees. "Did you have a nice time in town?" he asked.

She had except for making Bethanne cry. "I met Bethanne, Penny, and Sarah."

"Three lovely ladies."

They lapsed into silence, and Abbie was glad she didn't have to think of small talk to fill the walk to Crispin House. Being with Beau was soothing. She'd never seen him make an abrupt gesture, hurry with anything. Of course she hadn't seen much of him. But she had a feeling he was that way all the time. What could make a person so placid? Was he content?

Or was it that he just accepted life for what it was?

They were almost to the house when a creature darted out of the trees. The cat she'd seen the night before. It was huge with short black fur and a white bib. It glided straight to Beau, raising its rusty meow as it ran.

Beau laughed. "Old Moses knows he's gettin' a treat tonight."

"His name is Moses?"

"Yep. Found him in the marsh across the bay yonder. A feral litter, most likely. He was the only one I could find; guess the gators got the rest. Don't know why they didn't get him."

"Gators?"

"Oh, don't you worry; they're way on the other side of the bay. Don't cross salt water if they can help it. And when they do come out, they head for the golf courses." Beau grinned.

Abbie smiled back.

"Don't get too many snakes, either. A few garden ones maybe. But you won't see them much unless you go in the woods. Don't fret."

"I won't," Abbie said. Amphibians and reptiles she could handle. God knows she'd dealt with their human counterparts often enough.

Moses meowed and raced a few yards ahead before looking back.

Beau shook his head. "Hard to believe he used to be a tiny little thing. That was oh, goin' on twelve, thirteen years ago. And he hasn't slowed down one bit. Maybe I shoulda named him Methuselah."

They went around to the side door, where Beau stopped and pulled out a folded paper from the cooler. He opened it up and put it on the ground. Moses pounced on the fish heads and offal inside.

"Got all the bones out. Millie don't like to have fish cleaned near her kitchen so Silas and I always gut them 'fore we come home."

"Beau Crispin, is that you?" Millie's voice echoed from the kitchen.

Beau smiled at Abbie.

Millie appeared in the doorway, a white apron over her dress.

"Got us a mess of bream. Marnie has a way with fish," he told Abbie. He winked at her. "But Millie here makes a dog-gone good hush puppy."

"I'll hush puppy you if you bring any of that fish smell into my kitchen."

"I'll just go round back and clean up. Nice walking with you, Abbie." He deposited the cooler on the steps and picked up the paper that had been picked clean. Moses was nowhere to be seen.

"Did you have a nice time in town?" Millie asked.

"Yes, thanks. I'll just take my purchases upstairs, then come back and help with dinner."

"Oh, Lord no. You just go and enjoy yourself."

Enjoy herself. She was trying. She trudged up the stairs to her bedroom and tossed her gift shop bag and purse on the bed. Then tossed herself after them. Someone had opened the French doors, and a breeze floated in and ruffled the sheer curtains. She would make an entry in her new journal. Maybe describe her trip into town and meeting Bethanne, Penny, and Sarah. Get started on exorcizing her demons.

She dumped the bag onto the bed, chose a pen, and took it and the journal out to the veranda. It was shaded from the afternoon sun, which would be heaven in the summer but made it a little too cool for comfort.

But the beach was still sunny, and if she sat below the dunes, she'd be sheltered from the wind. She went back inside and down the stairs, thinking she was being absurd to worry about a few degrees of temperature, considering the life she'd led in the last few years.

She stopped in the kitchen to let Millie know that she was going out. The kitchen was empty, though there was evidence of food preparations on the counters. She backtracked into the foyer in search of one of the sisters and heard voices from the library whose door was behind the staircase.

She meant to stick her head in just long enough to tell them where she was going, but just as she reached the open door of the library, Marnie's voice rose in exasperation. "Just when were you going to tell me about this?"

"It just slipped my mind. I don't see why they keep botherin' us."

"Oh, Millie. You were supposed to give them a partial payment. Do I have to do everything myself? No, no, I'm sorry, I didn't mean that. But what happened to the money?"

Abbie knew she should creep away. This was family business she had no business listening to.

"Well, Rowena Thompkins's baby had a turn for the worse. I ran into her at the pharmacy. Rod's out of work still. They have no insurance. She couldn't even pay for her prescription. I just gave her a little something to tide her over."

"Two hundred dollars? Millie, there are agencies to help her."

"It's our duty to help out the less fortunate. Daddy always helped others."

Marnie barked out a laugh. "*We* are the less fortunate. Daddy should have seen to his own family."

"For shame, Sister. We are still leaders in this town. People look to us for guidance."

Marnie groaned. "And money."

"It was an emergency."

"This is an emergency." More rattling of paper. It must be a letter.

"I don't know why they just don't leave us alone; we've paid our taxes faithfully for years, and Daddy before us. They should be able to wait a little while."

"Not with beachfront real estate as profitable as this. They'll take the house and sell it to a developer and make a bundle off it, who will in turn make a bundle off it, while we walk away with nothing. How are we going to live then?"

Millie mumbled something that Abbie couldn't hear.

"And do you know what will happen to the other residents in town once we cave?"

"But she was in such dire need."

Marnie sighed. "We'll have to sell more silver. It won't fetch what it's worth, but it will keep the hyenas from the door for another year maybe."

"You can't. That's the last set, and it was Momma's favorite."

"Would you rather sell the house and grounds?"

"It isn't fair."

"No, but life isn't fair."

Millie began to cry.

Abbie tiptoed away. They were as generous as they could be. They'd taken in Abbie even though it was obviously putting a strain on their limited resources. She wondered if she should call Celeste. But what good would that do? Just worry Celeste because somehow Abbie doubted that the three would take money from their niece even if Celeste could come up with it.

Abbie left a note on the kitchen table saying she was at the beach and would be back in time to help with dinner.

She wouldn't impose on the Crispins any longer. She had some money, plus a life insurance policy Werner had not told her about. It wasn't much, but it would keep her afloat long enough to figure out what to do with her life. She wouldn't use the insurance money on herself unless she had to. She'd find a good cause and donate it all. And then she'd figure out what to do.

And that's where she began her journal. *What to do with my life*. She sat cross-legged on the sand, the wind rippling off the water and the late-afternoon sun warming her back. She stared at the first sentence and the subsequent empty page. Sort of like her future, a blank slate, a tabula rasa, a barren desert? It could be anything she wanted it to be, she thought. She could stay right where she was. Get a job. Maybe Bethanne would need help in the summer. She would work cheap if it included room and board.

Or she could travel. She could buy a car. Not a jeep or
Humvee, but something girly, small and low to the ground,
electric blue or silver.

She squeezed her eyes shut against the thought. The truth
was she had nothing to look forward to. But she wouldn't write
that down. Everything that was important about her had happened in her past, which would be okay if she was still on track.
But she'd been derailed, and she didn't know how the hell she
was going to carry on.

She didn't write that down either.

She wrote about Werner.

She'd just graduated from Ann Arbor and had gone down to
Guatemala to help build Habitat houses. The trip was a graduation gift from her parents. She knew a little about construction,
electrical work, plumbing. All the Sinclair children did. You
never knew when you'd be called on to help your neighbor
repair his roof or fix a burned-out fuse. And since she was the
only Sinclair who hadn't known from childhood which area
of selfless service she would make her life's work, she learned a
little bit of everything.

She studied communications in college. A degree that
landed her a job as a weathergirl at a Chicago television station, which if you had a really good imagination—and all the
Sinclairs did—you could count as a service job.

But she was ahead of herself. She was in Guatemala. Werner
was part of a Dutch filming crew who were making a documentary in a nearby village.

They camped along with the Habitat people because the
Habitat people had edible food, hot water, and decent living
quarters. She and Werner started talking over mess and talked
far into the night. He was older, wiser, so full of life, so determined to effect change, and so handsome.

In the early hours of morning, they went back to his room
and made love. They were together for another week, then the
documentary crew left for another location. The Habitat group
left two weeks later. Abbie settled into her job as weathergirl
for the same station Celeste worked for. They became friends.
Celeste was the person Abbie ran to when her world fell apart.

Abbie looked down at what she'd written. *What to do with my
life. Guatemala.* The rest of the page was blank. It seems that
Werner refused to be put on the page. It was so like him. Her
throat burned.

She closed the book, brushed the sand off her pants, and
went back to the house to help with dinner and try not to think
about Werner or how she had failed at the end.

Supper, as Millie called it, was served early that night. There
was fish fried in cornmeal, sliced tomatoes and onions, coleslaw, and stewed greens that Marnie said were collards. And
the famed hush puppies that were balls of deep-fried corn bread
filled with succulent pieces of onion.

It was delicious and filling, especially the hush puppies.
Abbie ate two. The greens were bitter but with a different taste
from broccoli rabe or escarole. Chewier, even though Abbie
was pretty sure they had been cooking since that morning
when Marnie brought them in.

A block of wood sat at Beau's elbow like an extra fork. He
must have completed the one he'd been working on the day
before, because this one was uncut. He didn't reach for it once,
but as soon as he finished eating, he stood up and put it in his
pocket.

"If y'all will excuse me, I promised Cab I'd come down and
help him with an electrical matter."

"You ask him what time he's coming for Abbie tomorrow,"
Millie reminded him.

"I will."

"Only if he has the time," said Abbie. *And the inclination,* she added silently. She didn't know if she was up for sightseeing with a person who so obviously didn't like her.

"He has plenty of time," Millie said.

"I have to get going too," Marnie said. "Leave the dishes until I get back." She followed Beau out, leaving Millie and Abbie alone in the dining room.

"I'll help you clear," Abbie said when Millie pushed her chair away from the table.

"That's all right, dear. I'll—"

"I insist. If you trust me with these lovely dishes."

Millie beamed. "Of course I do, but you don't need to lift a finger, just sit back and enjoy yourself."

Abbie needed to take a stand or she would be twiddling her thumbs until she left. "I appreciate your hospitality, Millie, but I want to help. I'm not very good at doing nothing, like Marnie said. And I'd feel a lot more comfortable if I could just be a part of things instead of the pampered guest."

Millie pursed her lips and placed her hand on her chest. "Oh, my dear, of course. You'll be just like one of the family."

They cleared the table, and Abbie scraped the dishes while Millie washed. "You know it's Beau's birthday come July."

"No, I didn't," Abbie said.

"I'm goin' to throw him a big party. Invite the whole town and a few friends from Charleston. But it's a surprise." Millie's eyes wrinkled in delight. "We'll open up the ballroom, and there'll be dancin' and a food table that'll stretch down the whole length of the room."

Abbie felt a little uncomfortable. Surely Millie couldn't be serious, not after the things Marnie had said.

"Momma and Daddy used to have glorious parties. It was a real honor to be invited to a party at Crispin House. Some-

times Beau would come home from the fleet. So handsome in
his uniform. All the girls were wild for him."

"He was in the navy?"

Millie's face clouded over. "No. The merchant marines."
Millie sighed. "We thought for a while he'd marry Susie Tolli-
ver, but he never stayed long enough for anything to come of
it. As soon as he could, he'd be off to some other foreign port.
Him and Marnie just couldn't seem to sit still."

Her eyes took on a glassy, faraway look. "Funny how we
all ended up right back here where we were born. And where
we belong," she added, almost defiantly. "Let's just let these air
dry. Would you like to watch some *Jeopardy!* on television? Or
would you like to see the ballroom?"

There was no question which one Millie wanted, so Abbie
said, "Ballroom, of course," and exchanged a delighted, if
somewhat faked, smile with her hostess. Millie led her past the
library to the back of the house and a wide double door made
from dark wood. It was divided into four panels with parquet
inlay, a testament to a richer, more elegant time.

Millie paused at the door, then turned back to look at Abbie,
her expression so delighted and conspiratorial that Abbie began
to catch her excitement. She could imagine Millie and Marnie
as children staring over the balustrade, watching the elegant
guests arrive. And later as young girls, dressed in flowing ball
gowns.

Or maybe these were just images she'd seen in a movie.

Millie pulled on both doors, and they stepped inside. The
room was dark at first, then gradually it became lighter at the
far side, and Abbie realized that the entire back wall was win-
dowed and looked out onto the sea.

It was breathtakingly beautiful.

And it was also unused. Millie found the light switch, and
a yellow haze spread through the empty space. A wide plank

wooden floor stretched across an expansive room. Along the walls, white tarps covered what Abbie presumed were chairs and settees and tables. A balcony overlooked the room; the orchestra surely must have played from there.

Millie walked to the center of the floor then turned back and motioned to Abbie.

"We'll have to take the dust covers off and give the floor a good polishing. And make all his favorite dishes. Not caterers. They never do things right, though I might ask Penny Farlowe to do the desserts. And we'll have to hire people to serve. And the invitations. I'll have to drive over to Georgetown to the stationers, and . . ."

The thought of Millie driving even as far as Hadley's was enough to rattle Abbie. And she knew there was no way all these preparations were even remotely possible. Surely Millie didn't really believe she could pull off such a large event.

But she was right about one thing. It was a grand ballroom and a pity it was going to waste. Abbie wouldn't mind seeing it lit up in all its former glory, herself.

"And dancin'. Not a fiddle and a piano, either. A string quartet . . . We always had an orchestra. Sometimes when it was hot, the party would spill over to the lawn and the orchestra would move to the summah house."

It took Abbie a second to translate her words to *summerhouse.* The gazebo.

"All the guests would dance in the moonlight. You could hear the waves each time the orchestra stopped playing." Millie walked to the window and peered out into the dark night.

"I think I saw it yesterday when I was out walking," Abbie said.

"When Beau was a boy, he would spend the whole day out there, even in the winter, paintin' the sea and whatever else he came across. He wanted to go to art school, but Daddy put

his foot down and sent him off to the Citadel. There was a big
set-to. It happened right down there in the summah house. I'd
never seen Daddy so angry. He—"

She shuddered and turned from the window. "Then Beau
left for school. Momma got sick and the parties stopped and
nobody went down there anymore.

"But why are we talking about that horrid old thing when
we have this lovely ballroom. It's perfect for Beau's party."

Abbie suspected Beau would enjoy something a little more
informal. She could imagine Cabot the third dressed in a tux
and waltzing his way around the room, but the idea of Beau or
Silas being comfortable in bow ties and dance shoes eluded her.

Millie wasn't being rational. Should she say something to
Marnie? Or should she just mind her own business?

The world is our business, Abbie, Werner had once told her.
She'd just tossed a handful of change to a small beggar boy.
He was immediately set on by other boys who wrested the few
coins from him, then shoved him to the ground. *It's hopeless,*
she'd cried. *What are we doing? Nothing will ever change.* He took
her by the shoulders. Held her firmly until she looked up at
him. *We can't change it all. But we sure as hell can try.*

And they had tried. Chipping away, incident by incident,
horror story by horror story. Sometimes effecting a brief re-
spite, sometimes not making a ripple.

Over the years Werner had moved away from documenting
people's lives and got more involved with stopping injustice.
At first she'd been swept along on his fervor. It had been exciting, important work, stories of waste and war and greed.
But Abbie cared about individuals more than causes. And their
work began to gnaw at her, break her down. It killed a little
piece of her. Maybe a big chunk of her.

Werner noticed it, and he was understanding. "Everybody

burns out along the way; just hang in and it will pass." She believed him; she believed *in* him. But it didn't pass.

He began spending more and more time on editing, distribution, and fund-raising. She didn't remember exactly when she first realized their lives, their hopes, their desires were diverging.

She'd hung in until the end, but her fervor had only grown dimmer. He'd left her behind and never even noticed.

He risked his life more than once to get his film. Times when he could have turned his back, taken an easier route. Times when she begged him to do just that, tried to convince him that he couldn't make things better if he was dead. But he wouldn't pull back. It was as if a stronger fire had ignited within him. And in the end it killed him. Not angry villagers, or an epidemic or widespread rebellion, but greed.

He was murdered to keep him from exposing the practices of a multibillion-dollar company who refused to pay the barest decent wages or lift a finger to save the countryside they were exploiting.

"Do you waltz?"

Abbie jerked back to the present. Millie was standing a few feet away swaying to some unheard music, her arms outspread as if resting on her hoopskirt.

"No," said Abbie. "I never learned to dance."

"Well, we'll teach you before the party. Beau was an excellent dancer in his day. And so was I." Suddenly she dropped her arms. "Let's go see if *Jeopardy!* is still on."

Abbie followed her silently out of the room, still disoriented from her flashback and even more disoriented by Millie's strange behavior. Abbie wasn't the only person living in the present and longing for the past. She'd found a kindred sprit, a fellow sufferer in Millie, but as much as she was beginning to care for the older woman, she didn't want to be like her.

Millie flipped the light switch, and the room was plunged into darkness. They felt their way back into the hallway.

The television, an unwieldy box with rabbit ears, was in a small den behind the parlor with an overstuffed sofa and chair, two battered leather ottomans, and a metal stand holding four floral-printed television tables.

Abbie sat down on the sofa. Millie sat down beside her and pressed the remote buttons until the game show came on the air.

"Aristotle was the teacher of this world conqueror."

"Who is Alexander the Great?" Millie called out the correct answer a second before the contestant.

"Beau says I should be on this show," Millie said with a mixture of pride and disdain.

"Why don't you?"

"I wouldn't presume," she said and answered the next question.

Chapter 6

Cab stood in the dark, listening. He could barely hear the waves in the distance. He groped for the light switch. The light flicked on, casting a low glow over its surroundings. And there she was. Midnight Lady. Black and sleek. Flanks tense. Nostrils flared, head tossed and straining to break free. He ran his hand over her back, slapped her shoulder. *I'm here.*

How many times he came back to her, how many times he left again. From the time he could first reach the stirrup, he'd hoist himself up, throw his leg over the saddle and they would gallop away. Down to the beach, over the world, with Cab on her back, slicing the wind, unfettered, happy—free.

How many times had he taken that ride in the past only to lose his way again?

She was older now and so was he. What a huge amount of time he'd wasted trying to get ahead, when as it turned out all he wanted was to come home.

"Cab, are you in there?"

Beau was here. "Coming." Cab slid a hand down the horse's side in a final caress, carefully pulled the blanket over her, and turned out the light. When he came out, Beau was down on his haunches staring into the wooden engine housing.

"Didn't expect to see you this early," Cab said.

"Always eat early on Mondays. It's Marnie's meeting night."

"Ah, lucky for me. I've been dealing with the damn thing for days. It runs for a bit then starts clanging like she's spitting nails."

Beau nodded, stood up, and wiped his hands on a white handkerchief. Millie would kill them both, Cab thought. Beau for ruining the handkerchief, Cab for letting him use it.

"You crawl in there and start her up," Beau said. "And let me have a listen."

Cab moved past him and fired up the engine. There was a click, another click, a grinding sound, and the engine began to chug. The apparatus lurched forward, sputtered, ran for a few more seconds, then ground to a halt. Cab turned off the engine and looked over to Beau.

"For starters, you need a new starter." Beau waggled his eyebrows. "Bollinger oughta have something that will work. Besides that, my guess is you got a cranky clutch. I'd just go on and get a new one if you can. Then . . ." Beau looked overhead, squinting and craning his neck one way then the other as he contemplated the rafters. "You also got some cracked teeth or a bent suspension rod."

Cab looked up into the mechanism. It always reminded him of some high-tech architectural design, and yet it was close to a hundred years old. And unlike Ned's five-year-old microwave, it still ran—barely, but with a little TLC he knew it would last for a long time to come.

"I was afraid of that. I'll have to order the replacement parts, but I can get by Bollinger's tomorrow. Except I promised Millie I'd take your guest around. Maybe I should—"

"I don't think Abbie'll mind taking a little detour."

Damn, cut off at the pass. Though Cab didn't get why he was so conflicted about taking Abbie Sinclair on a tour. She wasn't his type, though his type had turned out to be a big bust. And he did want to get her alone so he could find out just why she was here. At the same time he didn't want to have anything to do with her.

"Well, you gonna stand there gaping, or do you wanna go to the trouble to disconnect the engine from the mast, and see if we can clear up that hitch you've got?"

Cab retrieved his tool kit from the workbench. When he returned, Beau was standing on the wooden platform, hands in his pockets, surrounded by a forest of steel rods. "I remember when Ned bought this setup. *He* had to replace the engine. It had been running on steam before that.

"You coulda bowled us over with a feather when Ned ups and buys the damn thing. Didn't know he had the inclination or the money. But he fooled us. He had both. Worked like a dog, though. Those days the beach was built up and the tourists flocked in. We were going great guns for a while."

"I remember," Cab said, joining him on the platform.

"And he sure loved you. The summers you spent with him was the icing on the cake, he said. Never had his own children, but he had you, and you would be the next generation to enjoy the fruits of his labor."

"He said that?"

"Sure did. I know he's lookin' down saying, that's my boy. You and this old thing meant everything in the world to him." Beau sniffed, chose one of the wrenches, and bent over the engine. "He'd be tickled that you've taken over for him."

The wall phone rang. It was the first time it had rung in days, and it startled both of them.

"Better answer that," Beau said. "Might be an emergency."

"Maybe." Cab walked toward the phone, but instead of answering it, he listened to the caller leave his message.

"Hey, Cab, it's Frank." Frank Toohey, his colleague back

in Atlanta. "Where are you? I know you're there. Unless the gators got ya." A hearty chuckle; Frank loved his own repartee. "Anyway, Tony and I are gonna be up in Myrtle Beach this weekend. Thought we'd stop by on our way up. See if you've had enough of backwater living. So find us a decent place for dinner if there are any." There was a pause. "Oh, and just so you won't be surprised, we're bringing Bailey. See you in a few."

The call ended and Cab erased the message, though he felt more like tearing the phone off the wall.

Beau was watching him. "Woman troubles?"

"Not anymore." Over the months he'd gotten to know Beau, he'd told him about his past life and his aborted engagement. He'd been hurt when Bailey had called it off, but not all that surprised. He'd gotten over her. He'd gotten over it all. He really, really didn't want to be dragged through it all again.

Abbie was ready the next morning at ten sharp. Cabot had called the night before to make the arrangements. He hadn't talked to Abbie directly but passed the information through Millie, who took the opportunity to reiterate what a lovely young man he was.

Abbie let it pass. She was pretty sure she wasn't going to have to defend herself from untoward advances from Cabot the third. He plainly wasn't interested, and Abbie hoped the tour would be short.

At ten fifteen, Cabot called to say he was running late. Again Millie took the call, reiterating what a lovely man he was and adding that he worked just too darn hard.

When he finally showed up at twelve thirty, Abbie was playing Solitaire at the kitchen table, listening to Marnie and Millie squabble over which tomatoes were the ripest.

Millie ran out to meet him, and Abbie followed reluctantly behind. Since it was a sightseeing tour, she'd opted for dark-washed jeans and a V-neck sweater. Conservative but not fussy. She could tell the minute she stepped off the stairs earlier that morning that Millie did not approve. She probably thought Abbie should wear a dress and heels.

Cabot was standing in the foyer, and she was relieved to see him also in jeans. Though he looked anything but casual. He looked as trapped as she felt. She got a sudden image of her junior prom and facing the boy she'd invited to go with her. He'd been smart and sort of gawky, and she invited him because she felt sorry for him. It had been an excruciating evening for both of them. Cabot the third was far from gawky, but that didn't assuage her doubts about the coming day.

She adjusted the strap of her shoulder bag and smiled. "Sure you're up for this?"

"Sorry I'm late," he said, ignoring her question.

Millie walked them to the door and practically pushed them out to the porch. "Y'all have a good time and don't worry about hurryin' back."

"We won't be too long," Abbie and Cabot answered together.

"Oh, pooh, you two stay out as late as you want." Millie frowned down at a silver newer-model Range Rover that was parked at the front steps. It was covered with splashes of dried mud and a layer of red dust.

"Don't say it, Millie. I've been busy. If Ms. Sinclair doesn't mind, I'll stop by the car wash on our way to Bollinger's." He turned to Abbie, charming smile back intact. "Or I could run out there first and come back for you. I have to run a couple of errands and then the day is yours."

Abbie just looked at him. The day was already half over. But Cabot the third smiled, and Abbie could practically hear Millie's heart pattering.

Abbie only felt the underlying bite of hostility beneath that façade of Southern charm.

"Don't stop at the car wash on my account," said Abbie, leaving him on the porch and trotting down the stairs to the Range Rover. Before he could get to her, she'd opened the front door and climbed into the passenger's seat, scandalizing Millie and forcing a reluctant grin from The Third.

"See you later, Miz Millie," Cabot said and went around to his side of the SUV.

Abbie settled back in her seat determined to enjoy the scenery, even if her tour guide was less than congenial. There was nothing either of them could do except get through it; then Millie would be happy, and their obligation would be fulfilled.

"Hundred-year-old red oaks," Cabot said as they passed down the drive to the street.

Abbie started. It seemed that Cabot had begun his tour duty.

"They're beautiful."

"Yes, they are."

They lapsed into silence. Abbie usually didn't have trouble drawing people out, which is why Werner had depended on her for choosing who to interview and later had her conduct the interviews on camera as well.

Had she lost those skills, that empathy people trusted? Did Cabot Reynolds feel threatened for some reason? Or was it because she felt threatened? By what? The Third's pedigree? She wasn't sure he had one. Maybe he was just a mongrel trying to be something he wasn't. Or had she reached the point where she just needed to hold everyone at arm's length?

They passed out of the trees, stopped at the end of the drive, then Cabot turned the SUV toward town.

"Are there more houses down the other way?" Abbie asked.

"Yes. Is that what you want to see?"

"Not really, I was just wondering."

"There are several, but only the Crispins have ocean frontage." His lips tightened as if he'd exchanged a confidence he shouldn't have.

Abbie leaned back and looked out the window. She was getting a little tired of his surliness. Maybe he'd forgotten to take his medication. She tried to think of crazy fictional characters from the South, but she couldn't imagine him in an undershirt, yelling "Stella!" at the top of his lungs.

"What's that for?"

"What's what?" she asked.

"The smile."

She was smiling? That had to be a good sign. "Nothing. Do I have to have a reason to smile?"

He didn't answer, but expelled a breath—the long-suffering hero—and they'd been gone less than five minutes. If she were smart, she'd bail while they were still close enough for her to walk home.

"This is town. If you look to your right, you'll see the pier—or what's left of it. The last hurricane destroyed it, the beach, and most of the buildings at this end of town."

"The town decided not to build it back?"

"They would if—there's no reason to. The beaches have eroded almost to nothing. The roads from the highway are narrow and nearly impassable when it rains. And as you'll see as we pass through the three blocks of downtown proper, there's no entertainment to speak of."

"I hope you aren't in the habit of giving guided tours."

"Why?"

"You don't make Stargazey Point sound very appetizing."

"Well, it's nice enough if you don't want much. No room to grow. Got a national park to the northwest, highways to the west, and not much usable shoreline."

"Well, I think it's beautiful." She said it partly just to be difficult, but also because it was the truth. Stargazey Point had a quiet charm about it. An oasis in the bustle of crowded board-walks and congested highways. And if its beach wasn't very wide, it made up for it in the softness of the white sand. And the people she'd met, with the possible exception of her driver, were laid-back and friendly.

They passed the building with the cupola and she was going to ask him what it was, but Sarah Davis stepped out from the community center, grinned, and waved. Abbie waved back.

Cabot slanted Abbie a dark look. "It has no attractions like Myrtle Beach, no theme parks. No hotels and no room to build any," he added quickly. "Same thing goes for golf courses."

"I think the inn is lovely and the lack of amenities might be a drawing card for people looking for a quiet, charming place to vacation."

"They can go to Hilton Head or Charleston and get all the charm they want."

"Ah," she said, suddenly understanding what was going on. "You just don't want any tourists mucking up your home, is that it?"

"Tourists? We could use some tourism. But I might as well lay it on the line. We don't want some big corporation coming in, razing the place, and then locking everybody out."

"I don't blame you."

"Or any small corporations or individual developers either."

"Good."

Cabot just kept frowning at her, which was odd. Maybe he had his own plans for Stargazey Point.

As they drove through town, Cabot the third dutifully pointed out each business. But he never stopped the SUV.

A little white church marked the end of town. It had a stubby steeple and small sunny cemetery off to one side. Abbie closed her eyes until they were past.

On the outskirts of town, they slowed down in front of a white clapboard house with the popular blue trim where an old woman and a little boy sat on the front stoop. The woman was shelling peas into a plastic bowl, but she looked up and nodded when Cab beeped the horn. The boy jumped up and dashed out to run alongside the Range Rover. Cabot slowed down and played along for a few moments, then waved out the window as they left the boy behind.

"Everyone seems to know you," Abbie said conversationally. "The beauty of small town life."

"The beauty and the bane."

Okay, conversation was going to be stilted at best and painful most of the time. Except that she kept coming back for more. *The way to get to the real truth,* Werner told her whenever she stopped short in an interview. *Badger them until they finally open up or get caught in their own lies.* But did she really want to know more about Cabot Reynolds the third? Did she care?

He might be a plumber or independently wealthy or just shabby genteel. His jeans were Levi's not Calvin's. But his car was strictly upwardly mobile. He owned horses, according to Sarah. But he hadn't volunteered anything about himself.

"Are your 'people' from around here?"

"My people," he said, mimicking her tone, "are from around Boston."

"Boston? What on earth are you doing down here?"

His frown deepened. "Showing you the sights."

They lapsed back into silence.

The houses became sparser, less tended. Each hugged the road, tethered to telephone lines by sagging wires. The last house was a deserted wooden shack, balanced precariously between a patch of dirt that had once served as a parking lot and a slash of bulldozed earth at its back. A rotting sign above the boarded door spelled out COOK'S BB. The rest of the sign had fallen to the ground.

"A friend of mine used to own that, best barbecue on the coast," Cabot said.

Abbie looked back and saw the brick smokehouse standing alone among the scarred ground. "What happened? A hurricane?"

Cabot shot her a sideways glance. "Developer. Bought it for a song."

"Doesn't look like they've done much developing."

"No." His tone was harsh. It was pretty obvious where he stood on developing the coastline. She didn't blame him. It had a certain wild, but gentle beauty, a tenuous balance that even the most conscientious builder couldn't keep from disturbing. And the fact that some were unscrupulous enough to cheat the people who had a real claim to the land brought out her crusader spirit—but it wasn't her business, not anymore. Not their histories, their needs, their desires, their stories. She no longer had the right to enter their lives.

Cabot sped up and they left Stargazey Point behind. He concentrated on the road, not bothering to make conversation. Abbie just breathed in the fresh air and tried to enjoy the scenery. Tried to forget why she was here. Tried not to worry about where she was going.

"Something wrong?"

She glanced over at her driver, who was frowning at her. "No. Why?"

"You sighed like maybe you wished you hadn't come."

"You mean you're hoping I'll change my mind and free up your day?"

"No. Whether we like it or not, neither of us can avoid this little tour. Millie has a way of getting her way."

"Nothing's wrong. I was sighing with pleasure."

That gained her another frown.

They drove over a causeway, but instead of coming to signs of civilization like the shopping malls and highway hotels she had passed on her way from the airport, they seemed to be going farther into the wilderness.

A patchwork of marshes and dry land dotted with clumps of scrub oak and spindly pines spread out from the narrow road in all directions. In the distance, black-trunked oak trees stood above the landscape like something from Dr. Seuss. Closer to the road an occasional billboard stuck out of the marshy grass; sometimes a distant trailer glinted in the sun.

Time stretched and warped as it tended to do when you had no idea where you were going or how long it would take. They could be on an abandoned planet for all the people she saw.

Abbie had covered remote mountains, deep jungle, rain forest. The countryside they were passing through looked just as deserted, though she knew there would be hidden pockets of humanity—and inhumanity.

Then suddenly they rounded a curve into an unexpected, rolling, cultivated landscape of perfectly manicured lawn. It was such a shock after the desolate country they'd driven through that it took Abbie a moment to recognize it for what it was.

Then she saw a sign ahead. SALTAIRE PLANTATION. SOUTH CAROLINA'S FINEST PRIVATE GOLF COMMUNITY.

Private golf community. She turned to look out the window. There was no one playing golf. She didn't see one car parked in front of the condos that appeared as an oasis of wood and glass in the distance.

And they actually called it a plantation. Not exactly politically correct.

She glanced over to Cab, who kept his eyes on the road.

"Do you play golf, Cab?"

"On occasion; do you?"

"No. And it doesn't look like too many people are playing here."

"That's because they've glutted the area with condos and gated communities. SaltAire is only half full in season. Building has slowed to a crawl."

"Is that what happened to your friend's barbecue place?"

"Pretty much. They bought it and then didn't have the funds to build anything in its place."

"They should have thought about that before they razed the land and left his business to rot."

"You're against progress?"

Abbie shrugged. "No, just exploitation."

He looked sharply at her, then back to the road. "Good. Too many people like Silas get cheated from some suit who's never spent an hour here. Just sent an underling to make an offer. Before you know it, they've lost their homes, their businesses, and everything they've ever owned. Most folks around here have managed to eke out a life for decades. Now it's harder for them to keep up with expenses. No health insurance, no pensions. Silas wanted his granddaughter to go to college. Turns out she got a scholarship."

"So he didn't really need to sell."

"Nope, and he got screwed."

"Silas? Beau's friend?"

"Yes. How do you know Silas?"

"I met him and Beau coming back from their fishing trip."

Cab started to say something, then just grunted and went back to watching the road. "I have to make one stop, and then I'll take you over to Myrtle Beach or down to Charleston, though it's bit of a hike."

"Why don't you do your errand and we just see the local sights?"

"Why?"

"Because I came here for peace and quiet, not bright lights and big cities. Even charming ones."

"Why did you come here?"

Abbie hesitated. "I wanted to go on a quiet vacation. My friend Celeste suggested I come here. Frankly, I think she's a little worried about her aunts and uncle, and since she wasn't able to come, I'm sort of her proxy."

"How long have you known Celeste?"

"Since I went to work at the same station as her. Eight years, give or take a few months."

"You work at the television station?"

"I did."

"Doing what?"

"I was the weathergirl."

"The weath—You were the weathergirl?"

"Yes."

"A weathergirl." Cabot shook his head. Chuckled.

"And what's so funny about reporting the weather?"

"Nothing at all. I thought maybe you were in real estate."

"Real estate? Why?"

"It's just that the Crispins have been pestered to death about selling Crispin House. It's prime oceanfront acreage. It could make somebody a fortune . . . just not anyone who lives around here."

"And you thought I would use my best friend to weasel my way into a land deal?"

"Sorry. But I've never met her. It was a natural assumption."

"A jaded assumption."

"Maybe."

"She's very busy." They both had been busy; both had neglected their families. But she had a feeling that the Crispins felt it more than Abbie's own family. Hers didn't mind not seeing her as long as she was out making the world a better place. They kept in touch by e-mail and Skype. She wondered what they thought of her now.

"She really does care. She asked me to check up on them. Make sure they were okay." It hadn't been quite that straightforward, but if Abbie found out that anyone was trying to cheat them, she knew Celeste would be on the first available flight to help them out.

"Okay. I apologize. But you have to admit, it seemed like a natural progression. And in view of certain situations—well . . ."

"Something like unpaid taxes?"

Cabot stared at her. "They told you?"

Abbie shook her head. "I'm afraid I was walking past an open door and overheard."

He was looking straight ahead, and Abbie took the opportunity to scrutinize his face. "What's your interest in the Crispins?"

His head snapped toward her. "Interest? They're my friends. I've know them since I was a kid. Beau even taught me how to whittle. I was abysmal."

Out of the blue, Cabot the third smiled. It was an amazing transformation that sent a little thrill to her stomach. It was also extremely short-lived. An old man, with an older nag pulling a cart, moved out of a dirt path and onto the shoulder of the road.

"Watch out!" Abbie yelled.

Cabot jerked the steering wheel, and the Range Rover swerved into the other lane.

The old man led the horse to the shoulder and continued on his way. Then he raised a hand in an afterthought of a wave. Abbie raised her hand in return then snatched it back as the man began to dissolve before her eyes, shimmering pieces cascading to the ground and evaporating into nothing. Abbie blinked, blinked again, but all she saw was his hand still lifted in the air.

Chapter 7

Sorry about that," Cab said as he pulled the Range Rover back into the lane. "I was looking at you instead of where I was going. But he wasn't in any danger." Granted, he hadn't been paying close attention to his driving, but he hadn't come close to hitting the old guy. She'd way overreacted.

"What?" She turned slightly toward him; there was perspiration on her forehead. She was gripping the handle so hard that he wouldn't have been surprised to see it come away in her hand.

"Are you feeling all right?" *Please don't throw up in my car,* he thought. "Should I stop?"

"What?" she repeated, then shook her head. She released the handle, sat back. "No, I'm okay."

Thank God for that, because she *was* okay. More than okay. If she was being straight with him. Her compassion for Silas's situation, and her seeming aversion to development. She could be playing him. Hell, he'd been played by women before. Of course, in those days he had been a player himself, so all was fair. But he'd left that behind.

"But maybe we should go back."

He slowed down and pulled onto the rocky shoulder, came to a full stop. She looked ready to bolt.

"Look. I apologize. For my bad manners, my bad driving, my bad whatever else set you off. The Crispins are my friends, and now they're your friends. The least we can do is try to be friends, too."

She wiped her mouth with the back of her hand, a strangely sensual gesture. Took a breath. "Okay."

"Good. Now I have to stop by Bollinger's Electrical to pick up some parts for my generator, and then the day is yours. Deal?"

She looked reluctant, and for a second he thought she was going to turn him down, but finally she said, "Okay."

"Great," he said and hoped he wasn't making a big mistake.

Marnie cut down the overgrown path that led to Ervina's cottage. She could see a thin wisp of smoke rising out of the stand of palmettos ahead. Ervina had the fire going.

Warmth for old bones. Hell, how did she get to be so damn old? Seems like just a few weeks ago, she was in her prime, strong, not bad looking, with a purpose in life. Even now, she'd wake up in the middle of the night, which happened more and more the older she got, and she'd forget where she was. Think she was on her road somewhere, or reach for the warm loving body beside her, and she would feel a tingle of expectant excitement, mixed with sorrow. Then she'd recollect, and the excitement would dissipate like the driest desert sand, to be replaced with not resentment, not anymore, but with a kind of peace. Knowing she was home.

Now she was relegated to puttering about the garden. No, not puttering, but working her butt off, breaking her brittle old back. The garden was a necessity. It was the only way they could make ends meet. Keep up the façade of living. Feeding them and bringing in a few dollars by selling the surplus to a farm stand down the road. And it was all about to go up in smoke, like Ervina's chimney.

She stepped into the clearing of hard dirt in front of Ervina's shack. The shack had been white sixty years ago, but the paint had long since melted and flaked away. Too much time, too much weather. The house was still standing. The porch sagged a bit. It creaked beneath her feet.

She pulled the front door open, stepped inside to the familiar smell of clean linoleum and heady herbs. She peered into the shadowed room.

"Thought you might be showin' up today."

Marnie prided herself on not jumping out of her skin; she was used to Ervina's shenanigans. Ervina reveled in her witch-doctor status, the belief that she could weave magic, that she could read thoughts, know the future, that she could save you from yourself. It was mostly bunk, but it didn't change the fact that Ervina could "see" things and she was the wisest woman Marnie had ever known.

Marnie eased herself down in the lumpy chair. The spring was out. Ervina or someone had covered it over with a quilt, but it still poked right into Marnie's bony butt.

"What do you want with ole Ervina? Miz Millie don't want me to come play step and fetch again to impress yo' guest? Not that I think it fooled the girl for a minute."

"You only agreed to do it to get a closer look at her."

"You right about that."

"I still want to thank you."

"You oughta be thankin' Jerome. He was scared spitless carryin' that big old soup tureen. He was sure he was gonna dump it in somebody's lap."

"Well, tell him Miss Millie appreciates it."

"Miz Millie don't know the difference. That woman got

her head in the clouds, has done since she was a baby. That's all right though, whatever gets us through the day."

Ervina shuffled over to the cast-iron stove and poured hot water into two round cups that were waiting on the table. She set one cup down by Marnie's chair, took another one for herself and squatted down facing Marnie, the fabric of her long skirt billowing over her knees.

"Damn, how do you still do that?" Marnie asked.

"Just do, that's all. But that's not the question you came all this way to ask."

"No," said Marnie. "I'm just not sure how to ask it."

"Huh. Well, here's the answer. You need that girl and that girl, she needs you. Be patient and we'll see."

Bollinger's Electric seemed to spring miraculously out of the marshes. It was a one-story flat-roofed bunker, made from concrete blocks and painted a grayish green.

There was one car in the parking lot. Cab pulled in next to it.

"I'll just be a minute." It was obvious he wanted her to wait in the car.

Maybe it was curiosity or maybe pure perversity that made her open the car door. "I'll come, too."

He held Bollinger's door for her, and she stepped into a utilitarian rectangular room that was trisected by an arrangement of partially filled metal shelves.

A man, dressed in khaki work clothes, got up from a stool behind the counter. He lifted his chin, which was stubbled with a reddish beard. "Cab, my man." He switched his focus to Abbie.

"A friend of the Crispins," Cab said. "I'm showing her the sights."

"Abbie Sinclair," she said, putting out her hand.

The man grinned, displaying tobacco-stained teeth, and

shook it. "Howd'ya do. Quincy Bollinger. You staying up at Crispin House?"

"Yes. I'm on vacation."

Quincy glanced at Cab. "You don't say. Well, I'm sure they're glad of the company. Got your stuff in back." Quincy nodded to Abbie, then he went through an open doorway to a crowded storage room.

A few minutes later he came back pushing a loading pallet that held a heavy cardboard box and two spools of electrical wire. A big brown mongrel lumbered behind him, then stopped to turn lugubrious, bloodshot eyes toward Cabot then Abbie.

"Bubba, you leave Cab and his girl alone."

Bubba rolled his head, padded past Cabot, and snuffled Abbie's hand.

"Bubba," Quincy commanded halfheartedly.

"He's all right," Abbie said. She leaned over and took Bubba's jowls between her hands. Gave them a good scratch.

"Bubba, he's got a way with the ladies," Quincy said. "He sure does." He chuckled. "Uh-huh, he sure does. Let's load this stuff in your truck, Cab."

The two men headed outside, leaving Abbie and Bubba to get better acquainted. The merchandise was loaded, Cabot paid cash, and they were back in the car in a matter of minutes. Cabot handed her a bottle of hand sanitizer.

"Thanks," she said. "Bubba was very effusive in his affection." Abbie scrubbed her hands then wiped off her cheek where Bubba had given her a parting slurp.

Cabot puffed out air.

"What?"

"I gotta say. I wouldn't have been surprised if you had been totally grossed out by Bubba. Some women . . ."

"Oh, please, I've—" She stopped abruptly. She'd been about

to say, *I've been around a lot more intimidating animals than an old coonhound.* "—always liked dogs," she finished lamely. "Though Bubba has some serious slobbering going on."

Cabot laughed. It was a warming sound, and Abbie realized that she hadn't heard him laugh before. Of course she hadn't been doing much laughing herself lately.

"So where to? There's Myrtle Beach, amusement parks, bars, and restaurants."

Abbie shook her head. "I'm not a theme park kind of girl. Something low-key would be fine. Though I'm not partial to alligators."

"Neither am I," Cabot said. "Anyway, we're a little over-populated for them. Just stay out of the swamps."

"Not a problem."

"How about a quaint, historic, not-too-over-tourist-populated town with a nice harbor, good seafood, and a better sunset?"

"Sounds great."

"I'll call Millie and tell her not to expect you for dinner."

Abbie felt a serious stab of panic; she breathed it away. They'd gotten a late start, and even though it was still early afternoon, they hadn't seen much outside of marshes and electrical stores.

About twenty minutes later they came to a bridge, actually two bridges, that spanned converging rivers. A WELCOME TO HISTORIC GEORGETOWN sign greeted them at the far side.

"It's not much when you first enter it," Cabot said as they drove down a four-lane street with fast-food places, motels, and industrial buildings. "Most people pass right by without stopping."

"I'm not sure the local businesses are as happy about that as you seem to be."

"They get enough business." He turned left, leaving the

industrial area behind. They drove down a tree-lined street flanked by white clapboard houses, grass, and shrubs.

"Feel like walking a bit?"

"Sure."

Cabot made another turn and parked at one of the spaces that ran along both sides of the street. They walked along the sidewalk, shaded by thick live oaks. Here each house was marked with a historical designation, and Cabot pointed out special features as they passed by.

"They've done a good job of preservation and renovation," he said. "Hard to imagine wars were ever fought here."

"Definitely serene looking," Abbie agreed, though she had no problem imagining blood and gore here—or anywhere for that matter. And that disturbed her. She didn't want to be like that. She wanted to breathe easy and be happy again. Live in a house like the ones they'd passed. She'd wanted that for longer than she cared to admit, but it made her feel doubly guilty.

They crossed the street, and Cabot stopped her to point out an oriel window almost hidden by the trees. As they walked along, he explained the difference between Italianate and Georgian style. The way he talked about finials, cupolas, cornices, and gables was almost reverent.

His enthusiasm was catching, and Abbie found herself asking questions about architecture. She also found herself thinking about Cab Reynolds and wondering if she had misjudged him.

A few blocks later they came to a large Southern-plantation-type house that overlooked a river. The house was open to the public, but they didn't go inside. Instead Cabot led her through a park and onto another street where shops painted in charming colors lined both sides of the street. Abbie couldn't help comparing these well-tended stores with their cheerful façades and colorful flower boxes with the struggling, straggling stores at Stargazey Point.

Is this what Cabot wanted for Stargazey? Is this why he took such an interest in keeping developers out. Did he have his own plans for Stargazey Point? Why else would someone from Boston be living in a back-of-beyond near ghost town.

"Are you really from Boston?" she asked as they stopped at the corner to let a car go by.

It was like she'd pulled the plug. His face, which had been animated, became passive, and his voice lost its fervor.

"Partially," he said.

"And which part of you would that be?"

"I spent my teenage years there with my father and step-mother."

"And before that?"

He frowned slightly. "I was born and raised in Charleston. Why?"

"Just curious. Occupational hazard."

"From being a weathergirl?"

"From working at a television station, I guess." She'd recovered smoothly enough. She didn't love the idea that he thought she was still the weathergirl, but it was better if she just let him keep this misconception. She could easily talk about the weather. She couldn't talk about what she had been doing for the last eight years. It was too painful, too raw, too humiliating. Too final.

"So how did you wind up in Stargazey Point?"

Cabot shrugged. "I spent every summer in Stargazey Point with my uncle. I went to college, worked in Atlanta for a while—"

"As an architect by any chance?"

He dipped his chin in acknowledgment. "I found I didn't really like the job so I came back here."

"Where you raise horses?"

Cabot smiled. "Who told you that, Beau?"

"Sarah."

"Sarah? When did you meet her?"

"In town yesterday. I met Sarah, Bethanne from the inn, and Penny Farlowe, who owns Flora's."

Cabot's eyes narrowed. "What did they have to say?"

"Well," she began. "I went in to buy some paper and Bethanne was just going over to Flora's and invited me to go along. Sarah came in. Then, you might as well know, I said something that made Bethanne cry, she ran out, and I left."

"It doesn't take much to set her off. What did you say, if you don't mind me asking?"

Abbie sighed. She had a feeling he'd find out anyway, so she might as well tell him herself.

"Sarah said you were showing me around; she called it a date. Just as a joke. I merely said it wasn't a date. Bethanne burst into tears and ran out of the shop."

Abbie had often gotten unexpected truths from people she was interviewing and usually took it in stride. But Bethanne's reaction had hit her out of the blue and hit her where it hurt.

"Her husband died. It's been hard for her," Cabot said. "She cries a lot. It's healthier than keeping grief to yourself."

She searched his face to see if he was talking about her but decided she was just being paranoid. Celeste had promised not to tell the Crispins about her reasons for the visit.

"It might do her good to have someone to talk to. You know, someone who doesn't know everything about Jim's death."

Abbie shook her head. She wasn't going to encourage any kind of friendship with Bethanne. The two of them would end up crying into their appletinis and commiserating like two old widows.

"So what does Sarah do? Her accent doesn't sound nearly as thick as everyone else's. Is she from around here originally?"

Cabot took her elbow as they stepped off the curb "She's

from here, but she's lived in New York for about ten years now. She teaches at Columbia in cultural studies and is taking some time off to spend with her great-grandmother until she goes back in the fall. She runs the after-school program at the community center—by default. The last person left without notice."

He led her down to a wooden walkway that ran along the edge of the water. There was a cool breeze and Abbie was glad she'd worn long sleeves. Alfresco dining places were lined up side by side, the different establishments marked off by low wooden fences or glass surrounds. Upscale dining and wine bars rubbed elbows with hamburger joints and crab shacks.

"I suppose she gets lots of opportunity to study culture around here," Abbie said.

"Yeah, but mainly she's paying back. The community got together to send her to school."

They stopped to look out over the water.

"Don't feed the alligators?" Abbie asked, looking at a metal sign posted on the railing. "Is that sort of like no shoes, no shirt, no service?"

"Actually, it's serious. Not only is it bad for them, but the restaurants don't want to encourage them to get any closer."

Abbie shuddered.

"Not to worry, I don't believe they've ever tried to get in without a reservation."

"Very funny."

"Really, don't worry."

"I'm not worried."

They stood side by side, looking out at the river and watching the sun set. It was later than Abbie realized. She also realized she was having a good time.

She wasn't sure that she should be having a good time. She should be taking solitary walks and trying to figure out what came next. But somehow Cabot the third made it easy to forget the reason she'd come here.

"Nothing like sunset over the marshes," Cabot said.

"No, there isn't." She'd watched the sunset from the beach the night before. She could almost be standing on the beach now. She tried to imagine Crispin House as a popular museum. Stargazey Inn filled with people year-round, the shops thriving. A smaller version of this town.

She sighed. More than likely the businesses would continue to go under, the house would gradually fall down around the siblings' ears, destined to be razed to build a private gated community like the one they'd passed on the way to Georgetown. And another little bit of the past would be swept away.

"What?"

She started. "I was just thinking about the Crispins. It seems a shame that they couldn't get some help restoring the house. It must date back from plantation—real plantation—days. Why doesn't it have landmark status?"

"I doubt if it qualifies. Much of the land was sold off years ago. The storms have destroyed some parts of the house and had to be rebuilt. Most of the antique furnishings have been sold. It's an interesting part of history, but the house is mainly just old.

"Now. Would you rather dine with linen tablecloths and an extensive wine list or eat crab legs off a newspaper chased by microbeer."

"Newspaper and beer," she said automatically.

"Great. I know the place."

They walked down the boardwalk to the marina where wooden tables were crowded around a weather-beaten shack. Strands of lights were draped over a latticed roof suspended over the dining area. Almost every table was filled, but just as they walked in a couple at a table next to the water stood up.

A busboy cleared their table before they reached the exit, and a hostess hustled Cabot and Abbie toward it.

As soon as they were seated, she began rattling off things in an accent so thick that Abbie had trouble following it. They ordered beer and crab legs that came in a huge metal pot, which a muscular waiter dumped onto the table.

"Wow," Abbie said, contemplating the pile of crabs before her. They were beautiful; bright orange against the black and white of the paper, as if the setting sun had found a space in the lattice overhead and spilled onto the table. Beautiful and heart wrenching, but mostly beautiful.

Please, please, Abbie prayed. Let it all stay beautiful—just for a little while.

Chapter 8

Millie stood watch at the parlor window. "They've been gone for a long time."

"Isn't that what you wanted?" Marnie said, looking up from where she was stretched out on the sofa reading a magazine.

"I suppose. And I hope they hit it off. Don't you?" Millie turned from the window.

Marnie looked back at her over the rims of her reading glasses. "I think that would be very nice."

"Oh, you. And you, too, Beau."

Beau looked up from his carving. Marnie noticed that he'd placed yesterday's newspaper at his feet to collect the shavings.

"I've been hopin' Cab would find a nice girl ever since he came back. At first I thought maybe Bethanne, poor soul, but I just don't think they would suit. Do you?" Getting no response, she went on. "Well, I don't. It's goin' to take her a long time to get over Jim passing like that. Why, she might never marry again."

"Mm-huh," Marnie said. Beau leaned over, rolled up the newspaper and shavings, and stood up. "You leave the boy be. He'll find somebody to marry in his own good time."

"Hmmph. Something you would know all about, being an old confirmed bachelor."

"That's right, Sister." He strode over and gave Millie a peck on the cheek. "I'm going on down to town for a bit. If I see the two of them, I'll tell them not to miss curfew." He paused at the arch. "And you never know, I might give him a run for his money with that girl myself." He grinned and left the room.

"He was kiddin', wasn't he?" Millie asked as soon as they heard the front door close.

"I don't know, Millie. He charmed many a girl in his day. I don't think he's lost a bit of that charm over the years."

Millie felt behind her for a chair and lowered herself slowly to the cushion. "Oh, dear," she said. "Oh, dear."

He liked her, Cab realized as he watched Abbie dig into the pile of crab legs. He liked her energy. The way her eyes lit up on occasion only to be quickly extinguished, as if she had some sadness that she couldn't quite escape. It made her interesting.

He no longer thought she was working for a developer. But he also didn't see her as a weathergirl. She'd said she was between jobs.

"Are you looking for another job as a weathergirl?" he asked.

Abbie froze with half a crab leg shell in each hand. "Weathergirl?"

"You said you were a weathergirl but between jobs."

"Oh, yeah. I was, but I'm going to do something different now."

He watched that darkness descend and then dissipate with a flick of her hair.

"Actually, I thought Bethanne might need help when the tourist season starts."

Cabot stared. She was going to stay in Stargazey? It wasn't exactly the place to get ahead. And along with the sadness, he'd sensed an underlying energy in Abbie that never seemed to rest. He didn't see her as being content to make beds for a living. "I'm not sure if she'll . . . really . . ."

"There's a tourist season, isn't there?"

"More or less."

She'd picked up her beer but put it down with a thud. "What's wrong with that town?"

"Nothing," Cab said.

"Look around. These people are going great guns, and as far as I can tell they don't even have the ocean."

"And your point is . . ."

"Don't be obtuse. Stargazey Point has businesses, some anyway, and Crispin House could be a drawing card like the house we saw. Maybe they could do tours or something. There's a beach . . . It must have something to offer tourists. I know you don't really care for tourists, but—"

"I don't mind tourists, but I don't want it to become another resort that none of the people who live there could afford."

"Well, that's a relief. I was afraid you had plans for Stargazey yourself."

"I do, just not those plans."

She leaned forward and rested her elbows on the table. "What kind of plans?"

"Why do you care?" Cab asked, more sharply than he'd intended. She wasn't just making dinner conversation. She was really curious. Suspicion crept back into his consciousness. He couldn't help it; suspicion was in his nature.

"Because . . ." She picked at the beer label. "I like the Crispins, and I don't want to see them lose their home."

"Neither do I," he said.

"So what kind of plans do you have?"

He shrugged, attacked another crab leg.

They ate in silence for a few minutes. But Cab sensed a

storm brewing across the table. He couldn't remember knowing someone whose moods shifted so quickly. Bailey had two
moods, satisfied and not satisfied, shoes, salads, sex—it was all
the . . . He stopped himself, unnerved that he'd been comparing Abbie to his ex-fiancée.

He had barely thought about Bailey in the last few months.
An indictment of the happiness of that relationship. Actually
Bailey had just been a symptom of his former life. It must be
the call from Frank. He'd have to call him back and make up
some excuse for them not to come. He didn't want to share his
new life with any of them.

"Coward."

Cabot knocked his beer over and barely righted it before it
spilled over the table.

"Did you just call me a coward?"

"Well, yeah, but I was just trying to get your attention. I
guessed it worked."

"I guess it did." He couldn't help himself, he started to laugh.
For a second he thought she'd pulled an Ervina on him and was
reading his mind.

"So are you going to tell me or is it a secret?"

He studied her face. She didn't flinch or look away but met
his eyes, intense, interested, and suddenly very appealing. "I'll
go you one better. I'll show you."

Ervina peered into the flames even though the smoke from the
fire burned her eyes. The storm was a-comin' right over that
horizon. It was beginning.

Oh, Lord, it had begun years ago with Mr. Beau Senior and
his heavy-handed ways. He set these things in motion just as
sure as he was the puppet master hisself. But now he was gone.
His three children were out of his reach. And now this girl.

Ervina smiled through the smoke. Old Mr. Beau be rollin' over in his grave if he knew what was comin'.

Cab began to get cold feet on the drive back to Stargazey Point. He'd been rash to offer to show Abbie what he was working on. She might have the same reaction as his friends had when he announced he was quitting the firm. Or as his father and stepmother when they learned he'd given up everything to follow in Ned's footsteps.

Still, it wouldn't kill him to try it out on a stranger. He knew the advantage of beta testing. And she was the only new person in town. He tried not to think of how he would feel if she laughed in his face. Or dismissed him summarily like his father and his fiancée had.

And so what if she did? She was just one person. He was doing this as much for himself as for the future of Stargazey Point. It could turn out to be a gigantic failure. Unfortunately for a lot of people, it had become the panacea for putting them back on the map.

It was dark by the time they stopped in front of the community center. The center was dark. Most of the town was dark. Cab got out of the car.

"Look at that moon," Abbie said.

The moon had risen over the derelict old pier, its light picking the broken boards out in stark relief.

"When I was a kid, there were games on the pier, and food and dancing at night out at the end." Cab pointed to the remnant of the old pavilion. "It survived a bunch of storms. Was rebuilt time after time. But after a while, most of the vendors moved on."

"And no one bothered to build it back," she said.

"I don't know that it was a question of not bothering. There just wasn't the need for a boardwalk with Myrtle Beach only a drive away. We just kind of slowly gave up."

"Hmm," Abbie said, and he wondered what she was thinking. He didn't ask. He'd spent a whole day with her, and she knew more about him than most people would in just a few hours, or even in a few weeks. But he knew very little about her. It wasn't that she was evasive exactly. She just seemed much more interested in the sights he showed her, which was nice, and in him, which was even nicer.

"Is this what we came to see?" she asked.

"What? No. This way." He led Abbie over to the plywood door, opened the lock, and pulled the panel across the dirt.

"This is yours?" she asked.

"Yes."

"I thought it must be a church or an old meeting hall. You don't live here?"

Cabot laughed. "Sometimes it seems like it, but no. I have a house a few blocks away.

"It's kind of dark. I'll get the switch." On the other hand, he might as well go for the full effect. So what if he appeared ridiculous. "Close your eyes."

"What?" she asked nervously. Another of those lightning-fast changes of energy. "This isn't going to turn out like etchings, is it?"

"Nothing kinky. I just want you to get the full experience. Promise."

He heard her take a deep breath.

"Are they closed?"

"Yes."

"Okay, just come this way a little . . . a little more." He maneuvered her farther into the space, turned her around. Had second thoughts. "It's not finished. There's a lot of work left to do."

"Okay. What is it?"

"Just a second; stand right there. Don't move."

He hurried to the old power board. Hoping that he didn't blow a fuse, which would be a terrible anticlimax to his buildup, he pulled the levers. Lights flickered.

"What's happening?"

"Just hold on. We're almost there." The lights popped on one row after another: white, yellow, red, green. Some were still missing, and one row at the base of the platform was still completely out, where he hadn't rewired yet.

He moved to the engine. It started on the first attempt. Bless Beau. The platform began to move, the lights refracted into the mirrors. Shining on the painted panels, only half of which had been restored. Not a figure in sight, just metal poles going round and round to their own silent music.

"Okay, open them," Cab yelled over the engine noise. He stood holding his breath. His stomach was churning so much, he could have been a boy, waiting for his first date, his first kiss, his first time of making love.

She opened her eyes. The anxiety left her features. Her eyes widened, sparkled in the whirring lights, her lips parted.

"It's a carousel." She turned to him and smiled. "It's a carousel."

He smiled back at her, relieved and gratified. But she was no longer looking at him. She was watching the lights circle past, then slowly she stretched out her arms, and turned with them. "It's fantastic. It's yours?"

"Yes."

"That's why you aren't working as an architect anymore? You're restoring the carousel?"

"Yes."

"That is so cool."

It was strange, but all his hard work, his sacrifices, his self-questioning seemed justified when he looked at Abbie's expression. Okay, she was only one person and she might feel the need to be polite, but her amazement seemed real. Cab was so pleased that if he could carry a tune, he would have sung.

The engine began to clank, and he quickly turned it off. "Still has a few bugs."

"It's wonderful. You've done all this yourself?"

"Beau and I. Silas and some others have lent a hand now and then."

"Where are the animals? Did you have to send them out to a carousel restorer? Are there such people?"

"There are, and I had to send some of the most damaged ones out, but most of them are in decent shape. Do you want to see?"

"I'd love to."

"I keep them in storage. We bring out a few at a time to work on them, then send them back until we're ready to reassemble the whole structure." He led her over to a heavy door. "The workroom is climate controlled, concrete, and as hurricane proof as you can get."

He unlocked the door and turned on a light. "I can only turn on a few lights. With the carousel lights on, I'll blow a fuse if I turn on the work lights. The whole place needs to be rewired. I have a licensed electrician working on it, but it's slow going."

"That's what all the wire you bought was for. I was wondering."

"Yep. Careful. You'll have to come back when I'm running at full speed and get a really good look in the daylight."

He walked over to the workstation where Midnight Lady lay on her side. Her head and legs were protected by a bed of foam rubber, and she was covered with a tarp. She looked like a bundle of old cloth. He hoped that Abbie could see enough to really appreciate her beauty.

"This one . . . She was my favorite ride when I was a kid. Still is." Gently, he took the edge of the tarp that covered her head. Lifted it up, carefully avoiding pulling it over Lady's delicate ears.

He smiled; she always brought a smile and pack of good memories. "This is . . . Midnight Lady." He turned his smile on Abbie, and it froze on his face.

She was staring at Lady's head, her face stricken. Her eyes wide beneath questioning eyebrows. As if she couldn't believe what she was seeing.

"Abbie? What's wrong?"

Her mouth twisted, her hand went to her throat.

"Abbie, what's going on?"

She shook her head, took an awkward step backward, then turned and stumbled from the room.

At first Cab could only stare after her. He didn't understand. She'd been so enthusiastic just a minute before. He looked back at Lady. Her eyes wild and free and powerful. Her mane curving in the air as if a heavy wind danced at her head. She was beautiful.

He caught a glimpse of Abbie as she ran past the carousel and out the front door. And he stood there, torn between two women. Lady was faithful, Abbie was obviously crazy. Bipolar or something. She might be dangerous to herself.

Lady would wait. He rushed out of the room, still careful to close the door behind him, ran across the open hall, and into the night.

It was so dark that it took a second for his eyes to adjust. And then he saw her, a ghostlike figure jumping down to the sand by the pier and running to the waves.

God, where the hell was she going, and what was she going to do? Panic seized him. He called after her, then he started to run.

He was just passing the community center when a specter

stepped out of the dark. Cab stuttered to a stop. "Dammit, Ervina. I wish you wouldn't do that. I don't have time for hoodoo. I have to go."

"No, you don't. You leave her be. She got a sickness inside her trying to get out."

Cabot turned on her. "Yeah, I get that, but I'd better make sure she's okay."

"She not gonna hurt herself tonight."

"How do you know? The girl's not stable." He understood it now. The quicksilver changes from delight to sadness, from fun to anger. "Damn, I knew I shouldn't have gotten involved with her, but I told the Crispins I'd look after her and I'm going to look after her—at least for tonight."

"When you gonna start listenin' to Ervina? You stay away. Mr. Beau will see to her."

As she spoke a shadow rose from the seawall and moved slowly toward the water. Beau's gangly stature was unmistakable even in the moonlight.

"Did you know he was sitting there?" Cab asked suspiciously.

Ervina looked hard at him, shook her head. "Ervina got the eye. She knows. Oh, she knows."

"You creep me out when you talk that way."

Ervina flashed him a look. Her chill-your-bones look. "It is Ervina's way."

"That's just what I mean."

Ervina laughed softly, and Cab began to get annoyed. He had one crazy lady running out on the beach at night. And another one standing next to him making arcane statements and laughing like a lunatic.

Abbie stopped at the edge of the water. Thank God for that. He'd been afraid that she might keep running until the waves swallowed her. He shuddered. "She's not going to do anything rash, is she?"

"Rash ain't always a bad thing. Look at you, boy."

"Yeah, I'm beginning to wonder if I'm not as crazy as Abbie Sinclair."

"She ain't crazy; she got a sickness."

Beau had reached her, and they stood side by side looking out to sea. Then Abbie turned toward him. Beau put his arm around her; she fell into him and Cab was stabbed by a shard of jealousy.

Ervina chuckled and mumbled under her breath.

"You better not be putting any spells on them, Ervina. I mean it. Beau is almost eighty years old."

Ervina cackled. "But you ain't."

"And don't put any damn spell on me."

"Now, boy, you know you don't believe in no spells."

"I don't."

"Then don't you worry none."

"I'm not worried. Not about you, anyway. But what about her?" He lifted his chin toward the beach where Beau and Abbie stood almost as one in the light of the moon. "Just what kind of sickness does she have?"

"The angry sickness. An' it's gonna eat her up if she don't drive it out first."

Abbie didn't know how Beau appeared out of the darkness; she didn't even know how she got to the edge of the sand, so close to the water that it lapped at her sandals. But he was there, large and calm, and she collapsed against him just like she'd known him all her life. Just like he was the grandfather she'd never known. Like a wise man come to save her.

And Abbie broke. Months of holding in hurt, fear, and anger poured out against Beau's plaid shirt. She didn't even try to stop or pull herself together. She let it go, and even when she'd wrung out the last drop of heartbreak and reentered the here and now, she didn't feel embarrassed, or foolish, or anything, but exhaustion.

She looked up at the wrinkled face, saw neither shock nor pity nor disgust. Just a quiet acceptance.

They walked back to the house without speaking. During her breakdown, Beau hadn't uttered one word of comfort. Now he asked for no explanation. And Abbie felt no need to explain. She didn't feel much of anything. Just the weightlessness of a burden lifted.

They parted at the kitchen door. Abbie went inside, and Beau wandered off into the night. She tiptoed up the stairs and fell into bed and a deep sleep.

She knew exactly when the dream began. Knew and couldn't stop it. She might even be awake and this might be the point at which the nightly dream followed her into reality.

Her chest tightened as if it were being pressed by a stone or a ton of mud. She couldn't breathe. She was so tired. *Please. No more.* But still it came.

The rumble of earth. The screams. She stares helplessly as the hillside collapses. The boy tumbles down the hill, his mouth, his nose filling, drowning in mud. Her mouth opens, but nothing comes out but a silent scream. And she's being borne down with the rest. She looks back at Werner and sees him watching, helpless to stop her. He picks up a video camera. She struggles to her knees. Werner aims the camera. She stands, turns, and lifts her arm. There is a gun in her hand. She sees his eyes widen; he drops the camera and she pulls the trigger. I love you, she says as he falls to the ground.

Someone screams. Abbie sits up. She's alone in bed. It's dark. She doesn't move; her dreams come in two parts, and she waits for the second act to begin. The bedroom door creaks open. Marnie is standing in the light of the hallway.

"Are you all right?"

"Yes," Abbie says. "I'm fine." And then she realizes she's really awake.

"Oh, God, Marnie. I'm so sorry. Did I wake you?" She gripped the comforter. "It was just—Sometimes I have this—these dreams. Did I waken everyone?"

Marnie shook her head. "I wasn't asleep. That's the only reason I heard you. Would you like some hot chocolate? A brandy?"

"No, thank you. I'll just go back to bed. It's nothing, really." Marnie nodded. "Then see you in the morning."

"In the morning. Good night."

Ervina woke with a start. She didn't move, just counted her breaths, playin' possum. The angry was out.

She listened for Jerome sleeping in the other room. He was mumbling in his sleep. He felt it, too.

Hush up, boy. You don't want that angry findin' a settlin' place.

Silence from the other room. Ervina smiled to herself. It was gone. No landin' place here. It would go back to the big house. Try to get back in. She slid her feet to the floor and into her shoes.

"Jerome, get up. Fetch us up some juniper and ash wood. I need me a good, strong fire."

Chapter 9

"Did you find out what she was so freaked out about?" Cab asked, reaching for the bag of sausage biscuits Beau had brought from the Tackle Shack.

Beau sat down on the carousel platform next to him and handed him a cardboard cup of sweet coffee.

"Don't know for sure. She just stood there sobbing like there was no tomorrow. Enough to make a grown man cry. 'Course I didn't 'cause it wouldn't do any good both of us blubbering out there on the beach."

"She didn't say anything? 'Cause if it was something I did, I'll apologize, but for the life of me she was fine. I turned on all the carousel lights and she acted like she thought it was great, then I took her back to show her Midnight Lady. And she freaked, ran out, I couldn't stop her. I didn't do anything."

"Son, I know you didn't. And anybody who knows you knows you didn't, so don't worry about it."

Cab bit into the flaky biscuit; the sausage was juicy with a tang of hot pepper to it. He savored it for a second then chased it with a swallow of the sweet coffee.

"Did she ever tell you?"

Beau rested his elbows on his knees and looked at the plastic top of the coffee cup that he held in both hands. "At first she just cried. Every once and a while she'd say something. Mostly gibberish about horses, and Bethanne, and somebody named Werner."

"Bethanne? What does she have to do with anything?"

"Beats me." Beau pushed the last bite of sausage biscuit in his mouth and brushed off his lap. "And then she said how she had to leave."

"She's leaving?"

"That's what she says. I think it's a mistake, myself."

So did Cabot, though he didn't quite like his own reaction to the news. She'd done nothing but cause headaches since she'd arrived. Had it only been four days ago? It seemed much longer. And he felt like he'd known her for much longer. Some parts of her anyway. There was obviously a vast part of her that he didn't have a clue about. And that he should probably steer clear of.

"Less hassle for you and Millie and Marnie, not having a stranger underfoot. Has to have put a strain on you all."

"That's where you're wrong, Cab. Millie's showed more interest in life in the last few days than she has in I don't know when. And Marnie? The girl could be her daughter, well, granddaughter. That's something most folks don't know about Marnie. She wasn't always so standoffish. She has a real soft spot for orphans. And I think Miss Abbie is an orphan of sorts."

"No family?"

"Oh, yeah; I think a big one, too."

"Why didn't she go there for vacation?"

Beau grunted and pushed himself to his feet. "You and I both know about families. She might feel the same about hers."

"There's nothing wrong with my family." Except they had pretty much disowned him since his announcement that he was going to run Ned's carousel for a living.

"There's nothing much wrong with mine," Beau said. "But they aren't real restful, if you know what I mean."

Cab knew exactly what he meant.

"I'm thinking you might help encourage her to stay."

"Me? No thanks." Cab wadded his sandwich wrapping into a tight hard ball and shoved it back in the paper bag.

"Up to you."

"Why would I even want her to stay? She freaked out over a carousel and because I didn't see an old man walking on the side of the road. I wasn't anywhere near him but—She just went crazy. She's bound to be more trouble than she's worth."

Plus he had come to like her over the course of their sightseeing. It was bad enough witnessing her breakdown last night; he didn't want to see her go through that again.

"Like I said, it's up to you. I think she can do some good here."

"How?"

"Don't know. I just feel it."

"Dammit, Beau. You're beginning to sound like Ervina."

"A wise woman, that Ervina."

"Oh hell, I don't have time to worry about some demented friend of *your* family. She doesn't even like me. Now I got work to do." Cab tossed the trash into an oil drum near the exit doors and climbed over the barrier to the generator and began wrestling the housing into the open space.

"Uh-huh."

Cab stopped and looked over the top of the wooden panel.

Beau was grinning. "Would you like some help with that?"

Abbie found Marnie in the garden the next morning. It was after nine. She'd spent most of the night sitting in one of the balcony rocking chairs with Moses draped over her lap.

Marnie looked up as Abbie lifted the latch and stepped inside.

Abbie gave her a half smile and walked closer, a sudden stab of affection for this older woman throwing her off guard. She swallowed. "I think I have to leave."

"Mmm, leave as in the house for a walk or as in a taxi to the airport?"

"The latter." Abbie had trouble getting out the words. She'd thought for a minute Stargazey Point could be the place where she could let go of the past and start building a future. But it wasn't. She'd done nothing but screw things up since she arrived. Beau had said to give it some time. But she didn't see how time would do anything but make it worse.

"Why? If you don't mind me asking."

"I really appreciate all you've done, opening your house to me, your hospitality, your . . ." Abbie shrugged; her throat felt tight and swollen.

Marnie pushed herself to her feet and walked down the row of beans to the bench that ran along the brick wall. She sat down, patted the place next to her. An invitation. A summons. Abbie walked forward and sat down.

"Now tell me about it."

It was hard getting out the first words. Last night, standing with Beau on the beach, the words had gushed out. She couldn't have stopped them if she tried. Wild words, incoherent she was sure. Beau just listened. It was ridiculous. On the beach, in the dark, bawling into the shirt of an octogenarian gentleman she'd know for less than three days.

She felt like a fool. She was a fool. To think she could outrun her demons, that she could hide, that she could put her life back together, that she could find a place to call home, that she could do anything without carrying the ball and chain of her past around with her forever.

How did people do it? Why did they want to? "Did Beau tell you what happened last night?"

"Beau? If you haven't noticed, Beau keeps his own counsel. Plus he was gone when I got up this morning. He and Cab are working on something."

Abbie groaned.

"*Did* something happen? Millie was worried when you went straight upstairs last night that Cab had made improper advances." She snorted. "That Millie, you have to love her."

Distracted, Abbie said, "She didn't, really?"

"Like I said."

"Well, of course he didn't. At first he thought I was a real estate developer. Of all the dumb things."

"Well, don't take it personally. We have them buzzing around our heads all the time, especially lately, now that the beach is beginning to renew itself. A few of the people around here have been burned pretty badly by some less than honest speculators."

"Cab showed me Silas's barbecue place."

"Silas was just one of several. Damn fool." Marnie laughed. "Though people in glass houses . . ."

"You haven't sold Crispin House, have you?"

"Not yet, and don't you dare say a word, but I don't see how we can keep hold of it."

"What will you do?"

"Don't know. I'd buy a smaller house nearby, except that we won't be able to afford it. Once Crispin House is sold, the prices will shoot up, and the others won't be able to survive."

"Cab's carousel?"

"He told you about the carousel? He's usually a little circumspect about what he's doing. People tend to make fun of him."

"He didn't tell me. He showed me."

Marnie's eyes widened. "Did he, now."

"He showed me, and I freaked out and ran away."

Marnie frowned.

Before she could ask what happened, Abbie said, "What will he do if he has to sell the carousel?"

Marnie nodded. "I don't know. He may have enough money to move it somewhere else. Not much solace in that when he gave up a successful career and a wedding on the horizon for this."

"Would you still sell if you didn't have to?" Abbie paused. "I'm sorry, but I was looking for you yesterday and I overheard you and Millie talking about the taxes."

"No, of course not. It's a pain in my butt, and the acreage has dwindled down to a precious few. But we're all getting on. The taxes are skyrocketing, and it's getting too hard to keep up with the chores. We had hoped to leave the property to Celeste. After that she can sell if she wants to. We won't care. But this is the only home Millie has ever known. Beau is comfortable here." Marnie straightened. "But that's not what we should discuss at the moment. Why do you want to leave?"

"I don't want to. Not exactly. It's beautiful, and you three have been so kind. But I'm an imposition and a strain on the household."

"Nonsense. You've brought the old place and its old occupants to life in a few days. You must see that. I think Stargazey can be good for you, too. Now tell me the real reason, if it isn't too painful."

Abbie looked up. Marnie had surprised her, and she owed her an explanation.

"I—years ago—I met a man."

Marnie smiled.

"It's not what you think," Abbie added hastily. "Well, it is. But it's more."

"I wasn't smiling about that. Years ago I met a man too, but that *was* years ago. So how did you meet this man?"

Abbie told her about Guatemala, and how later she left her job at the television station to work on Werner's documentaries. The stories they'd brought to viewers, the sense of accomplishment, the excitement of new places, getting to know new people with lives so different and yet not different, from her own.

She actually found herself speaking with enthusiasm of some of their projects. And suddenly she was at the end, and the words stuck in her throat.

"I learned so much from him. But Werner was not just a great filmmaker; he loved people and he was driven to tell their stories. Some were heart wrenching, some were beautiful or amazing. Then he changed. He just got angry at what the world was doing to them. He became more . . . callous and more cause oriented. He didn't just want to reveal the plights, the lives, the fears—he went after the bad guys." She stopped, wondering how she could put what she didn't understand into words.

"And you thought he was wrong?"

"No. It's like he outdistanced me. I wanted to do good stuff, but I didn't have his vision or his fire."

"It sounds like he stopped caring so much about the people he was documenting."

"Not exactly, but his interest shifted; he lost touch with the individual." Her hand closed over her mouth as if she could keep such traitorous thoughts at bay. "It wasn't wrong, what he was doing. He was a genius." Her voice broke. She gripped her fingers in her lap. "And then . . ."

She took a breath.

"He went after a mining company that was strip-mining a plateau above a small village. There were spies and company security people everywhere. So a skeleton crew clandestinely filmed the mining practices while I took the rest of the crew to cover human interest stories in the village.

"On the last day, the whole crew was in the village. There had been several small mud slides because of the flooding of the lodes, and Werner wanted to take some footage from the village perspective.

"I should have seen what was coming. That we were bound to be caught. Cause the village trouble . . .

"I'd made friends with the women and some of the children. One of the boys tended his grandfather's donkey. He liked to parade that donkey in front of the camera, and the cameraman would pretend to film him.

"He'd just left us. He turned, smiling, to wave good-bye; the earth began shaking, and the whole mountain side fell." Abbie stopped to drag in a breath. "It took everything in its path, the schoolhouse, the children, huts, the boy, his donkey. It covered everything, dragging them down the hill and burying them alive. It was over in seconds.

"And the—the boy and donkey—I could see the boy's arm sticking out of the mud, his fingers stretched wide—like he was reaching for help.

"I ran along the edge of the slide, screaming for someone to help me, but everyone had panicked. I tried to crawl across the mud to get to the boy, but it just kept sucking me under, and I couldn't reach him. The donkey was still alive, but buried in mud up to his neck.

"Its eye rolled toward me, panicked, crazed, but there was nothing I could do. People were screaming and running, and I could hear Werner's voice yelling to the cameraman to keep filming as I started to dig for the boy.

"Then something whizzed past my head, and the donkey collapsed. An old man of the village had shot him. My ears rang, but I kept digging for the boy, digging until my fingernails broke and my skin bled. But the mud filled in as fast as I could scoop it out. His little fingers began to curl. I couldn't reach him.

"I was hardly aware of what was happening around me, but jeeps had roared into the village. The security police jumped out, herded people away. They broke the cameras, confiscated our computers. The villagers dragged me into the bushes, and we watched them take Werner and several other members of the crew away. I wanted to go with them, but they held me back. They probably saved my life.

"I never saw Werner again. He died in their jail. I know they killed him."

Marnie's hand covered hers. "I'm so sorry."

Abbie shook her head, flinging tears. "I should have gone with him. He didn't have to die. And all for nothing. Only a fifteen-second video that was taken with somebody's phone. It showed up on YouTube the next day. And all you could hear was me, yelling. 'Werner, goddamn it; stop filming and help me.'

"Those were my last words to him. After all the good he had done. But in that second, I knew that he cared more about the film than he did about the people, or about me."

And there it was. Abbie had wanted more than Werner could give.

They sat, silent, while tears rolled down Abbie's cheeks

After a few minutes, Marnie pulled a white handkerchief out of her pocket and handed it to Abbie. "So what will you do?"

"I don't know. I was hoping to figure it out while I was here."

"Hmm," Marnie said, frowning. "Might take more than three days, and we could use some help around here."

Abbie managed a wobbly smile. "Like manual labor for the soul?"

"Well, I could use another hand with these beans. But I was thinking Millie would love to have someone to conspire with about Beau's birthday party. She loves surprises. Does it every year. Beau knows it's coming, but he always acts surprised and pleased anyway. What?"

"The party," Abbie said, suddenly remembering Millie's plans for opening the ballroom.

"She's not still planning a huge bash?"

"I'm afraid so. She took me to the ballroom when you were out Monday night."

"Oh, Lord."

"And she was talking about caterers and hiring an orchestra. And I feel like a traitor for telling on her. But I don't know how serious she was."

"You never know with Millie. Three-quarters of the time she acts like someone out of a Tennessee Williams play; then when you least expect it, she comes on like Shirley MacLaine."

"In *Steel Magnolias*?"

Marnie grinned. "Only worse." She grew serious. "Give us a try; stay another week. Then if you still want to leave, I'll have Cabot drive you to the airport."

Abbie shuddered.

"But not until you go back and face that carousel. Now let's pick some beans." Marnie pulled Abbie off the bench.

Somewhere between the second and third row of beans, Abbie had an idea. "Marnie?"

"Hmmm," came the reply from the next row over.

"Millie said Beau used to spend all his time in that old gazebo I saw at the end of the lawn."

"Uh-huh."

"I thought maybe . . . what do you think if I tried to fix it up for his birthday?"

Marnie's head appeared above the teepees of green plants. "Sounds like a plan. Let's put these beans in the kitchen, and we'll take a look."

A few minutes later, Abbie and Marnie stood on the grass looking at the old gazebo.

"Maybe this wasn't such a good idea," Abbie said.

"Well, it isn't a bad idea either. What it is . . . is a big idea."

Maybe too big, Abbie thought as she looked at the gazebo. Yesterday she'd looked at it with the joy of discovery; today, she regarded it with a realistic eye. It was still standing, but that was about all. At least two sections of railing were missing. Several pieces of trim had broken away from the eaves. The whole structure needed serious scraping and repainting. Patches of shingles were either loose or had torn completely away from the pitched roof. At its peak, a spire had broken off, leaving jagged splinters jutting skyward from its base . . .

Abbie swayed, forced her mind from the image those splinters evoked. Made herself stare at them until they became just broken pieces of wood. She'd replace it first thing; she bet Cab would know where she could buy a new one. Which meant she'd have to face him sooner than later.

"Having second thoughts?" Marnie asked, breaking into her thoughts.

"No. No. I'm not. I'm making plans."

"Good for you. Let's take a closer look." Marnie started toward the gazebo steps.

Abbie followed close by while Marnie tested the steps, the floor, peered under broken benches, rattled loose railings.

"Not bad, not bad at all." Marnie brushed sand off her hands. "I don't think I've been out here since I've been back. A shame, really. It's lovely."

"It's beautiful. And it must have been elegant in its day."

"It was. Too bad it's been neglected. But you know how things are. Out of sight, out of mind."

And out of money, Abbie thought, but she kept the thought to herself. "I can do most of the work myself. I have a little experience. And I'll pay for paint and whatever else I need."

Marnie turned, looking stern.

"I have the money. It will be my birthday present to Beau."

"A rather extravagant present and a lengthy project. It might take several weeks to complete. And you'd need to enlist some help for the grunt work. Are you up for it?"

Weeks. It would take weeks? Could she commit to staying that long?

Only a few minutes before she'd been adamant about leaving that very day. What if she started feeling trapped like she did in every place she'd visited since returning from South America? What if she had to bail before it was finished? The gazebo would sit there, half finished, but still broken, a reminder that she'd left without doing what she'd promised.

Half finished, still broken. Like me, thought Abbie.

"Well?"

One word. Yes or no.

She could say no and be on a plane maybe even by this afternoon. *And where would you go? Back to Chicago?* Tell Celeste her family was in dire straits and Abbie had bailed on them? That after all their kindness, she'd left them to fight for their survival alone?

"Yes. I'm up for it," Abbie said.

"Good, and if you tell Millie you're doing it as a surprise for Beau's birthday, she might be convinced to have a 'garden' party. She used to love the teas and soirees Momma used to give."

"I thought maybe we could ask Silas to make barbecue,"

Abbie said. "Everyone could bring something, and we wouldn't have to hire a caterer."

"Reeks of potluck. A word that isn't in Millie's vocabulary unless it's at church and for a worthy cause."

"She said she might ask Penny to do the desserts. Maybe we could convince her that she would be helping the local businesses."

Marnie shook her head, and Abbie felt a stab of disappointment.

"What?"

"You said 'we.'"

Chapter 10

Cab glanced at his watch. Almost three. He and Beau had finally gotten the engine up and running. As soon as the parts he'd ordered arrived they should have a working carousel.

"Let's knock off for the day," he called to Beau who was meticulously scraping paint from the decorative panels that would be returned to the roof of the carousel when finished.

"Suits me. It was a good day's work," Beau said. He pushed himself out of the straight-backed chair he used while painting and fingered the wood Cab knew was in Beau's shirt pocket.

"What are you working on?" Cab nodded toward the pocket, not expecting a definite answer. Beau never said outright what he was carving.

"Somethin' for Abbie," Beau said and patted the pocket affectionately.

For Abbie. Cab didn't know whether to be charmed or worried. It was becoming pretty obvious to him that all three of the Crispins had taken a liking to her, and if she was about to leave them without a thank-you, they would be hurt.

"But if she's leaving," Cab began.

"If she leaves, I'll send it to her when it's finished."

They locked up and parted ways. Beau went down to the

seawall where he would carve his mysterious gift for Abbie, and Cab walked home to grab a late lunch before coming back to put in a few more hours.

He was halfway across the street heading toward Hadley's when he changed his mind. Three o'clock. Chances were Bethanne and Sarah would both be over at the tea shop. Maybe they knew more about what was going on with Abbie than he or Beau did. And then he could decide if he should get involved or not.

When he got to Flora's, he didn't go in but peered over the blue-checked half curtains to see inside. The Oakleys were sitting over by the wall, and he could have gone all spring without running into those two, but Bethanne was sitting practically under his nose. She looked up and motioned him in.

"You practicing to be some kind of Peeping Tom?" asked a voice behind him.

"Jeez," Cab said, turning around to face Sarah. "You're getting as bad as Ervina."

"Huh."

"Actually I came looking for you . . . and Bethanne."

"Just like a man, come sniffing around to find out what he could just ask outright. Come on in." Sarah marched past him into the tea shop, a petit, wiry whirlwind.

He nodded to the Oakleys before he sat down. Sarah ignored them completely.

"How long have they been here?" Sarah whispered to Bethanne.

Bethanne leaned across the table. "They were here when I came in, and I thought they were almost finished."

"When there's a chance of gossip flowing? Maybe Penny will put hot sauce in their second pot of tea." Sarah smiled at Penny who was carrying a second teapot over to the far table.

"Shh," Bethanne said but snorted a giggle.

"And to what do we owe the honor of your visit, Cab?"

"Feeling like a cup of tea."

"The hell you are," Sarah said. "He wants to know what we know about Abbie Sinclair."

"Shh," Cab said and frowned at Sarah before cutting his eyes toward the middle-aged couple. Not everyone's favorite people, since Robert Oakley was the tax assessor.

"You staying, Cab?" Penny asked when she stopped by their table.

"For a bit. I'll have a coffee."

"Just a coffee?"

"Yeah, and whatever the ladies want."

Penny laughed. "High tea for three. And a coffee. You are so easy." Shaking her head, she struck off toward the kitchen.

When Cab turned back to the table, Sarah and Bethanne were grinning at him.

"You never learn, do you?"

"Hell, I can afford to buy you two highfalutin' tea."

"You better watch yourself. You're startin' to sound just like one of those raving rednecks down at the Backwater."

"Yeah," Cab said. "Like that'll ever happen."

"Stranger things have happened," Sarah said darkly.

"What? Like you turning into your great-grandmother? Wring any chicken necks today?"

Sarah punched him in the arm. Penny returned with sandwiches and cakes and enough cookies for two tables. They all dug in.

"We haven't been seeing much of you these days, Cab," Bethanne said.

"Busy," Cab managed between bites. Suddenly he was ravenous.

"You think you'll get it up and running by June?"

"That was the plan, but I don't know. There's a hell of a lot of work still to do."

"Well, I just hope we have some tourists," said Bethanne, pouring tea. "Jerome helped me set up the inn's new website. Thank the Lord for folks like Jerome. He works, he goes to school, he's over at the community center every spare minute. And helps out whenever I need him. What are we going to do when he goes off to school?"

"Has he heard from any colleges?" Cabot asked.

"A few," Sarah said. "But we haven't heard anything about financing."

There was action at the far side of the room. The Oakleys were leaving. They stopped by the table on their way out.

"Cabot, Bethanne . . ." A pause . . . "Sarah."

"Miz Oakley. How are you?" Bethanne said brightly. "How's your spring been?"

"Oh, fair to middlin'; been an awful damp April so far if you ask me." She looked over the table, but no one asked her.

"Come, my dear, and let's let these folks have their tea." Mr. Oakley didn't leave but leaned over Bethanne's chair. "Now you just think about our little talk, okay?" He patted her on the shoulder, nodded, and went to pay his bill.

"What little talk?" Cab asked as soon as the Oakleys were gone.

"He's offered to help me find a buyer if I decide to sell the inn. After all the work Jim and I put into it? He seems to think I can't run a business because of my bereavement. My bereavement," Bethanne repeated, teary-eyed. "If I weren't a good Christian, I'd hire the Mafia to take him out."

Sarah grinned. "Then it's a good thing you are. Now let's forget about both the Oakleys. They can't make you sell. And Cab's here to get the scoop on Abbie Sinclair."

"I am not," Cab protested.

"Don't start without me," Penny called from the kitchen.

Two minutes later the closed sign was up, and three expectant faces were all focused on Cab.

"We don't know a thing," Bethanne said. "Sarah was kidding her about you two going on a date, and I got upset and ran out and I should go apologize, but it's so embarrassing. I don't know how I could do something so stupid."

"And don't look at me like that, Cabot Reynolds," Sarah said, her eyes wide. "It was just a little joke. Before I could kiss my grits, Bethanne turns into an afternoon shower—"

"I did not."

"And I was left staring at Miz 'It's All My Fault' before she plunked down a twenty and bolted and I was left looking at nothing and wondering what the hell had happened. I think it must have been *your* fault."

"Mine?" Cab said. "Why would it be my fault? Millie trapped me into taking her around. That's the long and the short of it."

"And it was so awful that you ended up bringing her back here and showing her the carousel."

"You didn't," Bethanne said, widening her eyes at Sarah.

Penny fanned her face with her fingers. "Well, Lord bless us. It *was* a date. And, Bethanne, don't you dare cry."

"I won't. I don't know why I did then. It was just the way she said it. For a split second, it was like I felt her pain, and she felt mine."

"Oh, God," moaned Cab. "Have you all gone hoodoo on me?"

"It's in the water and it'll get'chu, too." Penny crossed her eyes and broke into a fit of maniacal laughing.

"It's not a magic thing," Bethanne explained. "It's a girl thing."

"Uh-huh. And that was it?"

"That was it. Why?"

"I just thought she might have told you something about

herself." Cab leaned back in his chair. How much should he tell them about what happened last night? They obviously didn't know any more than he did.

"You mean you spent the whole day with her and didn't find out anything about her?" Penny asked incredulously.

"Pretty much." He'd spent a lot of time last night going over the events of the day. After a rocky start, they'd had fun. They'd talked enough, but for the life of him he couldn't remember what they'd talked about. Georgetown, its architecture, and how the town had developed a tourist industry, about how Stargazey might do the same. But he had told her a lot more about his life than she had told him about hers. All he knew was that she was no longer a weathergirl.

How had she done that? And the big question. Had she done it on purpose?

"So why do you want to know about her?" Sarah asked innocently.

"It's not what you think," Cab countered.

The three women exchanged knowing looks.

"Then why don't you tell us what it is?"

"I don't know. She's like a woman without a past."

"Oh, puh-lease. Didn't you ask her about herself?"

Penny snorted. "Just like a man, gabbing on about himself and not letting her get a word in edgewise."

"She talked."

"But not about herself."

"Exactly."

"So why didn't you ask her?"

"I think I did."

"Oh, jeez," Sarah said.

"Did you google her?" asked Bethanne.

"No, of course not."

"Why not?"

"I don't know. I'm trying to get away from that kind of life."

"The kind that makes you interested in other people? You content to live with a bunch of wooden animals that don't talk back?" Sarah said at her most Southern.

"God, crawl off, okay? I don't want that. I have friends."

"You don't have girlfriends."

"What about you three? You're not friends?"

"You know what kind of girlfriends we're talking about."

They were getting into dangerous territory. "I will when I'm ready."

A chorus of groans from his tablemates.

"Please tell me you're not pining over Brittany, or Tiffany, or whatever her name was."

"Bailey."

Sarah rolled her eyes.

Cabot rubbed his hand over his face. He'd almost forgotten about Frank's phone call.

"What?"

"Be warned. Bailey's making an appearance this weekend."

Three dumbfounded women stared back at him.

Sarah found her voice first. "Are you crazy? Or are you having a change of heart?"

"No and no. Some colleagues are in the area for meetings. They're bringing her along."

"Sounds suspicious to me," Penny said.

"Sounds like we might need to plan an intervention," Sarah said.

"God, no. I'm meeting them for dinner. Period. I didn't think quick enough to get out of it. I don't need anybody intervening or sticking their noses in my business."

"This from the man who showed a virtual stranger his prized possession."

"Sarah!" Bethanne exclaimed.

Sarah gave her a look. "I meant the carousel."

"Oh."

"What day are they coming? I'll make sure to keep the inn's restaurant open."

"Thanks, and you know I'd eat at the inn every night if you were open, but not this time, not with Sarah and Penny lurking behind the potted palms."

He stood up, paid for tea, and left before they could ask any more questions. Most people in town thought he was independently wealthy, which he wasn't, slightly eccentric, which he guessed he was, and following in Beau Crispin's path toward bachelorhood. After the first few months, everyone had stopped trying to set him up with dates.

He didn't mind the kidding; it was all good-natured, and he really did count them as friends. He wasn't sure why he blanched at the thought of them meeting Tony, Frank, and Bailey. He wasn't afraid of what people thought he was now, but maybe he didn't want anyone to see the way he had been. He didn't want any part of that life encroaching on his new life. Not even the woman he'd once asked to come with him.

Instead of going back to the carousel, he went home. He'd gotten a good deal of work done today and he deserved a night with his feet up in front of his flatscreen, one of the few things he'd brought with him.

He stopped on the sidewalk in front of his house and marveled as he did most nights at how he could be content with an old house in need of some major TLC. He'd given up a contemporary apartment with cutting-edge everything and a skyline view for a rotten porch, broken windows, and peeling paint. And he was content.

At least he had been until Abbie Sinclair arrived and his former life decided to make an appearance. He just hoped it didn't snowball from here.

The first part of Cab's evening went as planned. He got a beer out of the fridge, took off his boots, and turned on the television. Turned it off again. Walked into the spare bedroom that he'd meant to use as an office but had never gotten around to unpacking.

His laptop was sitting on a cardboard box. It was plugged in, though he hardly ever booted it up. He occasionally ordered something online, but most of the time, he just called the suppliers. He'd canceled his Facebook and Twitter accounts. He no longer surfed the web or played online games. He did have two websites, one for the carousel and one for his restoration business that he paid Jerome to keep updated.

He didn't miss it. But tonight it beckoned. Information about Abbie Sinclair was just a couple of clicks away. She would be there. At least mentioned as the weathergirl, and she probably had a social media presence, too. It would be so easy, and it would set his mind at ease.

With this innocent motive in mind, he opened the laptop, typed in her name. And got over eight thousands hits. A whole slough of Facebook, Twitter, and LinkedIn accounts.

Great. He refined his search to Abbie Sinclair weather. And he was in business.

He read for a while, got a little background. Found out a bit about her family, large, parents still alive, five brothers and sisters. All seemed to do a lot of volunteering, do-gooders or activists or both.

Opened up images and scrolled through photos of a younger Abbie with a pointer in her hand, a map behind her. It made him smile. An even younger Abbie standing with a group of students by a bus that would take them to Guatemala to build houses for Habitat for Humanity.

Following the family tradition, he supposed. And he'd thought she was a developer. He'd been way off the mark. And then he came to another photo and learned who Werner was. And what he looked like. A documentary filmmaker. A handsome guy. His search took a detour as he followed Werner Landseer. Werner had a list of impressive credits, and further search showed exactly when Abbie had joined his team. She hadn't been a weathergirl for over eight years. She'd been with Werner.

Why had she let him think she was between jobs?

The places they had been pretty much covered the globe. The last one he found was in Peru. Cabot had read something about a documentary team that was filming in Peru when a landslide buried half the village. It had been a year ago. He thought back. Brought up another site. And his stomach turned.

The article was short. The leader of a documentary team, Werner Landseer, had been arrested while filming the mud slide. Abbie wasn't mentioned, but several locals who'd worked for them were also jailed. And then he saw the YouTube entry.

He sat staring at the screen, not really wanting to know what it contained. Got another beer and stared some more. And finally he pressed play. The video clip was taken by a cell phone, and it was more gruesome than he had imagined.

Chaos as the person holding the phone runs to another position. Dirt and tremors, the back of a cameraman. A deafening rumble. The phone rises to show the side of the hill sweeping away a wooden building as if it were made of matchsticks. More chaos, screams, and people fleeing, and then quiet. Like the eye of a tornado.

The phone scans the rubble, stops on the solitary figure of a woman on her knees digging frantically in the mud, her white-blond hair catching the light. Two villagers drag her away, as she kicks and screams and tries to return to her effort. The phone jerks, and the screen goes black, but not before Cab saw why she was digging.

He covered his face with his hands. He should have never looked at that heartbreaking moment. Abbie digging in the mud; the buried donkey, wild eyed and panicked and struggling beside her; the small arm that stuck out from the mud.

No wonder she was so skittish. It was amazing she wasn't stark raving mad. And how was he going to face her and pretend like he didn't know?

He shut down the screen. Closed the laptop. Went to the kitchen for another beer, then out to the porch. There were a few lights in the houses along the street; some were vacant. He looked up at the sky, but he couldn't stop thinking about the YouTube video. And he knew just as sure as he was standing there that he'd go back and watch it again, and he would read more.

Because information at your fingertips was a constant siren call, a temptation, and when it was about someone you knew . . . He gave up and went back into the house, opened the laptop, and sat down.

Two hours later, he'd found little more than he already knew. A couple of small articles about Landseer's arrest. Another announcing his death. Cabot read it twice; the man was forty-four.

And his first thought was not about Landseer's death or the mud slide, but what was Abbie doing with a man probably fifteen years older than her?

He read on; learned about the subsequent disappearance of the local men who had assisted the camera crew.

There was no investigation of Werner's death or the other missing men. No retribution on the company whose shoddy practices had caused so much damage and tragedy.

And no more mentions of Abbie. It was like she had dropped off the face of the earth. Perhaps she had. Perhaps that was why she was here.

Chapter 11

Abbie began work on the gazebo the next morning. She'd stayed up late, drawing plans in her as yet unused journal. And though she was no artist, she was thrilled with the way the gazebo had turned out in her mind. Now to make it a reality.

She stopped by the garden shed to get her hat, which the sisters insisted she wear; gathered up rake, broom, hammer, and a makeshift toolbox; and hurried down the path. She swept off the sand, pulled the weeds away, tested the flooring, poked and prodded, shaded her eyes and inspected the roof. The old summerhouse appeared to be structurally sound, which was a bit of a miracle considering all the storms it had withstood. It would make her job easier.

She worked with a vengeance all morning. There was really no rush to get it finished, and she knew that her desire to repair the gazebo was only part enthusiasm. The other part was avoidance. She'd have to face Cab sometime soon and try to explain why she'd reacted the way she did. And she wasn't looking forward to that.

When the summerhouse was clean, she stopped to look out

over the ocean. The view was breathtaking. She'd seen a few such views on her travels, those that actually stopped your breath, like a camera shutter closing, while discovery hovered shimmering before you, until the shot was taken and the whirr and click of the camera brought you back to earth, and appreciation became a conscious thing again.

Stargazey Point was majestic but personable, vast yet comforting, formidable but engaging. And if she stood here waxing about the scenery, the gazebo would still be a dilapidated old outhouse when Beau's birthday finally arrived.

She went back for the hammer, placed a box of nails on one of the benches, and began her systematic search for loose boards. Some she merely had to reinforce by driving finishers at an angle against the floor joists. Some needed to be replaced and she marked these with a black marker.

Several splinters and a mashed thumb later, she was forced to put on a pair of work gloves that she'd found with the rest of the tools. They were cumbersome and slowed her down considerably. After several minutes, she threw them off in frustration. One flew right out of the gazebo to the ground. She stood, looked over the railing, and came face-to-face with two small ebony faces peering up at her.

A boy and a girl, looking so much alike they must be twins. They couldn't be over five or six.

"Hi," Abbie said.

They didn't say a word, but turned and ran off toward the beach. Abbie watched them run over the sand, wondering what they were doing alone so close to the water. When she saw them turn and disappear down a path through the dunes, she went back to work.

She'd just completed the floor and was starting on the railings when the lunch triangle rang. She reluctantly packed her tools, slipped the toolbox under one of the benches, and climbed the hill to the house.

Marnie was waiting for her on the kitchen steps. "Productive morning?"

"Very, but I need to buy some lumber and find someone with a skill saw."

Marnie's eyebrows lifted.

"Oh, it's not bad, just a few pieces of flooring and a couple of the benches. It should only take an afternoon—or two." She smiled. It felt good. "You don't happen to own a skill saw do you?"

"No, but I know who does."

Just the tone of her voice set off Abbie's alarm bells. "If it's who I think you mean, thanks, but no."

"Hell, Abbie. You ran out on him without explanation. You might have hurt his feelings."

"Whose feelings?" Millie asked from the doorway. "Now you two hurry up. I've got pimento cheese sandwiches all made."

Marnie pulled a face. "Just saying," she said under her breath and went through the open doorway.

"It wasn't a date," Abbie said under her breath, following close behind.

"Are you two tellin' secrets?" Millie looked eager to join in.

"No, Abbie was just asking who owned a skill saw."

"Skill saw? Why on earth?"

"Abbie is going to refurbish the summerhouse for Beau's birthday."

A frown creased Millie's face. "That old thing. It's practically fallin' down."

"Which is why it's getting a spruce-up."

"And it will be a nice place to sit on warm days," Abbie added.

Millie shook her head. "I would never go out there. I won't."

Shocked at her vehemence, Abbie glanced at Marnie.

Marnie looked thoroughly disgusted. "I think we'll have some early beans in a week or so."

"I'll be glad to have fresh beans," Millie said without missing a beat. "Don't know where the ones at the supermarket come from. Probably some South American country where you don't know what kind of conditions they've been grown in. And the seafood. The Publix last week had shrimp caught in Thailand. What kind of fools are those folks? We have more shrimp than we can eat right here without going to Timbuktu and back for what's right in our own backyard. Jerome might be able to come over here after school lets out. He's good with his hands."

"Why didn't I think of that?" Marnie said perfectly seriously. "I'll call over to Hadley's and ask him to go over to the community center and ask him."

After lunch, Millie went upstairs to listen to the radio. Marnie made the call to Hadley, and she and Abbie walked outside together.

"She's fine, you know," Marnie said when they were some distance from the house. "She's dotty, strays from the point, and gets confused sometimes. But she's always been like that. 'One to chase after her own thoughts,' Momma always said. But she's a good soul under all that superficial prejudice. She wouldn't let a person starve no matter what their pedigree—or their color."

They parted at the garden gate, Marnie to nurture the nascent beans, Abbie down to the gazebo. She wasn't alone. Her two visitors from the morning were back, and they'd brought three friends. They were sitting in a circle on the grass playing some kind of game with stones, but they stopped and turned to watch Abbie as she came toward them.

Two of the new kids were older. A girl, maybe twelve, with

fire engine red hair pulled up to the crown of her head into two ponytails and freckles so thick across her face to almost be a mask. The other was a serious-looking boy, of maybe ten, with stringy blond hair that fell over his eyes. Abbie wondered why they weren't in school. A girl, who looked hardly old enough to walk, stood on the edge of the circle rocking back and forth between two feet.

Abbie smiled but didn't try to approach them. She'd met lots of kids in her work, and she'd learned you couldn't push friendship or trust on them, especially when their culture was different from yours. And so far, just about everything about Stargazey Point was different. It could almost be a foreign country.

There wasn't much more she could do without Jerome. But she could take a closer look at the roof while she was waiting for him to arrive. She dragged a heavy wooden ladder out from the shed and wrestled it up the side of the gazebo. When the top rested against the most solid-looking eave and the feet were braced in the long grass, she tested the first rung, then climbed up.

The ladder groaned, shifted, and bowed beneath her weight. She carefully took another step, and another. And was suddenly surrounded by the five children, hands grasping the ladder to steady it and looking curiously up at her.

She smiled down at them. "Thanks."

"What'chu doin', missus?" This from the new boy.

"I'm fixing up the gazebo."

He nodded seriously. "What'chu doin' that for?"

"I want to make it beautiful again."

"What'chu climbin' that ladder for?"

"To see how bad the roof is."

He nodded again. The heads of the other four lifted and fell as they followed the question-and-answer session.

"It's bad. It gotta hole in it." He smiled, broad and proud.

The other four giggled. He cuffed the closest one, who happened to be the boy twin. He didn't cry, just frowned and rubbed his ear vigorously where the blow had landed.

"Well, I figured it might be bad, but I want to repair it. What do you know about roofs?"

He screwed up his face, looked up to the sky. "Roy, he crawled up on our roof and fell off. Broke his arm. Got a cast and everybody wrote their name on it."

"A good reason not to climb up on a roof," she said.

"Then why are you goin' up on it?"

"I'm not, I'm just taking a look to assess the damage."

"Huh."

They were silent while Abbie inspected the roof. There was definitely a hole in it, and some of the shingles had broken off. The eaves seemed to be solid enough, though it would take someone more knowledgeable than her to repair it. She climbed down the ladder.

They all held on until she reached the ground, then they dispersed as rapidly as dandelion down, stopping about five feet away.

"I bet'chu could use some help."

"I might." Though Abbie didn't know what she could find for five children under twelve to do.

"What'chu gonna pay?" the smallest girl asked.

"She ain't gonna pay you nuthin'," said the boy twin and cuffed her on the ear.

The trickle-down principle, thought Abbie, *as efficient here as with any corporation.*

The girl stepped away, mumbling something Abbie couldn't hear. Then she stuck out her tongue and ran away.

"JuJu Jenny, JuJu Jenny," chanted the older boy. The other three joined in and ran after her. Abbie watched until their cries were drowned out by the waves and they were mere dots

on the beach. Then she lowered the ladder and dragged it back
to the shed.

When Jerome arrived a little after four o'clock, Abbie was sitting in the gazebo, staring out to sea. She watched him come
down the walk with long bouncing strides and she thought
how much more comfortable he looked in jeans than he had
wearing that ridiculously small waiter uniform her first night.

Someone was with him and at first she thought it must be
Marnie showing him the way, but as they got closer, she recognized Bethanne.

"Hope you don't mind that I traipsed along with Jerome,"
she said a little breathlessly and Abbie thought maybe a little
nervously.

"Of course not," Abbie said. "I'm glad to see you." She *was*
glad to see her even if it meant she had an apology to make.

"It's beautiful," Bethanne said.

"It will be," Abbie said.

Bethanne stepped closer to look, and Abbie took the opportunity to talk to Jerome.

"Yes, ma'am?"

The ma'am made her feel ancient. "My name is Abbie."

"Yes, ma'am, Miss Abbie?"

Abbie gave up and told him what she needed.

"I got a gas skill saw," he said and leaped onto the gazebo
floor.

"I marked out the worst ones," Abbie said.

Jerome nodded, placed one foot on the marked board, and
tested the strength. He tested the next and then the others she
had marked until he returned to the entrance. "You need some
two-bys; I can probably get Otis to take me down to the lum-
beryard and get some scraps. Fix up those seats, too."

"Great, when do you think you can get started?"

"Saturday? Want me to pick you up some paint, too?"

"Yes, please. An exterior white that is weather resistant."

"Do better with whitewash, 'cause nothin's weather resistant down here. It won't be fancy, but it'll last."

"Whatever you think best." Abbie reached into her jeans pocket, where she had several folded twenties on the outside chance Jerome got by today. "How much do you think it will cost?"

Jerome looked over the gazebo frowning and nodded to himself. "I'd say about forty, if I can get scrap lumber, fifty if I have to buy whole."

"And the paint?"

"I know a fella."

"Ah," Abbie said. "Let me know, okay?"

Jerome nodded. "Yes'm. You want me to fix that roof, too?"

"If you can."

"I can. Might have to get Otis or somebody to help me some."

"Good." She unfolded sixty dollars and handed it to him. "Will this get you started?"

At first he just looked at it, then he gave her an appraising look and pocketed the bills. "I'll be back on Saturday. Shouldn't take more'n four hours for repairs. You want me to do the paintin', too?"

"I can do the painting."

"All right. See ya on Saturday. Ma'am, Bethanne." He tipped his chin and started back up the walk.

"Wait, Jerome. How much do you charge?"

He looked at the ground, suddenly the uncomfortable boy in the dining room. "Don't usually charge the Crispins."

"I'm not a Crispin," Abbie said.

"I don't know. Mr. Cab usually gives me fifteen an hour."

"For helping him?"

"Yes'm and for when I do stuff for the Crispins. But don't you go and tell 'em, please."

"I won't."

So Cabot was playing anonymous benefactor, Abbie thought as she watched the sturdy teenager walk back to the house. She didn't know whether she should like him more for that or be affronted by his high-handedness. She decided to give him the benefit of the doubt. Besides, she wanted to like him. Did like him. And owed him an apology.

Which brought her right back to Bethanne who was examining the gazebo like someone who had just discovered the mother lode.

"I had no idea this was back here. And that view. It's gorgeous. A perfect place for a wedding."

"You're—"

"Oh, not me, but for someone's wedding. I know it's weird a widow talking about weddings, but it's something I've been thinking about doing for a long time.

"Jim and I were planning to expand into the next building. Turn it into a reception hall where we could host weddings. We were going to call it Weddings by the Sea. But this really is weddings by the sea."

Abbie looked around, trying to see it through Bethanne's eyes. With a little paint the gazebo would be charming, but for the rest of the venue, she just saw a huge amount of work. The grass was brown and patchy. The trees were partially consumed by a trailing vine that made the whole ambience kind of creepy.

Rosebushes had been left to straggle, and bare beds that must have been perennial borders at one time or another lay dormant. The wall around the vegetable garden was almost hidden by ivy.

It would need some major landscaping, and the house would

need to be painted. White, with deep green shutters, not the faded grayish color they were now. Bridesmaids entering from the ballroom doors walking down the brick walk, followed by the bride surrounded by yards of lace and tulle— Yeah, she could see it.

It would certainly be a possible income for the Crispins, but it would take a lot of money and time to get the place in shape. What the Crispins needed now was an immediate infusion of cash.

And somehow she just couldn't imagine Millie going for it.

"Would you be able to handle the inn and a wedding business by yourself?"

"Well, no. But Penny has already agreed to be the caterer; I'd have to hire a staff." She sighed. "I've saved some startup money but not nearly enough for something like this."

She reluctantly turned from the sea. "Listen to me, carrying on about weddings when what I really came for was to apologize for asking you to tea and then deserting you. I don't know what you must think of me. I'm sure Sarah told you about Jim and all about what a crybaby I am."

"She did, and you're not. You have every right to grieve."

Bethanne shook her head. "It's been over three years, and I just can't seem to move on."

Three years? Three whole years? Already tears were pricking the back of Abbie's eyes as her throat tightened on the familiar pain. She didn't want to become someone everyone else had to tiptoe around in order not to upset her; she didn't want to be pitied. What she really wanted was to have her old life back and knew she never could.

"I lost someone, too."

Abbie watched her words sink in. Bethanne grasped her hand. "I'm so sorry. Your husband?"

"We weren't married. But he was my friend, my lover, my mentor, and—" She stopped. She hadn't intended to say that much, but she must have unlocked the floodgates by crying on Beau's shoulder and telling Marnie about Werner the day before.

She pulled her hand away, looked out to sea.

"Do you want to talk about it?"

"No. But thanks," she added as an afterthought. She didn't want to talk, didn't want to relive, didn't want to share. It was time for her to move forward.

"I know nobody can ever know how another person feels about that kind of loss," Bethanne said. "And I wish with all my heart you hadn't gone through it too. But it's a little help to have someone who gets it, don't you think? Sarah thinks I should just get over it and get on with it. She tells me that all the time. She just doesn't . . ." She took a big breath, whooshed it out. "Anyway, I just meant to come apologize. So what are your plans for the gazebo?"

"Well, Beau's birthday is coming up in a couple of months, and Millie said how he used to paint out here when he was a boy, so I thought it might make a nice present."

"You're going to stay for a few months? That would be great."

"I'll have to wait and see. I have to start thinking about getting another job."

"Would it be nosy of me to ask what kind of job?"

"No. But I'm not sure. Something . . . interesting."

"Ever think about weddings?"

Abbie shook her head. "No."

"It takes a lot of people to hold a reception, waiters, catering, a cake person, rentals, a photographer—"

"No. But thanks for the offer."

Bethanne shrugged slightly. "It's just a pipe dream anyway. Come have tea sometimes, okay?" She smiled. "I promise I won't cry."

"Sure," Abbie said as they started up the path.

When they reached the gate, Bethanne turned back for a last look at the sea.

"One more thing. It's not my business, I know, but it is a small town. Cab's sorry he upset you. He didn't say what happened. But he's a nice guy, so maybe you could give him another chance."

Chapter 12

Abbie walked to town with one purpose in mind. Apologize to Cab. Just walk into the carousel building and say she was sorry. Simple, except he deserved an explanation of why she'd acted like a nutcase, and she would have to tell him that she *was* a nutcase, and then he'd either be horrified or feel sorry for her and that would be that.

Better to get it over with.

But when she reached the carousel, a red late-model sports car was parked outside. Behind it, the door to the community center opened and Sarah came out, motioning frantically to Abbie with both hands.

Abbie hurried across the tarmac. As soon as she reached the porch, Sarah pulled her inside.

"What's wrong?" Abbie asked.

"Didn't you see the car? You don't want to go in there right now."

"I saw it and I was going to come back later."

"You can wait at the center. Come on."

She practically dragged Abbie through the front room, a square area that was cluttered with old couches and chairs, chalkboards, and an old television.

That's all Abbie saw before she was being propelled down a narrow hallway to a smaller room where a variety of old tape recorders, video cameras, and computers littered a wide shelf that ran the length of one wall.

Abbie took a quick look around as Sarah guided her toward the one window. Next to the window a larger monitor sat behind two VCR players. Someone was making a movie with equipment that had become obsolete years before.

And Abbie got a terrible suspicion that she was being set up. How had they found out? Did everyone know? Bethanne with her Weddings by the Sea photographer, now Sarah and her outdated equipment.

Sarah paused long enough to give her a look. "From my defunct family history project. But that's not important at the moment."

"And what is?" Abbie asked guardedly.

"I have a favor, sort of."

Abbie automatically shook her head. No way was she going to help with any video project.

"Look, I know about your freak-out at the carousel the other night. Hell, you can't sneeze in this town without everybody ducking. And I won't ask you what it was all about, though I'm curious, naturally. And Cab was, let's just say, confused about your reaction."

Abbie sighed. "I know. I was going over to apologize, but he has company."

"That's the favor I want."

"Oh." Abbie slumped with relief, then immediately became suspicious. "What kind of favor?"

Sarah pulled her over to the window and looked out. They had a full view of the red car and could just see the entrance to the carousel. "Do you know whose car that is?"

"No."

"Two of Cab's old colleagues from Atlanta."

"And? I'm sensing an 'and' here."

"And they brought Cab's ex-fiancée."

"Oh."

"Her name is Bailey." Sarah rolled her eyes. "Bailey," she repeated and shuddered dramatically before breaking into a grin. "What we need here is an intervention."

Abbie opened her mouth, then shut it again, amused but still wary. "Exactly what kind of intervention are we talking about?"

Sarah glanced out the window then back to Abbie. "How much did Cab tell you about himself?"

"Just that he'd been an architect in Atlanta and moved here last year. He didn't say anything about the carousel or an ex-fiancée."

"Just so she stays that way."

Abbie lifted her eyebrows in question.

"Oh not me, hon. We're not that kind of friends. Besides I have my own work. I have to be back in New York no later than the middle of August. I've taken way too much time off already."

Abbie was intrigued and would have liked to hear more about Sarah's work, but Sarah had one thing on her mind.

"If he lets them coerce him into going back, he's liable to let Bailey"—she moaned out the name—"talk him into marrying her."

"I'm taking it you don't care for Bailey?"

Sarah gave her a look. "Have you seen her?"

"No. I didn't even know about her." And then she said something she'd never say. "It's none of my business." *The world is our business.* Werner's words echoed in her mind. "Not this kind of business," she muttered.

"Huh?"

"Nothing. Do you think he'd let himself be coerced into something he didn't want to do? He didn't strike me as spineless as that." Just the opposite, in fact. Cab seemed perfectly comfortable in his skin and happy with his life.

"Honey, he's a man. And he wouldn't be the first to follow his penis down the aisle." She grabbed Abbie's elbow. "Someone's coming out."

The carousel door opened, and Abbie caught herself leaning forward to get a better look. But it was only one man; he was in his late thirties, wearing a short sleeve sport shirt, and he had an incipient pouch overhanging his belt. He reached into the car and came back with a long tubular mailer. The kind that might hold architectural plans. Helping Cab out with some specs on the carousel—or trying to lure him back to the city?

She and Sarah exchanged glances, then craned their necks to get a better view.

They'd barely been here for fifteen minutes and Cab couldn't wait for them to leave. It had been awkward, beyond awkward at first. Tony and Frank were obviously embarrassed. Bailey alternated between acting aloof and aiming darts of derision at him. Cab decided within a couple of minutes that he wouldn't be having dinner with them.

Bailey was one thing. There was bound to be animosity on her part. But Frank and Tony were his friends as well as colleagues. He should be glad to see them. Yet he couldn't wait for them to leave.

Tony had run to the car under the pretense of getting some specs he wanted Cab to look at. Frank had petered out on some story he'd started to tell. Bailey wandered off and was fastidiously inspecting his workbench.

With her back turned to him, he had the chance to really look at her.

She was a beautiful woman, tall, thin, with perfect skin, silky hair. Normally, just seeing her made his pulse kick up, made his thoughts start running in one direction.

Seeing her now he felt nothing. Not even regret. It made him realize that physical attraction had been the biggest thing they'd had in common. And his money, which was now academic, since he'd sunk a bundle into the carousel and his father had cut off the rest.

He didn't blame her for being pissed; she'd signed on for one life and he'd changed the rules on her. He could tell by the spark whenever their eyes met; the spark that had once been desire was now just anger, and he didn't blame her for that either.

He didn't regret her decision—or his. Actually he was relieved. He was happy and satisfied in his work, even the smaller renovation jobs he'd taken on in the last few months. And now that he'd met Abbie, he would never be able to date someone like Bailey again.

Bailey was beautiful, the kind of woman that any man would be proud to have on his arm. Yet as he looked at her, all he could think of was Abbie, her corn-silk hair wild about her face, digging frantically in the mud.

He shoved Abbie from his mind and concentrated on getting rid of his visitors.

Bailey turned back at that moment, and for a moment her eyes flicked with interest. He quickly looked away; he'd been staring at her and thinking of Abbie. He didn't want to give Bailey any encouragement to think he might change his mind. He hadn't.

"So where can we look at this?" Tony said striding back into the room with a cardboard tube in his hand. "After all, it was your baby."

Cab turned away from Bailey, knowing he'd made the right

decision. "I'll just move this stuff and you can lay it out here."
He shoved some gears aside. Pushed oil cans and sandpaper
away and covered the table with a fairly clean scrap of canvas
he kept for cleaner work. It would have to do.

Tony unrolled the spec sheets. "Remember the east exit
gates?"

Cab nodded, looking over the familiar sheets. "They're still
insisting on that? You did tell them it would dump thousands
of people into the parking lot and the main exit artery?"

"Yes. They have brains like sieves." Tony shot his fingers
through his hair. "Jesus, Cab. When are you gonna get over this
back-to-nature crap and come back to work. We need you, man."

"Not going to happen," Cab said distractedly. Bailey was
moving toward the back room where the animals were stored.

"Bailey," he called.

Bailey turned slowly, gave him that look, the look that once
had seduced him into doing whatever she wanted. Could have
him taking her in a closet of an empty condo they were considering buying, on the deck of her lake house while a party raged
on inside . . . but not here, not ever.

"That's off-limits."

True to form, Bailey stepped inside.

Cab headed after her. "Bailey, stop, it's climate controlled."

"Jesus," said Frank coming up behind him. "Are these what
I think these are?"

"You're working on a goddamned merry-go-round?" Tony
asked. "You left Bloomquist and Ryan and moved to Hicksville
for this? You been smoking funny cigarettes or something?"

"Originals?" Frank asked, stepping around Cab and going
to inspect Midnight Lady. "Do you have any idea how valuable
these are?"

Cab sighed. "I do; that's why they're in a climate-controlled
room."

"A bunch of merry-go-round horses?" Tony asked. "You're shitting me."

"No," Frank said. "I've heard of these babies going for thousands apiece. Are these by somebody famous?"

"No shit. Hey, I know a guy who can set you up on eBay," Tony volunteered.

"They're not for sale," Cab said through gritted teeth. He really wanted them out of here.

"Come on, you can't be serious about running a carousel." Tony glanced at Bailey and lowered his voice. "You can't make a living doing that. Especially not here. Have you looked at this town? It's on its last leg. Come back to the firm and do this on your free weekends. It's a hobby, man, not a way of life."

"I'm doing some architectural work," Cab said.

"Yeah? Anything interesting?"

"Interesting to me," Cab said, but he didn't elaborate. A few missing newel posts for the Crispins. A small renovation job on a historical cabin in Platteville. A few others, none he was willing to share.

Tony shrugged. "You at least have time for a couple of drinks?"

"I really need to get going," Bailey said and shot a look at Cab that could freeze men's balls, and all he thought was, *yes, please leave.*

Tony and Frank exchanged confused looks.

Cab didn't try to dissuade them. He waited for them to file out of the room. Bailey was last; she didn't look at him or comment. Her silence said it all.

He turned off the lights and closed the door with a sigh of relief.

Here they come," Sarah said, practically jumping up and down. She leaned close enough to the window to fog the view. "Man, don't go with them, Third." She grabbed Abbie and yanked her away from the window. "Come on, it's intervention time."

"Sarah, no. Leave the guy alone." But Abbie let Sarah pull her back through the house and out onto the porch without much resistance. It might be awkward, but she wanted to get a close look at Bailey, herself.

Abbie had just enough time to suck in a breath before Sarah opened the front door and they both walked nonchalantly onto the porch.

Three people came out of the building followed by Cab. Two men and a woman, tall, with dark, shoulder-length hair that swayed when she walked. She was "done" from the red nail polish Abbie could see from where she was standing to the expensive slacks and silk tee.

"Bailey," Sarah breathed in her ear.

She was beautiful. Next to her, the two men looked like car salesmen and Cab looked working class.

They stopped at the car.

"Just let us know if you change your mind," said the driver. The two men got into the car, which left Bailey and Cab staring at each other across the hood. Abbie suddenly really wished she hadn't let Sarah push her outside. It was such an intimate moment that it made Abbie feel sick, just watching it.

Then Bailey broke contact, shook her head. "You are pathetic. Your daddy was right about you. You're an insult to the Reynolds family name." She snorted, and even that vulgarity was done with breeding.

And Abbie hated her for it, because she could imagine what Cab's father might have said when Cab gave up everything to run a carousel. And she hurt for him.

Bailey turned away, and her eyes met Abbie's. Her expression changed. Her eyes narrowed, and her mouth hardened

into a sardonic smile. She looked back at Cab then leveled another look at Abbie.

"So," Bailey said, her words dripping disgust. "I should have
known. You've got a little piece of white trash on the side. You
better watch yourself, love. She'll end up barefoot and pregnant
and after your portfolio, then where will you be?" She opened
the car door and gave him one last sultry look. "Peter Pan." She
flicked a nasty look at Abbie and got inside.

The car backed up and sped away, and Sarah and Abbie were
left looking at Cab.

Cab had been watching the car, but now he turned back to
Sarah and Abbie.

"Oops. That was a little more successful than I intended."
Sarah slipped away; Abbie heard the screen door slam behind
her and wished she had followed. That way she could pretend
that she hadn't heard, that she hadn't been caught eavesdropping. She wanted to tell Cab not to listen to Bailey or anyone
who tried to make him feel bad, to pretend she hadn't been the
brunt of Bailey's insinuations. But she just stood there.

"Well," he said. "Do you think I'm pathetic?"

Abbie shook her head.

He stood there, angry, defiant, and obviously expecting
more of an answer than a shake of the head.

"I think you have a right to live your life the way you want.
Save that surly attitude for your friends."

Cab stepped back as if she'd physically slapped him.
"Sorry—"

"Look, I just came to apologize for acting like an ass the
other night. I guess I had a lousy sense of timing."

"You mean Sarah had a perfect sense of timing."

Abbie smiled in spite of herself. "She wanted to stage an
intervention."

He fought a smile then gave up. "She doesn't let up. But for once I'm grateful. I thought they'd never leave. And you don't have to apologize."

"Yeah, I do. I overreacted when you showed me the carousel. I loved carousels as a kid. I just had an experience that um—and it took me by surprise. So don't take it personally." She began backing away. "So thank you for the tour and for dinner. And everything. Bye."

She spun around to make a run for the porch.

"I know, Abbie."

She stopped, staring at the screen door, praying that he hadn't meant what she feared.

"I didn't understand why you were the way you were, so I did something I don't like doing."

"You googled me."

"Yeah. I saw the YouTube video."

Her stomach lurched. *Don't turn around, just go inside.* It would only take one step, the rest would follow. If she ran, she wouldn't have to hear what he thought, see his sympathy, feel his disappointment.

But she was tired of running. It was time to face it—to face him. "So now you know . . ."

"Some. At least it helped me understand why you freaked."

"I didn't freak."

"Why Lady *upset* you, then." He stepped toward her. "It was the donkey, wasn't it? Seeing Lady's head, you saw the donkey."

She nodded.

"And it wasn't because I nearly hit that old man and his cart, was it?"

She shook her head.

She was afraid she might burst into tears. Something she was doing a lot of these last few days.

He stepped closer. "I'm sorry. I wouldn't do anything to cause that kind of pain."

"I know, it's fine. Neither one of us meant to hurt the other's feelings. We're even. I've got to go."

She stepped off the porch. There was no chance of her making a new life for herself here. They would all know soon and pity her. You couldn't start a new life surrounded by pity.

But you can't start a new life if you don't stop running.

"I'm sorry about the stuff Bailey said. She can be pretty caustic when she doesn't get her way."

"It's okay. She's angry and had to take it out on someone. Let's just forget it." But she would be sure to thank Sarah later for her idea of an intervention; if anybody didn't belong together, it was Cab and Bailey.

He nodded but didn't say anything.

"You know, I'd like to meet Lady for real, if you'll give me another chance."

Cab looked at her for a long moment. "You sure?"

"I'm sure."

He waited for her to reach him, then they walked side by side through the open plywood doors. Cab paused just inside the room, and she thought he probably did that every time he entered the room, his pride and delight as palpable as if he'd explained it in words. She felt it, too. The magic was still there, waiting for someone—Cab—to bring it back to life. A thrill shot up her spine.

Without a word he walked her toward the back door. In the light of day, she saw that it was made of reinforced metal. Inside, the lights were blindingly white. Midnight Lady was lying on her side fully visible; a long gouge scarred her flank.

Abbie repressed a shudder and felt Cab slip an arm lightly around her shoulders.

"What happened to her?"

"Don't know. They were all moved inland several times during storms. It might have happened in the last move. Maybe vandals. She's almost a hundred years old." He laid his free hand gently on the scar before he led her to another horse, this one standing: a white high-prancing beauty, with gold mane and tail and a bright red, white, and blue saddle. One leg was unpainted, a replacement for the original, which was lost or damaged beyond repair.

They moved through the crowded room with its smell of linseed oil and turpentine.

"A pig," Abbie exclaimed, stopping before a huge, round beast, its pink snout riding above a smiling red mouth.

"There's also a dolphin, a sea horse, a lion, and two chariots in addition to the horses."

"And you're restoring them all?"

"Little by little. But it's a mongrel setup. Not one of the classics. The animals come from different places. I'm trying to get the major repairs done before I open. After that, I'll rotate them out to finish the job."

A rumble filled the air and Abbie jumped, even as she told herself it was just some kind of ventilation system.

"We use some pretty volatile chemicals, so I have an air exchange system to keep us from getting high or sick."

"We? I'm thinking I know who might be helping you."

He smiled and motioned her to follow him. They went through a narrower door and stepped down into a square room filled with daylight. Rectangular panels lined the walls in various states of cleaning. Some were barely recognizable for the grime and fading. A few looked brighter but still indistinct; two on the end had been completely restored to a colorful scene of Victorian families at play.

And at the very end of the row, seated on a straight-backed chair, was Beau Crispin, oblivious to their presence as he leaned forward, carefully detailing a figure in black.

So that was where he went off to every day. When he wasn't

fishing or sitting on the old pier pilings carving his little piece of wood, he was helping Cab restore the carousel.

"Did he do the replacement parts, too?" Abbie whispered.

"A few of the smaller, decorative pieces, but I really needed his painting skills. He balked at first, no matter what I said to persuade him. But he couldn't stay away." He stopped, and they watched in silence as Beau's brush ran fluidly over the wooden panel.

"He's good." Millie had told her about Beau painting in the gazebo—until his father "put an end to it" and sent him to military school. Was painting his first love? Was this Beau Crispin's guilty pleasure?

He glanced up as she came to stand behind him, winked at her, slowly like all his other gestures, and went back to his work.

Abbie peered over his shoulder at the wooden panel he was working on. Unlike the others, this panel was new wood, treated with something white but not previously painted. He'd sketched out a scene: tall, pointed trees on the right, cypress trees maybe, and a point of land, the beginnings of the ocean in the background and a tiny boat out to sea.

It was the view from the gazebo, Abbie was sure of it. And Beau was painting it by heart. Something wrenched in her own heart, though she didn't know what.

Cab nudged her, lifted his chin toward the door. They tip-toed away. It was like being in church, Abbie thought, the peace, the beauty; an image of Michelangelo flashed across her mind. Beau in his workshop.

"Just so you know," Cab said, when they were back in the main room. "We don't talk about Beau spending so much time here."

"Millie and Marnie wouldn't like it?"

"Oh, Marnie wouldn't care, but Millie has some strange

ideas about the way things should be. It's just better to keep the peace than stir up unhappiness."

Abbie frowned at him. She hoped he would say more, but if he knew more, he was keeping his own peace. "Does Beau do all the painting?"

"Most of it. I do some detailing. I'm a craftsman, not an artist."

"I wonder."

"Well, don't. I designed utilitarian buildings when I was an architect; I know how to follow directions and stay in the line." He grinned. "But I can appreciate others' artistry. What about you?"

"Me? I can barely draw a straight line. I'm not sure about staying in the lines. In my family you were taught to think and color outside the box."

"What about the films you made?"

"I didn't make them. I did the interviews. The local color, the history."

They had crossed the floor and come to the carousel platform.

"Sounds pretty creative."

Abbie shrugged. "In my family you learned to be creative, but for the purpose of helping others, outwitting red tape, getting things done. It wasn't art. At least not in my case. I was kind of the throwback."

They had sat down on the platform, angled slightly toward each other.

He frowned at her. "So you became a weathergirl?"

"Stupid. I know. I studied communications. I was egotistical enough to think I could change the world by reaching the most people at once. But I couldn't figure out how to do that. The only job I could get was weathergirl." She laughed. "Like I said, stupid. And arrogant. And look where my arrogance got me."

"Hey, Stargazey Point isn't so bad."

"That's not what I meant."

"You did good work. The documentaries."

"It was Werner's work. He had the vision, the ability. I couldn't get past the individuals." She swallowed. It hurt. "And in the end, I couldn't even help them."

She stood up. "Sorry, I don't know why I said all that. Just forget it. I'd better go."

Cab grabbed her wrist. Not hard but strong enough to prevent her from leaving.

Her first impulse was to wrench away and run, but she'd displayed more theatrics than she was entitled to. "I really have to go. Millie will wonder where I am."

They stood there for a long moment just looking at each other. Then he let go, reluctantly it seemed to Abbie, and there was nothing left to hold her back. She seemed to have lost the will to leave. He stepped toward her and she headed for the door.

"You did what you could," he said. "It's all any of us can do."

"But it wasn't good enough."

Chapter 13

Cab sat on the platform of the carousel and watched the plywood door, half expecting—no, wanting—her to turn around and come back. She'd delivered a zinger and slipped out before he could even recover. He should have stopped her.

He pushed to his feet just as the door opened. His pulse skipped a beat before he recognized Sarah.

"What did you do this time?" she asked, coming inside.

"Don't you ever let up?"

"When hell freezes over. I don't have all the time in the world. Life awaits me in Manhattan. And don't ask what's stopping me from going back there now."

Cab grinned even though he didn't feel much like indulging her. "I wasn't. I was going to ask you why you're here. Don't you have a whole bunch of kids to keep out of trouble?"

"They're busy. And I have plans for them for the weekend. What I'm wondering is what are your plans?"

"Working. Like always."

"That's what I figured." She slumped and shuffled toward the door, shaking her head.

"What?"

"I sure was hopin' I wouldn't have to get Ervina to make me a potion."

"What do you need a potion for?" Cab asked suspiciously.

She grinned over her shoulder. "To give it to you." She slipped out the door.

"I hate it when you do that," he called after her.

" 'Hate' is a powerful word," said Beau from the doorway to the workshop.

"I'm having a rough day."

Beau nodded slowly. "Women can make a day rough all right. 'Course they can also be good for what ails you."

"You're not suggesting that—"

"I'm not suggestin' nothin', just saying." He walked over to the workbench and picked up his jacket. "I'll be gettin' on now. Millie'll have supper on the table and wondering where I am. Evenin', Cabot."

In another minute, Beau was gone, and Cab was sitting alone with his empty carousel. It was Friday night. He could have been dining with Frank and Tony except that Bailey would be with them, and after the way she'd insulted Abbie, he never wanted to see her again.

He could have asked Abbie to dinner, that's what he really wanted to do. But hell, just when you thought she was beginning to relax, something set her off again. He didn't like to see anybody hurting, and he especially didn't like to see Abbie that way. She didn't deserve to think she was a failure just because some guy didn't know enough to save himself when the authorities swooped down on them.

When it was obvious she wasn't coming back and it was too late to go after her, Cab decided to knock off work and go home. He unplugged equipment, checked the dehumidifier and thermostat, and looked over his wooden menagerie, trying not to make any analogies about the route his life was taking.

He stopped by Midnight Lady. She was never fickle, never ran, never played games. Then again, she wasn't real. He stroked her flank. Ran his fingers over the hard, wooden mane and turned out the lights.

The nightmare came near morning.

Abbie turns, in slow motion, to Werner. Help me, but Werner keeps filming. A car slams to a stop behind him, the thugs jump out. She yells to warn him, but he doesn't hear. They run toward him, she screams. But they pass him and grab her instead, pull her from the donkey and his boy. She fights but they're too strong. They drag her to the car and throw her into the backseat. Werner, help me! Werner turns the camcorder on her and films them taking her away.

Abbie struggled to sit up. The sheets had tangled around her legs, tethering her to the bed.

"It wasn't like that," she moaned. She pressed her hands to her face. *He* wasn't like that. Or was he? Would he have sacrificed her to save his work? Because it was his work. Her work had been the donkey boy, the woman who showed her the handwoven wedding dress she'd been making for her twelve-year-old daughter for the day she would wed.

Her daughter who had perished in that schoolhouse—and she still pressed a packet of food into Abbie's hands as the embassy car came to extract her from the jungle.

What had happened to that woman? Would she finish the wedding dress for someone else or pack it away with her memories and her dreams? Would she drift back to anonymity because Abbie's interview had perished alongside her child?

Abbie felt feverish, her skin hot to the touch. She wrestled the covers away, sat up. It was tragic, but she'd done her best, and she wanted to be free. She wanted to live life again. Make friends. Make love.

Anger and frustration washed over her in suffocating waves. Maybe she was selfish, but she wanted to be happy. Useful. But mainly happy. She needed to move on. And she knew the only person who was stopping her was herself.

She got out of bed, dragged on jeans and a sweatshirt, and slipped downstairs. The lawn was heavy and wet with dew, bathed in moonlight. Cold on her bare feet. She walked to the edge of the dunes and looked out into the darkness.

It was a damp night; the wind off the water was chilled, but inside her was warm and she knew what it was. Hate, anger, frustration. And she wanted it gone.

She took a breath, her throat seized, but it had to be done; she was ready.

"You have to let me go," she said aloud. "I wanted to keep you but I can't. I can't change the past. I'm scared, but I have to go on alone. I need you to be okay with that."

She listened to the wind, to the waves. She didn't really expect to hear a voice, so she jumped when a voice came out of the darkness.

"Abbie?"

Abbie sucked in air.

"It's me. Beau. I didn't mean to frighten you."

"Oh. I was . . . just out for a walk." She shrugged. "Couldn't sleep."

He nodded. "I saw you from my window. I'm glad you came out tonight."

Abbie looked up at his face. *Why?*

"I made something for you. A *petit cadeau*, if that's not being presumptuous."

Abbie shook her head. She couldn't think of anything to say. She couldn't imagine why Beau would want to give her a present.

He fumbled in his jacket pocket, brought out a flat packet covered in tissue paper, and handed it to her. Slowly she opened it and held it to the moonlight. It was a small star, with five delicate points, each highly ridged. It was carved from a dark wood and was attached to a silver chain.

"It's beautiful."

"It's a nautical star. So you'll always be able to find your way home."

Marnie dreamed of Paris, of jazz trios and absinthe. Cigarette smoke and long thin loaves of bread. Of hot nights and hotter sex. Of a time long gone by.

She awoke with the sense of having been on a journey. And was a little disoriented to find herself at home. *Home.* There was a time when she detested that word. She'd suffered her entire childhood under Daddy's heavy-handedness and Momma's all-consuming love. She would have left as soon as she could, even if Daddy hadn't driven her off first. And the scoundrel let everyone think she'd run away. She never let on any different. Even to this day. Let Millie have her illusions about their family. She and Beau knew better.

They never spoke about it. Like they had just cut off that early part of their lives like you cut off last year's garden growth. She didn't know about Beau. She only knew about herself. She'd made her peace with things—with herself. Millie was the one who was still fettered to the past.

Abbie was wearing Beau's necklace when she came downstairs the next morning. She went straight to the coffeepot on the kitchen counter then carried her cup to the table, where Marnie and Millie were sitting over their midmorning cups of coffee. They'd been up for hours and Abbie had just managed to drag herself out of bed.

"Good mornin', Abbie," Millie said. "What would you like for breakfast? Jerome stopped at the back door to bring us some fresh eggs from Ervina."

"Jerome is already here?" Abbie looked at the kitchen clock. She'd overslept, but it was only nine thirty. Abbie drank her coffee as fast as the heat would allow.

Millie turned to her. "Now there's no need to hur— What a lovely necklace."

Abbie's hand went to her throat. "Beau gave it to me."

"Beau?" Millie squinted, trying to see better.

Abbie stepped closer so she could see.

Marnie pushed her chair back, glanced at the necklace, and raised an eyebrow. "I'm thinking you better get outside and oversee Jerome."

"Oversee? I meant to help him." Abbie turned from Millie, rinsed off her coffee cup, and put it on the drainboard.

"I'll walk you out," Marnie said and hustled her out the door.

"Beau made that?" Millie said from inside.

"Should I not have worn it?" Abbie asked and raised her hand to the wooden star.

"Of course you should. It's just unusual, or rather unheard of, for Beau to show a finished product, much less give it as a gift."

Strange that Beau didn't show them his carvings, didn't tell them about his work on the carousel. Abbie didn't understand why it should be kept a big secret. She wanted to ask Marnie why Millie would care, but she was stopped by the sound of children playing.

"Did you hear that? I heard them earlier and thought I must be dreaming, but now I hear them again."

"Well, it is Saturday and sunny. They may be down on the beach. They're welcome. Or—" She stopped by the garden gate and lifted her chin toward the gazebo.

The first thing Abbie saw was Jerome dressed in ragged overalls, dark muscular arms catching the sunlight. He was standing with his feet apart, pointing at something with the paintbrush he was holding.

And then she saw the source of the chatter and laughter. The gazebo was surrounded by children all holding paintbrushes, stroking the wooden boards and flinging paint as they cavorted with their friends.

"Well, well, well," Marnie said. "Looks like you've got a workforce."

Abbie had a momentary vision of Tom Sawyer before it was replaced with thoughts about child labor laws and the safety of whitewash.

"I see, but should they be helping? Isn't whitewash made with lye? Is it toxic?"

"It's safe enough. Most of these children are exposed to things kids in the suburbs have never heard of. It's the way of life here. Nothing too dangerous, but no pampering. You have to be tough to get ahead in this world. Especially these kids.

"Besides, Sarah wouldn't let them do anything that they're not capable of doing or anything that might hurt them. For all her Yankee ways, she's still one of them."

"Why would Sarah think we need help? Not that I mind it, but . . ."

"I've been around for a long time, seen lots of places, and the one thing I learned was that it sometimes takes a village, not largesse handed down from the haves or the has-beens—something that my sister would do well to learn. Not that I expect that to happen in this lifetime.

"But Sarah understands and I suspect you do, too. Let them have their fun." She lifted the latch and went through the gate; Abbie headed down to the gazebo.

Abbie stopped by Jerome. "Was this your idea?"

He shook his head. "No'm, but it's a good one. Get the job done faster, and since it's all white, they cain't make a mess. You don't want 'em here?" Alarm flashed through his eyes.

"It's fine, but is it safe?"

"Yes'm. Safe enough. Me and Clarence'll do the high stuff and the paint's safe enough outside. They'll wash off good afterward."

Abbie laughed. "How did you get them to give up their free morning to work?"

Jerome shrugged one shoulder. "They all come to the center on Saturdays if they don't have chores or after they've finished. And today they got the choice of getting tutored or painting the gazebo out in the sun. Which one would you choose?"

"I'm not sure it's legal to use children."

"Sure it is. It's a part of our oral history project."

"I thought that project was dead."

"Oh, well, it's the new paintin'-the-historic-Crispin-gazebo project. See over yonder? Dani and Joe are documenting it."

Dani and Joe, the twins from the other day. They were attempting to hold up a heavy old video camera. The camera tipped wildly as they tried to aim it at the painters.

Exasperated, Dani tried to yank it from her brother's hands. A tug-of-war ensued while the video continued to run. They'd end up with nothing but erratic shots of ground and body parts.

Sarah appeared at Abbie's side. "Looks like they could use some help."

"Of course. I should have known. This was your idea," Abbie said.

"Thought it would give them something useful to do while still being out in the fresh air," Sarah said, not taking her eyes from the group. "Daniella, you two cooperate or you'll never get your story."

Dani grabbed the camera from her brother, lifted it against her chest, and held it with both hands while she arched to hold the extra weight.

"Dani, I mean it."

The girl huffed out a sigh and handed the camera to Joe. He snatched it out of her hands and nearly fell over backward.

"It's too heavy for them," Abbie said.

"It's the lightest one we've got."

"Don't you at least have a tripod?"

" 'Fraid not," Sarah drawled. " 'Spect they could use some help."

Abbie should have seen it coming; both times she'd heard Sarah lapse into a drawl was right before she asked for something.

"Go ahead," Abbie said, refusing to take the bait.

"I have to oversee." Sarah shot her a complacent smile. "Seems like it's the least you could do, seeing how we're painting your gazebo."

Joe was jumping around Dani waving his arms and whining for her to give him a turn. At this rate they'd break the camera; it was so old it was amazing it still worked at all.

"Well? You gonna just let them struggle like that?"

Abbie looked back at the twins. *Okay, big talker,* Abbie told herself. *You wanted to be free. You wanted your life back. Here's your chance.*

With a theatrical sigh, she marched off toward the twins. They immediately stopped fighting. Abbie reached for the camera. Dani reluctantly gave it up and stepped back, cowering.

Abbie squatted down to make herself the same height, and she motioned the two over. When they were in front of her, she said, "This is really heavy, isn't it?"

Slow nods.

"Want me to show you a trick to keep the camera steady?"

Joe nodded uncertainly, but Dani looked up with a smile so broad that it tightened Abbie's throat.

She faced the gazebo and sat down with her knees up in front of her and patted a place on the ground next to her. "Sit down beside me."

There was a moment's tussle and they plopped on the grass, one on each side.

"To get a good sequence—a good picture—you have to find a way to keep the camera steady. So if you don't have a tripod or a bench or something, you can use your knees." Abbie rested the camera on her knees, noticed that her hands were shaking.

"Now the camera will stop jumping around as much. Do you want to try?"

Dani's eyes widened. A nod.

Abbie transferred the camera to Dani's knees, positioned her hands to give maximum mobility without blocking the lens with her fingers. Joe crawled over Abbie's lap to get a closer look.

"Now look through the eyepiece and pick a subject."

Dani's eyes cut toward Abbie.

"Pick the people you want to take a picture of."

"Oh." Dani bent over the camera biting her lip in concentration.

"Now gently press the record button. Easy now."

They reviewed the shot. Dani smiled, then Joe took a turn.

"It works," he said and gave Abbie a duplicate smile.

"Thanks," Sarah said, and there was no trace of the drawl now.

"You're welcome." Abbie cut her attention back to the twins. They were intent and serious, both leaning over the camera and slowly panning across the gazebo.

"Maybe you'd be willing to help with the postproduction."

Abbie stood. "I'm not really an editor." The shakes had moved from her fingers to her legs, which was stupid. It was just some kids taking pictures. Nothing bad would happen if she helped them.

She squatted down. "You want to try some close-ups?"

Two enthusiastic nods.

"Great." She took the camera, and Dani and Joe scrambled to their feet.

When she looked up, Sarah was gone.

Chapter 14

Around noon Marnie came down the walk, pulling an old red wagon behind her.

"Lunch," she announced. She found a flat place on the lawn and began opening containers and laying them out on the grass. "Jerome, clean up these children and let 'em take a break."

Everyone moved at once.

"Mind your manners," Jerome ordered in a calm round tenor. The kids stopped where they were.

"Now you all line up and put down your paintbrushes on that piece of cardboard there. Then you go over to the hose and Grace will make sure you get washed up good. Then you go over and wait your turn for Miss Marnie to hand you somethin' to eat."

There was a minor tussle before they all lined up to deposit their brushes and get their hands washed. Within minutes they were all sitting in the grass eating peanut butter and jelly sandwiches and drinking red Kool-Aid.

"Best Millie could do on short notice," Marnie said, handing Abbie a sandwich.

"Well, tell her thank you; they're gobbling it up without a complaint."

"I expect they're glad to get it."

"Sarah said most of them are in foster care. That's a lot of kids for such a small town."

"Foster care, ha. Some of them, like Dani and Joe, live with relatives or with a working parent who leaves them with friends. What constitutes family isn't always cut and dried in these parts. Just suffice it to say, none of them is going to turn down a free meal."

Abbie watched the children dig into their sandwiches, some eating from one corner to the other. Some eating a crescent out from top to bottom until the edges flopped over. Joe started in the middle making a big hole that he looked through, then he laughed so hard he fell over onto the grass.

Abbie smiled, caught herself. She was not ready to get involved with any children. Even though she had to admit she was intrigued by what Marnie had said about how they lived. Had they fallen through the cracks of governmental support systems? Or had they avoided them on purpose.

Whichever it was, at least they had a nurturing place to go after school and on weekends. Though she did wonder who would take over when Sarah returned to her work in New York. It would be hard to find someone to fill her shoes.

After lunch, the kids filed by Marnie and dropped their trash into the brown grocery bag she held out. They were less than enthusiastic about returning to painting, and Abbie saw more than one yawn.

Jerome chose one of the older girls to take the younger ones back to the community center. That left two girls and two boys to finish the job.

Joe and Dani lay in the grass, the heavy camera held between them, fast asleep. But when Jerome woke them, they clung to the camera and groggily refused to leave.

In the quieter atmosphere, the gazebo got its final coat of

whitewash while Abbie sat on the grass watching. Joe and Dani sat beside her, the camera going on and off as they filmed each other's feet, a line of ants, and what they swore was an alligator, but which on closer inspection turned out to be a stick that had washed up from the tide.

One of the older girls began to sing in a contralto, a beautiful melody that Abbie assumed was an old folk tune until she began to pick out the words " . . . a long and winding road . . ."

Abbie listened for a while then turned Joe and Dani over to Jerome and made her way back to the house. No one was in the kitchen, but the Kool-Aid containers sat unwashed in the sink.

She pushed up her sleeves and washed out the two containers, thinking she should make a contribution to the community center in exchange for their help, their very messy help, today. The gazebo was mostly finished though there seemed to be as much paint on the grass as on the structure.

She dried the Kool-Aid containers and briefly considered going into town for a latte, but she settled for a cup of instant coffee.

Marnie came in while Abbie sat at the table drinking her less-than-satisfying brew.

"Instant?" she said, wrinkling her nose.

"I only wanted a cup so it didn't seem like it was worth getting out the percolator."

"We actually had a Mr. Coffee, but it gave up the ghost months ago. Can never remember to pick up a new one when I go out." She poured a cup of water from the kettle and added some instant coffee.

Abbie made a mental note to buy a coffeepot when she went into town next.

There was a quiet knock at the back door.

"I'll get it," Marnie said. She returned a second later.

"Somebody for you," she said seriously.

Abbie went to the door, saw no one, and opened the door.

Dani and Joe stood at the bottom of the steps, both holding the video camera.

"Miss Sarah said for you to keep this for us," Dani said. They thrust the camera toward Abbie. She grabbed for it as it wobbled in their small hands.

"Thank you. Did she say what I was supposed to do with it?"

They shook their heads, so synchronized to be almost funny. "Jus' we s'pposed to give it to you," Joe mumbled.

"I'll take care of it for you and bring it by the center tomorrow, okay with you?"

The heads bobbed up and down simultaneously. Then they broke and ran around the house and out of sight.

Abbie looked around—no Sarah, no Jerome, just a white gazebo sitting in the sun.

She would take the camera back, but if Sarah thought she was going to help with the filming, she could think again.

Abbie fell into bed exhausted that night, which was odd, since she had done very little work during the day, just hung out with the kids. She slept soundly until morning when the slamming of a car door woke her up and she heard Millie greeting the Oakleys, who took her to church every Sunday.

She showered and dressed and went downstairs, intending to return the camera and walk home again while everyone was at breakfast or in church.

The town was deserted, and it occurred to her that the community center would probably be locked.

She crossed the tarmac and tried the door. It opened. She stuck her head through the opening. "Sarah? Are you here?"

No one answered, and no lights shone from the back. Abbie stepped inside and closed the door behind her.

She carried the camera back to the video room she'd seen the other day. The room was dark since the only window opened onto the narrow walkway that ran between the center and the carousel.

She put the camera on the work shelf and looked for a piece of paper to leave a note. Smiled when she saw an old cassette recorder that reminded her of one her mother had saved from college. Out of curiosity she pushed the play button.

"I come here from across the water up from Beaufort. My fambly raised hogs. But my mama brung us boys over this way where her boyfriend ran the motel out on Highway 17. It ain't there no more." She pushed stop. No wonder Sarah was having trouble focusing the children.

She found a tablet and a grease pen. Wrote, *Brought your cam back. Got some interesting footage. Abbie.*

She folded the note and tented it on top of the camera.

"You lookin' for somethin?"

Abbie cut back a screech. "Who's there?"

Ervina stepped into the doorway.

"Ervina, you startled me."

"You didn't answer my question."

"I was returning the camera. The twins were using it yesterday and left it at the gazebo. I was just leaving a note for Sarah."

Ervina cackled a laugh. It sent gooseflesh up Abbie's arms. Of course from what she'd seen of Ervina and what Sarah had told her, she was pretty sure that's just what Ervina intended.

They stood looking each other over. Ervina wasn't exactly short or tall, not even medium. It was hard to describe her, except her hair was gray and cornrowed close to her head. Her skin also had a grayish tinge. Old age or bad diet. She was dressed in an old housedress that buttoned up the front and was soft and nearly transparent with washing.

Abbie smiled. "Could you please tell Sarah I came by?"

"You not gonna get free if you keep acting this way."

"What way?" The words escaped before she could stop them.

"You stuck."

"Well. I'll try harder." She forced another smile and tried to squeeze past the old woman, who was blocking the doorway.

"Cain't get there in a hurry."

Abbie sighed. She knew Ervina wasn't talking about her walk home, but Abbie had no intention of being the subject of her arcane folk wisdom.

"Good to see you." And though she hadn't seen Ervina move, the doorway was clear. "Bye." Abbie stepped into the hallway and headed for the front door.

"Girl, you so busy lookin' behind you, you cain't see what's up ahead."

Abbie stopped, turned, gave Ervina a steely look. "That's not what my therapist said."

Ervina spit. "Man's a fool."

Abbie couldn't agree more, but she wasn't about to say so.

"The only person fixin' you is gonna be you."

Abbie gave up trying to escape. She sat down on the arm of a sagging easy chair. "I'm not doing such a good job of it."

"No, you ain't." Ervina shuffled across the floor until she was standing in front of Abbie. She leaned over and squinted into Abbie's eyes. "You holdin' down that poor man's soul with yo' anger and yo' grief. You need to let him go."

Abbie was so stunned she could barely breathe. "It's not like that. You can't hold on to someone when he's dead." *But he can hold on to you.*

"He don't want'chu, girl," Ervina said. "He's got a better place he needs goin' to. You're bein' selfish. Let him go to where he belongs."

God, those betraying tears were building at the back of her eyes, just waiting to spill over.

"Let him. Go." Ervina leaned even closer, reached out, and touched Beau's star with one gnarled finger. "You won't get lost." She moved away. "Sarah's here." She shuffled to the door and opened it just as Sarah reached for the doorknob.

"Jeez, Granny E. What are you doing here?"

"Just came to have a talk. I'm goin' home now." And she went out the door.

Sarah saw Abbie sitting on the edge of the chair. "Oh, shit. Ervina's been practicing her conjure, hasn't she?"

"How—"

Sarah waved her hand. "I've seen that look on the faces of some of her other victims."

Abbie ran a hand over her mouth. "I'm afraid she was pretty on target."

"Yeah, she tends to be."

"But you don't believe in her . . . whatever you want to call it."

"Gift? Powers? Bullshit? Hell, I don't know. Actually I think it's fascinating. Worthy of a dissertation; I just wish I wasn't in line to inherit whatever it is." She shuddered. "Okay, I just weirded myself out. What do you say we run over to Penny's and have some lunch. Then we can discuss a proposition I have in mind."

"Lunch sounds great. I'm not so sure about the proposition."

"Hey, my kids painted your gazebo, you owe us." Sarah grinned.

She was as sure of getting Abbie to agree as Ervina was about Abbie's holding on to Werner. They were both right. It was time Abbie started looking forward.

"My treat," Abbie said.

"Oh, no. Don't think you can buy me off that easy."

Abbie laughed. "Fine. You buy."

"Dutch treat. Come on. We want to beat the after-church crowd." Sarah led the way, stopping only to lock the front door.

"Your door was unlocked when I came this morning," Abbie told her. "I left the video cam the twins were using in the media room."

Sarah let out an over the top guffaw. "Media room. Love it."

"Couldn't you get a grant or something?"

Sarah gave her a look. "We're trying to keep a low profile. Once you ask the government for something, they slap you with a bunch of rules and regulations so that it's impossible to get anything done. We'd be building a handicap ramp, and hardwiring smoke detectors, filling out forms to get, then keep, our not-for-profit status, get regulated by a bunch of state politicians who never even heard of Stargazey Point much less give two shits about anything but bringing more tourism to South Carolina. And the kids get lost in the shuffle."

"Feel strongly about this, do you?"

Sarah grinned. "Ya think? We're content just to scratch along."

They passed the carousel where sounds of a power saw whined from inside. "The Third is a workaholic. Least he's doing something useful for a change."

"What did he do before?" Abbie asked, hurrying to keep up with Sarah's long stride. Sarah was a good six inches shorter, but she outdistanced Abbie with every step. "I mean I know he was an architect, but he really didn't say what he designed. I guessed houses, since he spent the whole day pointing out architectural details on the historic homes of Georgetown."

"He did that?" Sarah groaned. "The man's an animal."

"It wasn't boring, if that's what you mean."

"We were hoping it moved to the more personal. Say maybe you liked him."

"I did, I do. He's very nice." She did like him; it was disconcerting how much she liked him.

"Oh, gack. The man needs a love interest. We live in constant dread of Bailey having a change of heart and moving here. There's only room for one witch in this town. And Ervina's got that sewn up. That only leaves bitch, and we sure as hell don't need any more of those. But to answer your question . . ."

Abbie laughed. "Please do."

"Convention centers, hotels, shopping complexes, sports arenas."

"The Third?"

Sarah nodded, tightening her mouth, which created dimples in each cheek. "A sad commentary on a bright mind. Fortunately he saw the evil of his ways and dumped it all for no money, no fiancée, and no job security."

"That takes guts," Abbie said. She'd had him pegged all wrong. She'd always prided herself on her ability to see the real person. She'd missed big-time on Cab Reynolds.

"I guess."

"You don't sound too impressed."

"Well, it's not like he gave up something that could change the world. Just making a bunch of money for cluttering the country with surplus buildings."

"Still, it's something he'd obviously had to spend years training for. And—" Abbie took a breath. "It's not so easy to change the world."

Penny's was already half filled, but they managed to get a table in the corner. Abbie was surprised to see Bethanne waitressing.

"She helps Penny out on the weekends in the off-season and during the season, Penny makes the pastry for the inn's dining room."

"A win-win relationship," Abbie said.

Bethanne plunked down menus. "The spinach artichoke quiche is to die for."

"Works for me," Abbie said. "And a double latte."

"Make it two, but I'll just have seltzer with lime." Sarah handed back the two paper menus.

"I was talking to Penny about the gazebo," Bethanne said, before scurrying away.

"What about the gazebo?" Sarah asked. "No. Wait. Let me guess. Weddings by the Sea."

"She thought the gazebo would be a perfect venue."

"Right. Like Miss Millie would go for—" Sarah took a breath and drawled, "Openin' the house to the puh-blic. Nev-uh."

"And they would have to, wouldn't they?" asked Abbie. "You'd need more than a gazebo. Like dressing rooms and a place for catering and a backup plan in case of rain?"

"Beats me, I'm more of a theoretical kind of girl. Can we forget weddings for a sec? I want to talk about something else."

Abbie braced herself. Cab must have told Sarah about her background; why else would Sarah have sent the kids down to "document" the gazebo being painted? Maybe Sarah had even looked on the Internet herself. There was no way to get around it anymore.

"I suppose you want to know what happened in Peru."

Sarah snorted. "Nah, twenty seconds of you digging in the mud was enough for this lifetime. Don't say anything; here comes Bethanne, and tears will flow."

Bethanne placed their plates and drinks on the table. "Anything else?"

"Nope, but that corner table over there is trying to get your attention."

"Yell if you need anything else." She hurried over to them.

Abbie cut into her quiche. The pastry was flaky, and the quiche was golden and delicious. The accompanying salad was simple, a perfect accompaniment to a light lunch and so fresh that Abbie guessed Penny had her own garden nearby.

"Here's my proposal," Sarah said between mouthfuls. "You're

on vacation, I know. But I could use some help." She held up a preemptory hand. "You can do vacation things all morning, and then come in and give me a hand in the afternoons.

"I'm trying to get these kids interested in doing something besides getting into trouble or contemplating their navels. But I'm kind of winging it here. And I can't be everywhere at once. I got two kids I'm trying to get into college. One of them is Jerome, the other a girl named Talia. Forms, forms, and more forms. Trips to Beaufort. Letters to Columbia—the state capital not the university. And I actually do have my own work, not that I've been doing any of it. I could use some backup."

"What about Bethanne or Ervina?"

"God, no. Besides, you're new. Being from the outside carries a certain cachet. I want to make use of you while you're still an oddity."

Abbie laughed. "Thanks a lot. I'll think about it. Okay?"

"Better than nothing. But don't take too long. "

By the time they finished, the tearoom was filled, and there was a line waiting to get in.

"This is great," Abbie said. "I was afraid Stargazey Point was on its way to being a ghost town."

"Could still happen, but we've managed to hobble along from one summer to the next. So far anyway."

They paid the bill. Sarah insisted on paying. "You can drop Cab's lunch off on our way back, I gotta meet up with Talia."

"What lunch?"

Penny came out of the kitchen, holding a paper bag aloft. "Don't forget Cab's lunch."

Abbie took the bag, and they edged past the waiting crowd toward the front door. The day had turned overcast while they'd been inside.

"April showers," Sarah informed her. "Are like none you've ever seen before."

"I've been in the rain forest, remember."

"Right. Well, looks like you might be meeting the low-country version of them before the afternoon's out."

The cutoff Chevy was parked in front of the community center. A young guy with orange-red hair was sitting on the hood. Abbie had gotten a glimpse of him her first day in town.

He jumped down when he saw them.

Sarah lifted her eyes to the sky. "Oh, God, what does he want?"

"Talia has to stay home and babysit. I told her I'd come get you and bring you on over there."

"Damn. Okay. Let me go get my books and leave a note. You got a top for that crate?"

"Got a piece of plastic if it rains. You wanna ride or not?"

Sarah took off toward the center.

"Hi, I'm Otis. You must be Abbie."

"Yep. Nice to meet you, Otis. Well, I have to go drop this off. See you later."

She walked toward the carousel, but stopped at the door and listened. The skill saw had stopped, but another machine had taken its place. She knocked, then realizing no one would be able to hear her, she pulled the door open and went inside.

Chapter 15

Cab was leaning over a plank of wood that was balanced between two sawhorses. He was wearing jeans and a white T-shirt. The single work light above his head cast his body into deep contrast and defined the muscles of his back and arms as he ran the sander the length of the wood.

He looked strong and powerful and lean and agile at the same time. A little thrill swept through Abbie, a treacherous, betraying thrill, and she recoiled. How could she even be having these feelings? It was too soon.

Castigating herself, she marched forward to hand over the sandwich and get the hell out.

He lifted his head and, seeing her, broke into a smile. He cut off the sander and stood up.

"I didn't mean to interrupt. Sarah asked me to bring your lunch. I was just on my way back to Crispin House." Abbie thrust the bag at him. Noticed the tremor in her fingers.

His smile faded.

She cast around for a flat surface. Reached over and deposited the bag on a nearby table. "Bye." She turned to go.

"Abbie, is something wrong?"

She shook her head. "Just want to get back before it starts to rain. Sarah warned me about afternoon showers."

"Rain wasn't forecast for today. But you know how wrong these weathermen can be."

She stopped. Turned slowly to see what she expected. The smile back in place. He was teasing her. Nobody had teased her in years.

"I didn't bring lunch for Beau."

"Beau isn't here. It's Sunday, remember?"

"Does he go to church with Millie? I heard her leave this morning."

"God, no. I don't know what he does on Sundays, though I do know they 'visit' in the afternoon and have an early dinner. To which . . ." he added, "I've been invited. Thought I better give you a heads-up."

He was coming to dinner? Her heart made a traitorous bump.

"Well, I'll see you then . . . then."

He chuckled. Chuckled. Christ.

"Hear you've been doing some painting. Maybe you'll volunteer to paint here when the time comes."

"Sure. Just say when and I'll bring my paintbrush. If I'm still here."

"Why wouldn't you be?"

"I'm just visiting, remember. I'll have to go out and find a job pretty soon. Since as you know, I don't have one."

"Abbie." He stepped toward her.

"Don't."

He stopped, his eyes focused on her chest. "I was just— Is that what Beau was carving for you?"

"What?" She swallowed. "Oh. Yes. It's beautiful, isn't it?"

"Yes." He leaned in to study it more closely. So close she could smell the sawdust and shampoo in his hair. He lifted a finger and lightly touched the star. "I've never seen anything he's carved before. It's exquisite."

She was having trouble breathing. She stepped back. "You better eat that sandwich before it gets cold."

"It is cold. Turkey and Swiss."

"Or dries out. I'd better go."

He smiled and her whole body tingled. "Abbie. Wait a minute."

"I'm—"

"I know, you want to beat the rain. You also want to get away from me. Is it something I've said or done?"

She shook her head. "Of course not."

"Look. This is a small town and we're going to be running into each other all the time. I don't want to make you uncomfortable. I want . . . well, for us to be friends."

He grimaced. Abbie bet she had a similar expression. Friends? "Sure. Fine."

"So let's make a pact. I won't push, and you won't run. Deal?"

She nodded.

He stuck out his hand. "Shake on it."

She looked at his hand; time seemed to freeze while she ordered herself to put her hand in his. Slowly she reached up and his hand enclosed hers. An electric shock shot up her arm. She flinched but didn't pull away.

"Static electricity," Cab said. "Maybe it *is* going to storm."

Abbie had no doubt that it would, but not the way he was talking about. A storm was already raging inside her. It had been bad enough when she'd thought she had no future. It had just gotten worse now that she began to hope she would.

She realized he was still holding her hand.

"Deal," she said and tried to pull her hand away.

He held on. "You don't have to be afraid. I'm pretty harmless. I would never do anything to hurt you."

"I'm not. I know—"

"And if I do, you have leave to slap me upside the head."

She laughed; she couldn't help it. Just when she'd started to panic, he'd brought out the comedy relief.

"Deal." This time when she pulled her hand away, he let it go.

"See you tonight."

"See ya." She held the smile until she made it outside. Then she stopped to take several deep breaths. She wasn't afraid of him. How could he even think that? He just kept her off balance. Just like Ervina or Sarah did.

Who was she kidding? It was different. Way different. She cringed when she remembered the way her body had reacted to Cab's touch. That was certainly different, and she was so not ready.

She was castigating herself for being a coward when she passed the community center. She abruptly forgot about herself.

The twins were sitting on the stoop looking forlorn, but their faces lit up when they saw her. They popped up simultaneously from the step and made a beeline for her, both talking at once.

"Miss Sarah says we cain't see our pictures by ourselves," Dani explained in a rush.

"Have to have a grown-up," Joe added. "Miz Sarah's helping Talia with her sittin' test."

"Her sitting test?" Abbie asked, her concentration taken up with the hands pulling at her clothes.

"To go to college. Her sittin' test."

"Her SAT?"

Joe nodded so hard that Abbie was afraid he might hurt himself. "S . . . A . . . T. Sat. That's right, her sittin' test."

"I see," Abbie said. "Her sittin' test." How could she resist? She took their hands. "Come on, let's see what you've got."

Dani let go of her hand long enough for Abbie to open the

door, which she noticed Sarah hadn't locked, most likely for the same reason she'd probably left the twins on the stoop—to sucker her into helping. But they looked so innocent she couldn't hold it against them or Sarah.

She had to hoist each of them onto the high stools in order to reach the worktable. Then she found their tape and, after hunting through a pile of used electronics, found an adapter that actually worked.

For the next hour they ran portions of the videotape, re-watched every bouncing out-of-control frame of the gazebo painting twice while the twins giggled and pointed and accused each other of making the camera wobble. Finally they reached steadier footage, and the twins grew quiet as they watched the camera pan across their friends.

Abbie saw their faces transform to wonder, and she was suddenly glad that Sarah had left them to waylay her. She relaxed into a scenario where she belonged. Working, one-on-one or one-on-two or -three. Up close and personal. This is what she did best.

Other children began to dribble in, and by two o'clock, seven more children had arrived at the community center. Abbie settled them into games or homework and went back to finish up with Dani and Joe.

A deafening boom made them all jump. In one movement, the twins glommed themselves to Abbie.

"Wah's dat?"

"Shootin'," Dani said in a whisper that stuttered with her quaking body.

Abbie gave them both a squeeze. "I don't think it's shooting, just thunder."

Another boom made the windows rattle. "See." But she became vibrantly aware of all the electrical equipment surrounding them. She hadn't noticed any surge protectors.

"But I think we're finished here. Let's go in the other room."
With the twins glued to her sides, she quickly unplugged the
equipment. No reason to tempt nature or the electricity, which
by Sarah's admission was ancient. As they left the room they
were confronted by seven wide-eyed children standing in the
doorway to the media room.

"The little kids are scared," said Kyle. He was putting up a
good front, but from beneath his shaggy blond bangs, his eyes
kept darting to the ceiling as if he expected lightning to strike
through the roof.

"Well, there's safety in numbers," Abbie said. "Let's go find
something we can all do." Then the rain started. A heavy down-
pour that clouded the windows and drummed on the tin roof.

They stood surrounding her as close as they could get.

"How about we read a book?"

"Aw, no readin'. I already done my readin'."

"Tell us a story," begged Dani, just as another clap of thunder reverberated through the room. Everyone pressed closer.
Abbie toppled backward and landed on the lumpy overstuffed
chair. Dani and Joe climbed onto her lap before she could
extricate herself. All the others crowded around, sitting on
the rickety arms, leaning over the back. Huddled at her feet.
JuJu Jenny managed to find a place perched precariously on
Abbie's knee.

The lights flickered and went out. They all scooted closer.

"Well . . . Once upon a time there was a little town called
Stargazey . . ."

Marnie hung up the kitchen wall phone. "That was Ervina. I
told her the weather was looking too bad for her to come over
tonight."

"That was very considerate of you," Millie said.

"Actually she said she had no intention of coming anyway.

That our guest knew which end was up and we could just serve ourselves."

"She's just too old to be working for us."

Marnie turned away to hide her impatience. Ervina didn't work for them. Hadn't worked for them in decades. They couldn't pay her even if she wanted the job, which she didn't.

Millie sighed and looked up from the peas she was shelling. "I'm sure Abbie will understand. And besides, a more intimate dinner might give her and Cabot a chance to get to know each other better. I think they would be lovely together. Don't you? But where is she? I hope she's not stuck out in the rain some- where."

"I'm sure she's fine."

"Well, I think you should call Cabot and ask him to look out for her. She'll need a ride back in this weather."

Rather than arguing, Marnie picked up the phone again. Her call went to Cab's voice mail. She left a message, sat back down at the table, and reached for a handful of pea pods.

"Do you hear that?"

Marnie stopped to listen.

"It's that cat again. I don't know why he can't find some- where else to stay when it rains."

Marnie pushed out of her seat and went to the kitchen door. She opened it just wide enough for Moses to shoot through, not slowing down but streaking through the kitchen and out the door to the hallway.

Millie looked up. "Beau, don't you let that cat get my fur- niture all wet."

A muffled reply from another room.

Marnie sat down and reached for another pea pod.

Cab knocked off work when the rain clouds made it too dark to see. He covered over the new exterior doors he'd been working on, checked that there were pails under all known leaks and went into the back workshop. He checked the humidity setting and the temperature and locked the room. With a final look around he called it a day.

He was halfway home when the first bolt of lightning split the sky. It was followed almost immediately by a deafening clap of thunder. Cab picked up his pace then broke into a run as the sky began dumping water on the streets. By the time he reached his house he was drenched to the skin.

He kicked off his shoes just inside the door and quickly crossed the living room, stripping out of his wet shirt as he went. The layer of sawdust and grime that seemed to cover him had turned to mud on his final sprint home. He went straight to the bathroom and turned on the shower. He stripped out of his clothes while the bathroom filled with steam, then he climbed in.

Feeling human again, he toweled off and went to find a beer. His phone message button was blinking. He picked up the receiver and was relieved to hear the message was from Crispin House. He listened to Marnie ask that if he saw Abbie in town to drive her home.

Abbie had left him more than four hours ago. He thought back trying to remember if she'd mentioned where she was going. But he drew a blank. Something that had happened more than once when he was with her.

His mind would drift away from her words and he'd find himself just looking at her wondering how someone so—*fey*, the only word he could come up with for describing her pale ethereal beauty—could manage to thrive in all the places she'd worked. Extreme weather, topography, disease, natural disaster, death.

Her body was lithe, fragile looking. Her hands appeared too delicate to dig in the mud even to save a child. He wondered how she became so strong and where she would go next. And he'd begin to wonder other things, which were definitely not in order, and he'd jerk his attention back to what she was saying and try to jump back into the conversation.

He remembered she'd had lunch with Sarah.

Well, if she wasn't back at Crispin House, she'd either be at Penny's, Bethanne's, or with Sarah at the community center.

He made some calls. Neither Penny nor Bethanne had seen her since lunch. He called Sarah's cell.

"She's not with me. I'm out at the Howard place tutoring Talia for her SAT."

"Who's at the center? I saw a light on."

There was silence, then Sarah said, "Ha. Maybe, just maybe, she's there."

"You sound very satisfied with yourself."

"I will be if you find her there."

Cab dressed for dinner and took the SUV to look for Abbie.

The rain was really coming down. Even with the wipers on high he could barely see. He drove slowly and pulled up to the steps of the community center. He should have called Marnie back to see if Abbie had a cell phone, not that she would have reception in this weather. Besides, this way . . . Cab reached over the seat and fumbled for the stadium umbrella he kept in the back pouch.

He opened the door, unfurled the umbrella, and sprinted up the steps to the porch. Stood for a few seconds to shake off the rain from the umbrella, then leaned it up against the house.

He tried the door. It opened and he stepped in to find a gang of children all huddled together.

"Hey, what's going on?" he asked, suddenly alarmed.

"Thank goodness," said a familiar voice.

The children parted to reveal Abbie holding three sleeping children and surrounded by several more.

"I could use a hand here," she said.

Cab just stood, watching. *A reluctant Madonna,* he thought, dressed in jeans and sweatshirt, surrounded by a ragtag assortment of children wearing hand-me-downs and bargain-store clothes. She was beautiful. They were beautiful.

"Sarah's not back and they're still here. How do we, um, when do they go home?"

"They'll stay forever."

The look on her face was priceless. He couldn't help himself. He smiled, he grinned, he felt exhilarated. "Who needs a ride home?"

Everyone's hand went up. Dani and Joe sat groggily up, pushing Jenny to the floor. The three of them raised their hands, though Cab doubted if they even knew why.

"Why don't you call Marnie and tell her we're going to be a little late; this is going to take two trips. Okay, who lives the farthest away? I've got room for five."

It took Cab over a half hour to deposit the first group. Some lived out from town, either close to the road or up unpaved drives where the rain ran in rivulets through the sand. It was slow going, and he was anxious to get back to Abbie.

By the time he returned to the center, the rain had stopped and the sun was shining low in the sky. Abbie and the last four kids were waiting by the door.

"Had enough?" he asked as she handed the smallest ones to him and he strapped them in.

"Had a lot," she said. She glanced at her charges. "But we had a good time, didn't we?"

"We made a video," Dani said.

"All by ourselfs," Joe added; then he looked sheepish. "Abbie helped."

"And she told us a story," Dani said. "About all of us."

"All in a day's work?"

"All in a rainy day's work," Abbie said. "I'll be ready for that glass of Millie's sherry."

"I can do better than that. As soon as we drop this batch off we'll stop at the inn for a quick happy hour."

Abbie sat in the passenger seat trying not to look at Cab. She didn't want to take the chance of feeling that shock she'd felt in the carousel again. She wasn't so naive as to think she would never love again. At least have sex, though she hadn't even thought about that possibility until today. Only for the briefest second. And it was only natural. Hell, it had been eight months. Longer. She was young and . . . Why was she thinking like this? It was impossible.

You have to let that poor man's soul go.

Was that what she was doing? Holding on to the past, so tightly that she was going to strangle it? At first it was too raw and painful to share. Later she'd thought she could keep what was precious to her by keeping it to herself. Now she was afraid it had become a habit. Ervina had rattled her.

She thought with chagrin about the money she had wasted on that therapist. Ervina should set up a shingle. She could finance the community with her advice.

Cab stopped the SUV in front of a weather-beaten two-story shack. There was a postage-sized porch over the doorway. Several rusted cars sat at various angles in the front yard. Only one appeared to be running.

Kyle slid out of the car. He turned to wave back at them, then ran around to the back of the house.

They let the next boy, Pauli, off at the house they had driven by on their way to Georgetown, and for the first time Abbie recognized the boy who had run alongside the car.

"Thanks, Cab, Miz Abbie." He trotted off to where the old woman was waiting for him on the porch.

The twins were the last to be taken home. If you could call

it that. The house was small and sagging. The yard was packed dirt; a few straggling weeds were matted down by the rain. Cab got out and opened the back door. Lifted them down and walked them to the front door. None of the three seemed in a hurry.

A curtain was pulled back in a front window and let fall. A minute later the door opened and the twins went inside. The door closed. Cab stood for a second longer before he turned and came back to the car.

"Yeah," he said to Abbie's unspoken dismay.

"Did someone bring them to the center today?" she asked.

"I expect they brought themselves."

"They can't be more than five or six years old."

He gave her a funny look. "You don't have to go to South America to find kids who need attention."

She felt as if he'd slapped her. She turned away and stared out the window.

"Hey, I'm sorry. I didn't mean that as a judgment on your work."

Maybe not, but it sounded like a judgment. She didn't want to be one of those people who gave all their attention to third world countries while their neighbors needed help. Is that what had happened to her?

Cab reached across the console and squeezed her hand. "I swear. I'm not saying anything except these kids need someone to care about them just like every other poor kid in the world."

She frowned at him. "Is that what you're doing with the carousel?"

"Hardly." He returned his hand to the steering wheel. He laughed, almost to himself. "I come from a long line of pedigreed money-acquiring Charlestonians."

"I thought you were raised in Boston."

"Yeah, but I was born in Charleston. We moved to Boston

when my father married my stepmother, a Bostonian Brahmin. She hated Charleston, and he pretty much hated Boston. They traveled a lot. I spent summers and holidays with my uncle Ned, my father's brother, at his carousel."

Abbie smiled. "It seems like a wonderful way to spend a summer."

"It was, though I worked my butt off. It takes a lot of upkeep. And I had to sell tickets and stuff like that."

"But you became an architect."

"I love architecture, too."

"I can tell."

He smiled. It happened again, that warm zap of excitement when you feel a connection, both emotional and physical, to someone else. Not such a shock this time.

"So that was the brief history of Cabot Reynolds. Are you ever going to tell me about yourself?"

Chapter 16

I was born in California," Abbie said when they were sitting at the nearly empty bar at the inn. "But we moved a lot." She paused, took a sip of her chardonnay. "My parents worked for different nonprofit organizations. My father is a lawyer—liberal—and my mother is . . ." Abbie chuckled. "An ex flower child.

"They met in the Peace Corps and now fund-raise for reclaimable water.

"I have three brothers and one sister. Well, two brothers now. My oldest brother works for Doctors Without Borders. John runs a group home for runaways. Adam died in Afghanistan; he was an army medic. My sister is over there now, though I think her desire to bring democracy to the Middle East is more about avenging his death than anything else. She was studying to be a special ed teacher."

"I'm sorry."

"My parents didn't love the idea of him being a marine, but they were open-minded enough to know that we all have our own paths to take."

"That sounds like a quote."

"My father when mom got on her peace and freedom, anti-military horse."

"All the Sinclairs work in the not-for-profit sector?"

"Pretty much. So before you ask how I became a weather-girl—I had trouble finding the right 'path' for me."

"I take it you didn't find it being a weathergirl."

"Nope."

Cab turned his glass around, looking at it as if he was contemplating something, and she was afraid she knew what was coming next.

"And not when you were making documentaries?"

"I thought I had, for most of eight years. Toward the end I wasn't sure, but now I am. I learned a lot, maybe did some good, but it was someone else's path, not mine."

"Maybe you'll find yours here."

"Maybe." She reached for her glass, realized it was empty. "But for now, I'm here, thanks to Celeste and the Crispins' generosity." She smiled though it was a little difficult. "Not a weathergirl, not a filmmaker." She shrugged. "Not even a conniving real estate agent. Just some lost soul on her road to somewhere else."

Cab burst out with a laugh. "Sorry, sorry. But did you ever think maybe you should become a writer?"

She laughed, too. "I tend to get a bit dramatic."

"A bit, but it's a hell of a story."

"And not over yet." She stood up. "But we'll be late for dinner, I mean supper, if we don't get going."

Beau was waiting for them on the porch. "Millie and Marnie are in the parlor. Millie was worried."

"Oh dear," Abbie said. "We called to say we were taking the kids home and would be late."

"That don't have anything to do with Millie being worried." Beau glanced at Abbie's throat and the necklace. A hint of a smile as elusive as a breeze. Then he turned and held the front door for them to enter.

"I think I love him," Abbie whispered as they made their way to the parlor.

"I think I might be jealous," Cab whispered back.

Abbie's step faltered.

"Here they are. Home at last," Millie said, beaming on them.

"Sorry we took so long. But I somehow ended up with the kids at the community center. I didn't want to leave them unsupervised."

Marnie snorted. "I know just how you ended up there."

"Yes," added Millie. "Don't you let Sarah impose on you. She will, you know. Cabot, fix you and Abbie a glass of something."

Cab was already standing by the Queen Anne drinks cabinet, which contained myriad bottles and glasses and where a silver tray held a permanent array of cut glass decanters. He looked as uncomfortable as Abbie felt. Surely that quip about being jealous was just flirtation.

He poured Abbie a glass of sherry and spent the next few minutes conversing with Millie.

Marnie excused herself to serve the dinner. Abbie offered to help.

"We wouldn't hear of it," Millie said. "You just sit over here and visit with Cabot and me."

Abbie felt she'd already visited with Cab enough that day, told him more than she intended, felt more comfortable than she should. But she stayed put and listened to them chat.

Cab left right after supper, and Abbie, after yawning through a half hour of television, took herself off to bed. She was exhausted, but oddly content. She opened the notebook, turned past the page that said Guatemala and the pages with her notes on the gazebo, and wrote down the date. She started her journal with the decision to paint the gazebo, then moved on to the carousel, the twins, the storm, and the way the children lived.

They were a motley group, different ages, races, attitudes, from homes not even close to middle class. When she'd mentioned it to Cab, he'd said, "Of course we have rich kids. They just don't come to the center." He paused. "They don't need to."

That had to be the longest Crispin dinner in history, Cab thought as he kicked off his shoes and began to channel surf. Not timewise, unless you counted the way it seemed to crawl after his unthinking quip about being jealous.

It had just slipped out. Ordinarily it would have been the kind of flirtatious remark that women were flattered by. Not Abbie—she'd seized up, right back to where she'd been until the last couple of days.

And the hell of it was, he meant it. When he'd walked into the center earlier that night and saw her surrounded by children, her pale blond hair haloed by the reading lamp in the semidarkness, his world tilted.

And later in the car, watching the twins return to that wretched hovel, the look in her eyes pierced straight to his heart. And he knew in that moment that while Abbie Sinclair was in Stargazey Point those kids would have a champion. And so would he.

He'd once compared her to Bailey, but he'd been dead wrong. She required just as much energy, maybe more, but unlike Bailey, Abbie gave back, even though she might not want to, even when she didn't realize it.

Hell, Beau had carved her a star, gone to Bethanne's and bought a silver chain to put it on. And she wore it in full view, seemingly unaware that it was the first Beau sculpture to see the light of day, at least since Cab could remember.

All three Crispins came alive when Abbie entered the room. Bethanne, the kids, even Sarah, though she'd deny it if pressed, him—they'd all been touched by her in some way. And it wasn't just pity or compassion or curiosity. Abbie had come here to get her life back on track. Heal her wounds. But she was doing a lot more, and they were all benefiting from it.

She had a lot more strength than she gave herself credit for. They all saw it, now if only she would.

Or maybe he was full of shit. He got a beer from the fridge, put his feet up on the coffee table, and settled down to watch the last half of a Celtics game. Even down here he couldn't leave Boston completely behind.

Abbie didn't remember dreaming. She wasn't ready to hope the nightmares might be going away, but she awoke refreshed and tripped down the stairs just like her life wasn't still in shambles.

She had toast and coffee and went out to check on the gazebo. Jerome had said it would take several days for the whitewash to cure. And they'd only had two before the storm. It looked okay from where she was standing. Better than okay. It was charming.

Marnie didn't need her in the garden, so she grabbed a hoodie and hair elastic and took her notebook out to the beach. The day was warm and sunny. A breeze blew in from the water, and she stopped to pull her hair back into a ponytail. The waves seemed a bit choppy, probably left over from the storm or maybe from a storm farther out to sea. At least the storm within her had subsided a bit.

She had no doubt it would be back. But for now, she just breathed in the air and decided to stay at least another week. She sat on the end of the wooden walk and took off her shoes. Wiggled her toes in the sand. It would be nice to be at the shore when the summer began, put on a swimsuit, splash in the waves. Be here for the carousel opening. Beau's birthday.

She'd have to get a job long before then, but every time she thought about calling Celeste and asking about work in Chicago, her stomach tied itself into a knot.

Soon, she would decide what to do. Soon but not today. She pushed herself to her feet, rolled her jeans up above her ankles, and tied her sneakers around her neck, which gave her a momentary sense of déjà vu. How many times had she forded a stream with her shoes tied about her neck?

She pushed the thought away and walked to the water's edge. Stepped gingerly into the surf. Cold but not freezing. She began to walk north, letting the sea air take away her thoughts almost before she thought them.

Before she knew it, she was standing in front of the old pier. She wondered if it would ever be rebuilt or just left to rot away. As she stood there, two men came to stand at the edge of the parking lot. She recognized one of them as Robert Oakley, the tax assessor. They stood side by side, while Oakley pointed at the pier, then swept his hand in a wide arc from the carousel to the point of land beyond Crispin House.

Heart suddenly beating faster, Abbie headed toward the parking lot, trying to look like she was just out for a stroll, straining to hear what they might be saying. She even stopped to put her shoes on just below them. But they stopped talking, and she had no choice but to continue on.

Feeling an inexplicable sense of urgency, she hurried across the way to the carousel. The lock was off; she pulled on the doors and let herself in.

Cab looked up, surprised.

She motioned him toward her. "Come here."

His incipient smile changed to concern. He dropped a paintbrush, and wiping his hands, he walked over to her. "What?"

"The tax assessor is out there with another man."

Frowning, Cab peeked around the edge of the open door. "Ah, shit." He strode out the door and across the parking lot. He stopped Oakley as he got into his car. They seemed to be chatting amiably, and Abbie wondered if she had overreacted.

After a few minutes, Cab came back inside. He looked grim. "You've got some kind of instinct. He brought a state engineer to look at the pier. They'll probably make us tear it down."

Abbie let out a huge sigh. "Is that all? He pointed over here and then toward the Crispins'."

"The town owns the community center. I own the carousel, and my taxes are paid. However, the Crispins are behind. He's probably stopping there next to remind them their taxes are delinquent and the county will begin proceedings to put the property up for sale. As if Marnie needs reminding."

"Can they do that?"

"Yes. It happened last year, too. They managed to sell some silver or something and paid the tax and the penalty."

Abbie bit her lip. "I think that's what Marnie was planning to do next week. Millie was upset."

"Millie doesn't always have a firm grasp on reality." He flipped the paint can top over and banged it shut with a hammer. "I think I'll just take a ride over there. Oakley's a fair enough assessor. But his hands are pretty much tied. Want to come?"

"No. I'd better wait for Sarah. But let me know what happens."

She stood in the parking lot until Cab's SUV turned into the Crispin drive. Then she sat down on the stoop of the community center. She didn't have long to wait. Otis's heap rattled to a stop; Sarah jumped out and headed for the center. She did a double take when she saw Abbie.

"Well, well, to what do I owe the honor?" Sarah said in a slow drawl.

Abbie frowned at her.

"That's Southern talk for, so you decided to show up." She walked past Abbie and unlocked the door.

"Excuse me?" Abbie said. "Who was here all day yesterday by myself? Who waited until Cab could take a dozen kids home? Who drove along on the last batch? And if you want to insult me, I'd rather you'd do it in your normal voice and stop blaming how you feel on some part of the country." Abbie clamped her mouth shut.

Sarah grinned. "Guess you got up on the wrong side of the bed today."

"Guess you did, too."

Sarah sighed, dropping her attitude. "I did," she said in her own voice. "Talia filled out one of her forms wrong and they're making her do it again, which means she'll miss the deadline for the spring SAT. And this morning Jerome's daddy calls me saying no son of his is going to no art school and call it college. He don't, and I quote, see why he should go anywhere 'cause Jerome is going to take over the family business."

"Which is?"

"Collecting old cars for parts. He has an outbuilding on his property that he calls a shop. Hell, Jerome doesn't even live with him. He stays at Ervina's to look out for things. But suddenly his daddy thinks he's got the right to—" Sarah marched through the house, Abbie following. "I swear, I don't know why I—" She stopped her tirade long enough to yank open the ancient refrigerator's door. "Bother."

"I'd tell you," Abbie said, parking one hip on the old Formica table. "But it's too cornball."

"Then don't. I want to be pissed off for at least another hour." Sarah took two bottles of water out of the fridge and handed one to Abbie.

"Well, here's something that might keep you pissed off. The

tax man cometh, and he brought a state engineer. Then they drove off toward Crispin House and Cab followed them."

"Damn the man." Sarah pulled out one of the aluminum chairs and sat down.

"But it's not just that. He was pointing to the community center."

"That all? The town owns it, and they aren't going to sell unless they can sell the whole package, and that is never going to happen, because Cab will never sell."

"And what about Crispin House?"

"That's a problem; they barely eked through last year, and I think Cab helped them out. The problem is the county keeps reassessing the property. Taxes around here have tripled in the last few years, and Cab isn't made of money. In case you haven't noticed, he's sunk a load into the carousel."

"He's taking a big risk, isn't he?"

"It's what he loves. He thinks it's worth the risk. You should understand that."

"I do. At least I did. Sometimes the price is too high."

"Is it?"

The outer door opened and slammed shut. Loud voices and scuffling followed.

"They're here," Sarah intoned in a creditable imitation of Jack Nicholson.

Abbie stood up. "I'm on it." She tossed her empty water bottle in the recycling bin.

Sarah grabbed her elbow as she walked past the table. "You know. You're not half as screwed up as you think you are."

Abbie left the room, openmouthed. How could Sarah possibly know how screwed up she was? On the other hand, maybe she was right.

That commitment that inspired Sarah to help Talia and Jerome to get into college, that led Cab to reopening the carousel—Abbie had that fire, too. It was still inside her. It had been derailed for a while by the disaster of the last project, the destruction of a town, the loss of so many lives, including Werner's.

But her work with him had given her a firm foundation, solid ground to rebuild her life on, if she didn't let it sink her. It was time to make it her own, just hers. And she'd start with that rowdy bunch of kids in the front room.

Chapter 17

There were ten of them, though she didn't see Dani and Joe. Abbie felt a bit overwhelmed. She'd seen kids playing and reading when she'd come by before, but now they were all facing her. Waiting.

"Do you guys have projects you're working on?"

Nothing. Just ten intent faces.

Finally Sarah came through the door. "What's the matter with you kids? Cat got your tongues?" Several shook their heads, and finally Kyle said, "No."

"Well, good, 'cause if you don't start answering, I'm gonna take y'all off to do math problems."

"Aw, Miz Sarah."

Sarah gave him a look.

"Yes, ma'am."

"Lucy and Max. Come with me." Lucy, the girl with the red pigtails, and Max, a tall lanky boy Abbie hadn't seen before, grumbled but dragged their backpacks to the other side of the room where a beat-up table was stacked with books and papers. At one end an old aqua iMac was hooked up to an older printer. Which was stupid; printers didn't cost that much.

"I guess the rest of you come with me to the media room," Abbie said.

"Where's that?"

"Back here where the film stuff is. This is hereby the Stargazey Point Media Room."

"Like at the tee-vee station?"

"Our version of it. Who's been to the television station?"

No one had.

"Okay, everyone take a seat. Where are the twins today?"

"Dunno."

One of the girls giggled. "Ole Eddie. He probably skunked again. He lock 'em up so they won't get in trouble when he's out carousin'."

"Well," Abbie said, trying not to think of the two children locked in the closet while the man who was supposed to be taking care of them was tying one on. "Why don't you bring me up to speed."

No one said a thing.

"Speed is what cameramen say when their camera is rolling. 'Speed.' Before then, if you started filming, the film would be all wobbly."

"Our film's all wobbly anyhow."

"Well, we'll work on that. Everybody got a seat? Good. Now I'm not sure if Sarah has already been over how to plan your interviews."

"Sarah don't know squat about interviews," Sarah called from the front room. "You're on your own."

Two of the boys grinned.

After her cursory look at the equipment and the amount of footage they'd gotten so far, it didn't seem like much work had been going on.

Kyle blew his bangs out of his face and said, "We bring what we got to Jerome and he fixes it."

"Edits it," Pauli said and poked Kyle in the ribs. Kyle stood up. "Who you pokin'?"

"Hey," Abbie said. "No more pokin' or asking who's pokin'. Got it?"

Her entire audience stared at her.

"Glad we understand each other."

"We don't understand nothin' you say, missus. You talk funny."

"Why don't each of you tell me a little bit about what you've been doing so far. Any volunteers to go first?"

There were no volunteers.

Finally Kyle said, "Mainly we just ask questions and write stuff down. Sometimes we get to check the video camera out and take some movies. Then we bring it in and Jerome . . . edits it for us." He shot Pauli a smug look.

"Jerome is gonna be busy studying for college," Sarah called from the other room. Was she eavesdropping? "Abbie's gonna help you do it like real professionals."

"You know how to do this stuff?"

"I do."

"How come you know how?"

"I used to work for a television station."

"What'dja do there?"

"I was the weathergirl."

Big grins. "You had one of them little sticks and everything?"

"I sure did."

"It's not funny," said one of the girls. "I'd like to be a weathergirl."

"It's a great job," Abbie said.

"You learn to make pictures when you were a weathergirl?"

"No. After that I"—she took a breath—"I worked with a documentary filmmaker."

"Did you go to Africa?"

"On two projects. Once to Kenya and once to Soweto."

"You been to Paris?"

"Yes, but just on vacation."

"You been to Antarctica?"

"No. Have you?"

Everybody had a good laugh at that.

While they were laughing, Abbie found a cassette player and an empty cassette. She slid it down the work counter to Pauli.

"Okay. Pauli, why don't you tell us something you learned about your family that you didn't know before."

After that, everybody was anxious to tell some story of theirs. Some of them were probably true. There was nothing wrong with their imaginations. She just needed to figure out how to ignite it.

Jerome came in while they were all crowded around the computer table indulging in a snack of granola bars, juice packs, and boxes of raisins. He was holding the twins by each hand. They carried overstuffed backpacks, and Dani was also carrying a cloth bag that bulged under the weight of whatever was in it.

Sarah nodded and looked closely at the two children.

Dani came to stand in front of Sarah, her shoulders slumped, her eyes looking at the ground. "Unk says we cain't do his hist'ry. And to get that fuckin' thing outta his face. He mad. He broke it." She put the bag on the floor and wrestled a mangled piece of plastic out of it. The twenty-year-old cassette recorder would never tape again.

Joe stepped up, but kept behind his sister. "We're sorry, Miz Sarah."

"Well, heck," said Sarah, recovering while Abbie stood there burning with anger. "That old thing was on its last leg anyway." She took the recorder from Dani, gave it one look, and tossed it into the trash. "Don't worry about it."

Jerome's nostrils flared. "He was drunk. Had 'em locked up.

Dani and Joe are spending the night with me and Ervina to-night. If he wants them back, he'll have to come for 'em." His hands curled into fists.

Abbie shot a look to Sarah, whose mouth tightened. "You don't really expect trouble from him, do you?"

"Don't know, but if he comes looking for trouble, he'll get it with interest."

"You shut your mouth, Jerome. You're never going to make it in the world if you slide to the lowest level every time some piece of scum acts true to his nature. You take the high road. And that goes for the rest of you."

"Ervina gonna put the curse on him," Dani said defiantly.

"Ervina is not going to put a curse on anybody. Let me think."

"Couldn't you call social services?" Abbie asked.

Sarah laughed. "You're kidding, right? How do you think they got where they are?"

The twins turned to the door and started walking slowly toward it.

"Hey, where are you going?" Abbie blurted out. She was a visitor here, had only known the twins for a few days, but she was with Jerome. Just let anyone try to hurt them.

"We got no fambly hist'ry now," Dani said.

Not one they wanted to remember anyway, Abbie thought. "But you already took some footage—some pictures—of the gazebo, that's part of the town's history."

"That's all done up," Joe mumbled.

"But there's something else that needs its story told that I don't think anyone has done yet." But that would keep every-body's interest.

Two hopeful children turned back to her.

"The carousel," Abbie said, hoping she wasn't promising something she couldn't deliver on.

"Huh?"

"The merry-go-round. Has anyone thought about documenting it?"

Their eyes grew rounder. "Mr. Cab's merry-go-round?"

"The very one. It's a big part of Stargazey Point's history. And it should get to be documented, too." Abbie mentally crossed her fingers that Cab wouldn't mind having a couple of children underfoot while he was trying to work.

"We'll have to ask him first if it's okay."

"He'll say no."

"Maybe not," Abbie said.

Sarah shook her head, but she was smiling. "Well, you're in luck, 'cause I think I just heard his Range Rover pull up outside."

"Well, let's go ask him," Abbie said, not feeling nearly as enthusiastic as she sounded. Surely Cab wouldn't disappoint the twins further by not allowing them into the carousel.

Nothing ventured nothing gained, she thought and almost laughed. It sounded like something one of the Crispins would say. She took each twin by the hand. "Come on, you two, let's go talk to a man about a horse."

In the end, the entire group plus Abbie, Jerome, and Sarah were waiting for Cab when he got out of the car.

Cab turned to see a whole boatload of kids surrounding his SUV, but it was Abbie he saw first.

"Is something wrong?"

She shook her head, a little spasmodically, then she smiled, narrowed her eyes at him in what he thought must be her attempt at the evil eye.

"We've got an offer you can't refuse." An even more intent stare.

"Okay," he said slowly. She was trying to send him a message. Something he couldn't refuse. He just hoped he could say yes and not disappoint her and evidently everyone else.

Dani and Joe, the twins, flanked her and they leaned into her. She was too thin for them to hide behind.

"We were just discussing how good for business it would be if there was documentation of the carousel renovation."

She sounded so stilted that he had trouble not laughing.

"I've thought of that myself,"

"And the twins need a project," she said. Moving closer, she added under her breath, "They won't get in your way; just take a little footage to make into a tape."

He took one look at those kids and the others surrounding them and knew he was suckered.

"Excellent idea," he said and watched Abbie's face relax in relief.

Sarah gave him a nod of approval, and the twins, miraculously recovering from their shyness, jumped up and down. "We gonna film the merry-go-round! We gonna film the merry-go-round!"

Damn if it didn't break his heart. "I'd better go tell Beau."

He headed for the carousel and realized he was being followed by the entire group. Abbie gave him a look that said it was out of her control. He tried not to smile. He wasn't even sure if he'd be patient enough to let the twins be underfoot, much less a dozen of them.

He didn't really have any experience with children. But that wasn't entirely true, he realized as he stopped at the door and turned to face the group again. Every summer of his boyhood, he'd seen faces like these waiting in line to ride the carousel. He'd shared the excitement and the wonder. Hell, that was part of the reason he'd come back.

"I'll give you a quick tour, but stick together and don't touch anything. I don't want anyone getting hurt," he said in an afterthought. He was actually more concerned about his animals than he was about the kids and that was surely the wrong way around.

He took a breath and opened the door. They all piled in, and the delighted sighs and squeals that he'd been imagining for the last year became a reality. And he felt damned good.

Beau must have heard them, because he came to the door of the workshop, looking slightly dazed. He quickly disappeared again. Beau didn't share his work and it had been a hell of a time convincing him to work on the carousel at all. Cab didn't know what had happened all those years ago that made Beau give up his art, but whatever it was, Beau was still not willing to acknowledge his gift.

Cab hoped to hell having the kids here wouldn't drive him away. It would take the two of them and more to get the carousel up and running by summer.

For a second Cab felt that sick drop of his stomach when he actually considered what might happen if he failed. Or if he became bored or went broke. He could always get another job as an architect or contractor; that's not what scared him. What scared him most was that his dream would turn out to be bogus, and all the work and love and hope he'd put into it would betray him in the end.

"Thank you." Abbie's voice drew him back to reality.

"For what?"

"For giving these kids something to look forward to. It's been a bad day for them."

"One of many." But he felt unjustifiably touched by her thanks. Whether he deserved it or not was another question.

"This has got to be a quick one, because some people"—Sarah stopped to look at certain members of the group—"have tutoring today."

"No, Miss Sarah. This is better."

"So it is. But Cab has work to do and so do you. I'm sure he'll let us come back."

"Uh, yeah," said Cab.

He showed them the platform. Moved them back while he turned on the engine and the platform jerked to life.

"But there're no horses," Lucy complained. Her pigtails swung as she followed the moving rods.

"They're getting a fresh coat of paint. You can look in at the door, but you'll have to wait to get a closer look."

Cab stepped inside the workshop, and the others crowded into the doorway. Joe squirmed to the front of the line.

"I'm gonna ride that one." Joe pointed to Lady, half covered by a tarp.

"She was my favorite, too. Her name is Midnight Lady," Cab said. He managed to grab Joe as he darted forward. He handed him back to Abbie, who looked apologetic. "But her mane was just painted, so she can't be touched until it dries."

There was pushing from the back, but before pandemonium broke out, Abbie had moved the front group to the back and maneuvered another batch to the front. They looked at the animals, and she moved them on, too. In a few minutes, everyone had gotten a firsthand look.

"Now I have to get back to work," Cab said, trying to sound chipper as all hell. Actually he was feeling a bit overwhelmed.

"Well, thank you for having us," Abbie said.

The two of them had to physically force the group out into the parking lot.

"See ya tomorrah, Mr. Cab," Dani said, all smiles.

Cab nodded. "See you tomorrow."

"Thanks," Abbie said. "I mean it." And she hurried after the group before he could even respond.

"I want to work on the carousel history, too," Kyle said.

"Me, too."

"And me, too."

"Me, too. Me, too."

"We all want to work on the carousel."

Abbie turned, and their eyes met over the heads of the children. And how could he say anything but "Fine"?

I've never seen them so enthusiastic," Sarah said as they climbed the steps. "The carousel's so close that if it was a snake it would've bit me, and I didn't even think to make use of it."

"You wanted to do family histories. Something that should be done."

"But not by kids."

"This will be the start, and we'll see where it goes from here."

"Works for me. Hey, you guys calm down and listen to Abbie. She's gonna tell you what to do next."

They started by cleaning up the media room. Two of the older kids printed out a sign that said MEDIA ROOM, and they hung it on the door. They moved equipment and labeled shelves, then talked about the carousel.

It was almost six before Abbie realized she wasn't going to make it back to Crispin House in time to help with dinner.

She called Marnie and apologized profusely. "I just started a project and it's taking longer than I expected."

"Don't worry. We'll leave you a plate in the oven. Or get Cab to take you out to dinner."

"Thanks, it's just that I told the kids . . ."

"It's my meeting night, and Millie will be content with *Jeopardy!* Go have some fun."

Several kids left for home. A few minutes later a woman came in and spoke to Sarah. She looked over at Abbie, gave her a lengthy once-over, then Sarah brought her over and introduced her as Jenny's grandmother, Momo. She was young, probably not over forty years of age. She was polite and curious.

As soon as the last batch left, Sarah began turning off the lights, and Jerome reluctantly shut down the computer. He gathered up the twins who were practically hidden by the couch cushions where they were watching a snowy rerun of *Flipper*. He turned off the ancient set, collected their backpacks, and led them out.

Sarah plopped down on the couch the twins had just vacated. Abbie collapsed beside her.

"Tired?"

"Exhausted."

"Just wait until summer. Most of them will come first thing in the morning and stay until we kick them out."

"Summer? You're using that 'we' awfully freely."

Sarah lifted her eyebrows. "I'm counting on you."

They were staring at each other when the door opened and Cab walked in.

"Sorry. Am I interrupting something?"

"Depends," Sarah said.

"Depends on what?"

"On what you're offering."

"Dinner?"

"Sorry, I already got a date."

"Does she?" Cab asked.

Abbie shrugged. "No idea."

"What about you? Do you have a—" He stopped abruptly, remembering what he'd heard about the last time someone mentioned dates. "Something to do tonight?"

Sarah guffawed into her hand.

Abbie gave her a look and turned to him. "Do I have a date? No. But you don't have to ask me to dinner." Her eyes narrowed. "Did Marnie call you?"

She knew in an instant that she'd guessed right. Cab looked totally guilty. It was pretty endearing.

Sarah had moved onto silent chortling.

Cab cleared his throat. "Well, yes, but I was going to come over anyway. I thought you wanted to hear what the assessor had to say."

The assessor. She'd forgotten all about him.

"I do."

"Not here, you don't. I'm locking up." Sarah jangled keys at them. "But the Silver Surfer is open nights, and it has a great ambience for talking if you don't mind screaming over loud music. Bet you haven't even been to that end of town, have you?"

"I don't recall seeing anything called the Silver Surfer."

"Up-scale beach bum." Sarah grinned. "Expensive junk food."

"Actually I was thinking barbecue," Cab told her. "What do you say? With Silas closed, Sonny's has the best barbecue in the county. It's about a half hour away, but it's worth the drive."

Abbie bit her lip. It was tempting. And she did want to hear about the assessor. Besides, now that he'd mentioned dinner, she realized she was starving.

"You had her at barbecue," Sarah said. "Now get the hell out of here. This mess ain't going anywhere overnight. See *you*"—she pointed to Abbie—"at two."

Sarah waited for them to go out then locked the door behind them.

"Sure you don't want to go?" Abbie asked.

"Yep."

"You want a ride home?" Cab asked.

"Nope," Sarah said and walked into the night.

"She certainly has a theatrical streak," Abbie said, watching Sarah's slim retreating figure.

"She learned it from the best."

"Ervina?"

"Uh-huh."

"Is Ervina really . . ." Abbie groped for a word. Not a witch.
A wisewoman? She was certainly that.

"Full of crap?" He sighed. "Not really. But it's hard to always
tell what's real and what's posturing." He opened the car door
for her, and she climbed agilely into the front seat.

The town looked deserted. The porch light was on at the
inn, but only one lamp shone in the first-floor window, and the
windows above were all dark.

Abbie wondered if Bethanne was sitting alone at the kitchen
table, missing her husband. Or maybe she was out drinking
margaritas with Penny at the Silver Surfer, which was open
and lit up like a giant pinball machine. Cars were parked along
front and in the spaces across the street.

It seemed to be the only hot spot in town.

"Do you still get tourists in the summer?"

"Some. It was at an all-time low a couple of years ago, but
with the beach rebuilding, they've started coming back. Last
summer Bethanne had most of her rooms let out for most of
the season." He sighed as he looked ahead to where the head-
lights carved out a cone in the darkness. "But 'most' isn't good
enough if you want to make a go of it. For the inn or any other
business. We're working on it."

He turned down a road that curved away from town. It was
black as pitch, and she couldn't imagine where this place was. It
felt like they were at the end of the earth. They were. She'd felt
it more than once since she'd been here. The end of the world,
the end of the line.

She mentally shook herself. *Barbecue,* she reminded herself.
Not philosophy, not psychology, but barbecue.

Gradually the dark lessened. Soon they were passing through
the outskirts of Myrtle Beach.

A few minutes later, Cab slowed down and pulled off into

a sandy parking lot, filled with cars, trucks, and motorcycles. Lincolns and Mercedes rubbed fenders with rusty pickups and battered heaps, though SUVs seemed to be the vehicle of choice. They were packed haphazardly into two ragged rows.

"Lucky I know the owner," Cab said as they searched for a place to park.

A white stretch limo pulled into the parking lot and stopped at the entrance. Abbie unconsciously pulled the rubber band holding her ponytail in place and finger-combed her hair.

Cab looked over and smiled. "You look fine."

Right. She was wearing jeans that had been crawled in, squatted in, had apple juice spilled on them, and were covered by inky fingerprints. But her escort didn't look much better. His jeans were paint splattered, and his sweatshirt was faded and stretched out at the neck.

As the limo's passengers, who seemed way overdressed for a barbecue joint, crowded through the entrance, Cab squeezed the Range Rover into a space that had been meant for a much smaller car.

"Can you get out okay?"

"Think so," Abbie said, looking out to the narrow opening between them and a ten-year-old Ford. "Not sure about after dinner. Depends on how good the barbecue is."

Cab smiled so openly that she wondered how she could have ever thought of him as a conniving usurper.

As she squeezed out of the car, the smell of hickory wood and roast pork filled her nose and surrounded her.

Sonny's was little more than a shack with a long screened-in porch filled with picnic tables and people. Smoke belched from behind the building. People moved from counter to tables in a constant stream.

The inside of the shack was a tad more upscale, though the smell of barbecue permeated the air even here. Tables and booths were crowded together, and through an opening in back, Abbie saw another dining room just as crowded.

She thought about Silas and his lost smokehouse.

"Cab, great to see you." A tall, barrel-chested man strode up to them.

"Hey, Sonny, thanks for squeezing us in."

"Good thing you called ahead. There's an hour's wait. Had some kind of big conference this weekend. Still got a lot of overflow. Fine by me. They can stay all spring if they keep coming like this.

"I've got you a table in back. Quieter. Out here you can hardly hear yourself think. Come right this way." He nodded to Abbie, then began weaving his way through the room.

They were halfway across when a loud voice called out. "Cab, over here."

Cab stopped, looked around, found the source. "Oh, shit, maybe this wasn't a good idea."

Chapter 18

A man was standing at a table halfway across the room. He waved.

"Jesus, what are the odds," Cab said under his breath. "Just hang on, and I'll get this over with as soon as possible."

Their host stepped aside and waited while Cab maneuvered Abbie toward the table. She was acutely aware of the heat of his hand resting on the small of her back, and she reined in the direction her thoughts were taking.

"Good to see you, George, how are you?" Cab reached over the platters of ribs and fries and shook hands with a man a decade or two older than Cab, deeply tanned and well dressed.

Cab nodded to the other men at the table, none of whom stood or shook hands.

"I'd be better if you were heading this project."

"I've retired. But it's good to see you. I'd like you to meet Abbie Sinclair. Abbie, George Erickson, a local developer."

George half rose from his seat. "Abbie, I'd shake hands, but I'm covered in sauce. You must try the short ribs."

"They look delicious," Abbie said.

"So are you the reason for Cabot's disappearing act?" George smiled at her, smooth as silk and deadly as a snake.

She smiled back. "We just met." She'd had to deal with people like George before, rich men enamored of their own success, poor men with chips on their shoulders, powerful men surrounded by beautiful women or security people with automatic weapons. All totally self-involved.

"Why don't you two join us," George said. "I'm sure we could rustle up a couple more chairs."

"Thanks," Cab said smoothly. "But Abbie and I have some business to discuss."

George frowned. "Well, see if you can talk some sense into him. This will make your career, Cab. There are more projects down the road. Big projects. Don't throw it all away."

"I'm retired, George. Nice running into you."

"If you don't want to go back to the firm, I'll hire you myself. I'll pay you as a consultant."

"Thanks, but I've moved on to something else. Not architecture."

"Well, if you change your mind . . ." George reached in his breast pocket and thrust a business card at Cab.

Cab looked at it, then took it.

"Call me."

Cab turned away. "Sorry to keep you waiting, Sonny." He pushed Abbie along behind their host.

He sat them at a table on the far side of the back room and took their order, something Sonny called the house special.

"What would you like to drink?" Cabot asked. "They have a great microbeer."

"Sounds great."

"Oh and, Sonny, can you throw this away for me?" Cab handed him the business card. Sonny took it and hurried away, then returned almost immediately with two bottles of beer.

"If you don't mind me asking, what work did you do for him?"

"A totally self-sufficient resort community. Two towers,

gardens and parks between, with complete shopping facilities underground and connecting the towers, plus pools, a stocked lake, and direct access to the beach."

"Sounds major. And you designed it?"

His face clouded over. "Yes."

"Does that mean you don't want to talk about it?"

"I don't mind. It's a hell of a design if I do say so. Big, bold, self-sufficient, and depends a lot on solar panels."

"It sounds wonderful ecologically," Abbie said, wondering why he'd left it behind.

"It is; unfortunately, they plan to raze three old motels, a local shopping area, and several blocks of low-income homes to do it."

"Oh. Is that why you pulled off the project?"

He put down his beer. "When you design, you hand it over to a contractor, maybe you're on-site a few times. I wasn't naive. I knew that in most cases for buildings the size we designed, something had to be torn down to make space for it. Sometimes that was okay. I turned my back on the details. But this one. No. It was too much. Too callous. I just couldn't be responsible for that many people losing their homes.

"When I said so, they pretty much told me to stick to designing and leave the rest to the developers. I couldn't do it. I quit." He smiled a little crookedly. "Guess I won't be lunching in that town again."

"Have any regrets?"

He cocked his head, gave her a funny look. "Oh, I have lots of regrets. But none about leaving the firm—or the fiancée. You met her at the carousel." He sighed. "I don't know what the hell happened to me. Then Ned left me the carousel, and I knew I couldn't do what I was doing anymore. Nobody gets it." He stopped to look at her.

"I get it."

The food arrived. Two oblong plates piled high with sizzling ribs glazed to a shine, corn on the cob, coleslaw, sliced tomatoes, crunchy dilled cucumbers, and a plastic basket of thick slices of corn bread.

The smell was a heady mixture of sweet and spice all steaming together, and within seconds they were both licking sauce from fingers and sighing.

"Incredible," Abbie said between bites.

"Told you."

For the next few minutes they just ate, drank, and sighed with satisfaction.

"So what did Oakley say?" Abbie asked, reaching for another piece of corn bread.

"The usual. The Crispins are sitting on prime property and a lot of it. They could make millions if they sold."

"And Stargazey Point would become a golf course resort."

"Pretty much. But nobody wants that to happen, even Robert Oakley. That would be the end of the town and a lot of people's homes and ways of life."

"Including yours."

"Including mine."

"And the threat of auctioning off the house and land?"

"Oakley suggested they think about parceling it off so it wouldn't have to go to auction. That would see them clear for a few years. But it would be like taking the finger out of the dike." Cab licked a spot of sauce off the corner of his mouth.

Abbie almost forgot what they were talking about.

"It doesn't matter whether they sell to individuals or developers, the tax base will go up again. The Crispins would be able to pay their taxes, but everyone else would be out of luck. There would be a mass migration. We've lost enough of the local populace already."

Abbie sighed. It wasn't a future that she wanted for Stargazey

Point, and she'd only known it for a short time. But now she understood Cab's initial hostility to her. He'd given up everything not to be a part of the land grab monster, and now he might become its victim.

"What do the Crispins want to do?"

Cab took a swallow of beer. "I think Marnie would be glad to be rid of the responsibility. But she's loyal to the town. And to the family in her own way."

"Millie?"

"I think we both know she won't go down without a fight."

"And Beau?"

"I don't know about Beau. You never really know what he thinks about anything that touches his own life. But he's pretty astute. He gave you that necklace."

Abbie touched the tiny star. Just knowing that it was there made her feel at peace.

When they finally left the restaurant, there were only a few patrons left. The table where George Erickson had sat was now occupied by a young couple with a sleeping baby.

"You know," Abbie said, watching the lights of Myrtle Beach blur by as they drove toward home, "Bethanne came out to the house the other day while we were painting the gazebo. Well, while the kids were painting the gazebo."

"Ha. So that's how Sarah lassoed you into working at the center."

"Bethanne told me about her idea for a business called Weddings by the Sea."

Cab nodded. "She and Jim planned to expand into the building next door, but then Jim got sick and the owners sold to an antiques dealer from Beaufort."

"It sounds like a good idea. She said she would have done that big wedding that Penny was making cheese straws for, but the inn was too small. She thought the gazebo would be a perfect wedding venue, and I have to admit, looking through her eyes it was pretty romantic."

"What about your eyes?" He glanced over long enough to give her a provocative smile then went back to watching the road.

"I wouldn't know," Abbie said, slightly flustered. "Are there enough rich people having weddings to make any money?"

"Yeah. The venue would be great. And the ballroom would be perfect for large receptions, but she'd have to advertise, hire a large staff, waitpeople, ushers, caterers, bartenders. She'd have to do all the rentals, tables and chairs and whatever else. She'd need dressing rooms and bathrooms for the guests; you can't have a wedding with porta-sans lined up across the lawn. Landscapers. The house itself would have to be spruced up—"

"Okay. I get it. A money pit. But I hear they know a pretty good architect who might be able to advise them."

"Sure, but it would cost, and it takes time to build a business. Bethanne would eventually make money probably. But not in time to save the Crispins."

Abbie frowned. "You sure know an awful lot about catering weddings."

"Not me, but Bethanne has been talking about this so long, it just kind of rubbed off on me."

"I like that."

"What. Talking about weddings?"

"No. That everyone is trying to figure out how to save the Crispins."

"And themselves," Cab said.

"And themselves."

It was only ten o'clock when they drove through Stargazey. The Silver Surfer was still lit up, though most of the cars had left. The rest of the town was dark. Even the moon had shrunk to a sliver, and the night was black.

Cab slowed down near the carousel, checking to make sure

it was safe, Abbie supposed. But when he got to the entrance of Crispin House drive, he stopped.

"Does this mean I have to walk the rest of the way?"

"It means—" She heard him take a deep breath. "It means I'm not ready to take you home yet."

"Oh?"

"And since there's no place open to have coffee or a nightcap, and I don't want to scare you away by asking you if you wanted to stop by my house, and I'm not really up for visiting with Millie and Marnie, I'm kind of stuck for an idea."

"How about a walk on the beach?" She heard herself say it and couldn't stop. She knew she should just get back to the Crispins' where life was safe. But she didn't want the evening to end either, and that scared her.

Everything was churning around inside her, the relief of being able to talk to someone who didn't feel sorry for her or judge her in any way. She was also feeling a little attracted to him—a lot attracted. She didn't want to; she didn't trust it. As Marnie said, he was the only act in town, and she didn't need to have anything like that going on in her life right now.

Hell, she couldn't even say it. She was turned on; she knew he was, too. It was the beer, the food, the dark night. She wasn't sure about Cab, but she was afraid she wasn't ready. And she didn't want to risk it.

"Good idea." Cab made a U-turn and parked near the pier.

They climbed down the old seawall, and Cab took Abbie's hand to guide her over the broken concrete. She didn't really need help, but she appreciated the gesture. They walked side by side to the water where the sand was packed and easier to walk on.

They stopped to look out at the sea. The forlorn pavilion, the deserted stilt houses, the dark businesses. Far off in the distance the lights of Myrtle Beach glowed along the shoreline, a beacon or a mockery.

It was a clear night, crisp and invigorating. Abbie zipped up her hoodie.

"Cold?"

"No. Not much."

"Would you admit it if you were?"

"Of course." Wouldn't she? She was used to carrying her own weight . . . plus equipment. She didn't complain about the heat or the cold, the rain or the drought because it was part of her job. Part of what she was. Or so she had thought. "Are there plans to rebuild the pier?"

Cab accepted the change of subject gracefully. "I don't think so. Every now and then someone mentions it, but as you've undoubtedly noticed, the town is barely making it; there's no money for improvements."

"It's a shame."

"It's life."

She looked sharply at him, but his face was calm, and there was no rancor in his words.

"I just mean, sometimes you have to roll with the punches. Stargazey was once a thriving little beach town. Family oriented. An arcade and the carousel and miniature golf along the main drag. A few stores, cafés, the old hotel and another motel that didn't survive Hugo."

"Hugo was twenty years ago."

"Yeah, it tore away the beach and a lot of the oceanfront property. A lot of damage in town, too."

"But the carousel was saved."

"Miraculously. The building was flooded, and we lost part of the roof. That was the last summer I spent here. I'd left to go back to school two weeks before it hit, and when I learned that

Ned wasn't rebuilding, I thought that the damage was worse than it actually was."

"But you came back to fix all that."

Cab laughed, the sound snatched away by a sudden gust. "Twenty years later. I went to school at Virginia Tech and he'd come to see me, but I never came back here until he died. Too busy, too involved with my career and my future. Too busy to care about the man who cared about me."

"So you feel like you're carrying on his legacy?"

Cab looked at her, smiled slightly. "Hell, it was the furthest thing from my mind. But he named me executor, and I had to come to settle the estate, such that it was. The house was neglected, the carousel building a disgrace. Not one character was left on the carousel. I figured he must have sold them off."

"And did he?"

"No. He'd managed to move them inland to a friend's shed. And they were still there, covered and protected. It was amazing. I saw Midnight Lady and my fate was sealed."

"Can you make a living running a carousel?"

"No. But that's not the point. Ned was my anchor growing up. He taught me what was important in life. I'd come work for him all summer long. I'd do odd jobs, take up the tickets. I think it was maybe fifty cents. I kept noticing that he would give tickets out even when the kid didn't have enough money. He'd take buttons and bottle caps, marbles. It was crazy.

"I told him he should raise the fare and not let any of the freeloaders keep riding. That the carousel in Myrtle Beach was charging twice as much and he could make a lot more money. He said he'd never turn away a kid who didn't have the money for a ticket.

"He told me about the Stargazey Carousel when he was a boy. The rich summer kids would come every afternoon and night to ride the carousel, sometimes three or four times. He and his buddies didn't have enough money for tickets, so they just sat outside and watched the others ride.

"When he made his money, the first thing he did was buy the carousel. Put it back together after years of neglect. Saved it from more than one storm. And all that time he never turned a kid away because he couldn't pay.

"So I guess you could say this is part of his legacy. But it's also part of mine."

She smiled. "It's wonderful. Will you tell it again for the twins to tape?"

"I guess." He shook his head. "Why?"

"I think people would love to hear that story. But if you can't support yourself following in your uncle's footsteps, what will you do?"

He shrugged. "I'll set up an office in town and take on some restorations. That's the part of architecture I really love. It's what I always intended to do. I don't know how I got sucked into that other—And you've done it again."

"Me? What did I do?"

"Got me talking about myself. While I still don't know that much about you."

She shrugged. He knew more about her than she liked. "I just have a natural facility for drawing people out, I guess. I was pretty good at getting interviews."

Cab stopped and turned toward her. "Is that what you're doing? Interviewing me?" His eyes glistened in the starlight.

Against her will, she leaned toward him, drawn by a mutual energy that she refused to name. She was vaguely aware of his hand moving toward her, and she knew if she stayed, he would pull her into him and she would go willingly.

She laughed and stepped back, breaking the connection. "Of course I wasn't. I'm just interested, that's all."

He started walking again. "You think that running a carousel is interesting?"

"Yes. I think anything that a person is passionate about is interesting."

"Huh, I never thought of it like that, but you're right. This carousel is my passion. I liked architecture, too. I was really good at it. But the moment I unwrapped that first horse, I knew where my future lay."

"I'm envious."

"Get out." Cab laughed and gave her a little push. It was playful, almost boyish, a side of him she hadn't seen before but had guessed existed.

"Really. I never knew what I wanted to do. My family traveled all over the world, ready to leave at a moment's notice. Nothing throws them off their game. They're caring, loving people, and every single one of them had a plan. Except me."

"What about Guatemala and Habitat for Humanity?"

"A graduation present from my parents."

"What?" Cabot laughed. "I'm sorry. But . . ."

"I know. Whose parents give manual labor in a third world country for a graduation present? A car, a trip, a new condo. Hell, a gift certificate."

"Not any that I know of."

"Don't get me wrong. I loved working on those houses."

"I'd like to meet your family. They sound fascinating."

"Well, good luck getting them all in one place."

"They never have family reunions?"

"Hardly ever. It's part of the territory when you're a member of Do-Gooders Without Borders. But when they are together, it's pretty amazing."

Cab smiled, a brief flash of white teeth.

They walked on in silence, closer than before, almost touching, but not quite. Occasionally their shoulders bumped, but neither moved away. The only sound on the beach was the waves and their breathing.

They were nearing the walkway to Crispin House, when Cab stopped and grasped her shoulder. "Wait," he said, but he didn't have to warn her. She'd seen him, too.

A solitary figure, tall and lanky, standing feet apart in the gazebo. He was facing the ocean, and he didn't move.

For a moment they, too, stood still, then Cab touched Abbie's arm. "Let's not disturb him," he whispered and motioned her away. They walked back the way they had come, this time hugging the dunes.

When they were out of sight of the gazebo, Abbie said, "Millie said no one ever went out there."

"Looks like Millie was wrong."

"I thought it would be good to fix it up, but I wonder—"

Cab turned and took her by both shoulders. "You are not responsible for other people's lives or how they choose to live them."

For a minute they stood locked eye to eye and then his grasp loosened; instead of pulling away, Abbie swayed toward him. His arms came around her, gently finishing the movement she'd begun. And they swayed together in the night ocean breeze. Hearts pounding much faster than the waves.

Abbie didn't want to look up, break the sense of peace that cartwheeled along with awakening desire. So she stood taking it all in, feeling every sensation. Then she pulled away.

"I guess you know I was about to kiss you," Cab said, his voice breathy and rough.

She shook her head.

"Isn't that why you pulled away?"

Again she shook her head.

He pushed a strand of hair behind her ear. "It wouldn't be so bad. Actually I'm pretty good at it."

A laugh breathed out of her. "Can I take a rain check?"

"Sure thing. Just say the word."

They veered off the beach along a path through the dunes, and Abbie was surprised when they came out near the side of Crispin House. The porch light was on, and he walked her up the steps and to the door.

Abbie stood indecisive.

Cab reached across her and opened the door. "Go on now." He smiled at her. "And if anybody asks, I was a perfect gentleman. Much against my wishes. But don't tell them that." He pushed her in the door. "Good night, Abbie."

"Thanks. I had a lovely time."

"So did I."

"Don't forget about the twins tomorrow."

"How could I," he said. "I'll see you then."

"Bye."

"Shut the door, Abbie. We're still friends."

She closed the door. Heard the soft tread of his feet as he jogged down the front steps. Friends. She was afraid if she didn't pay attention, they might become more than friends.

Chapter 19

Marnie and Millie were both at the kitchen table when Abbie came downstairs the next morning. Neither of the sisters looked as if they had slept much the night before.

Abbie immediately felt contrite. She should have come back to keep them company after the assessor's visit. Instead she was out having fun.

She poured herself coffee, asked if either of them wanted more.

"No, thank you, dear," Millie said in a tight, resigned voice.

"I've had my quota," Marnie said, but she made no move to stand up.

Abbie deliberated whether to take her coffee outside and leave the sisters their privacy or to jump in with both feet.

She chose the latter, though she knew she had to be subtle.

"Is everything okay?" she asked looking from Marnie to Millie.

"Yes, dear. Everything is just fine," Millie said. "Would you like some toast and eggs?"

"Oh, for crying out loud, Millie. The girl doesn't want toast. She wants to be informed. She'd have to be blind not to see what's happening here."

"Sister, the idea." Millie's lips trembled, and she pleated her paper napkin.

"I didn't mean to pry," Abbie said quickly. "'I just thought maybe I could help."

"You're our guest."

Abbie cut her eyes toward Marnie, who rolled hers in return.

"You're sweet, but what I really am is a refugee. I had no place else to go."

Millie's eyes widened. "Why, sugar, how horrible. Well, you have a place here as long as you want."

"Thank you, but what I mean is . . ."

Marnie sat back in her chair watching the two of them dance around the real issue.

"I saw the tax assessor yesterday when I was in town. I saw him come here."

Millie sighed and deflated like a forgotten balloon. "It's all my fault."

"Oh, for heaven's sake, Millie." Marnie stood up; the chair skittered across the linoleum. "You're a pain in my butt, but it's not all your fault." She leaned on the table and peered at Abbie. "Here's the long and the short of it. We can't pay our taxes—or next year's taxes—we can never pay our taxes. We live on Social Security. Though that's a misnomer if there ever was one. Beau doesn't even get a pension because he was in the merchant marines instead of the navy."

"Daddy wanted—"

Marnie rounded on her sister. "I don't want to hear about what Daddy wanted. If he wanted us to be able to keep this white elephant, he shouldn't have squandered the family fortune by trying to out-Rockefeller everyone around him."

Millie brought the napkin to her mouth and held it there to stop whatever words were about to escape.

Abbie sat across the table like a pinned bug, wishing she'd

never gotten involved. Just spent the week and left with a big thank-you and a fruit basket that would arrive after she was gone.

But she had to admit she wasn't ready to leave. She wanted to work with the kids, get to know Bethanne and Penny and Sarah better. She hadn't even been into Hadley's yet and she wanted to meet him.

And Beau. Beau standing like an enchanted prince in the gazebo. And Cab. She wanted to see the carousel in operation. Hear the music. Laugh as the twins rode round and round. Maybe, welcome that almost kiss.

She pulled herself back to earth. The twins might never ride the carousel. Social services would send them back to their hateful uncle and that would be the end of that. To Penny, Bethanne, and Sarah, she was just an out-of-season tourist. She'd go to Hadley's tomorrow and buy a Coke like a real native. And her vacation would be over.

Then she looked at Millie, so frail, and Marnie, so disgusted, and she knew she couldn't walk away.

"Do you—" Abbie had to clear her throat to get the words out. "Do you have a plan?" And almost laughed. She was the last person on earth to ask about plans.

"Ha!" Marnie said. "Here's the plan. Start packing."

"How could you?" Millie cried. "It's Beau's home, not yours."

Abbie saw Marnie flinch. Millie pushed herself to her feet and tottered out the door.

"She didn't mean it," Abbie said, just because there was nothing else to say.

"I know. Neither did I. I just tend to go all caustic when I'm frustrated. But at least she's right about one thing. It isn't her house, either. Nor is it her decision to make. She'll feel slighted for a few days, roam the upstairs like Mrs. Rochester, and get

over it. And I'll do what I always do. Find more hidden silver
to sell. And keep us afloat one more year."

"I think I should wrap up my visit."

Marnie rounded on her. "Will you cut it out? You sound
like a broken record. I have enough on my hands without worrying about you."

Abbie was stunned. "I'm sorry. I don't want you to worry.
You don't need to worry. I've had a wonderful time. You've
been so kind, but I don't want you to be inconvenienced in any
way." She stood up.

"Sit down. You're the best thing that has happened to this
house in years. You may not have noticed, but Beau's not here
a lot. With you here, Millie has someone to fuss over instead
of harping on him all the time. She's cooking and dusting and
getting out the fine china. Hasn't had that much interest or
energy in years. I swear, if you cut out on me, I don't know
what I'll do."

Abbie stared at her. Surely she hadn't heard Marnie correctly. "I don't understand."

"Didn't Ervina talk to you yet?"

"Well, yes, but all she said was I looked back too much and I
should be looking ahead. Or something like that."

"Well, there you have it. Please stay. Now, finish your coffee
and eat some breakfast and come help me in the garden."

You can come out now," Cab said and watched Beau, Silas,
and Hadley ease back into the carousel room. The state electrical inspector had just left.

"We passed."

"Hallelujah," Silas said.

"Amen to that," Hadley said.

"Then let's start putting the rounding panels back into place,"
Beau said. "Cab, you get on my end, Hadley you take the other."

"What're you in such a hurry for?" Silas asked. "Thought we'd take a break and go down to the Tackle Shack for some catfish. Jonesy might even break out some of his applejack in celebration that we're not gonna burn the place up."

"Amen to that," Cab said. Now if they just passed the safety inspection, they could paint and start moving the animals back to the platform. They might be able to open by summer after all. Cab positioned himself at one edge of the painted panel and motioned for Hadley to take the other end.

"Don't have time for that today," Beau said. "I gotta go make sure the girls haven't pulled each other's hair out while I was gone."

"They fightin' again?"

"Taxes," Beau said. "Don't know why Hugo couldn't've taken the damn place when it washed out the pier and the arcade."

Hadley took the other side of the panel. "Come on, Beau. What would you have done if Crispin House was destroyed?"

"I'd've taken the insurance money and built me a barbecue place. I'd get Silas here to cook and you to run it for me. We could build in that space where the arcade used to be."

"But what would *you* do?" Cab nodded to Hadley and they lifted the wooden panel.

Beau frowned and watched them maneuver the panel to the center of the carousel and slide the panel into its frame. Hadley crawled behind and screwed it into place while Silas and Cab held it steady.

"Me? I think I'd build me a boat . . . and sail away. But don't tell the sisters. It's too high up on your end, Silas."

Silas let the panel slip down a fraction of an inch. "Nobody's stopping you from selling it."

"I know and if I could sell it without it going to some greedy bastard, I might do it. But the way those developers are swarmin' around, I know that they'd gobble it up bit by bit if they had to. And build a golf course, and where the hell would any of us be? Where you gonna live, Silas, if that happens?"

"They already took my place of business; they'll hafta carry me out in my coffin 'fore they take my home."

Hadley slapped Beau on the back. "Don't worry, there's always the next hurricane."

They all laughed and went back to work. But when the panels were hung and Silas and Hadley had left, and Beau had returned to his work in the workshop, Cab thought about what he'd said.

If Cab had the money, he might consider buying Crispin House, himself. It had great bones in spite of the neglect it had suffered. But they could get millions for it. Hell, they could get millions for a couple of quarter-acre border properties. He didn't have millions. And by the time he finished refurbishing the carousel, he would have less than squat.

And like Beau and his barbecue place, as soon as it was up and running, Cab would find someone to run it for him. He'd go back to work, in Stargazey Point if he could pull it off. That way he could keep an eye on the carousel, tinker with it in his spare time while he made a living at his second passion, restoration.

The twins were waiting for Abbie when she reached the center early that afternoon. They were sitting on the steps on either side of Ervina, huddled against her like two appendages. Their faces lit up when they saw Abbie. Ervina shooed them away and struggled to her feet.

Abbie looked from Ervina to the twins. "Shouldn't you two be in school?"

Two slow unison head shakes.

"They're sick . . ." Ervina said.

Dani and Joe looked up at Abbie with such hangdog looks that she could barely keep from laughing out loud.

"But it ain't catchin'," Joe blurted out.

Ervina snorted, straightened her faded shirtwaist. "Now, we don't know that for sure. They sick with longin' for someone to take an interest in them."

"I see." Abbie rubbed her chin like a television doctor. "I think I know just what to do."

"What's that?" Dani asked warily.

"We don't want no med'cine," Joe added and made a spitting noise.

"How about a trip to a carousel? We can get started on the carousel history. I don't think Cab will mind if we come early, do you, Ervina?"

Ervina smiled. "I don't think he'll mind at all. You chil'run behave," she said and walked off down the street.

Abbie opened the door to the center. Of course it was unlocked. She'd come early with the intention of looking over the equipment, seeing what actually worked and what could be repaired, but that would have to wait.

She got the video cam off the shelf. Looked for an empty video cartridge and called the twins over to learn how to load the camera. It was simple, just pop the cassette in and push the button to close. Still, it took each of them several tries before managing to get through all the steps correctly.

She's learned early on that if you did things for people instead of teaching them how, they ended up letting you do it for them and forgetting how as soon as you left.

She sat down hard, staring at the video camera.

"Miss Abbie, what's the matter?" Dani tugged at her T-shirt.

"What? Nothing, Dani. I'm fine. I was just teaching myself a lesson."

"Huh?"

"Like learnin' to put in the tape?"

"Exactly, Joe. Like putting in a tape." *Or getting your life back on track. Who did she think would do it for her, if not herself? What the hell was she waiting for? And why had it taken her so long to figure it out?*

She checked to make sure the tape was empty then herded the two outside. As soon as they reached the porch they ran toward the carousel.

"Wait a minute, you two. You're getting ahead of yourselves." They ran back to her.

"We're going to tell a story about the carousel, right?"

Two simultaneous nods.

"So where does a story start?"

"You messin' with us. It starts at the beginning."

"So where are we going to start the carousel story?"

"Front door," Dani said and grinned.

"Right." She'd leave establishing shots and camera angles for the older kids.

There was a squabble over who was going first. A quick game of rock, paper, scissors ended the debate.

She opened the lens wide, then knelt down behind Dani who placed the camera on her knees like Abbie had shown her.

"Okay, Dani, find your picture in the viewer. Got it? Okay. Gently push the red button."

Dani pushed the button.

"Cut. That means stop taping. Now, Joe, you're going to take a picture of the door to the carousel."

"Can we go inside now?"

"Yes," Abbie said.

The two children took off at a run.

"But wait until Cab says it's okay to go in."

They skidded to a stop at the plywood door. It was ajar, and their heads disappeared inside. Then the rest of them.

Abbie hurried after them. "Hey, you two, what did I say?"

They were jumping around Cab, pulling at him, begging for him to show them the horses. He looked over their heads at Abbie.

"I'm sorry. I told them to wait."

"We are waitin'," Joe said.

"We asked p'litely," Dani added, looking suddenly wary.

When Abbie stepped toward them, Dani stepped back, knocking up against Cab. Abbie stopped, squatted down. "I'm sure you did," she said softly. "But there are a lot of things that can hurt you in here. Sharp and pointed things," she clarified to let them know it wouldn't be Cab or her or Beau "Besides, if you're going to tell the story of the carousel . . ."

"You have to start at the beginning," Dani said.

"We done the beginnin' already," Joe groused. "I wanna see the horses."

A voice echoed from the open door to the workshop. "I need a strong boy to help me with something."

"That's me," Joe said. "That's me." He jumped up and down. "That's me."

"I don't know," said Cab. "Better let me see your muscle."

Joe pulled up the sleeve of his T-shirt and made a muscle. His arm was so skinny that Abbie's throat tightened.

Cab bent over and felt the muscle. "I guess you're right, Joe. That's some muscle. It must be you."

"I got a muscle, too." Dani held up an even skinnier arm for him to inspect.

"You do have a big muscle," Cab said and looked over her to Abbie for help.

"We need a strong girl in here for something else."

Dani made a face at her brother.

"We both strong," Joe said.

"They have to be," Cab said under his breath. "Okay, Joe,

go straight back to Beau and don't touch anything on the way. Can you do that?"

Joe nodded, and Abbie noticed that Dani nodded, too.

Joe walked carefully across the room with the others watching.

"Beau will take it from here," Cab said, standing up.

"What about me?" Dani asked.

"You get to decide what to film next."

Dani chewed on her lip and looked around. Looked back at Abbie and shrugged.

"Well, what do you do after you come inside?"

"Dun'no."

"What do you need before you can go on any ride?"

"Ticket," Dani exclaimed.

Abbie looked around the half-finished room. "Ticket booth?" she asked Cab.

"Uh, demolished," Cab said apologetically. "But I can show you where the booth was, and when we build the new one, you can film that, too. Before and after. Oh, hell. Get the camera ready."

Abbie readied the camera while Cab walked over to the entrance.

"Action," he said.

Dani and Abbie grinned at each other. The video camera rolled.

"This is the former site of the Stargazey Carousel ticket booth. It was destroyed by a hurricane. But the new booth will stand where its predecessor stood. Right here."

"Say 'come an' get yo' tickets,' Mr. Cab," Dani mumbled from behind the lens.

Abbie broke into a grin. A director in the making.

Cab looked mulish for a second, then took a breath. "Tickets, tickets, come get your tickets for the carousel."

"Cut," Abbie said.

Dani released the record button. "You did that good, Mr. Cab. I'm proud of you."

"Why, thank you, Dani. I aim to please."

"Now what do we take pictures of?"

"That's all for today. You need to save something for the others."

"Aw, Miss Abbie."

"It's getting late, and everyone will be here soon. And we need to get started on our storyboard."

"Storyboard. What's that?"

"I'll show you when we get back to the center."

They collected Joe from the back. At the door Abbie stopped. "Thanks again for letting us do this, and thanks for being such a good sport about the tickets."

"Not a problem." That smile again.

"Come on, Miss Abbie. We're ready to make that board thing."

They met the other children filing up the steps to the community center. Sarah had left a message saying she'd be late. Jerome had a night class. Abbie was on her own.

"We gonna make a board thing today," Dani announced.

"What's a board thing?"

"I wanna make one."

"Me, too."

"Okay," said Abbie. "We're going to make a giant board thing."

They had a quick snack, then all settled down in the media room, where Abbie explained what a storyboard was, and how filmmakers used it to tell a story. "It's like a big comic book, only ours will be on the wall."

It took most of the afternoon, but by the time everyone left for the evening, they had covered one wall in a black-taped grid of uneven squares and squiggly lines and a big sign that read BOARD THING.

It was getting late, and only Kyle and the twins were left.

She settled them down at the media room work counter with video math games, while she made an inventory of the equipment. It was primitive, and some of it didn't work at all. Even the Scotch tape she'd tried to use wouldn't stick. They'd ended up making the storyboard with electrical tape she borrowed from the carousel.

She heard the front door open. "We're in here," Abbie called. "Jerome's here. Go get your backpacks. He'll drop you off, Kyle. I don't want you walking alone at night."

Dani and Joe slid off the stools and started toward the door. Then they stopped, slowly pressed into each other.

A man was standing in the doorway. But it wasn't Jerome. Abbie had never seen him before. But when she saw the twins cowering in the doorway, their eyes round and frightened, she knew who he was. Their abusive, drunken uncle, Eddie Price.

"Can I help you?" she asked, coming forward briskly, and easing herself in front of the twins.

He didn't answer just peered at her through bloodshot eyes for a second before lifting a threatening hand. "Came to get them children. You come on now." He could barely stand he was so drunk. And the smell of alcohol and unwashed body was enough to make her gag.

Abbie resisted the urge to step back. Instead she stepped forward, confronting the man and his stinking breath and trying to push him out of the room.

"We're closed for the day. I'll have to ask you to come back tomorrow and speak with the director." She didn't expect him to leave, but she thought it might befuddle him long enough for her to signal the twins to run.

Abbie took another step, gradually working the man back into the hallway. From the corner of her eye she could see Kyle pulling the twins farther into the room.

"I come for them kids," he slurred, looking around her to

the two frightened children. Abbie could hear one of them mewling, and she saw red.

"Well, you can't have them," she said without breaking eye contact. "Dani, Joe, Kyle, go out the back door and get Mr. Cab."

"Don't'chu move."

The uncle lurched forward; they screamed and moved farther back into the room.

Abbie lunged for his arm and held on. "Go!" she cried. Kyle took one frightened look back at the twins and shot past the drunken man and was gone.

Price was drunk, but he was strong, and he flung Abbie out of the way like a piece of lint.

He grabbed for the twins; they jumped out of his way and he fell against the counter. He struggled to gain his balance and knocked two cassette players onto the floor. Plastic and metal and batteries exploded across the room.

Abbie threw herself between them. "Stop, damn you. You're trespassing."

He lurched forward and pulled the old video camera onto the floor. "Shut your skinny white mouth or I'll shut it for you." He stalked toward the twins. "Come here, ya little bastards, I come to get ya."

Abbie grabbed one of the video games and flung it at his head. It barely slowed him down.

"Cain't keep 'em from me. I'm their legal guardian. Ain't I?"

"Not if I can help it."

He grabbed a stool and threw it at her.

She jumped aside, then lunged for the man, hoping it would give the twins time to run. But Dani pulled Joe toward the window away from the door. Abbie just hoped, prayed, that Kyle actually went for help and wasn't hiding somewhere in fear.

"Puttin' all kinds of nonsense in their heads. Fill 'em up with stupid ideas. They ain't never gonna amount to nothin' are you, ya little bastards. So leave 'em alone, leave 'em all alone."

He started to turn and Abbie caught him in the forehead with a second video game.

He fell against the counter, stunned. Then he got mad. He grabbed the VCR and swept it to the floor.

He was destroying all their equipment. Their ancient, decrepit equipment.

The only equipment they had.

"No!" she screamed just as he hurled the editing machine to the floor. It bounced and landed with a thud, barely missing the twins.

"Damn you, damn you." Abbie grabbed the nearest stool and swung it at his head. She was vaguely aware of footsteps running across the front porch. The door opening and banging shut.

"In here!" she cried and moved to the door to block the drunk's escape.

Suddenly aware that someone was coming, the drunk man lunged past her and into the hallway only to be stopped in his tracks by Cab Reynolds's fist.

The man reeled back, and Beau pushed him to the ground, where he lay moaning.

"Where's Kyle?" Abbie asked.

"He's safe," Cab said. "We sent him to Hadley's to call the police. Are you okay?"

"I'm okay."

"If he hurt you, I'll beat the crap out of him," said Cabot.

"And I'll hold him down while Cab does it," Beau added.

The twins rushed to her, clawing frantically at her. She knelt down, gathered them up. "It's all right. You're safe."

"We don't wanna go with him," Dani wailed.

"You don't have to," Abbie said. Surely not even social services would allow him to take them back after what had just happened.

The police were just taking the twins' uncle away when Sarah and Otis drove up.

"What the hell happened? Is that Eddie Price? Damn him. Where are Dani and Joe? Are they okay?"

"We're here, Miss Sarah," Dani said from the computer table where Hadley was feeding Kyle and the twins Cokes and Cheez Doodles.

"We're all doin' fine," Hadley said. "You just go on and take care of business."

"What business?" Sarah asked, looking from Cab to Abbie to Beau.

"The police are going to keep him overnight on drunk and disorderly. Abbie's a witness to his attempt to harm his wards. And you are going over tomorrow to press charges for destruction of property."

"What property?" Sarah asked, looking around.

"All the equipment," Abbie said and stepped aside as Sarah rushed into the media room.

"Son of a bitch. He's gonna pay for this." Sarah leaned against the wall so fast she smacked the back of her head. "All that work, all that effing work on old useless equipment, and some effing drunk has to destroy even that. What the hell is the point? Hours of studying and filling out forms for nothing. Effing . . . stupid . . ."

"Take a breath and calm down," Cab said.

Sarah turned on him. "Eff you, too. Calm down? I'll calm down. I quit. I'm going back to New York. You can't volunteer to do something with nothing forever. I have real work to do back in New York."

"You can't just up and abandon these kids."

"Why not? It won't ever change. Jerome's father refused to sign his application papers. Talia barely passed her SATs. The equipment is wrecked. What's the damn point? Nothing will ever change around here."

Abbie slumped against the door frame. How many times had she felt like giving up. Said the exact same things: what's the point, nothing will ever change. And maybe it wouldn't, but Abbie knew she would keep trying.

"You can't leave," Abbie said. "At least not like this. The twins' uncle said they'd never amount to anything, and if you go, you'll prove him right. Is that what you want?"

Sarah turned on her. "Advice like that from you?" Her eyes widened, her mouth opened. "God, I'm sorry."

"Don't be. You're right about me. But don't you make the same mistake. It will haunt you forever. I didn't have a choice; my work was snatched away. But you do have a choice. You can make a difference."

Sarah groaned. "I feel a rendition of Up with People coming on."

Abbie grinned. "Was I pontificating?"

"A bit. And as much as I hate to say it, you're probably right. But look at this shit. What are we going to do with them for the whole summer?"

"We'll think of something."

"Uh-huh. Well, let's think of it tomorrow after I get back from the police station. I'll get Otis and Jerome to cart this crap away in the morning."

Cab drove Abbie and Beau home, though none of them felt much like talking.

Beau and Abbie agreed not to mention the break-in to Millie, although they did tell Marnie. And Abbie went upstairs right after supper. She'd been pretty unnerved by the whole thing. And there was no guarantee it wouldn't happen again. She stood looking out at the stars and the dark waves for a long time, thinking about Sarah and about herself. And trying to erase the image of Eddie Price from her mind. And she came to a decision.

She went inside, pulled her largest suitcase out of the closet, and hoisted it to the bed. Grasped the metal zipper pull and worked the zipper around the case.

She should have done this before, but she was being selfish. She needed to start thinking about someone beside herself. The choice was hers: continue to hold on to the past or set herself free. She knew what she needed to do.

She opened the suitcase and reached inside.

Chapter 20

Only Marnie and the cat were in the kitchen when Abbie came down the next morning. Marnie was at the stove cooking sausage; Moses sat at her feet, looking up expectantly.

"Millie's taken to her room over that damn silver. Beau ran out before seven. Since he's not fishing, I assume he and Cabot are working overtime."

"You know about the carousel?"

"Of course. I, unlike my sister, live in reality. She was never one much for reality even as a child. Worshipped our father, the bastard." Marnie shook herself. "Don't know why we're talking about that.

"So it's just me, you, and Moses this morning." She stopped to study Abbie's face. Nodded. "Looks like you've begun sleeping through the nights."

She speared the sausages, dropped them onto a plate, slipped bread into the toaster, and carried sausages to the table while Moses did his best to trip her up on the way.

"Have I? I guess I have." Abbie got a cup from the cupboard. "More coffee?"

"Please. So what are you going to do this morning?"

Abbie shrugged. "Garden, then I guess I'll go down to the center early. See if anything can be salvaged."

"Do you think it can?"

"Honestly? No. It was barely working to begin with."

"I'm sure you'll figure out something."

Abbie smiled, but she didn't feel nearly as optimistic. They'd been working on a wing and a prayer before the destruction of the equipment. This was more than a setback.

Anger swelled inside her, at Eddie Price, his ignorance, his poverty, his fear. But anger didn't make things right. Surely she'd learned that in the last months. What she needed was a clear head and a plan.

Marnie pushed the plate of sausages toward her. "You're banned from the garden today. But you can take a basket of lettuce to Penny for me on your way to the center, if you don't mind. She was running low, and I just happen to have a surplus." She pushed back her chair. "I'd better get that lettuce picked."

Abbie started for town a half hour later with a canvas carryall over her shoulder and a basket of crisp green lettuce in the crook of her arm.

The village seemed busier today. Several cars were parked along the street. The real estate office was open. A woman was washing windows at the antiques store next to the inn.

The sound of the vacuum cleaner met Abbie as she stepped into the inn. Bethanne was down on hands and knees running the wand beneath the Queen Anne sofa. Abbie waited until she stood up then yelled her name over the whine of the vacuum.

Bethanne saw her and shut it off. "Hey. I heard what happened last night. Is everybody all right?"

"More or less."

"That Eddie Price is a poor excuse for a human being. I hate to think of the twins being returned to him."

"So do I. I'm hoping that his behavior will make social services pull his foster status."

"They certainly should. Where are you going with all that lettuce?"

"To Penny's. I stopped by to see if you wanted to go for coffee."

"I'd love to. Let me just get my purse."

Spring break," Bethanne said as they walked to the tea shop. "Most of my rooms are booked for the weekend. Penny convinced me to put an ad with a coupon in the Beaufort, Georgetown, and Charleston papers. Between that and the website Jerome designed, I'm getting a lot of traffic."

"Does it stay busy from now through the summer?"

"Fingers crossed. Things calm down a bit during the week, but the weekends should be pretty steady. There have been some articles about the beaches replenishing, so hopefully we'll pick up some tourist traffic because of it."

She waved to the window washer. "That's Geraldine Fanning. She owns and runs the antiques shop. She'll be opening Thursday through Sunday until June. Then seven days a week after that."

Bethanne held the door while Abbie angled her way into the tea shop. Several tables were occupied, and a man was leaving with a cardboard tray holding four cups.

"Dom," Bethanne said, her face lighting up. "Here midweek? To what do we owe this?"

Dom smiled, showing perfectly even white teeth. He was in his midforties. His hair was stylishly long, and he was wearing khakis and a pin-striped shirt open at the collar. He gave Bethanne a kiss on the cheek.

"Rotating the exhibits. Bringing some classical seascapes down for next week. Spring. A time for redecorating." He lifted his eyebrows. "And what better than a seascape over that new couch." His smile broadened, a mixture of charm and irony.

"Abbie, this is Dominic Gaillard. Dom, this is Abbie Sinclair; she's visiting the Crispins."

Dominic nodded with an elegance that made the gesture a bow. "I'd shake hands but as you see . . ." He lifted the tray.

"Dom is the owner of the Gaillard Gallery across the street."

Abbie nodded. She'd wondered how an art gallery managed to stay in business here. Having met the owner, she imagined that he sold on pure charisma.

"And don't listen to anything he says. He has wonderful pieces on display."

Dom turned his smile on Bethanne. "Saw your ad in the *Courier*. I'm thinking about taking one out myself. Now I must get going. The troops will mutiny if their cappuccinos are cold."

"Does he live around here?" Abbie asked as she watched Dom hurry down the sidewalk.

"He has a gallery in Charleston, too, but he spends most of the summer here."

Penny came from behind the counter to relieve Abbie of her basket of lettuce. "Bless you. And thank Marnie beaucoodles. Sit down. Just give me a minute to put this away."

Bethanne waved to two women sitting in the corner. "They run the gift and souvenir shop." She sat down. "I always love this time of year. Before the tourists come and everyone is gearing up for the season." She sighed. "It always seems so hopeful."

"Well, I predict this season will be wonderful," said Abbie with forced enthusiasm. This end of town might turn into a quaint little seaside resort, but it made her end of town seem all the shabbier.

"Bethanne, why don't they fix up the other part of town? Everyone has to pass through it to get to the beach, don't they?"

"Pretty much, and it is an eyesore. But what can you do? The pier can't be salvaged, and the town can't afford to rebuild it. Several of the buildings were abandoned by their owners. They've been begging Hadley just to paint the front façade, and he just won't budge. I don't understand why he has to be so stubborn."

Abbie thought she knew. Hadley was holding on to what he knew, where he was comfortable, with the only thing he had left.

Penny brought new-looking menus. "I recommend the blueberry crumb cake. It's darn good if I do say so myself."

They ordered the crumb cake.

"I've got to stop eating like this," Abbie said. "Between Millie's cooking and Penny's desserts . . ."

"You might be in danger of fitting back in your clothes."

"I'm beginning to." Abbie had bought the jeans after she returned from South America. She'd lost weight and continued to lose since then. Stress and grief and anger could do that to you. She took it as a good sign that she was on her way back from despair. Marnie was right; she hadn't had a nightmare or an overwhelming attack of grief in days.

Bethanne reached out. "Are you all right?"

"Yes, actually. Yeah. I think I am."

Bethanne smiled, but she looked a little sad. "It's hard to let go, isn't it? You're going along and suddenly you realize that you weren't sad for five minutes, then one day it's several hours and you wonder if you're doing something wrong, and if you deserve to be happy."

Abbie just looked at her. "Why wouldn't you deserve to be happy?"

Bethanne shrugged. "It just seems like cheating."

Penny deposited plates and cups on the table. "You two

don't look like you're looking forward to my spec-i-al-i-ty. I know what happened last night at the center. Ran into Kyle's mama at the market this morning. But it isn't all bad. You and Sarah will think of something. Now eat." She bustled away.

They spent the next few minutes digging into the rich cake, moist with berries.

"Have you thought any about our conversation at the gazebo?" Bethanne asked. "About Weddings by the Sea."

"Sort of."

"I could use a partner."

"Me?" Abbie shook her head. "Bethanne, I appreciate it, but you need someone who knows what she's doing."

"I need someone who knows how important the inn and Weddings by the Sea is to me. It was Jim's and my dream." She smiled tremulously. "You could live at the inn for free."

Abbie had toyed with the idea herself, but only for a second. Bethanne sighed. "It was just an idea."

Penny appeared at the table. "I'm seeing frowns over here. You two don't want people to think you don't like my blueberry crumb cake, do you?"

Abbie shot her a relieved look. "The crumb cake is delicious."

"That's what I thought." Penny gave Bethanne a look. "And what about you?"

"Yummy. It really is."

"That's better. Now no more frowning. Summer is almost upon us. Time's a-wasting."

As Abbie walked back to the center she thought about Bethanne's proposition. Weddings by the Sea. Somehow she didn't think Werner would approve of using his insurance money to start a wedding business.

On the other hand, how else could she support herself in

Stargazey Point? She wasn't ready to leave. And it wasn't just because she had no place else to go. She liked it here and was becoming attached to the people who lived here.

She was tired of the nomadic life. Always moving on, never putting down deep roots. She was raised that way, moving from one town to another as her parents moved from one project to another.

"Where's your sense of adventure?" her mother would ask when any of them wanted to stay in the same school for another year, when they longed for a room that was just theirs and not shared with siblings, stray animals, or stray children who needed to be fostered.

And look at them now. All of them still moving, still living project to project.

Abbie didn't want to be a citizen of the world. She wanted to be a citizen of one spot on earth. One little town. Maybe one like this town. Maybe this town.

The sound of hammering brought her back to reality. She needed to get online and look for real work instead of thinking about working for Bethanne and kissing Cab.

"Watch out!" A sheet of roofing slid off the carousel roof. Abbie jumped back, just managing to get out of the way as it crashed to the ground. And she realized she was standing amid the rubble of the previous carousel roof.

"Sorry. Didn't see you," the workman called from the roof.

"My fault," Abbie yelled back. "I wasn't paying attention."

Because she was fantasizing about a life that was clearly not meant for her. She readjusted her bag and picked her way through the detritus.

She met Cab coming through the carousel door. "Is everything okay? I heard yelling."

"I wandered too close to the roofers." She blew a stray bit of hair out of her eyes. "New roof. It looks nice."

Cab pulled his gaze away from hers. "Yep, and a new coat of paint day after tomorrow. Then we'll reinstall the animals . . . if I can ever figure out the order." He shot his fingers through his hair, which was looking a little longer than usual.

"Does there have to be a specific order?"

"Yes."

"Besides aesthetic reasons?"

He laughed slightly. "Well, besides my stubborn desire to bring it back the way it was, it would make the rejoining a lot smoother without having to stoop to trial and error that can damage the horses and the rods. The standers are larger than the jumpers and since the circumference of the circle diminishes as you move inside, it's pretty important to get it right."

"Are there photos of the original?"

"A few. Do you want to see them?"

"I would love to see them, and I still have some time before the horde arrives."

He took her inside to where three flatscreen computers were set up near the carousel. One screen showed a grainy black-and-white photo of a close-up of the carousel. The next was a wider color shot of an entire horse. Abbie could see the nose of the horse behind it. She looked back at the first screen. It could be the same horse.

"See? A pretty frustrating endeavor."

"Yes." She was sympathetic, but mainly she was thinking what she'd be able to teach the kids at the center if she had a setup like this. But that wasn't the point. "What about Silas and Beau and some of the older people in town? They might remember."

"I've already asked. This is pretty much what we've come up with." He clicked on a file and a schematic of the carousel appeared. Abbie moved closer to look at the circles that represented the rods. Some of them had a letter inside. Some were blank, and others had two letters separated by a slash.

"This represents the leader." Cab pointed to a circle in red. "I remember he came behind the Neptune chariot."

"Neptune chariot?"

He opened a picture file. "I took these as I unwrapped it."

It looked like a chariot, only instead of wheels, it rode on aqua-painted waves that curled along the sides. In front, Neptune arched like the prow of a ship, wild haired, golden crowned, trident raised in his hand. And in back an enormous tail curved above the heads of the riders.

"It's magnificent," Abbie said.

"It is. And this is the leader."

Another photo, this one of a large palomino decked out in full regalia, a red-and-gold bridle studded with jewels, plated armor, and festooned saddle. Even in a computer image he appeared larger than life.

"I can't wait to see it. It's strange, but I just felt that thrill that I used to get as a child. When will you have it up and running?"

She turned from the computer to look at Cab.

He was looking at her, not the images, and he hadn't seemed to hear her.

"Cab?"

"Huh? Soon I hope. I just need to find the right setup."

"Maybe the kids can ask their parents."

"Good luck. I've already asked everybody in town. One person remembers one way and the other something entirely different. I guess when you're enjoying yourself, you don't pay much attention to what's around you." He paused, shrugged. Smiled. "I don't."

Cab stood staring at the computer screen long after Abbie left to go to the center. She'd been excited, really excited. Evidently it was easier to relate to his carousel than it was to him.

But he couldn't complain. She was about the first person besides Beau who didn't question his rationale or his sanity.

She was genuinely excited about what he was doing. More
excited than she was about him.

And so what if she was. She was obviously not ready for any
kind of relationship. And neither was he. They would just keep
having dinner and talking about carousels until she decided it
was time to go.

And that could be any time at all. She was just a bit unpredictable. Okay, a lot unpredictable and he didn't need that
kind of woman in his life. And what the hell was he thinking
anyway? If it were summer and they were two different people,
they might have had a vacation fling. But not the way things
were now. Was he crazy?

She was carrying way too much baggage. Emotionally
fragile. Intriguing but unstable. In need of saving? He was no
savior, and the only white horse around here would soon be
circling the carousel.

Then he thought of her yesterday, a fierce tigress who took
on an out-of-control drunk to protect those two kids. Not so
fragile.

He pulled over a stool and sat down peering at the computer
but not really seeing anything but Abbie's face when they'd
rushed into the center last night. How her taut lean body was
poised for a fight. And how his body had responded.

Did she feel anything like that toward him? Could she?

"Making any headway?" Beau asked, coming up beside him.

"Huh? Not really." Especially since his concentration had
just followed a line of inappropriate thoughts about Beau's
houseguest.

"Well, you'll figure it out. Be patient." Beau braced his hand
on the worktable and leaned over the computer. "Neptune. I

remember him. Kissed a few girls under that tail." He chuckled, placed a reassuring hand on Cab's shoulder, and wandered
back into the workshop.

Abbie was testing broken equipment and disposing of most of
it, when Sarah arrived, carrying a tote bag half her size. She
walked right past the open door without looking or slowing
down.

"Hey," Abbie called and followed her down the hall.

She found Sarah leaning into the fridge.

"What's up?" Abbie asked, coming into the kitchen.

"Nothing but my blood pressure." Sarah brought out two
bottles of water.

Tossed one to Abbie and they both sat down at the table.

"Want to talk about it?"

Sarah snorted. "Sure. Why not. I woke up to a call from
the university; my paper for the *Review* is late. They want me
to come back and start structuring a minor in cultural anthro,
which we were supposed to work on this past spring, but *they*
got busy.

"That was followed by a trip to the police station, where I
filed a complaint for destruction of property, harassment, and
a bunch of other stuff, which took hours and won't keep the
bastard in jail any longer than drunk and disorderly.

"After that I had to go deal with social services. Ervina insisted on going along. She wanted temporary custody of the
twins. They took one look at that crazy old woman, and I
thought it was over. Then their supervisor comes over. Says,
'you give her custody.' There was no hearing, not even an interview."

Sarah smiled for the first time. "She knew Ervina from some
ungodly group and was afraid Ervina would put the conjure
on them. They signed those papers so fast we were out on the

sidewalk before I knew what was happening. First time I've ever been glad to have a crazy-as-a-loon great-grandmother."

"Is it legal?"

Sarah shrugged. "I don't think anyone will contest it. Eddie's already scared she gave him the scabies from the last time he tried to hurt those kids.

"Looks like my old granny is a new mama."

She scrubbed her face with her hands then took a long drink of water.

Abbie jumped in. "I was thinking. What if while we're filming the carousel, we interview the parents who remember the old one? We might even get a bit of family history along the way.

"We can set up an interview room here at the center and nab them when they come to pick up their kids."

"And you think they'll do it?"

"Yes. We just need to give them a little incentive."

"Yeah," Sarah said, her normal glint back in her eye. "We do have a not-so-secret weapon."

"Ervina," said Abbie. "But will she help?"

"Are you kidding? Right up her alley. It might just work."

"We'll use the carousel as an anchoring point, and I bet you money we'll get a lot more details about their family histories than asking them where they came from."

"You were good at this, weren't you?"

"Interviewing people?" Abbie considered. "Yeah. I think maybe I was."

"There's only one thing."

"What?"

"We don't have any equipment. Damn Eddie Price."

"There is that. But I'm working on it."

Chapter 21

Change of plans," Abbie said when the afternoon crowd had eaten a snack and were sitting around her in the front room.

"Yeah, old Eddie Price broke all the equipment," Pauli said.

So they already knew about that.

"Guess we won't be making no pictures of the carousel," Kyle said.

Dani and Joe looked like they might cry.

"Well, that's not necessarily so," Abbie told them.

"It was a dumb idea anyway," said one of the older girls, clearly disappointed, but trying to hide it.

"Does this mean we don't get a ride when it opens?"

"No, not at all, and don't be so quick to give up." She couldn't stand to see their disappointment.

"How? We don't have no camera."

Abbie lifted her shoulder bag to her lap. Let it sit there. Here was the moment of reckoning. If she encouraged them, she'd be obligated to see it through. She swallowed, felt a flutter of nerves. And realized they weren't nerves from fear, but from anticipation.

"Yeah, we do. I have a surprise." She reached inside the bag, pulled out the camera she had sworn she would never use again, and held it in one hand for all of them to see.

They all looked, some frowning, some scratching their heads.

"What is it?" Kyle asked, peering through overlong bangs.

"A video camera "

"Don't look like ours."

"That's because this one is a digital camera."

They moved as one, closing in on her. She passed it around and gave each one a chance to hold it, then she took them outside to practice shooting with it.

And they were sold. Everyone wanted to use it, but Abbie told them that in order to do that, they had to sign up an adult for an interview time. There was a rush toward the table with the sign-up sheet.

Abbie breathed a sigh of relief. Now if they actually showed up for their interviews, they'd be in business.

"Great," Sarah said, sidling up to her when the children had moved to the tables to finish homework and read. "Only thing is, we don't have a way to edit digital."

"But I do," said Abbie.

Ervina picked up the twins at six o'clock, and after they excitedly told her about the new camera, Sarah and Abbie explained what they needed her to do.

She pointed her finger at Abbie. "You take their picture, you steal their hearts."

"Souls," Abbie corrected. "Some tribes believe if you take their pictures, you'll steal their souls."

"You know so much. You wait and see. Ervina knows." She nodded portentously.

Abbie stepped back in surprise. Ervina led her two charges out the front door.

"She does that sometimes," Sarah said, coming up beside her. "I like to think it's all an act. But sometimes . . . well, sometimes, I just don't know."

Abbie met Beau as she walked out of the center on her way home that night. It was the first time they'd left at the same time, and they walked in silence for a while.

"I asked the children to ask their families what they remember about the carousel. Maybe that will help Cab figure out the order he's so insistent on reproducing."

Beau nodded. "He wants to get it right. It's his homage."

"To his uncle?"

"Yes, ma'am, and to a way of life."

"I thought we could help. The children are all anxious to film the carousel. I really appreciate him letting them film. I'll make sure they don't pester him."

"I don't imagine he'll mind as long as you come along to supervise."

Abbie looked sideways at Beau, and he winked at her. She felt the heat spread over her cheeks.

"Do you think anyone will remember anything specific that will help?"

Beau had taken a piece of wood out of his pocket and was fingering it like worry beads. "Somebody's bound to."

"Do you remember anything about it?"

"Oh, I remember lots of things." He smiled, but it was at something Abbie couldn't see.

"It's too bad there aren't more pictures of it. I saw the ones on the computer, but there were only a few."

Beau didn't reply. She glanced over at him. He seemed far away.

"Beau?"

"Yes, it's too bad." He took her hand and hooked it into the crook of his arm, and they walked down the drive into the dying light.

Dinner was strained. Marnie looked every one of her eighty-four years. Millie was tight-lipped but looked more like a sulky child than an adult. Beau placidly ate his dinner, but he got up with a mumbled excuse as soon as he finished eating. He gathered his dishes and took them into the kitchen. He didn't return.

When he was gone, Millie stood up and began clearing her and Abbie's plates. When Abbie tried to help, she brushed her aside with, "You just sit and relax."

Abbie didn't insist but let her go.

Marnie waited until the door closed behind her then turned to Abbie. "I told her I'm taking the silver in tomorrow to sell it. They will forgo the penalties we owe if I pay up tomorrow." She sighed, snorted. "It won't hurt for her to come into twenty-first-century reality for a change. Do you want coffee?"

"Thanks, no," Abbie said. "I've taken on a project for Sarah, and I want to get organized so it doesn't turn into a disaster. Unless you need help with anything."

"No, go ahead. And Abbie, don't let this upset you. She always pouts when she doesn't get her own way. Been like that since she was a baby. Always worked, too. Until now."

Abbie climbed the stairs thinking about what she should do, if anything, about the Crispins' plight. She had tried not to be nosy or judgmental. She'd just met them, but she knew Celeste and she knew she had an obligation to inform her of what was going on. Then if Celeste said stay out of it, she would.

She called Chicago.

"Hey. How's your vacation going?"

"That's what I'm calling about."

"You don't sound happy. Is something wrong?"

"No, no. Everyone's healthy as far as I know. And I'm fine, but we have a situation."

There was silence on the other end, the sound of the fridge opening. Celeste rummaged around for a few seconds then said. "Okay, I'm fortified with a glass of wine; hit me with the worst."

"The upshot is they can't pay their real estate taxes." She told Celeste about Millie giving the payment to a family to pay for medicine.

Celeste groaned. "How much do they owe?"

"I haven't asked. I *am* a guest. But I did mistakenly overhear Millie and Marnie talking when I first got here. I guess they've been paying quarterly. Marnie said they needed to come up with three thousand by this week.

"I don't have a clue to how much more they owe. But the assessor has been here several times from what I've heard, and he was here again the other day. They're delinquent and the property will have to be auctioned if they can't make a payment by tomorrow."

"The hell it will. You'll have to ask Marnie how much it is."

"Me? Why don't you?"

"Here's something about the South. They still see me as a child. The idea of me offering to give them money would be embarrassing at best and humiliating for sure."

"And it won't be coming from a virtual stranger?"

Celeste laughed. "You? A stranger? How long have I known you? Eight, ten years? And I've learned that no matter where you go or how long you stay, you always get involved."

"I just—"

"Don't bother to deny it. How much time have you spent on the beach?"

"Okay. You're right. I'm a buttinsky."

"No. You're a compassionate person. I'm kind of envious. With all the news that crosses my desk day after day, I've become inured to humanity's unpleasantness. God, I actually get excited when something bad happens. It makes for cutting-edge broadcasting. So let me do something good for a change."

"Okay, so what do I tell them?"

"Tell them I'm protecting my inheritance. How soon do they need it?"

"Marnie says she's going into town tomorrow to sell the silver."

"They still have all that silver? Let her sell it. I remember spending every Wednesday of my summer vacations polishing the stupid stuff. But try to find out how much they need. I don't want to get their hopes up. I've got savings but not nearly as much as I meant to have. I can write them a check for three thousand, but they won't get it by tomorrow. They do nothing online."

"Well, I've got some money saved, too. I'll spot you."

"Thanks. I'll deposit a check in your bank tomorrow. Promise."

"I believe you. But I want to contribute, too. They haven't let me pay for a thing or lift a finger since I've been here. I'm insisting on paying for my room and board for the summer, and you have to let me visit anytime I want when it's yours."

"Deal. How long are you staying?"

"Why?"

"Well, if you'll stick around until September, I'll try to come down for Labor Day."

"That would be great. I know they would love to see you. They talk about you all the time."

"Don't guilt me. I'll see if I can get off. I'm long overdue. But you didn't answer my question."

"Which was?"

"Are you planning to stay for the whole summer?"

"I'm thinking about it. I'm working on a project."

"I knew it. Oh, Abbie, that's wonderful."

"Not that kind of project, those days are behind me. I'm working with some kids and a carousel."

Silence, then a long "Okaaay."

"Like I said, no big deal. In the meantime, I'll try to find out how much they still owe in taxes, but Celeste, if they can't pay this year, how on earth will they pay next year?"

"I don't know. I'll figure out something by then. Thanks for helping them out. You're the best, you know that?"

She wasn't. She could thank Werner for his foresight in securing her future, even if it was a meager one. "I'll keep you posted."

Abbie waylaid Marnie the next morning as she carried a heavy box toward the garage. She waited until Marnie had deposited it in the trunk of the old Buick before she jumped in the front seat and shut the door.

"Do you mind giving me a ride into town?"

Marnie pursed her lips. "Not at all."

"Thanks."

Marnie kept her eyes trained on the driveway, and Abbie didn't mention the tax payment. They had a long ride to Georgetown.

They were on the open road before Marnie said, "Have anything special you want to do in Georgetown or are you just bored?"

"I noticed one of those big electronic stores when Cab and I had dinner there. I wanted to pick up a few things for the center."

Marnie glanced sideways at her then went back to watching the road.

"Does Sarah know about this?"

"Some. But I told her if she wants me to work for free, she has to let me do it my way."

Marnie laughed. "I would love to have been a fly on the wall for that conversation. You know if she hadn't gone off to school and become a professor, she'd have ended up just like

Ervina. Two peas in a pod, stubborn and willful and they both have the sight. Only Sarah's scientific mind is causing a big chasm inside her."

Abbie angled herself so she could see Marnie better. "Is she really here to take care of Ervina? It seems like Ervina can take care of herself. She's even taken in two of the town children."

"Dani and Joe. Sad story. Their daddy ran off, then one day their mama dumped them on her no-good brother's front door and took off after him. No one's heard from her since. God only knows what happened to her. Her brother keeps them because he gets state money."

"They'll be better off with Ervina, but it has to be a strain; can't they find a better situation for them?"

Marnie snorted. "We've all tried. But he always comes back for them, and social services doesn't want to rock the boat. They're understaffed as it is, and if there's a family member, it makes their life much easier."

Abbie thought about those two expectant faces, then she pushed them out of her mind. It was a common story. And not much could be done except what Sarah was trying to do for all of them.

"I think Ervina was hoping Sarah would stay and adopt them," Marnie said.

"You're kidding, right?"

"She's pretty much given up getting Sarah a husband. Guess she figures children would be the next best thing."

"She's not putting any spells on her, is she? It wouldn't be fair."

"Not that I know of. And what part of life do you think is fair?"

Abbie leaned back against the seat. She couldn't think of one.

"Never mind. I have an appointment in twenty minutes. Do you want me to drop you off at the electronics place and pick you up or do you want to tool around town while I'm inside?"

"I'll go with you." Now was the time. She couldn't put it off any longer. "I talked to Celeste last night."

"Oh and how is she?"

"She's . . . concerned."

The old Buick surged forward then slowed again. "About?"

"Look, Marnie, and hear me out—"

"I haven't said a word."

"No, but you will, and I want you to listen first."

Marnie huffed out a sigh. "Okay, if you must, but I'm not going to like it, am I?"

"Academic. I know you have your mother's silver in the trunk, and I know you're going in to sell it."

"Is that why you called Celeste?"

"I didn't say that I—"

"Academic."

"Okay, I did call her. I thought she should know about the tax situation. It is her inheritance after all."

The car surged again. This time when it slowed down, Marnie was frowning at her. "And did you two concoct this together?"

"We decided to try to make you feel guilty enough to let us—her—pay the taxes."

Marnie snorted. "Guilty. Good Lord, you have no idea. If I succumbed to everyone in my family or in Stargazey Point who tried to make me feel guilty, I'd never dig out. Better try another tactic."

"Okay, here it is. You can't pay the taxes. Celeste has a little money saved that she's willing to put toward them. I'm thinking of staying here through the summer, and I insist on paying room and board and I might as well pay it up front."

"You're our guest."

"Yes, and I'd be paying at least a thousand a week if I had to stay at the inn."

Marnie cut her a look.

"Would you rather I go there?" Abbie said slowly.

"Don't be absurd."

"Then it's settled. We don't know how much you need, but whatever we have we're going to put down."

Marnie didn't answer. Abbie wondered if she had insulted her.

At last Marnie cleared her throat, stared at the road ahead. "I have to pay three thousand today or it will go on the auction block. Celeste can't get money here in time."

"But I have the money and a checkbook. Celeste and I will settle later."

"I'm still selling the silver."

Abbie slumped with relief. "That's just what Celeste said."

They looked at each other and grinned.

"But will Millie ever forgive you?"

"She has no choice. I'm all she's got left. But don't tell her about Celeste."

Abbie shook her head.

"I'll let you spot me today, but you get paid back with interest."

Abbie knew when to back off. "Fine." Though she had no intention of taking the money back.

"And then I'm going to strongly suggest to Beau to sell off a block of the property."

They turned down Church Street, and Marnie pulled into a parking spot along the curb. Abbie carried the heavy silver box inside an antiques store. Five minutes later, they walked out still carrying the box of silver.

"I could spit nails," Marnie said. "I can't believe he wouldn't take that last batch. It's a service for twelve and the best of the lot. Damn. Now what do I do, go door-to-door until I find someone to buy it?"

"For probably much less than it's worth," Abbie said.

"Hell, we never get what it's worth. Everybody and their uncle owns generations of silver and china."

"Then put it back in the trunk," Abbie said.

They drove to the courthouse on Screven Street where Abbie wrote a check for the back taxes.

"Thank you. You've given me a few months before the next tax payment, and maybe by then I'll have a plan."

"You're welcome. Now, let's celebrate. I'll take you to lunch."

"We'll go to lunch. But I'll buy. It's the least I can do."

They ate at one of the trendier French restaurants on Front Street.

"It isn't authentic, but it's better than catfish," Marnie said and ordered a bottle of cabernet sauvignon.

"Did you ever go to France?" Abbie asked conversationally, while wondering if Marnie would be able to drive after a lunch of pâté de foie gras, steak frites, and wine.

"Oh, my dear, yes. Best time of my life." Marnie smiled, and Abbie saw a flash of the young woman she must have been. "Spent twenty years there."

Abbie stared. "You're kidding. I mean . . ."

"And New York, San Francisco, Tokyo, to name but a few. Close your mouth."

"So would you like to share?"

"Eventually. But the Reader's Digest version is, I ran away from home at sixteen, worked my way to France and got involved in the war effort. I met a man there, a jazz musician, and we lived wickedly and mostly happily ever after until about fifteen years ago when he died of cancer."

"I would never have guessed; you never talk about it."

"It was a scandal. It's never mentioned, and Millie pretends like it never happened. Beau . . ." She shrugged. "He has stories of his own, I'm sure."

"What made you come home, if you don't mind me asking?"

"It's home. Daddy was dead, at last. Jean Paul, my life partner—isn't that what they call it these days?—was dead. Crispin House was going to wrack and ruin, so I sold my apartment and rode in like the geriatric cavalry. And before you ask, in the twelve years I've been back, I've spent every dime keeping the house from going under the hatches.

"So now I grow vegetables and wear dungarees and let my hair go uncombed as my last act of defiance. But I can't in all good conscience let Beau and Millie go down with the proverbial ship. So I sell the silver and everything else that can be sold." She groaned. "It's all so pathetic, and so Southern."

She poured the last of the wine into their glasses and ordered dessert. When the check came, Marnie opened her wallet and pulled out a wad of bills. "My egg money."

Abbie narrowed her eyes. "I've never seen any chickens."

"That's because we only meet on Monday nights." She grinned. "My last guilty pleasure. Poker. Don't worry that I'll gamble away the family nonfortune; let me just say that I don't always win, but I never lose. But—"

"Don't tell Millie," they said together.

They wove their way out into eye-dazzling sunshine.

"Maybe we should walk to the electronics store."

Chapter 22

It was late afternoon when Marnie dropped Abbie and several huge shopping bags off at the community center. Sarah was in the back but came to the door of the media room while Abbie unpacked her purchases.

"What the hell is all that?"

"Some toys I bought for myself," Abbie said, continuing to unpack the bags.

"Then what are they doing here?"

Abbie pulled a tripod out of the box and began to set it up. "If you haven't noticed, I spend most of my afternoons here. Where I go, my toys go."

"Are you trying to guilt me? I told you—"

"Most of it was on sale. It's not a case of largesse from the plantation house, if that's why you're so bent. We can't do this with the two pieces of Neanderthal equipment Eddie Price managed to miss. You know, you should really get over this inability-to-accept-help syndrome." She stopped, shocked at both their reactions. "If you don't want it for the center, I'll take it with me when I leave."

"Fine," Sarah said and retreated to the kitchen.

Abbie sighed, not sure if they had come to an understanding

or if Sarah had just written her off as a friend. "You could at least show some interest in what I got."

Silence, then the slow creak of the floorboards as Sarah came down the hallway. She stopped in the doorway. "Hit me with it."

"Tempting, but what if we just look?"

"Snark doesn't become you." Sarah stepped up to the counter.

"I bought two of these to augment my video cam." Abbie lined up the camcorders on the worktable.

"Shit, those are camcorders?"

"Yes. Not high-end tech but better than a phone for basic video. And cheap."

"Cheap? How cheap?"

"About fifty each."

"Better *and* cheaper than a phone. Hmm." Sarah picked one up. "And not too heavy."

"Yeah, but not quality video. Still we'll be able to get some decent location shots with them and I really got them so the kids wouldn't have to wait so long until their turn with the digital."

She hoisted a box that held a video package—recorder, case, and tripod—to the countertop. Then she laid the additional tripod next to it.

"You can't keep momentum up when there's so much down-time in between turns at shoots. These babies will hopefully keep them busy, and if they get interested, maybe their parents will, too. The carousel story will just be the beginning. You can do all sorts of recorded histories after that."

"Except I'm going back to New York," Sarah said.

"Well, whoever takes over for you. For now let's concentrate on getting a tape of the carousel. That way if there's any decent footage, and I think there will be, Cam can use it for publicity, YouTube shorts, commercials, whatever. And when people see how it helps bring revenue to the town, they'll be even more cooperative the next time."

Abbie wound down. "In theory, anyway."

"Girl, you are something else."

Abbie frowned, suddenly serious. "You were right. I'm good with kids and mothers. It's sort of what I did. Let me help by doing what I know how to do."

"Why do you want to help?"

"You asked me to. Hell, you strong-armed me into it. And now you've giving me shit for doing it?"

"I did, but I didn't mean for you to spend any money on it. I can't pay you back."

"I didn't ask you to. This town gave me a safe haven when I needed it, the Crispins, Penny, Bethanne, even you, the biggest pain in the butt on the South Carolina shore. Let me give a little back without having to beg." She huffed out an exasperated sigh. "All this stuff cost less than five hundred dollars, including the coffeemaker I got for Crispin House."

"You bought them a coffeemaker?"

"Yes. And I hope *they're* not offended, but really, that percolator they use makes mud."

"I'm not offended. Well, okay, I'm kinda thin-skinned about that kind of stuff."

"Something you should work on. Maybe you should get Ervina to give you a potion."

Sarah scowled, her mouth twisted, then she broke into a grin. "You are one scary woman." She chuckled, then grew somber. "And a strong one. Thanks for the equipment."

"My pleasure," Abbie said and began opening boxes.

Abbie stopped by the carousel on her way home that night to see if Beau was ready to leave. It seemed to be becoming a ritual, the two of them walking back together at the end of the workday. If Millie ever wondered why they came in together each night, she didn't ask.

She found Cab perched on a ladder, paintbrush in hand. Abbie waited for him to finish what looked like a delicate task before she called up to him. "What are you doing?"

He looked down, his concentrated expression turning to welcome. "Hang on two secs." He put the finishing touches on a fat cherub, balanced the brush on the paint can, and climbed down.

There was a smear of pink paint across his nose. It made Abbie smile.

"We decided to do the finishing on the cherubs in situ instead of trying to take them down without damaging them, but I didn't want Beau to be climbing up there, so the job fell to me. You off for the night?"

"Uh-huh. I'm beat."

"Kids getting to be too much?"

"Not usually, but I went into Georgetown with Marnie today, we had lunch, there was wine involved. I bought a bunch of equipment. The kids got a little overexcited about using the new cameras. They were practically bouncing off the walls by the time they left. It was a long afternoon."

Cab smiled at her, and she felt a little flutter.

"You bought new video equipment for the center?"

"Yes. And before you get all snooty on me, I did it to make my life easier."

"Uh-huh."

"Well, I did, and besides everything was on sale."

"And Sarah's giving you a hard time about it?"

"Of course. Is Beau still here? I thought I'd walk home with him."

"He's in back. But he's probably close to finishing up . . . if you want to wait."

"I'll wait, but don't let me interrupt your work."

Cab glanced up the ladder and back at her. "Right. I'd like

to get these little angels done tonight." He climbed, reluctantly it seemed to Abbie, back up the ladder.

Beau came out of the back room a few minutes later, saw Abbie, and tipped his head. Then he called up to Cab, "I set the humidity and temperature. I'll leave the locking up for you. My young lady is here."

Cab stopped painting long enough to look down at them. "Lucky man," he said. "Good night." He turned back to the cherub, and Beau and Abbie walked out into the night.

"Boy's like a racehorse nearing the finish line."

"He does seem rather single-minded," Abbie agreed. "Has he had any more luck with organizing the menagerie?"

"Not yet. But he will." Beau's steps slowed as they reached the end of the drive. Abbie didn't blame him for not being in a hurry.

Marnie and she had discussed keeping the silver hidden in case of emergency, but in the end decided to give it back to Millie.

"She'll still sulk for a bit, just for form's sake," Marnie had said. "Then we can live in peace until the next time."

"It won't be long," Beau said.

At first Abbie thought he was answering her unspoken thought about Millie's bad mood, but then she realized he was still talking about Cab.

He fingered his shirt pocket and the block of wood she knew would be there.

She touched her own nautical star. And felt a calmness that must have mirrored Beau's. Ervina wasn't the only one around who had a kind of magic. The town, itself, seemed to nourish the unusual. There was Beau and his wood, Cab and his carousel, Sarah, Bethanne, Penny, Silas, Jerome. They were all special people.

Stargazey Point—A Place for Dreams. It would make a wonderful video.

Without thinking, she slipped her hand through the crook of Beau's arm. He patted her hand, and they continued to the house in silent comradeship.

Dinner was not the celebration it should have been with the return of the silver. As Marnie had predicted, Millie was still sulking. She sat primly at the head of the table, carefully not looking at any of them as she picked daintily at chicken and dumplings. Beau sat with his head bent, bolting down food like a starving man.

As soon as he'd taken the last bite of food on his plate, he gathered his dishes up, said "Excuse me," and took his dishes to the kitchen.

Marnie didn't try to coax Millie out of her mood but ate her own dinner, took a second helping of chicken, then announced that she would do the dishes. She too disappeared, and shortly after, Abbie excused herself and took her plate to the kitchen.

Abbie went straight up to her room. She had plenty to do. Her first set of parents were coming in to be interviewed the following afternoon, and she needed to make a list of guideline questions the kids could ask to get the ball rolling. She wanted to think through the whole project so they didn't fly off in too many directions.

At first she just sat on her bed staring at the empty page of her notebook. She finally gave it up and went back to the closet for her laptop. Cautioning herself to pull up a blank document and not look at anything else that awaited her there, she carried it out to the writing desk in her little parlor.

It wasn't easy. The YouTube link as well as her other work sat in full view on her desktop. She created a new folder, dragged her old work-related folders into the new one, then hid it in an unused file. Once it was out of her sight, she began to type.

It took a while. Her back grew stiff; she stood up, stretched, paced the room. She stepped out onto the veranda and looked out to the gazebo, but there was no one standing in the moonlight tonight.

She returned inside and sat back down. A half hour later, she heard a door shut in one of the other bedrooms. And a few minutes after that, another. The next time she heard a noise, she glanced at the computer's clock. It was almost midnight, and she had several pages of material.

She was tired, but her brain was racing with ideas. Excitement, something she hadn't felt in a long time, rose up in her as she imagined the finished project, and the carousel with a line of expectant people waiting to ride.

She'd start the film with a shot of the oldest people in town riding the new carousel, maybe intersperse it with some old photographs. Then she'd end with a new generation of children climbing on the newly restored animals, a nod to the past, hope for the future, and a story of a way of life. At least a slice of the story.

She stopped herself. This would be the children's story, not hers. She had to let them discover, with a little guidance, the richness of their community. See it through their eyes, not hers.

She sat down and began to edit her notes. A noise above her stopped her fingers. She held still, listening. Footsteps. A crash as if a heavy object had fallen to the floor above.

Marnie had told her the third floor had been closed up years before. So who was up there now? And why?

None of them should be wandering the house late at night. Especially in an abandoned part of the house.

The footsteps ceased and Abbie waited to hear them coming back downstairs, but all remained quiet.

Worried at the sudden silence, she went into the hallway to listen. Across from her, the door to the back staircase was ajar as if someone had let it shut and it hadn't caught all the way. The light from inside cast a yellow sliver across the floor.

Abbie started up the narrow, steep stairs. She reached the third floor and found herself in an identical hallway to her own. And where her own door would be was another door. It too was ajar. She listened but no sound come from inside.

Please don't let them be hurt or . . . worse.

Abbie tiptoed up to it and peeked into the opening. The room was her parlor's counterpart, except that cast-off furniture, trunks and cardboard boxes, and wooden crates rose in a precarious jumble on each side of the door.

The room was dark, but light came from the bedroom. Abbie crossed the floor and peered in.

The room was cleared of normal furniture. In its place was the most amazing sight Abbie could ever imagine. Shelves, tables, and stands lined the walls, trisected the room—all filled with wooden objects. Some large, some smaller than a thumb. None bigger than the pieces of wood Beau kept in his pocket.

This was where all the figures he carved and no one saw had gone. To a hidden space in a locked-away room.

He'd built a menagerie of animals, people, trees, houses. On one table was an entire village with stores and stop signs and a village green. On another, wild animals crowded around a painted oasis. Sea animals were lined up along one shelf, and a circus paraded on another.

There were hundreds and hundreds of them, exquisite in their rendering and their detail.

And in the midst of this, Beau sat at a table, hunched over his work, his back to the door. Surrounding him, leaning against chairs, walls, wherever there was space, were paintings. Canvases large and small, all colorful, fantastical portrayals of the carousel.

On the largest canvas, Midnight Lady, black as the night, tossed her head, her mane flying in wild abandon, as she strained at the bit as if she might leap from the canvas. Next to her with its nose pushing forward, hooves stretched almost parallel to the ground, a pinto with a blue-and-gold bridle raced with a golden lion. On the next was a green and gilt sea horse whose tail coiled beneath him as he rose toward the brass ring.

Sections of carousels turned giddily across the canvases, their colors vibrant and fantastical, yet real.

And before him on the table sat a wooden carousel no more than a foot high. Abbie recognized it immediately, though it was rendered in natural wood, no paint to distinguish it. It was the Stargazey carousel.

A pot of glue and a small brush were placed at his elbow, and several carved figures lay on their sides waiting to be attached.

"Beau," she breathed. Abbie moved slowly toward him, looking raptly at the miniature carousel.

He looked up and saw her. He quickly put his fingers to his lips. He slid off the stool and went to shut the door before coming to stand beside her.

"It's incredible," she said. "Did you do this for Cab?"

"The miniature," he said. "These others"—he peered around at the canvases—"were done many, many years ago."

She tried to read his expression, but it was far away, as if he were seeing them in a different time.

"Does Cab know you're doing this?"

Beau shook his head. "Didn't want to get his hopes up, if I couldn't remember."

"He'll be so excited. He'll have the order and the colors. Beau, this is wonderful."

But Beau didn't look like it was wonderful; he looked like a cornered man.

"You are going to show him, right? That's why you're doing it."

Beau nodded. "The miniature. Not the paintings."

"Why not?"

Beau didn't answer. And Abbie remembered Millie talking about Beau painting in the gazebo until "Daddy put an end to that." Is that why he kept them hidden from view? Because his family disapproved? Surely not anymore.

How much delight these paintings and objects could bring if they were on display. Instead they were shut up and locked away.

Abbie felt a pang so sharp that it took her breath away. What had happened that made him have to keep these hidden away from view? Abbie couldn't remember seeing anything like them displayed in the house. She would have remembered.

They'd been here all this time. And there were more. She could see the edges of frames standing on their sides in wooden storage racks against the far wall. Had they been here for decades, unseen and forgotten, while Beau traveled the world?

Curiosity finally got the better of her. "May I see the others?"

Beau hesitated. Fingered his shirt pocket. Dropped his hands and walked almost tiptoeing to the first cubicle. Abbie stood where she was, afraid of destroying the fragile moment. He looked back at her once, then he slid a painting from the rack and placed it on the floor.

He set another one to the side of the first.

Now that he had begun, Beau seemed to not be able to stop. Painting after painting came out to be displayed: landscapes in myriad greens and browns, seascapes with bright undulating waves, portraits of running children, smiling adults. All alive and vibrant in color and tone.

One especially caught her imagination, a nude of a young

African American woman, her hands lifted over her head as if she were carrying a basket, but she held only air. She was voluptuous, seductive, and innocent at the same time, and Abbie couldn't remember seeing anyone more beautiful. The painting captured the immediacy and universality of her, like a friend you've known for a long time, like an icon of womanhood.

"Beau, this is incredible. Did you do all of them?"

Beau stepped back and looked at the canvases framing the room. He nodded. "Yes, Abbie, I did, a long time ago."

They stood side by side taking it all in. Then with a jerk, Beau moved. He snatched the nearest painting as if he couldn't wait to get it out of sight. One by one, they were returned to the storage bin. He was like a man possessed, one who had shared a beautiful gift with her then regretted his decision.

"Beau, wait. Why are you hiding them? They're all beautiful. Have they ever been displayed?"

He shook his head and continued to return them to their places. And Abbie was filled with outrage that he was made, for whatever reason, to hide his extraordinary talent.

He systematically placed the paintings in their proper places, not even looking at them as he did. One after another, they disappeared.

Until there was only one left. The young black woman with the lifted hands. Beau seemed to run out of steam then. He stopped, looking down at it, and wound down like an old toy.

"What about the ones of the carousel, Beau? I'm sure everyone would love to see them. Does the town have a library? Or maybe at the inn. Or maybe Dom Gaillard would be interested in displaying a few in his gallery. He said the other day he was looking for seascapes, and yours are wonderful."

He turned toward her, his eye suddenly defeated and old. "No, Abbie, it would make Millie unhappy."

Abbie didn't believe Millie could be so selfish. She'd been

given a reprieve on the silver that nobody wanted. And she'd made everyone's life miserable until it was returned. Surely she wouldn't deny her brother his moment of recognition.

"Why? Why wouldn't she want you to display these? They're wonderful. I bet you could even sell them if you wanted."

There was a brief flicker of interest before his eyes clouded over again. "That wouldn't do, Abbie. I sold one when I was a young man. Made some decent money. But only the one— then I went off to the merchant marines and . . ." He paused, looked back at the now hidden canvases. "And these have been here ever since. We'd better go."

He led her out of the room, and they tiptoed down the stairs, Beau leading the way. He stopped at the bottom, listened. Then he beckoned her into the hallway.

Abbie was thrumming with excitement and indecision. She didn't want to interfere in something that was decades in the making. On the other hand, she hadn't missed that one split second of longing as he put the last painting away.

They walked down the hall and stopped at her door. On impulse, she stretched up and kissed his cheek. When she was inside her room, she stood at the door until she heard him walk slowly away.

Chapter 23

Abbie was surprised to find Beau waiting for her at breakfast the next morning.

"Millie and Marnie are in the garden. I'm taking the carousel to Cabot this morning. You can take one of the paintings to Dom if you want."

"Only if that's what you want. You don't have to agree to anything. He can just give you an appraisal, and you can decide what to do later."

Beau nodded brusquely. "All right."

They were about to leave the kitchen when the back door opened. Beau froze. Abbie whirled around.

Marnie stood just inside, a colander of snap peas in her hand. She eyed them speculatively.

Abbie looked at Beau for a cue. Saw the indecision in his eyes and butted in. "Beau has made a wonderful carousel to help Cab reconstruct the order of the horses." She hesitated.

"And I'm taking a painting down to Dom Gaillard to appraise," Beau said.

"Painting," Marnie asked incredulously. "Are you painting again?"

Abbie felt Beau draw back. "Just some old ones," he said.

"No kidding. Meet me in front. I'll go get the car."

Beau and Abbie watched openmouthed as Marnie dropped the colander of peas into the sink and quickly washed her hands. "Get going, you two," she said as she hurried for the door. "I'll meet you out front."

They were carrying the carousel and the painting out the front door to the Buick when Millie came around the side of the house.

"I thought I heard the car. What are you doing? Where are you going?" She spied the carousel and painting and began shaking her head. "What are you doin', Beau?"

Beau licked his lips; Abbie held her breath. She really didn't want to have to take the paintings back to the attic before Beau got his answer from Dominic Gaillard.

Marnie's head appeared over the top of the car. "We're taking Beau's painting to get an appraisal."

"You can't," Millie said, her fingers clutching at the skirt of her dress.

Beau started down the porch steps, Abbie by his side. As they reached the ground, Millie jerked to life. "You can't." She made a feeble grab at the painting Abbie was carrying.

"Millie, don't you dare touch that painting." Marnie rushed around the car faster than Abbie had ever seen her move. She stepped between her sister and Abbie.

Millie turned on her. "You knew about this?"

"About the paintings, no, but the fact that they might bring in some cash, I sure as hell hope so."

Millie's eyes darted from Marnie to Abbie to the painting she held. For a moment Abbie was afraid she was going to try to wrestle the painting from her.

"But Daddy would be so angry." She turned to Beau. "You know he would."

Abbie saw a flash of emotion pass across Beau's face that

frightened her. Then it was gone, and Beau was his normal placid self again; she wondered if she'd imagined the intense anger she'd seen there.

"Leave it be, Millie," Marnie snapped. "Daddy is dead. Beau isn't, and he's waited a goddamn lifetime to show what he loves best. Leave it be."

Beau was clutching the box that held the carousel in a death grip. Abbie sensed the moment when he caved. So did Marnie. He turned toward the porch steps, ready to put back what had been hidden for so long. Marnie grabbed him by the arm.

He shook her off. To their surprise, he walked straight up to Millie. "That's enough, Millie."

"Those paintings wrecked our family."

"No, Millie, it wasn't the paintings."

"But Daddy said he'd rather kill you than let you paint."

Beau just stared at her.

"I heard you, out in the gazebo, the night before you left."

"You don't know what you heard; leave it be."

His voice never even modulated, but Millie jerked back as if he'd physically slapped her.

"Beau, no." Millie clutched her chest.

"Go on in the house." Beau lifted his chin toward the door. "Go on now."

He turned away. "Get in the car, Abbie." He opened the car door for her. She slid the painting into the backseat and climbed in after it. Beau sat in the front looking straight ahead.

Millie clutched at Marnie's sleeve. "Sister, no! Don't let him do it."

Marnie pulled away. "Stop making such a fuss. You have your silver; let Beau have his life back."

Millie's chin quivered, but she lifted her head. "I'd rather never see the silver again if it comes from that."

"Think before you speak. Now go inside like Beau told you to do." Marnie got in the driver's side and started the car.

Abbie looked out the back window as they drove away. Millie stood where they'd left her, one hand gripping the railing, the other clutched to her chest, looking frail and frightened and totally defeated.

They dropped Beau off at the carousel. He didn't want to go with Abbie to the Gaillard Gallery. Abbie didn't try to persuade him; she had all she could do to persuade herself that she was doing the right thing.

"You're sure?" Abbie said as he got out of the car.

He nodded and carried his box into the carousel building.

Abbie scooted into the front seat. "Am I doing the right thing?" she asked Marnie.

"Yes, you're doing the right thing."

"But Millie was so upset."

"She'll get over it."

"Are you sure Dominic Gaillard is a reputable dealer?"

"Yes. We've all known Dom for years. He loves art, and he's honest and hardworking. Stop worrying."

"What if he says he can't show it or sell it? I don't want to crush Beau's expectations."

Marnie laughed. It was a bitter sound. "Then it will go back in the attic or wherever Beau's been hiding it all these years. And life will return to the travesty it was. Is this the only one?"

Abbie shook her head.

"How many?"

"I'm not sure. There were about seven renderings of the carousel that he was using to construct the miniature. He showed me several more landscapes and seascapes. Dom said he was looking for seascapes . . . so I thought . . . but I may have opened a can of worms for nothing. I don't want this to come between the three of you."

"Hell, Abbie, we're an old Southern family; we have more skeletons, more unacknowledged scandals, more innuendos and power struggles than you can even imagine. Our father was a bastard, not in the literal sense, but you know what I mean. He drove me away, he drove Beau away, and he crushed any sense of spirit Millie ever had.

"She was a compassionate child, but she idolized our father, and he crushed her. It's too late for her to change. I'm just glad Beau has found a champion." She shot a quick glance over her shoulder. "Or that you found him."

"But what about Millie?"

"It's time for Millie to stop protecting the old rascal. Eighty years is enough. The man is dead. He manipulated us all while he was alive, and he still manages to manipulate Millie now that he's dead."

"Do you mind if I ask, what actually happened between Beau and your father? Millie said he used to paint in the gazebo, but 'Daddy' put an end to that. And today she sounded like it was something really dreadful."

"I have no idea. Just part of the web of the past. 'What happened in the gazebo,'" she intoned and chuckled. "My family is a cliché, Abbie, we have to accept that. It's way too late to do anything about it. Except maybe let Beau fulfill his dream."

Marnie stopped in front of the gallery. "You don't mind if I don't come in?"

"No." Though Abbie would have appreciated the support.

"I talk a big game, but I still have my own issues with my family and the town."

The Gaillard Gallery was a storefront with two wide glass windows backed in black velvet. An abstract painting was displayed in one and a seascape in the other.

Abbie thought the seascape she held in her arms was much better. She was about to find out.

As she came through the door a man entered through a curtain from a back area. She recognized Dominic Gaillard.

"Mr. Gaillard," she began.

"Didn't I meet you at Penny's the other day?"

"Yes, Abbie Sinclair. I was hoping you could give me some advice about a painting I have here."

Dom's pleasant face went slack. "Yours?" he drawled.

"No," Abbie said quickly. She didn't want him to think she was asking for favors. He probably charged a fortune for appraisals, something she hadn't thought of when she jumped into this. "I found it in an attic, and I'm not sure what I should do with it. I mean I like it, but I don't know whether I should insure it or not."

Dom eyed her speculatively. "I can take a quick look, if you want. But I wouldn't be able to give you an accurate appraisal unless you left it. Of course, first we want to make sure it's worth spending the appraisal fee. Is that it?"

Abbie nodded and handed it over.

He carried it to a glass case in the back corner. He sighed, took a cursory look. Paused. Picked it up in both hands and held it at arm's length. Put it down and disappeared through the curtain. He came back seconds later with an easel that he set up alongside the counter and placed Beau's seascape there.

He reached in his pants pocket and brought out a jeweler's loop. Scanned the painting, resting on the lower-right corner where Beau had left his signature.

When he stood up and looked at Abbie, he was frowning.

Abbie's heart sank.

"Where did you say you got this?"

"In an attic."

"The Crispin attic?"

"Yes. And they know I was bringing it in for an appraisal. Marnie drove me here."

"I see." He leaned back over the painting, scrutinizing the signature once again. Then he stood up. "At the risk of sounding like the *Antiques Roadshow*, I'm pretty sure I've seen this artist before. And I'm also pretty sure one of his paintings recently went at auction for several thousand dollars. Caused quite a stir. No provenance and yet . . ."

"Several thousand—wow."

"I don't suppose you found any others?"

"Well, actually . . ." Abbie wound down; she'd seen the glint of anticipation in Dom's eye. She didn't want Beau taken advantage of. "Yes, there are some."

He caught himself and now he became polite and slightly disinterested, though Abbie knew people and she could feel the hum of excitement beneath his calm. She was feeling her own.

"If the others are the, um, same quality as this, I might consider showing them as an exhibit, say, at the end of the month."

"That sounds very exciting, but I'm not sure. What are your terms for representation?"

"I'm assuming the artist was a Crispin?"

"Yes. Is."

Dom's eyebrows lifted. "Is?"

"Beau painted them."

Dom's mouth literally dropped open. "Good God. But this wasn't painted recently. Has he been storing these in the attic?"

"Evidently."

"Do you think he would let me see the others?"

Abbie deliberated. "I don't know. I had to convince him to let me bring this for an appraisal. I'll talk to him."

Dom's eyebrows lowered until he was glowering at Abbie. "What's your interest in Beau's paintings?"

"Mine? I just think he should have a chance to show them. But he's very sensitive about the paintings and, uh . . ."

"Let me guess. Miss Millie thinks it's low class."

"Well . . ."

"You don't have to beat around the bush. I've known that family for years."

"I'll have to talk to Beau before we reach any agreement."

"Of course. Why don't you leave the painting here for a day or so in order for me to get a couple of additional opinions. I'll give you a receipt."

Marnie had said he was reputable, and though Abbie wasn't sure how these things usually worked, she knew she should take the chance. "I guess that would be okay."

Dom smiled slightly. "Then if things go as I expect, I'll have a gallery agreement drawn up. You might want to ask Leslie Tuttle to advise you. She's a local real estate lawyer, but she'll be able to broker a deal that benefits both parties."

It was all moving too fast. "I'll ask."

He retired to the back for an appraisal agreement, struck through appraisal fee and wrote complimentary, they both signed and Abbie was back on the street empty-handed.

She walked to the carousel trying to quell her excitement. A painting that might possibly be Beau's had sold for thousands. Dom was willing to show the rest. This might, just might, make them enough money to pay their taxes each year, maybe even have a little left over for themselves.

She quickened her pace, anxious to tell Beau. Now if he would only agree to letting them go.

Abbie knocked, but she got no answer. She pulled the door open and saw Beau and Cab bent over the workbench with their heads together. They were so intent that they didn't even hear her come into the carousel. She stood watching them for a moment, dark head against white. They could be two boys having just discovered something fascinating—a dead frog or a buried marble . . . or the key to restoring a carousel.

Cab finally looked up. His face was bright, eager. "Have you seen this?" he asked.

Abbie nodded and came to stand beside them. She smiled at Beau whose hands rested, quiet, on the table. She looked from him to the wooden miniature, even more beautiful in the bright work lights of the carousel building.

"What did he say, Abbie?" Beau looked eager and cautious, a mixture of vitality that she hadn't seen before.

"He said . . ." She broke into a grin. "He said he wants to see them all if you will let him. He kept the seascape so he can get an official appraisal. And that if the others are the same quality, which they are, he might be interested in giving them a show at his gallery." She stopped for breath. She didn't want to get his hopes up, but she had to ask.

"He said he thought a painting by the same artist had sold at auction for several thousand dollars. Could it have been one of yours? You did say that you had sold a painting years ago."

"I did sell one. Several thousand?"

"Yes, but Dom has to have it appraised."

"If he can sell it, we could pay the taxes." Beau couldn't seem to take it all in.

He could pay more than back taxes. "Let's not get too carried away until we hear from Dom. He said it would take a few days. But if it does sell, he'd like to see the others."

"He wants to see them all?"

"If you'll let him. And if he does think he can sell them, you could start painting again. You could be a working artist."

She knew the minute the words left her mouth that she'd said the wrong thing. Beau's fingers twitched. He reached for his pocket, fumbled the piece of wood out.

"Only if you want to. You don't have to do any of this. I can tell Dom you've changed your mind. I can get the painting back."

Beau licked his lips, glanced at Cab, and pushed himself off the stool. "You tell Dom to come up to the house. If you two will excuse me for a few minutes, I think I'll go talk to Silas."

He shuffled out the door, moving no faster than he did any other day.

Abbie sank onto the stool he had vacated. "I hope I haven't butted in where I shouldn't. What if it all turns out to be nothing?"

Cab shrugged. "Then life goes back to normal. They'll end up having to sell Crispin House, and nature will take its course."

"Thanks, you're making me feel so much better."

"But I have a feeling things are going to turn out fine for them. And for me. Can you believe he had this the whole time?"

"He didn't. I think he's been making it since you decided to restore the carousel. That's what he's been working on. But there's so much more, Cab. Shelves and shelves of figures, tiny ones, big ones, he has whole towns of little people and buildings. And the paintings.

"To my untrained eye, they're beautiful. One especially—" She stopped as the image of the young nude came to her mind. "They're a treasure trove."

"What's a treasure trove?" Sarah bustled into the workshop. "Whoa. What's that?"

"Beau made a copy of the carousel," Cab said.

"Huh, how about that?" She looked more closely, then looked at Abbie. "What's the matter with you? Don't tell me you're sick 'cause three mothers already stopped me on the street to say they're coming to get their picture made today." Sarah frowned at her. "Abbie?"

"I'm not sick; I'll be there," Abbie said. She'd been thinking about the painting of the young girl when Sarah walked in. It was the same face, the same swaying walk, but it must have been painted over sixty years before. Ervina? Was that what the fight with Beau's father had really been about?

Abbie let out her breath. "I'm fine. Just thinking."

"Hopefully about what you're going to do with those mothers this afternoon. Gotta run." She ran.

"So this means you can get the carousel finished," Abbie said, still a little befuddled from Sarah's likeness to the painting.

"Yes. It's amazing. We can start replacing the animals next week as soon as the exterior painting is done. And with the paintings out in the world, it's a pretty good day."

He slipped off the stool, grabbed her by both arms, and kissed her. For a second she just stood rooted to the floor. Then she gave in, and the kiss turned slow. They fell into a timeless moment until simultaneously they stepped away. Breathing hard.

"Don't run," Cab said.

"No."

"That was meant to be a celebratory hug."

Abbie nodded; she couldn't seem to speak. She knew how she felt, but she didn't know what she should feel. And she wanted to run; it was so much easier than having to face the fact that she wanted that kiss and she wanted more.

"Now what do we do?" Cab asked.

Abbie shrugged. "I think—" She didn't get a chance to finish what she was thinking, because Cab took her in his arms and kissed her again.

When Beau came back a half hour later, Cab was still feeling a kind of exuberance that he wasn't sure came from the miniature carousel or from kissing Abbie. He was afraid he looked like a starstruck simpleton, but Beau didn't seem to notice, just went straight back to work.

Even though Beau seemed as calm as ever on the outside, Cab could sense a different energy about him. An excitement. Both of their good moods were brought about by one girl, as skittish as ever, except for a few minutes that afternoon she'd let down her guard. Only a few minutes, a couple of kisses, but it had Cab thinking down the road. Something he didn't do much these days except when it came to the carousel.

He knew better than to put too much importance on the fact that he'd surprised himself and Abbie as well, and she didn't bolt. And neither had he. Could they both be ready for something more?

Then he thought about the Crispins and decided anything more than a few dinner dates would be out of the question. That was the downside of small towns, one of the few, but a major one.

He shook his head to clear it. He was steamrolling right along, and he wasn't even sure if she was really interested in more. Maybe he was just an exploratory experiment.

Best to leave it for now. He'd have his hands full and his time scheduled until he got the carousel up and running. For the first time in weeks he thought he just might have a chance to get it opened by the beginning of the summer season.

He moved the miniature over by the computer screens so he could begin making a schematic. As soon as that was done, he and Beau had decided they would ask Bethanne to display it at the hotel with a short story of the carousel and the opening dates.

He should have thought to ask Abbie if she would be interested in bringing the kids to see Beau's miniature, but he wasn't sure if Beau was ready to share, and he suspected he wasn't either.

He ran a finger over the tiny horse that was Midnight Lady. Beau had captured her perfectly in his four-inch carving. He'd

captured them all. He was more than a craftsman. He was an
artist, and if his paintings were anywhere as good as this, he
should be able to make some money from them. And at last
glean a little fame and appreciation.

Cab smiled. He just couldn't see Beau basking in the lime-
light of a gallery show, but that was probably because he'd only
really known Beau the last year. When he was a kid, he just
accepted Beau, with his block of wood, as a man who was kind
to children, but a man unto himself.

Cab tried to imagine him as young and dreaming of becoming a painter. It wasn't easy. But he could imagine old Beau
Crispin Senior putting an end to that dream and shipping him
off to a military academy. It was no secret that even though the
old man was generous toward the town, he had a mean streak
when it came to his children.

Ned had once told him that right before Beau had left for the
merchant marines, he'd come to his house, bloody and beaten.

"I think I killed my father," he said before he passed out in
Ned's kitchen.

But Beau hadn't killed him, just fought back when old Beau
had threatened to smash his hands. All over some portrait no
one had ever seen. Cab wondered if it was among the ones
hidden in the Crispin House attic. And whether it would finally be displayed.

Chapter 24

JuJu Jenny's grandmother, Momo, arrived at three o'clock for her interview.

"She's been pesterin' me and pesterin' me to come down here and tell y'all about that old carousel. So here I am."

"Thanks for coming." Abbie explained a little about the documentary and showed her to the interview area where she'd set up the tripod in front of a straight-backed chair.

Momo sat down on the edge of the seat, clearly nervous. "What'chu want me to do?" she asked.

"Just tell us what you remember about the old Stargazey carousel. But first let us get a test and a sound check. Okay, crew, are we ready?"

Kyle, with Jerome's help, adjusted the light for Momo's diminutive size. Jenny stood at Abbie's side with her questions written in large letters. Dani stood on a chair behind the camera.

Kyle moved away, and Abbie lifted her hand. "In three, in two, in one." She dropped her hand, Dani pressed record like they had been practicing. Abbie nudged Jenny.

"Momo, what'chu 'member about that merry-go-round?"

Momo straightened her skirt with both hands.

Abbie leaned over to Jenny and prompted. "First ask her her name and who she is."

"She's my grandma."

Momo shook her head. "My name's Momo. And I'm Jenny's grandma. Her mama was too little to remember that carousel, but I do. It was a mighty fine carousel. Mr. Ned always gave the local boys and girls a ride. Afore that it was owned by a Mr. Clayton. In those days nobody round here could afford to ride that carousel. Just the summer folks. Only cost about a nickel, but none a us had a nickel.

"But then Mr. Ned bought it and gave everybody a ride. All's you had to do was bring him a piece of garbage."

"Garbage?" Abbie asked.

"Yes'm. Like Coke bottles and candy wrappers and such. Mister Ned just took whatever we had, didn't make no matter to him. He'd just take it and toss it in this big old barrel, then let'chu go up and choose your animal. That was a fine thing to do on a summer's night. Mighty fine."

Abbie nudged Jenny and pointed to the next question.

"What was your favorite thing to ride?"

"Oh, I liked them all, but the ones that went up and down were the best. I was little then myself, but the older kids would sit in the Neptune chariot or one of the other seats with their sweethearts.

"And now young Mister Cabot's gonna bring it all back like it was."

Abbie thanked her and waited for Kyle's mother to take her place and for Kyle, and the twins, to go through the routine of setting up the shot.

"The carousel wasn't the only thing to do on a Friday night," Kyle's mother said into the camera. "But it sure was the most fun. The lights and the music just made you feel all fizzy inside. And if you didn't have your nickel, Mr. Ned wouldn't turn you away.

"Sometimes, he'd just give you the loan of the nickel. He didn't expect you to pay him back. Not in money 'cause none of us had much. We'd just pass that same old nickel back and forth all summer long. And our mamas would make him jam and corn bread and fried okra and all sorts of things 'cause he was so nice to us."

"What else was there to do on the boardwalk?" Kyle asked.

"Oh, there was an arcade, where you could throw things for prizes and guess the number of marbles in this big old bowl. And a machine that you could move around this claw thing and snag yourself a prize. And dancin' at the end of the pier, and car'mel corn. A guy with one leg shot off in the war sold cotton candy. And another one sold foot-long hot dogs out of a cart.

"And across the street there were shops with souvenirs. This building right here was a store that sold local crafts and such. But they all cost money. So we mostly hung out at the carousel."

Next up was Pauli's grandfather. "Yessiree," he said. "I proposed to your grandma on that carousel. It was in the Neptune car. Ya see, his tail sorta came over you so nobody could see. I thought that would be real romantic. Mr. Ned said he'd make sure nobody else got to it before I did." He winked. "Neptune was mighty popular with the young folks.

"Miss Sally Gentry she was in those days. And I knelt down right there beside the seat and asked her to be my wife. We been married goin' on fifty years now. I used to tell everybody if they wanted to ensure themselves a long, happy marriage, propose under Neptune's tail.

"We sure were sad when Ned closed it down for the last time. Glad it's coming back. It belongs down here."

An hour later, Abbie transferred the last of the interviews to her computer and closed up for the night. All the kids were gone. Several more family members had added their names to the list to be interviewed. There was a good bit of ambient noise on the footage, because they had no soundproof place to use for filming, but it gave the filming a sense of energy, like something exciting was going on just out of frame.

She added stills of the four interviewees to the pictures that were already posted to the "board thing."

She looked out the window at the carousel. All the lights were blazing. Cab and Beau were still working. They'd be working late for the next few weeks in order to finish in time for the opening. This might be a perfect time to take some of her own footage for a publicity trailer without the children underfoot. Besides, she wasn't really looking forward to facing Millie after that scene earlier.

She checked the camera battery and headed for the carousel, where she met Silas, Hadley, and two other men coming out the door.

They nodded. Silas stopped for a second. "They still in there. Working like they were possessed. We've finished for tonight." He tipped his head and joined the others as they made their way across the darkening street.

She stepped inside. Cab was at the workbench. He looked up, stood, started to cross to meet her.

She felt a little flushed. She hadn't seen him since that unexpected kiss, and the repeat performance. She was suddenly embarrassed to face him, and just a little giddy at being near him.

"Hi," he said.

"Looks like things are really coming together," she said, looking around instead of at him.

"Yeah. We might just make it. The storm windows are in. The painters are coming tomorrow, the exterior should be finished by next week." He took a deep breath. "And then we replace the animals."

"I can't wait," she said. "Everybody is really excited. We have a long list of people wanting to be interviewed."

He nodded.

"I know you're busy, but I do need to get some footage of you and Beau working, if that's okay. I'll take some for the carousel documentary, and then I can take some that you can use for advertisement. Free of charge as a thank-you."

"That would be great. I've been sending out some Facebook stuff, took a few stills." He heaved a sigh. "I really didn't want to have to do all that myself. Maybe I can hire someone down the road."

"So go back to work and I'll just roam around. I'll try not to bother you too much."

Light flickered in his eyes as he looked at her. "You can bother me anytime you want. I think I made that clear."

She laughed. "I'll keep you to that," she said purposely misunderstanding his meaning.

She set up some handheld shots, filming different aspects of the carousel from various angles. She moved in behind Cabot and zoomed in on the miniature carousel that sat on a block of wood on the workbench. He glanced up and smiled at her; she concentrated on the viewfinder and holding the camera steady. She moved away, and she felt Cab's eyes follow her as she moved to her next shot. It was an effort to concentrate on her work.

She didn't like how her body was betraying her. Her mind might not like it, but the rest of her . . . She was surprised and a little excited that she could actually feel that way again. And she felt the ties that held her to the past loosen just a bit more.

She went into the workroom, panned across the finished panels and the partially restored animals. Moved in to capture details. She hit her stride, entered that place where the work practically created itself—and was surprised when the sound of her own name rang as if from a deep well. She pulled herself away from her subject matter to see Beau standing next to her.

"We're closing up. Cabot and I think you've done enough work for one day."

She laughed and rolled stiff shoulders. "Is that a polite way of telling me to get lost?"

"No. You've been working at the center all day and now here. Time for you to take some time for yourself. Now let's go get Cabot before he gets involved in something else."

Cab was waiting for them by the front door. Abbie and Beau waited while he locked up, and then they walked across the tarmac together.

Beau stopped them. "I told Silas I'd meet him over at Hadley's, if you wouldn't mind walking Abbie home."

"I can walk—"

"I don't mind."

"Then I'll say good night." Beau ambled away.

"You really don't—"

"I'd like to. Besides, Beau won't let you walk alone and I don't think he's ready to go home and have to deal with Millie. I heard there was a dustup this morning over the miniature and painting."

"I can't say that I'm looking forward to it either. I just don't understand why she was so upset. Cab, they're brilliant. And they've been hidden away for decades. Why?"

"There's no understanding some things, and this may be one of them. Families are full of secrets and animosities that no one ever learns."

Abbie looked at him. Were they? It always seemed to Abbie that her family was too open about what they were feeling.

She and Cab walked down the road without speaking. It was a comfortable silence, which neither seemed eager to interrupt. They were halfway through the arbor of trees before Cab asked, "So when do you think you'll finish the documentary?"

"Hopefully for the opening of the carousel. I was thinking of having a guest viewing the day before, though the number of people the center can hold is prohibitive. Once the carousel opens, we could run a continuous loop, maybe at the inn or the art gallery."

"Then what?"

She looked up at him. "I haven't really thought. I may enter it into a few contests. There are organizations that accept student films."

"I meant with you. What's next for you?"

She looked into the darkness between the trees. Shrugged. "I haven't decided yet." She hadn't even thought about what she would do after she left Stargazey Point. She only knew that she wouldn't go back to being the weathergirl.

They fell silent again, and Abbie became very conscious of the space between them. What had begun as a calculated safe distance began to change, seemed to vibrate with energy, drawing them closer. Which was ridiculous. She was just feeling their mutual attraction.

She glanced at Cab to see if he was feeling the same pull. From the corner of her eye she saw a shadow move silently through the trees.

"Did you see that?"

"What?"

"Something or someone in the trees. I think they were watching us."

"Probably just a trick of the light." But he slipped his arm around her shoulders and pulled her close, and in another minute they stepped into the clearing before Crispin House.

Cab stayed only long enough for Marnie to answer the door.

Abbie watched from the window until he crossed the clearing and started down the drive, watched until he melted into the shadows of the arbor and disappeared from her view.

When she turned, Marnie was watching her. "I saved you a plate; it's in the kitchen. And don't worry, the coast is clear. Millie has taken to her room . . . again."

"I'm sorry if I've caused a rift between you and Millie and Beau. It just seemed like such a waste to leave Beau's paintings hidden away. And I didn't coerce him into agreeing to show one to Dom."

Marnie poured out two glasses of wine she kept in the mudroom. "You're right. It is a waste. I had no idea the paintings were there. And you didn't cause a rift. Whatever the big bugaboo is, it's between Beau and our father. Millie adores Beau, ordinarily. She wouldn't have reacted that way if Daddy hadn't planted it in her mind."

"But that had to be decades ago."

"For most of us. Not for Millie. Now don't give it another thought; she always does this, whenever she's upset or doesn't get her way, or if things are happening that frighten her or that she doesn't understand.

"You look dead tired. Go to bed. I'll worry about the dishes. And Millie."

Abbie trudged up the stairs wondering how long it would take for Millie to come out of the sulks this time. Or if Abbie's actions had pushed them into a permanent family rift. Whatever had happened all those years ago—it had to be fifty or more—it wasn't over yet. And she realized as she climbed into bed that she'd been watching it play out day after day after night since the first day she arrived at Crispin House.

She fell asleep almost as soon as she climbed into bed. And she dreamed not of Werner, or Cab, but of Millie and Marnie as young women, dancing beneath the stars.

A crew of painters were already at work when Abbie passed the carousel the next day. She had to consciously make herself keep walking. Her destination was the ramshackle community center, not Cab Reynolds or his carousel. Not today anyway.

She spent the morning leaning over her laptop, scanning the Internet, and was still there when the kids arrived, bringing several parents, some of whom weren't signed up for an interview. Word had traveled quickly about the carousel project. They seemed more interested in cooperating with carousel interviews than they had been with the family histories. Abbie wondered if Ervina had anything to do with that.

The first interviewee was an old man who had known Ned Reynolds personally. "Me and Ned used to come down to the carousel when we was boys. Never had a nickel. Hell, nobody much had a nickel in those days. We'd just go down and lie on the grass and watch them horses go round and round. We could stay there for hours watchin' the summer people bring their chil'run to ride. Ned said someday he was gonna make some money and buy that carousel and he wouldn't never turn nobody away." He slapped his bony knee. "And damn if he didn't do it.

"He ran that carousel every day, even in the winter. 'Course times were better then. People came here all year-round, even for Christmas. Ned would dress up those animals in red ribbons, put that cotton snow all over the center drum, and play carols. One year he got a touch of bronchitis so I went down to spell him. Don't know how he did it day after day. Nearly drove me crazy listening to that music all day long. If Ned hadn't gotten better fast, I mighta had to rip that music right clear out of the player machine."

"What you saying, Micah Jones?" A plump woman in a purple running suit hurried into the frame before Abbie could stop her.

She turned to the camera and said, "You keep that thing runnin', Dani. That music saved our bacon back in '84. Hell of a year, what with the hurricane sweeping half the town away.

"And the economy going down the drain. Folks were hurtin' I don't mind tellin' you. One night in the middle of the coldest night I can remember—it was a couple days after Christmas, I think—carousel music comes blaring out of the dark. It keeps playing and playing. Lordy, we were afraid it was judgment day.

"So my man gets up and gets dressed to go see what's up. He comes back a few minutes later. 'Get up,' he says. 'Get the kids up.' I'm scared outta my wits but I do and we all go down to the boardwalk and there's the carousel all lit up and there's Ned in a Santa hat standing in front of the old craft shop, this building right here, and the door is open and the lights are on and heat is blastin' and there's a long old table with a spread of food the likes of which you've never seen.

"We crowded inside and had us a feast. Ned said that food fell off the truck. But we knew better. Ned Reynolds never stole a thing in his life. So it's the least we can do to help young Cabot get the carousel up and running again. Maybe it'll bring prosperity back."

"That's right, Ivy Lee. You tell it like it is," came a voice behind Abbie.

"Amen," said another. Then another "Amen" and another. Several women had crowded into the doorway and stopped to hear Ivy's story.

"Those were good days."

"Gone forever," someone said.

"Aw, they weren't so good."

"Hell of a lot better than now. Everybody had their own houses. There was work to be had on the boardwalk, and the hotels and businesses out on the highway."

"And the fishin' was good, too. Not like now with so many rules you don't know if you're comin' or goin'." Micah Jones shook his head slowly.

"Amen to that," said Ivy Lee and wandered off toward the kitchen, followed by the other women.

Abbie took the kids into the media room to work on the storyboard. There was some fighting over whose relative went first on the board thing. Even after Abbie explained how things would move around as they developed their story, there was still some grumbling. So she settled them in front of her laptop and showed them what she'd found and edited just that morning. Several minutes of vacation clips people had posted to YouTube, blogs, or Google images. The pictures were grainy and the color was primitive, but it showed a busy Stargazey Point from decades before.

There was some snickering about the fashion as snippets of families darted in and out of the film, strolled along the crowded sidewalk, or posed, smiling, in front of brightly painted buildings. But as soon as the carousel appeared, running at capacity with happily waving children and a few adults, they quieted and stared, mesmerized at the footage. A few women wandered in from the kitchen to watch.

"Look, that's the center in the background."

"Where?"

Abbie rewound and slowed the tape to single frame.

"Would you look at that. That's from when we used to have the co-op here."

"You had a co-op?" Abbie asked.

"Sure did and a farmers' market and all sorts of things going on all year-round."

"We want to see more pictures of the carousel," said Pauli.

Abbie restarted the video. Everyone, including her, leaned a little closer to see.

When the tape had been watched through the second time, the women reluctantly gathered up their children and headed en masse out the front door. Abbie straightened up the media room, thinking about the past—Stargazey's past and hers.

She packed up her laptop and camera and locked the rest of the equipment in the closet. She wasn't taking any chances of someone, namely Eddie Price, ransacking the place again. She checked all the windows and the back door, then doused the lights and left. She was surprised to find Momo, Ivy Lee, and another woman standing in the parking lot. Momo was pointing at Hadley's or maybe one of the abandoned buildings that lined that part of the street. They must still be reminiscing, while their children climbed over the rotten pier.

They nodded as Abbie passed them, said good night, and went back to whatever their conversation was about. The painters had knocked off work for the day. In the light of the low-lying sun, the carousel fairly glowed with paint and expectation.

She didn't stop to see if Beau wanted to walk home. She knew they were planning to work late. She just kept walking, feeling a little lonely and not quite sure what she should do about it.

Chapter 25

Abbie awoke to thunder. The sheer drapes billowed through the open French doors of her bedroom. Raindrops drummed and splashed on the veranda floor. She slid out of bed and hurried to close the doors, shivering as her feet hit the cold floor.

The temperature had been climbing steadily as the month wore on. They'd even started leaving the center's doors and windows open to capture whatever cross breeze they could. But today they seemed to be cast back into winter.

She stood looking out at the rain slashing at a sharp angle and creating waves across the porch floorbcards. In the distance the sea swelled dark and gray. She'd gotten used to the afternoon rains that darkened the skies, dumped buckets of rain, and moved on within a matter of minutes. But today it looked like they were in for the long haul.

Which meant the center's roof would leak like crazy.

She thought of the pails always set strategically beneath known leaks as if they were permanent pieces of furniture. There was one in the media room, but for the life of her she couldn't remember seeing it there the day before. She vaguely remembered moving it aside to make room for working on the storyboard. But she didn't remember putting it back.

She quickly made her bed, showered and dressed in a matter of minutes, and went downstairs. She hurriedly drank coffee, while Marnie gathered up a slicker and an umbrella for her. Then she was out the front door and splashing through puddles that had collected in the drive.

She was running by the time she reached the parking lot. Light from the carousel shone hazily through the rain, but the center was still dark. She jogged up the steps, searching for the keys Sarah had given her. The door was partially opened.

Sarah must have had the same idea. Abbie deposited the umbrella and slicker against the porch wall and went inside to help.

"Sarah?" she called into the gloom.

A figure appeared from the hall. Large but unrecognizable in the shadows. Abbie stiffened. Had the town let the twins' uncle out of jail already? Her mind flew to her equipment.

"Damn you!" she yelled and ran. She'd have to get by him to see what damage he might have done. Instinct told her to run the other way, but pure anger drove her on. If he had destroyed those children's hard work, she wouldn't be responsible for what she did to him.

"You son of a bitch," she spit at him as she tried to pass.

"What?" He grabbed her and stopped her dead. "What the hell did I do now?"

"Cab?" She whooshed out a breath. "Thank God. I thought you were Eddie Price."

"And you were going to take him out all by yourself?"

"If he had touched that equipment or any of the interviews, I would have."

He seemed to be pulling her closer. Her smart self told her to ease away, but the rest of her just wanted a safe place to land.

"Do not," he said, holding her close, "do anything dangerous. This isn't the jungle or some desolate spot where you have to depend on yourself for survival. You have friends here. You have me, whether you want me or not."

"I—"

"Whether you want me or not."

There was no question as to his meaning, and a thrill of excitement and anxiety helixed up her spine. She tried to look up at him, but he held her closer so that she couldn't see his face. But she could feel his heart beating a rapid tattoo, and her own heart beating a betraying message back to his.

They could have stayed that way forever as far as she was concerned. It felt good, safe, seductive. Then a clap of thunder reminded her of why she was here.

"The leaks."

"Already taken care of," he said, refusing to let her budge.

"The media room."

He laughed. "Already done."

"There's a lot of equipment in there and hours of hard work. The kids would be devastated if something happened to the video."

"Under plastic just in case I missed something. We're used to this weather. We come prepared."

"I—"

"Have run out of excuses. And I know what you're thinking. It's crazy and probably stupid, but just give it a chance, okay?" He gradually let her go then put her back on her feet. "But don't think yourself out of it."

She shook her head, not sure whether she was saying no or telling him that she wouldn't talk herself out of what obviously they both wanted.

"I have to get back to work." He gave her a quick kiss on the forehead and left her standing there.

Abbie watched him go, already starting to think herself out

of getting involved. Of even having a summer romance. It was too soon. And what if it turned out to be a mistake? Every time they met it would be embarrassing and awkward. So awkward that she'd have to leave before she was ready.

And how many excuses could she throw in her way? She was ready to move on. The truth of the matter was even though she would always love Werner, she wanted to love someone living.

Love? Holy crap. She barely knew the man. She quickly checked the media room. The pails were set and everything was covered in plastic, just like he said. She stopped at the door, made one last sweep, then went back outside and put on her rain slicker.

Two minutes later she was depositing her umbrella in the inn's umbrella stand.

Bethanne was sitting at the registration desk, her chin resting in her hand, looking into space.

"Hey," Abbie said. "Want some company?"

"Sure. Come on back to the office. I just made some tea."

The office was a small room just large enough for a kneehole desk and several file cabinets, and though utilitarian, it was decorated in the same colors as the rest of the inn. At the back was a double glass door that led out to a narrow sunporch.

Bethanne poured the tea, and they went out to sit at a delicate white tea table.

"This is lovely," Abbie said, watching the rivulets run down the glass.

"It is," Bethanne said and sighed. "I serve breakfast out here in spring and summer."

Abbie sat down across from her and tried to read her expression. Was she missing her husband? It was the kind of weather to bring out the sadness. "You okay?"

"Me? Oh, yeah. Well, not great. The Hendersons' daughter, Sabrina, is getting married next spring and they're looking for a place to have the wedding and reception. Sabrina and I are pretty good friends and she wanted her wedding to launch Weddings by the Sea, but there's no venue in Stargazey Point big enough, not one with any kind of ambience." She sighed again. "That will be the second big wedding I've lost because I can't accommodate the guest list."

Abbie thought about Crispin House and Bethanne's reaction to the gazebo. It would be a perfect venue for a spring wedding. If it were restored. If the Crispins could be convinced to open their house to the public. Abbie just didn't see Millie ever allowing it.

"So what brings you here this early in the morning?"

Abbie hesitated then thought, *What the hell.* "I need some advice, sort of."

"From me? Sure, if I can help."

Okay, here she was, now how did she start? How could she phrase this without appearing nosy, not to mention rude. "You've been alone for a while now, right?"

"Three years and two months, and if I stop and think, I can tell you how many days, but I try not to think."

"Have you . . . have you seen anyone since then?"

Bethanne frowned. "You mean a therapist?"

"No," Abbie said quickly. "That's not what I meant. I mean like a man, a date, that kind of seeing." *A date? Jeez.* She sounded like a teenager.

"You mean have I been with a man since Jim died?"

"Uh, yeah. It's none of my business and you don't have to tell me. It's just—"

Bethanne tilted her head, her frown turned to speculation, then to a slight smile. "Have you and Cab . . . ?"

"No."

"But you're thinking about it. "

Abbie's face heated. She was bumbling around like a teenager about to lose her virginity. And in a way she was. She'd had plenty of experience before Werner. But after meeting him, she had never thought about life without him. Now he was gone, and everything was new and frightening and confusing. "I don't know."

Bethanne leaned toward her. "It's okay. It's hard being lonely all the time. And I hope when, if, I meet someone, I'll be ready to start over again. Or start from here anyway. So my guess is when it feels right, it'll happen."

Abbie groaned. "I was hoping for a more definitive answer. Don't tell anyone we had this conversation. I'm not taking a poll; I just needed to talk to someone who might understand."

Bethanne smiled suddenly. "Stargazey is a small town. We've all been wondering how long it would take you two to get together. Cab is a romantic at heart. He's gaga over you. And you seem to be the only one in town who hasn't noticed."

"Somehow that doesn't make things any easier."

"Well, if you really want advice, I'd say stop fighting it and let nature take its course."

Abbie returned to the center, heedless of the rain, and just as confused as she had been before talking to Bethanne. She didn't know if she trusted nature to do the right thing. And now she was embarrassed that she and Cab had been the object of speculation. Small-town curiosity. It was something she'd have to get used to if she stayed.

If she stayed? When had a vacation, a change of scene, a chance to regroup become a possible future?

I kinda propositioned her," Cab told Beau as they sat on the carousel platform, drinking their Tackle Shack coffees.

Beau shook his head. "Seems to me you went from zero to sixty pretty fast."

"Tell me about it. I also maybe told her I was available and willing even if she wasn't."

"What did she say?"

"Nothing. I might have cut her off before she could tell me to go to hell."

"And then?"

"I told her to think about it, said I had to get back to work, and left."

"Lord, son. Never give a woman time to think. She'll just make it more complicated than it really is. I thought you had better sense than that."

Cab studied the cardboard cup. "I used to. I don't know why this is not working out."

"None of my business, but you're not trifing with her, are you?"

Cab stood up. "No. I'm not doing anything with her." He sat back down just as abruptly. "I'm not usually so inept."

"'Spect you're just out of practice. If you want my advice, if she's the one, don't let her get away."

"How do I know? I thought Bailey was the one. And, boy, did I get that wrong."

"From everything you've said about that young lady, I think she was a just-settle-for."

Cab snorted. "Bailey? She was a prize."

"Do you wish you hadn't given her up?"

"No, but I knew where things were with her. Shoes, shopping, society, and me. In that order."

"Don't sound too appetizing."

"It wasn't."

"Then what's worrying you about Abbie?"

"I don't know. I keep getting mixed signals from her. She keeps me off balance. I can't seem to make it past that protective barrier. She's skittish and unpredictable and energetic and passionate."

"And independent."

"And," Cab said dejectedly, "she's still mourning Werner."

"Can't compete with a dead man."

Cab cut Beau a look. "Are you saying I should back off?"

Beau slapped his knee. "Sometimes, you sure are slow on the uptake. I'm saying, you're not dead, and neither is she. Hell, if I was even twenty years younger, I'd give you a run for your money." He chuckled. "One thing you gotta say about that girl. You'd never get bored."

"Did you ever meet the one?"

Beau lifted both bushy eyebrows. "Met a lot of ones. But not 'the one.' *The* one got away."

Cab cocked his head, waiting for more.

"It was a long time ago. I was real young. My family did not approve. My daddy . . . Well, I 'spect you've heard about our daddy. Son of a bitch. Gave me hell. Sent me off to join the navy. I ran off and joined the merchant marines just to be ornery. Best move I ever made. It was a good life. Hard work and a lot of good times."

"Did you ever regret leaving?"

"What's the use in that? When I was here, I got all the grief and none of the joy. I've had my share of fun since then. But if I had it to do again . . . I don't know.

"Don't let that happen to you, son. If you're serious, let her know it. Then you'll know if she returns your feelings and you can stop worrying about it." He pushed to his feet. "Now let's get this molding finished so we can start reloading the menagerie."

Cab tossed his cup in the trash can. Easy for Beau to say. Fortunately he wasn't twenty years younger, because Cab had a feeling in a contest for Abbie, Beau would win.

He didn't have a clue as to what to do next. He didn't have time to wine and dine the woman. He was working overtime at the carousel. And she had her own work at the center. She'd settled into a comfort zone, one that evidently didn't include him.

He followed Beau over to the new ticket booth and positioned the yellow trim for Beau to nail.

Was she the one? He'd only known her for a few weeks, and yet it seemed like it. Even when he'd first met her and mistrusted her, he couldn't stop thinking about her. And since then she'd become a constant presence even when she wasn't around.

Infatuation? Possibly. A quick summer affair? Definitely possible. But Beau was right. How would they know it was more if they didn't take a chance?

The rain kept up for two days. Abbie thought it might keep some of the children away, but she was wrong.

Family members trekked in and out of the center. Sarah had to hang a clothesline on the porch to serve as a coatrack, and Abbie sacrificed her wastebasket to use as an umbrella stand.

"Amazing," Sarah said. "Who knew wooden horses could garner such interest."

Abbie gave her a look.

"All right. You were right. And . . . you were right. Thanks. There might even be bits of real history to be gleaned from these reminiscences."

The center began to hum with voices remembering the past. More people came in to be interviewed and by the following week, the board thing was filled to capacity.

Mothers and grandmothers and aunts who had already been interviewed came anyway and sat in the kitchen until it was time for the children to go home. They drank tea and ate homemade sweets and sometimes helped out with the kids.

The sun finally broke through the clouds just before the weekend. And with the sun came the heat.

"Yep, summer's comin' on," Ivy Lee said as she passed Abbie on her way to the kitchen. "Come on back when you get a

chance and sample some of my sweet potato biscuits." She held
up a foil-covered package. "They're mighty fine with a glass
of sweet tea."

"Thanks, I will," Abbie said. She'd been hearing laughter and some raised voices for the last half hour. She grabbed
her video cam and headed back to see what was going on.
The kitchen was more crowded than usual. There were more
women than chairs, and someone had brought a picnic bench
inside. Tea glasses and mugs, paper napkins, and plates of cakes
and cookies littered the table.

Abbie stood just outside the door, listening to the women
talk. Reminiscing about the carousel had set off other memories, and they were lamenting the loss of the co-op gift shop
that had sold many of the local crafts.

Abbie booted her camera and stepped into the kitchen. The
voices stopped, all faces turned toward the door.

"Come on in and take a load off," Momo said.

Abbie held up her camera and looked a question.

"Sure, bring that thing in, we're gettin' to be right movie
stars, ain't we, girls?" Momo moved over to make room for
Abbie. "We were just talking about the shop that used to be
here. I sold my baskets there and Ivy sold cornhusk dolls. It had
all sorts of local crafts and things."

"And don't forget the farmers' market," said a heavyset
woman, who Abbie thought must be related to Pauli.

"Rayleen, you got rocks in your head," said Ivy, as she
poured Abbie a glass of tea. "That weren't no market, just a
handful of dirt farmers settin' in the parking lot."

"Same thing," Rayleen shot back. "Met every weekend
during the spring and summer and on Wednesdays for the local
people." She grinned. "Prices were better on Wednesdays."

Everyone smiled and nodded as they all shared the joke.

"Why did you stop having the farmers' market?" Abbie asked.

"Not that many farmers left," Ivy said.

"Got golf courses instead," said someone else.

"There are some."

Ivy shrugged and handed Abbie the glass of tea. "Not that many folks to buy from them. They gone over to Georgetown and Myrtle Beach."

"What? We don't look like folks to you?" Rayleen leaned her ample chest across the table and glared at the naysayer.

"I meant summer folks."

"We got us some," Momo said. "And we all have gardens. We could be sellin' the surplus."

"You crazy, woman. I suppose you think we oughta open up the arcade and the gift shop, too?" Ivy shook her head and reached for a slice of bread filled with plump raisins.

"And why not? With the carousel coming back and most of town lookin' good, we're gonna attract tourists again."

"Not our end of town," said Rayleen.

"We did it before."

"Hannah Stevens did it before," said Ivy. "And she just displayed things from us and gave us a percentage. Hannah's gone back to New Jersey. Might be dead for all we know."

Abbie panned the camera from one woman to the other.

"Well, I don't think it's a crazy idea at all," Momo said. "We've been sittin' around here for twenty years watching our property being sold off and our way of life disappearing. Heck, Sarah over there had to come all the way back from New York City to try to put us in history before we disappear altogether. And we didn't even lift a finger to help her."

The women all looked down at their plates.

"My man didn't like it." Ivy shook her head. "Anyway, his people ain't nothin' to write home about."

The woman sitting next to her patted her shoulder. "I don't even know nothin' about my family."

"Me neither. My Dermott tried to do one of those family trees. Didn't get too far."

"Heck, we got nothing to be ashamed of," Wanda, a big woman with a high soprano voice, said.

"No, we don't. Just took getting us talking to figure that out. What I want to know is why are we sitting here reminiscing about the good old days—"

"Weren't all that good, most of them."

"No," agreed Momo. "But we were all involved in our town. You saw them movies Abbie put together. Things were happening in those days. Now it seems we're just sitting back waiting for our young people to grow up and move away. I'm thinking we oughta start doing something for ourselves."

"Like what?" Ivy asked.

"Like maybe reopening the co-op and startin' up the farmers' market again. I could sell my basketry and such here instead of driving all the way to Beaufort or Charleston and sittin' out in the sun all day being a spot of local color and feelin' like a monkey in the zoo."

"And what about customers? You can make a living going to Charleston and Beaufort, but who's gonna buy your goods over here?"

"Tourists," Wanda said.

"And where are we gonna get us some of those?"

"Like I said. The beach is coming back, the carousel is reopening, and uptown is doing okay. We just need to spruce things up down this way a bit. Get us some paint and a sign 'cause people are gonna have to walk right past us to get to the beach."

"They sure do. That's a great idea, Momo. I vote we do it," Wanda said.

Ivy leaned back in her chair and rolled her eyes up to the ceiling. "Listen to you, Miz Rockefeller, you gonna buy this

old run-down building, kick out Sarah and the children, and
ren-o-vate it yourself?"

"Don't be dense, Ivy Lee. We'll use one of the other buildings. Maybe that vacant store by the post office."

"Foolishness. Besides it's too small."

"Well, what about the old arcade?" Wanda piped in.

"Too big. And anyway, we can't afford to buy no building,
even if whoever owns it would be willing to sell."

"Who does own them?" Abbie asked.

Nobody seemed to know, but everybody had something to
say. And Abbie was kept busy moving the camera from one
person to another as they argued.

"Bet we can find out from Mr. Oakley. He knows everybody's business."

"Oh, him. We're not gonna talk to him."

"We ain't gonna kiss him, just gonna ask him who owns the
boardwalk buildings."

"And he's gonna ask you if you owe him any taxes."

Murmurs shot around the table. It seemed that several of
them were sketchy about their taxes.

"I'm not gettin' near him," Ivy said and put her tea glass
down on the table in a way that said the subject was over.

"Me, neither," Wanda said. "He come around us twice last
year."

"I'm not going. That'd be like sticking your hand down a
snake hole."

Momo stood up and slapped her hands on the table. "Well, I
will. The Lord helps those who help themselves. And it's about
time we started."

Abbie and Sarah stood on the porch and watched the last of
the women and children leave the center. It was after eight, and
even so, Sarah had to force them to leave. It had been a free-

for-all for a while, but finally they settled that Momo would approach the town about renting one of the buildings at this end of town. They were still unclear as to how they were going to pay for it.

"You and Cab make some kind of team," Sarah said on a giant yawn.

"Me and Cab?" Abbie said. "Where did that come from?"

Sarah grinned at her. "Besides the fact that you two are just cute as buttons together?"

"Right," Abbie said at her driest. Cute wasn't exactly what she was feeling when it came to Cab.

"Beyond that, Cab getting the carousel back in shape gives this town a chance at a comeback, but without you pointing that out to them, they would have never realized it until it was too late for them to take advantage of it. And from the sounds of things in the kitchen tonight, I think there's going to be some changes going on pretty damn soon."

"I hope so, but I think they would have figured it out on their own. Besides, you're the one who got the center up and running, which, if you haven't noticed, is a hotbed of activity."

"I noticed. But we'd still be floundering around trying to concoct a history nobody thought they remembered until you started making this documentary about something else."

"Which I recall you pretty much strong-armed me into doing."

"And I could never get anyone to help out before they came to be interviewed. Now I practically have a staff. Whether I want it or not."

Abbie laughed. "Some of them are a bit opinionated."

"I'm hoping you're going to stick around to see it all through."

"Think I'll desert you before the opening of the carousel?"

"God, no. But I may have to desert you."

"What are you talking about?"

"I do have a job I have to get back to."

The statement caught Abbie off guard. She knew the university was pressuring Sarah to return early. Abbie would also be leaving at some point. But she wasn't ready for either. "Just when things are firing up? I thought you had until August. Who's going to take over the center?"

Sarah continued to look at her.

"No. I don't know anything about long-term organization. I do hit and run."

And wasn't that just what had left her empty before and threatened to make her even emptier now. Where did she go after this?

And how could she leave without knowing if Beau's paintings sold or if the new director of the center was nurturing and inspiring? How could she leave Marnie or Millie or Beau, the carousel or Cab, Bethanne or Penny? The children? Especially the children.

And what about Ervina? She was a walking repository of history. Someone should tell her story before she was gone.

"You turn to stone, girl?" Sarah stood looking up at her. Seeing Sarah with her hands on both hips reminded Abbie of the first day they'd met. That exaggerated drawl, and the sophisticated New Yorker blanketed beneath the country girl façade.

But today was the first time Abbie saw her as a person straddling two worlds, not willing to leave either one for good. She knew as sure as she was standing here, Sarah would be back. At least as long as Ervina was alive. And then what? Would Sarah become the witch doctor of Stargazey Point or would she leave it behind for good?

And what about Abbie? Where would she go from here?

"All right, we'll cross that bridge when we come to it."

Sarah stifled another yawn. "I don't know about you, but I'm beat. See you tomorrow."

Abbie watched for a minute and turned to go back inside. The door to the carousel opened and Cab came out.

Abbie's heart did a little skip and flutter that she was beginning to recognize.

"Got a minute?"

"Sure." She went to meet him. He pulled her inside to where Beau was waiting.

"You're not going to believe what just happened," Cab said.

"Dom Gaillard called," Beau said.

"What did he say?" Abbie's fluttery heart dropped into a churning stomach. She mentally crossed her fingers.

"He's in Charleston having my painting appraised. And someone came into the gallery, saw it, and put a retainer of five thousand dollars down." Beau sat down suddenly on the carousel platform.

"That's great." She frowned at Cab, trying to figure out if Beau was happy or panicked over the news. "So what did you tell him?"

"Huh?" Beau's eyebrows creased. "I told him to sell the damn thing."

Abbie laughed. "Beau. You didn't say it like that."

"No, he didn't," Cab said. "He and Dom talked for a bit. I tried to listen in, but Dom was talking a mile a minute."

"I told him to set a price that he thought fair. He wants to see more."

"Great," she said again, though with a little less enthusiasm. She didn't look forward to another scene when they tried to sneak the others out of the house. "What about Millie?" she asked.

Beau broke into a broad smile. "Dom's driving back tonight. He'll meet us at the house in the morning . . . after Millie leaves for church."

Chapter 26

Abbie, Marnie, and Beau watched as Millie climbed into the Oakleys' car. They stayed at the window until the car disappeared down the drive, then they let out their collective breath.

A few minutes later, a white van came up the drive and stopped in front of the house. Dominic Gaillard, dressed in khakis and a polo shirt, jumped out of the car. He was followed by Cab.

"Hope you don't mind that I brought Cab," Dom told Beau. "But if we come to an arrangement, I wanted to be ready to transport them." He looked back at the van. "She's specially equipped to insure against damage."

Beau nodded, and they all climbed two flights of steps to Beau's hideaway.

"Amazing," Dom said when Beau had unlocked the door and they'd all stepped inside. He walked slowly along the shelves and tables, bent over as he perused the wooden carvings.

Cab whistled.

Beau looked uncomfortable.

"I don't handle miniatures, but I know who would give his eyeteeth to get his hands on these." Dom glanced up at Beau without standing up. "If you're interested in selling them."

Abbie took one look at Beau's face and said, "Why don't you have a look at the paintings and talk about the figures later."

"Absolutely. That's what I came for."

Beau ambled over to the storage rack and stood facing it. For a moment Abbie thought he might change his mind. Then he resolutely pulled the first painting out of the bin and placed it on an easel that had appeared since the time she'd visited.

They all hovered close to Dom and he nodded, moved closer, stepped back. It was one of Beau's seascapes. The edge of a roof, the gazebo? On one side, two young girls in long dresses and sun hats, sitting on the sand, their skirts spread out around them.

"Oh my," Marnie said. "Oh my."

Beau pulled the next one out, held it to his chest. "I thought you might be interested in these," he told Cab. He turned it around, replaced the seascape with the head of a carousel horse, so vivid that it looked real in spite of the fanciful colored mane and the detailed body.

No one spoke as Beau stepped away from the canvas, though next to her, Cab caught his breath. Marnie covered her mouth with both hands. And Abbie watched Beau, his expression calm, but years of emotion and memories rippling just beneath.

"Good God, Beau. Are there more of these?"

Beau nodded.

"Let's see them, man."

Beau moved to the bin, Dom at his heels. He handed one out; Dom took it and handed it to Cab who leaned it against Beau's workbench. Another followed and another. When Beau at last stopped, eight carousel paintings lined the space, capturing the viewers in a magic circle.

"Would you be willing to let me show all these in the Charleston gallery? We get much more traffic there. A wealthier clientele. I'll keep a couple of the horses to put in the window of the gallery here. "What do you say?"

"All of them?" Beau asked.

"Yes," Dom said, drawing out the word. Abbie could practically see him calculating. "To coincide with the carousel opening."

"Wow," breathed Cab. "These are incredible." He turned to Beau. "Why didn't you tell me?"

"I kinda forgot about 'em till a few weeks ago. Ned kept the paintings for me all those years until I came back. Then I put them in here and just forgot. When I started carving that carousel for you, it all came back."

"That's why you remembered things so well."

"You didn't need these, son. You know what to do. You got it inside you."

Dom cleared his throat. "I hate to break up this Hallmark moment, but if you're going to let me have these, I suggest we get them in the truck before church lets out."

They all pitched in and carried the paintings downstairs until only one painting remained in the bin.

"What about that one?" Dom asked. Abbie had noticed that Beau hadn't brought out the picture of the young nude.

"Not that one," Beau said.

"Intriguing," Dom said. "But I have enough to bring out slowly over the next year or so." He glanced once more at the lone canvas and left the room.

Beau and Cab drove with him back to town to unload the paintings. And, Abbie suspected, so they wouldn't be there when Millie got home.

"Coffee?" Marnie asked.

"Absolutely," Abbie said.

They were in the kitchen when Millie returned from church.

She came straight into the kitchen and dropped her purse on the counter. Then turned and glowered at her sister. "What's this I hear about Beau and Cabot seen riding in Dom Gaillard's van this morning?"

Marnie shrugged. "Care for some coffee?"

Millie turned on Abbie, then back to Marnie. "This is her fault. Nothing's been the same since she came here."

"Bullshit."

"Millie," Abbie began.

"I don't want to hear anything from you. And after all we've done for you."

"Millie!" Marnie stood up so abruptly that she hit the table and coffee sloshed over their cups and spilled on the table. "You forget yourself. If anyone's done anything for anybody around here, it's Abbie. And you know it.

"If you must know, Dom has taken several of Beau's paintings to be sold. And I'll expect you to be glad for him."

The blood rushed from Millie's face and her lips pursed. "It's evil, evil."

"Oh good God in heaven," Marnie exclaimed. "Get a grip. You sound like some lunatic from an old movie."

Millie gasped. Abbie's mouth dropped open.

"Beau and I let you have your way in almost everything, but this has gone too far. I know it isn't your fault. Our illustrious father drove me from home and destroyed Beau's hopes of becoming a painter. I'll never forgive him for that, but mostly I'll never forgive him for what he did to you."

"He was good to me. He was a good man."

"He was an arrogant bastard. We got away from him, but he bullied you into submission while he was alive and you've never been able to escape. Fine. If that's how you want to live your life. But don't try to impose that on Beau . . . or me."

Abbie sat almost afraid to breathe. Had her actions been the
impetus that would tear this family apart?

"I—I— How can you say such things and in front of our
guest, too." Millie reeled and caught the edge of the counter.
"Abbie, don't you listen to her. Daddy was a fine upstanding citizen and he loved his family. Shame, Sister. Shame," she wailed.

"Perhaps you should go up to your room and calm yourself."

Millie turned on Abbie. "See what you've done? Everything
was fine until you came."

"Millie, go upstairs."

"No good will come of this. You mark my words. I want her
out of my house. Today. This afternoon. I won't have her stay
another day under my roof."

"Millie, it isn't your house. It's Beau's, and Abbie is his guest
and mine."

Abbie fought to find her voice. "No, Marnie, it's okay. I'll
pack and go. Millie, I'm sorry."

"Sorry, she says. I'll never forgive you. Any of you." Millie
groped for her handbag and rushed from the room.

Abbie covered her face with her hands. "Marnie, I'm sorry.
I never meant to cause such trouble."

Marnie laughed. "Hon, you just witnessed a first-class
Southern hissy fit. I didn't know the old girl had it in her."

"I should never have interfered."

"Stop it! Would you rather Beau go to his grave never
knowing that he had real talent? I didn't even know there were
paintings up there, and I doubt if Millie did. Maybe Celeste
would have discovered them and done something with them.
But more than likely, whoever buys this old dump would toss
them on the fire with the rest of the contents. You gave Beau
a chance to see his work, his passion, appreciated. Would you
take that away from him?"

"No, but—"

"Millie will get over it."

"Will she?"

"Of course. She always does. It might take her a day or two to work it around her convoluted sense of reality so that it makes sense. But, Abbie, don't despise her. It isn't her fault what she's become."

Abbie shook her head, so close to tears that she could hardly talk. "I don't. I love her, all three of you."

"That's good to know."

"But maybe I should stay at the inn from now until I leave."

"If you feel you must, but think about this. If you do, *I'll* be mad at you. And if you think Millie is dramatic, hon, I can leave her in the dust." She gathered up the coffee cups and put them in the sink. "I'm going to do a little gardening. I think you should go get yourself a real cup of coffee at Penny's, then drop by the carousel and tell the boys they've been found out."

Abbie pushed to her feet, adrenaline and shock making her knees weak. She was still shaking when she started down the drive toward town. She was tempted to look back at the house to see if Millie was watching from the window. She didn't understand what the big deal was about. And it didn't seem like Marnie did either. And as she went over all the things the siblings had said, she wasn't even sure that Millie knew what the argument between Beau and his father was really about.

It was none of her business. And to hell with it. She was glad Beau was getting a chance to show his work. He deserved that. But why did everything have to be so complicated?

Cab's phone rang. He checked caller ID and answered it. He listened for a few minutes, then hung up and looked over to where Beau was putting the finishing details on the drum.

"That was Marnie. Millie knows about the paintings; it

seems someone saw us riding in the van and told Millie about it at Flora's after church. Evidently she had a 'hissy fit,' Marnie's words, and blamed Abbie who is on her way into town."

Beau finished gilding the coronets on top of the music box, then sighed. "There's no reasoning with the woman."

"Which woman would that be," asked Cab, deadpan.

"In this case, Millie. She's gotten some strange notions over the years. Somehow she thinks everything fell apart when I left home. She was old enough then to know better. It started way before that. The old rascal drove Marnie away, drove me away, and finally drove my mother to the grave. For the life of me, I don't see how all that escaped Millie. Now she's latched on to this painting thing."

"Your argument wasn't over painting?"

"Every day of my life. But that last night before I left, it was about something else. Painting was a part of it, but not the part he hated most." He rested the paintbrush on a cloth and climbed out of the housing. "Guess I'd better go smooth things over with Abbie. Don't want the girl to feel bad. And I don't want her leaving. God knows she's the best thing that's happened to any of us in I don't know when. And that includes you, son."

God knew that was true, Cab thought as he watched Beau walk away. But she sure wasn't restful. Was always in the thick of whatever was happening, taking up the cudgels for some poor soul, whether it be the twins or Beau Crispin. Ervina had seen it right away; it took some time for the rest of them to figure it out.

He wondered if Abbie had figured it out yet. Understood how important she was to them all. And if she did, was it enough to make her stay?

Abbie looked up to see Beau ambling toward her. She dreaded seeing him and having to tell him what had happened; heat suffused her face. Today there was a spring in his step. He seemed so happy, and anger flared in her again when she thought of what Millie's reaction would do to him.

Well, she wasn't going to be the one to burst his bubble. Let the man have a little joy for a change. It was going to end soon enough. She forced a smile and went to meet him.

As soon as he reached her, he took her elbow and steered her toward the old pier.

"Heard you had some problems with Millie this morning."

Abbie stared at him. Marnie must have called him. So his energy hadn't been dampened by Millie's outburst. Unless Marnie had sugarcoated it. Then why tell him at all?

She let him lead her through the pylons and sat beside him on the concrete wall.

"Families are a strange beast," he began. "You think you can tame them, but you only fool yourself. One day you wake up and know you just have to accept them for what they are or leave them behind." He grew silent, looked out to the gentle waves.

Abbie understood what he meant, not that she'd ever been challenged by her family the way Marnie and Beau had been by theirs. But then she'd never veered from the family path. The fact that it was a very wide path made it easy. But what if she'd chosen to be a corporate lawyer or an investment banker? Her father might accept it, but her pacifist, we-are-the-world mother would throw a hissy fit to rival Millie's. The thought made her smile.

"Good," Beau said. "I was afraid Millie had upset you."

"Only because I don't want to cause dissension between the three of you. She was really upset."

Beau took her hand, patted it. "Millie is only a half-formed woman, Abbie. She's half child, dependent, needy, and, yes, selfish. Not much any of us can do about it. Just accept it and get on with life the best we can."

"That's so unfair," Abbie said; she couldn't help herself. No one should have to cater to someone so selfish.

"Maybe, but it's not worth fussin' over."

"But your paintings."

Beau smiled and squeezed her hand. "Are out there for the world to see. Thanks to you."

"But what if—"

"It's too late for what-ifs about the past. What-ifs are for the future. Me, I mostly just live in the present. Future doesn't have all that much adventure left for me."

Impulsively Abbie threw both arms around him. "You don't know that. You might become famous and have to go on an international tour."

Beau chuckled and patted her back. "Wouldn't that be something."

They sat that way for a few seconds, then Beau pulled away. "Now let's just wait and see. And no more talk about moving to the inn."

"But Millie—"

"Will forget why she's upset when she sees this." He fumbled in his breast pocket, but instead of a block of wood, he pulled out a folded check and opened it for her to see.

"Wow! Is that from Dom Gaillard already?"

"Yes. He inflated the price for the buyer in exchange for giving him first look at the rest before they go on sale. And he refused to take a commission if I agreed to let him handle the sale of the collection.

"Twelve thousand is a lot of money, for us anyway. Enough to pay off this year's taxes, with plenty left over. And, God willing, there will be more coming in."

"What will you do with it?"

"Marnie will have some for household expenses. I'll take some for a rainy day. And the rest I'll give to Millie to play with." He grinned.

"You know she's planning a big formal surprise party for your birthday."

Beau smiled beneath bright sparkling eyes. "She does every year. But this year she'll have something else to think about."

"What?"

"Cab is going to ask her to host the premiere of the Stargazey carousel video as a present."

"He is? She'll never agree, Beau. She practically threw me out of the house."

"You just place your faith in that young man and we'll see."

"I hope you're right."

"Absolutely. She'll bother you with so many ideas and plans that before it's over, you'll wish she was still mad at you."

He slapped his knee. "Now I need to get back to work, before Cabot comes looking for me. So start thinking about what you'll need for the showing. Silas has already agreed to make barbecue.

"Now let's go tell Cabot that you're staying with us and everything is fine. Though I think he'll be disappointed. He was hoping that he'd get you all to himself." He stood up and offered her his hand. "Enough time for that down the road."

Chapter 27

It was already hot when Abbie walked to the center the next morning. She'd left early to avoid any confrontation with Millie. She still didn't feel right about what had happened. But it was something the Crispins would either settle among themselves, or let slide and slip back into the way things had always been.

The sight of the newly painted carousel made her forget fights and misunderstanding and everything else except how wonderful it looked, sparkling white in the sun. The lattice was gone and removable storm windows had taken its place. A tricolored ball was perched atop the cupola, supported by a new green roof.

The painters had moved on to the community center, which she was sure was Cab's doing. The front façade was finished, and a man was painting the door the bright blue that the area favored.

"Keeps evil away and prosperity inside," Sarah said. "Wish it could do something about the heat."

"I told you I'd get us an air conditioner."

"I'm tempted, but we'd blow a fuse. Maybe we could run a power cord over to the carousel and pirate some of Cab's electricity. I bet he has plenty. Speaking of which, I heard rumors that he has some big secret exhibition opening the same week as the carousel."

Abbie grinned. "So I hear."

"I also heard he and Dom Gaillard were seen driving in Dom's van up to Crispin House."

"Yep."

"I also heard that Miss Millie threw a fit on account of it."

"She did that, too. Blamed me. Told me to leave."

"Sounds like Millie all right. Is she over it?"

"I haven't seen her since. Marnie and Beau say she'll forget all about it."

"Too bad. I'm sure Cab was looking for an excuse to have you move in with him."

"Sarah, we are so not there yet."

"Can't blame me for that." She stopped. The screen door banged, followed by footsteps. "They're already here. We should charge admission."

There was a pretty good crowd. The mothers, aunts, and grandmothers carried what looked like a bakery's worth of food back to the kitchen. Sarah rounded up the teenagers and took them to the tutoring station.

Abbie sent the rest of the kids to the media room and was about to follow them when Momo, accompanied by Kyle and Jenny, came in. Momo was dressed in a suit and two-inch heels. "Found him walking along the road to town. I told his mama I'd bring him when I brought Jenny, but I guess he couldn't wait to get here."

"You look great," Abbie told her.

"I got a meetin' I have to go to. Come on back to the kitchen for a minute."

Abbie followed her down the hall, to where the ladies were already setting up a feast.

"Would you look at Momo," Ivy said. "You got your days mixed up. Yesterday was Sunday."

"I know what day it is, Ivy Lee, because on Sunday I was in church."

"Amen."

"Amen."

"That's where I saw Mr. Robert Oakley. I told him what we had in mind, and he told me to come see him this morning. Turns out the town bought back several parcels down here to keep 'em from going piecemeal to developers. Owns the land the arcade sits on, too. They've been trying to get some interested party to set up a business. I'm on my way over there now."

"Girl, where are we gonna get the money to rent a store?"

"I'll put in my laundry money," Rayleen said.

"Rayleen, you fool. That wouldn't buy you a crayfish sandwich." Ivy looked disgusted.

"I got some savings," Momo said. "It's not much, but I figure if we can give him some good faith money, maybe I can get the board to take a percentage of the profits as payment."

"Why would they do that?"

Rayleen fisted her hands on her hips and scowled at Ivy. "Because it's better than having some sorry ass tear-down sittin' in the middle of a town that's tryin' to make itself better and get us some tourist dollars."

"Oh, hell," said Ivy. "If you can get them to go for that, I'll bring you some of my dolls to sell."

"Well, ain't you the philanthropist," Rayleen countered.

"Thank you," Momo said. "Now I gotta go or I ll be late. Wish me luck."

They all did, including Ivy who added, "She'll need it."

She was gone for nearly three hours.

We got the building!" Momo screeched as she burst into the kitchen. "I signed a lease on that place next to Hadley's."

Cheers went around the room.

Momo jingled a set of keys. "Well, what are we waiting for? Let's go see what needs to be done."

"That's right."

"Get off your butt, and let's go."

"Wait a minute. It takes more than a building to have a store, a building that needs a heck of a lot of work put into it. And then we have to get stuff to sell, then we gotta get people to sell the things, and how are we gonna do all this?" asked Ivy.

"We're gonna form us a committee," Momo said. "We're gonna call it the Stargazey Restoration Project. And you're gonna be the chairman."

"Me?"

"Yeah, you. But first . . ." Momo went to the back door, stuck her head out. "Men, when you finish up on the community center, just come on over and paint the new Stargazey co-op."

"Where the hell's that?" came the reply.

"We'll show you."

They marched out en masse. Abbie snagged a piece of gingerbread and followed them out to the porch to watch.

And that's where Sarah found her a few minutes later.

"Come on back. I gotta get some ice water." Sarah got her water and sat down, fanning herself with a paper plate.

Abbie told her about the lease for the co-op.

"Whew. I wondered what the hell was going on. You've created a monster."

"Me? Oh, no. *We*."

"Suit yourself. Damn, it's hot."

Within an hour the women were back and the center was

buzzing with noise, excitement, and more than a few mosquitoes. Ivy, now that she'd come on board, was the perfect leader, dividing the women into subcommittees and sending one group off to gather cleaning supplies, others to canvass their friends and neighbors for possible inventory, and setting the rest to help with lunch.

The twins were late and Abbie was beginning to worry about them when they appeared, dragging Ervina between them. Ervina was dressed in a long robe and wore a turban on her head.

"Ervina's ready for her inner-view," Joe said. His excitement was palpable. "You gonna sit over here. In this chair." He pulled Ervina over to the chair and turned back to Abbie. "Ervina remembers all 'bout that merry-go-round. She's gonna tell us for the doc'mentry."

"Excellent," Abbie said. "I'll get the camera."

She passed Sarah who was staring unabashedly at her great-grandmother. "Oh, Lord, has the circus come to town?" she asked under her breath.

"You watch your mouth, Miss Know-It-All. You settin' an example for these children."

"Uh-huh," Sarah said and went back to the porch where the summer school math tutorials were taking place.

"Ervina remembers the carousel," Dan said. "She telled it to us, but I didn't know how to write all the words, so she says she'll tell you for the movie."

Joe had settled Ervina in the chair, and she sat upright like an exotic, colorful bird. Or an African chieftain. The woman knew how to put on a show. But Abbie was beginning to think it wasn't just a show. Ervina had the habit of nailing things too often to be a sham.

"You have your questions for Ervina?"

"Yes'm, Jerome wrote 'em for us."

"Okay, who's going to film and who's going to ask the questions?"

"I'm gonna be the cameraman," Joe said.

" 'Cause I read better," Dani said.

"Nuh-uh," Joe said.

Abbie stepped in before things spiraled out of control, though she was glad to see them arguing rather than smacking each other in the head. Progress.

"Okay, Dani, you stand just there." She hoisted Joe onto the chair so he could run the camera. A crowd formed behind them and no one—kids, teenagers, mothers, grandmothers, aunts, Sarah—made a sound.

Ervina looked into the camera as if she'd done dozens of interviews.

Joe pressed play; Dani frowned at the paper and asked, "What chore name?"

Ervina sat even straighter. "My name is Ervina Eugenia Maxwell."

"Whose mama are you?"

Ervina pursed her lips. "I had me a son. He was killed in the war, but he left me a granddaughter. Her name was Sarah. And she had a daughter and she named her Sarah. And we had Sarahs livin' in this town ever since."

Behind Abbie, Sarah groaned and left the room.

"What'chu remember 'bout that carousel?"

"Oh, that carousel. I remember when I was a girl, the town was somethin' in those days, filled all summer with fancy people from Charleston and Columbia and even farther away. They brought their chil'run to the beach, stayed in the hotel before it burned to the ground. They'd stay all summer, some of them. That carousel music filled the air from morning to night. There'd be dancin' at the end of the pier, and if you sat out on the beach, you could hear a little bit of both.

"But if the man who ran the carousel ever caught one of us trying to sneak a ride, he'd pull us off that thing and throw us out to the ground. None of us ever had no money.

"Then Ned grew up and moved away. Never thought we'd see him again, but one day he comes drivin' into town in a big old black Mercury. He goes up to that feller, Clayton, I think his name was, and says, 'I want to buy your carousel.' We'd had us a couple a bad storms and that old man sold it to Ned that very day.

"From then on everybody could ride the carousel. Rich or poor. No matter what color. Those were good and bad days. Changing days. Then the hotel burned down, and they started buildin' these big old hotels up the way, and those big fun parks. Stargazey just got left behind." She chuckled. "And some of us got old. Ned got old. Now we got young Cab fixing it up again. We got a place for the children to come where it's safe and they can learn how to go on in this life. We gonna have us a new store."

"Praise the Lord," someone said.

"Amen."

Ervina held up her hand, a benediction, and looked at Dani. "We take care of our own. We take care of each other. We welcome strangers." She looked at Abbie. "If they don't wanna build no golf course."

They were surrounded by laughter, which somehow made Abbie want to cry.

"Now I got me two new children and that's all I got to say." Dani threw her arms around Ervina before she could get up from the chair. Joe slid off the chair and hurled himself at her.

Abbie took over the camera. This was a scene not to be missed.

"And we never leaving Momma Ervina," Dani said.

"And if uncle or the services try to take us, Jerome gonna shoot him."

Abbie stopped the camera.

"Lord, child," Ervina said, placing him on her knee where he could see her face. "Remember this. Nobody is gonna do no shootin'."

"Uh-huh," Dani said. "Uncle—he shoots people."

Ervina hugged them both close. "Lucky for people he cain't hit a barn. You got no cause to worry, now you go on and help Miss Abbie with her board thing."

The crowd dispersed, and conversation broke out where it had left off. Abbie seemed to be the only one disconcerted by the talk of shooting.

"Down here it's not always easy to be a pacifist," Sarah said. "I'm going back to the kitchen to get these ladies to start making some lunch."

Ervina scooted the twins away and waited for everyone else to leave before she stood.

"Thank you so much for coming in to do that," Abbie said. "It means a lot to the twins."

"I have somethin' to say to you."

"Okay," Abbie said, taken aback.

"I came here and talked nonsense. Now you gonna do something for me."

Abbie smiled inwardly. Like great-grandmother like great-granddaughter. Sarah and Ervina didn't mind a spot of tit for tat.

"You came here lookin' for somethin'."

"I came here on vacation."

"Uh-huh. You came here lookin' for somethin' and you found it. You got these children trustin' you. You got a responsibility now."

Abbie shook her head. "I'm sorry?"

"You can't take those children out of Egypt and leave 'em alone in the desert."

"I don't understand."

"Don't be dense. You know what I'm sayin'."

"I don't."

"Then I'm gonna tell you." She moved in close, drawing Abbie toward her. "It's too late to help those dead babies where you were before. It's time to start helpin' the ones who can still be helped"

She walked slowly toward the door, stopped when she reached it. "And don't you worry none about Miss Millie. She'll come around."

"And you can bet the ranch on that," Sarah said under her breath.

Ervina shook her finger at her great-grandaughter, and then in typical Ervina fashion, she was gone.

Her words, however, lingered all the way into the afternoon when they were distracted by the sound of a big truck, stopping out front. Everyone rushed to the window.

The back tailgate was open, and several men were unloading huge wooden crates. Everyone converged on the porch, and it took Abbie and Sarah both to keep them from running to get a closer look.

"Someone go get the camera," Abbie said, grabbing Pauli as he tried to sneak down the steps. "I bet if we all stay right here and out of the way, we'll get a peek at what's inside once they've finished unloading."

They watched and filmed for the next hour. Then as the truck drove away, Cab came to the door of the carousel and yelled, "Who wants to see what just came?"

There was no holding them back now. They broke for the carousel, and Abbie, camera in hand, and Sarah ran behind them.

Rows of wooden crates stood end to end in the octagonal room. Several men stood ready with crowbars to open the nearest one. Otis and Jerome and two other men were standing by a ladder and a cherry picker.

"Now listen up," Cab said. "You have to stay behind this line." He made an imaginary line with his foot. "I don't want anybody getting hurt. Got it?"

Everyone nodded.

"I mean it, because this lady could squash you like a bug."

The children took an extra step back.

"Good. Okay, gentlemen, man your crowbars."

Abbie readied Joe and the camera, hiding her smile. The first time she'd met Cab, she thought he was a charming huckster. Now she *knew* he was. And a great showman. He'd missed his calling as the ringmaster of a circus, or some other fanciful profession.

The men leaned over the box with their crowbars. Nails screeched as they were pulled through wood, then the men lifted the top and laid it aside, revealing foam packing material, which they carefully removed.

Beneath it lay a mermaid with pale yellow hair that billowed about her face. Her tail was a vibrant green with gold leaf accents. Her body curved gracefully in an elongated ess.

The men lifted her out of the crate, and everyone gasped in delight. Abbie caught Cab's eye across the heads of the children. He smiled, she smiled, and everything else blurred for just a second.

Then Cab turned away and directed the men as they lifted the mermaid to her slot on the wall. Everyone cheered as she slid perfectly into the cradle that had been prepared for her. Then they just looked in awe at the beautiful creature who smiled down at them.

When Cab turned back to the group, his face was luminous. His eyes sparkled as if his dream had just come true. Abbie thought that it had.

"Madame Mermaid has been restored to her place of honor,"

he said, grinning at his visitors. "Now out you go." He flour-
ished a hand toward the double doors and winked at Abbie.

"Aw, Mr. Cab. We want to see the others."

"Yeah."

"Yeah."

"Just one?"

"The rest is a secret." Cab ushered them out the door and
locked it behind them. It stayed locked for the next ten days.

Chapter 28

Abbie didn't see Millie the next morning, and she wondered if Beau had been too optimistic about her coming around. But there were other things to be optimistic about.

The carousel and the new co-op were nearly finished. The sound of hammering and sawing rang in the air. There seemed to be an army of men on ladders, women sweeping, garbage bags piled on the sidewalk, waiting to be hauled over to the Dumpster that had appeared overnight.

Wanda's huge person was perched precariously on a stepladder, scrubbing the dirt-caked windows of the new co-op. And in the center of the tarmac, framed by a semicircle of men with paint cans, stood Ivy and Hadley nose to nose. Though Hadley had to stand on his toes to hold his own.

"I ain't gonna paint," Hadley told her.

"You are too, you old hunk a junk. You are not going to bring this end of town down after all the hard work everybody's put into it. If you ain't gonna help, then move yo' sorry backside outta the way, 'cause one way or the other, we're gonna paint."

"Oh, Ivy, leave the man alone," said one of the men.

Ivy fisted her hands on her hips. "Albertus Brown. You

better not let your wife hear you; you know she's been workin'
herself half to death gettin' her afghans finished for the grand
opening of the co-op."

Albertus sighed and slumped, but then he gave in. "Come
on, men, let's get it over with. Sorry, Hadley."

The men trudged past him while Hadley and Ivy glared at
each other. Abbie passed by without slowing down.

The kitchen was already crowded with the publicity committee, mostly older women and a few teenagers, who were tri-
folding announcements of the carousel opening to be mailed to
nearby towns.

The editing of the documentary was mostly done, so Abbie
organized the kids into cleaning squads. She kept busy but was
randomly hit with pangs of anxiety.

What if the video was a flop? What if the kids were disappointed? What if Millie stayed angry? Then she'd remember
what Beau said about what-ifs and tried to live in the moment.

But as the day wore on, Abbie's anxiety increased. She hadn't
seen Millie since Sunday afternoon and Beau since Sunday
night. She'd hardly talked to Marnie. She felt like an inter-
loper, and it was driving her crazy. It would be better just to
find out what was going on.

While the mothers served lunch, Abbie went to the
carousel—and found it padlocked, as if Cab and Beau had left
for the day. She listened for sounds coming from inside but
heard nothing.

A hell of a time to take off, she thought, and a hundred pos-
sibilities crowded her mind. Something had broken and they'd
gone for a new part. There was trouble with a zoning issue.
Millie had suffered a heart attack.

Each possibility grew worse, and she considered going to
Flora's to see if they had gone there for lunch, but a crash from
the media room blew that idea out of her mind. She rushed

back to the center and down the hall, wondering if they'd just lost an important piece of equipment, and praying it wasn't her laptop with Final Cut Pro installed on it.

She reached the door to the media room just in time to see Pauli and Kyle crawling out from under the folding table they used for drawing.

"The legs collapsed," Pauli said.

"'Cause you didn't listen."

"'Cause they ain't no good."

"As long as you weren't hurt," Abbie said, stepping between them. "Now help me put the table back."

When she left the center that night, she heard men working at the carousel. That must mean that whatever happened must have been dealt with. She didn't stop. Even though she wished Beau would go with her, she knew he had more important things to do. And since it was Marnie's night out, that left Abbie to face Millie on her own.

As she reached Crispin House, the front door swung open. Millie came out and blocked the door. Abbie's stomach went south.

She climbed the steps ready to face the music.

As she reached the top, Millie motioned to her with both hands. "There you are. I've been waiting."

"Not to worry, I'll pack now and be out in half an hour."

Millie gasped in an intake of air. "Leaving? What are you talking about? You'll do no such thing. We have too much to do for you to go gallivantin' about."

"What?"

Marnie stepped into the light and made a face over Millie's shoulder.

"Well, come on in," Millie said and took Abbie by the arm. "Time's a-wastin'."

Abbie only had time enough to glance at Marnie as she was propelled forward.

Marnie cast her eyes toward heaven and followed them across the foyer to the parlor.

Millie stopped at an escritoire covered with catalogs and paper of various sizes. "I know it's going to be a public day, but we need to send formal invitations to certain members of the community. I'm leaning toward the oyster shell myself. Marnie likes the blue. What is your opinion?"

"Uh, oyster?"

Millie shot a triumphant look at her sister. "Now I need to order the tablecloths tonight from the Party Rental place. Plastic, I'm afraid, but it can't be helped. Beau is insisting on having barbecue out on the lawn. And you know what barbecue does to linen.

"But the poor soul misses Silas's barbecue so much, I relented, but I told him in no uncertain terms that I would not have barbecue in my ballroom. I'll have Penny Farlowe do canapés for the ballroom."

"Very wise," Abbie said and cast another look toward Marnie, who was hovering at a safe distance in the archway and hiding what Abbie hoped was a grin beneath her hand.

Ballroom. Public day. Had Cab actually asked her to host the viewing? And she'd agreed?

"We'll put chairs and the projector at one end and still have enough room for people to socialize. Once your little movie is over, I'll get Otis and Jerome to remove the chairs to give us more room. Not everybody wants to sit elbow to elbow at picnic tables."

Abbie didn't know what to say. Except that she must be dreaming. So she just nodded in agreement. Marnie snorted from the doorway. Millie didn't seem to notice. Two days ago she had stood in the driveway demanding that Abbie leave. Now she was consulting her about tablecloths?

"I'm not sure I understand."

"Didn't Cabot tell you? Well, isn't that just like a man. He and Beau dropped by for lunch this afternoon. And he was telling me how you're cleaning up the community center to show your film.

"I told him not to be ridiculous. After all the work you've put in with those kids and the carousel, everybody would want to come and there just isn't any room down there."

Abbie nodded, though she bet Millie had never even been in the community center.

"I told him just to plan to have the festivities at Crispin House. Our family has always supported the endeavors of the community. This is no exception. Now, I'd better telephone to Myrtle Beach and order those tablecloths. I think a dozen of the large rectangular ones should suffice. You had better make a list of equipment and things you'll need and let Otis know so he can pick everything up."

She took her catalog and tottered into the hallway where the telephone sat in an alcove behind the staircase.

Marnie stepped aside and watched her go. "Damn, that was a sight."

"I'm having a little trouble processing all this. What are you doing here?"

"Hell, I called in sick tonight just to see your face when you encountered the new and improved Millie."

"Want to fill me in?"

"Sure, but come on back to the kitchen. I think we both need a glass of something stronger than sherry."

It was a sight to behold," Marnie said, over a double scotch. Abbie was sipping a white wine spritzer. She wanted to be on her toes in case the wind shifted.

Marnie burst out laughing. "A public day. I swear we've

never had a public day in our lives. I think she must have gotten it out of an old movie."

"I can't believe it. She acts like nothing ever happened."

"To her, nothing did. Thanks to Beau's painting and the buyer from Charleston."

"She accepted the money?"

"Never saw a genteel lady move so fast. Did he tell you he got paid a bundle?"

"He said it was enough to pay the taxes and give some to Millie for pin money."

"Which reminds me, I can pay you and Celeste back."

"Forget that for now. Tell me how it all happened."

Marnie poured herself another scotch.

"Beau calls this morning and tells me to tell Millie that he and Cab are coming for lunch. So I haul my butt up to her room and yell through the door. All I had to say was Cab was coming to lunch, and open sesame, she's brushing past me and headed for the kitchen.

"She called Wilson over at the market and had him deliver shrimp. I'm surprised he didn't keel over from surprise on the spot." She looked over the rim of her glass.

"So they get here, and Cab's slathering on the charm and Beau's looking shifty and I know something's up, so I just sit back and watch.

"We're on our way in to lunch, like it was Sunday, and I see Beau slip something into Millie's hand. Her eyes grow the size of salad plates, then she quietly slips it into her dress pocket.

"So they all sit down to lunch and I start serving. Thank God she didn't have time to get Ervina to come over. She would have sat down next to us and laughed herself silly to witness the goings-on in that room.

"Cab flirted outrageously, extolled the virtues of Millie's

shrimp gumbo, and told her how her abilities as a hostess were wasted. I swear that boy could sell snake oil. And then he asked if she would please host the first Annual Stargazey Carousel Picnic.

"She didn't have a chance. She'd agreed before she realized that it meant having a barbecue on the grounds and showing the video you and the children made in the ballroom. He made moon eyes at her until I thought I'd burst a gusset from trying not to laugh. He was incorrigible.

"Once he told her he'd pay for everything, there was no going back. Because then she got to say she wouldn't think of letting him pay, that the Crispins had always supported the 'endeavors of the community,' and she would be pleased to continue the tradition. Of course she has no idea how much things will cost, and I'll have to find a way to curtail her spending, but Cab will pick up whatever goes over budget."

"Everyone was planning to bring a dish," Abbie said. "I'm not sure if any of them know how to make canapés."

"No problem. We'll say that it is an evening honoring low-country cuisine."

"So has she forgiven me?"

"Forgiven you? You've made her dream come true. At least she sees it that way. You and Cab." Marnie laughed. "I won't even tell you what she said about you and Cab."

"Does it involve cute?"

"Something like that. Oh, don't look so abashed. She's already seeing the return of the Crispin dynasty and naming your children. Let her have her fun; it will end soon enough."

During the next week, Millie was a picture of industry. She consulted Abbie whenever they passed each other, called her cell when she was working, asked her opinion on everything, and posed the same questions at least twenty times apiece.

Hadley's store had a coat of paint, and Hadley had been heard to say he didn't know how he'd let things go so long. He was seen every day wearing a not-quite-clean butcher's apron, washing and scrubbing and throwing out cans of food that had probably expired years before.

Women filed in and out of the new co-op, and, inside, the shelves filled with handcrafted gifts. A sign arrived and was hung across the front. Green letters spelled out SWEETGRASS.

Posters appeared on telephone poles, old billboards, the sides of abandoned buildings, and in store windows from Myrtle Beach to Savannah. It seemed that the inhabitants of Stargazey Point had friends and relatives everywhere.

The YouTube video Abbie posted had over a thousand hits the first week. Articles appeared in the local papers, in weekend circulars. Abbie, Sarah, Cab, and whoever they could corral who had access to the Internet posted on Facebook, tweeted, and left comments on the colorful website Jerome had designed.

Businesses throughout town opened full-time, and the inn served nightly dinners.

Abbie hardly ever saw Cab, and the carousel remained locked.

"What do you think they're doing in there?" Abbie wondered as she and Sarah sat on the front porch, drinking iced tea.

"Same thing they've been doing for the last week. Hammering and hollering and Cab shouting orders day in and day out." The blare of calliope music rent the air. Sarah clapped her free hand to her ear. The music warbled and fell silent.

They both grimaced.

"I sure as hell hope he gets that thing to work," Sarah said.

"He will," Abbie said and mentally crossed her fingers.

Everyone worked overtime. At Crispin House, preparations were in full swing for the barbecue and video showing. Beau paid Jerome to mow the grass and, along with his cash, handed him a letter that had come in the mail that day. He'd been accepted to Virginia Tech with a full scholarship.

There was an impromptu celebration on the newly mown lawn.

Friday came. Abbie awoke to the sweet smell of hickory smoke wafting through her windows. She went out to the veranda. Silas was already cooking, a long white apron tied over his coveralls, a red bandanna tied around his head. He waved a pair of tongs at her as he moved up and down the elongated grill like a marimba player.

The day was sunny, already hot. It would be a scorcher, but there was a breeze from the ocean down on the lawn. The ballroom might get a little uncomfortable, but Abbie was hoping the subject matter would keep everyone enthralled for the twenty minutes it took to show the video.

After much deliberation, she dressed in a boatneck sundress and sandals and went downstairs in a welter of emotions. Butterflies, excitement, and a bit of trepidation. It occurred to her that instead of taking a week's vacation, she'd spent almost two months here.

Inside the ballroom, Otis and Sarah were setting up video equipment. A cadre of men arranged folding chairs in rows facing a large video screen that someone borrowed from the community college. Everywhere women and teenagers swarmed about, dusting, polishing, and sweeping while Millie, looking very much like the lady of the manor, directed the activities.

"This is beautiful," Abbie told her.

"Isn't it? And this is the way it should be seen."

"Thanks again, Millie. Cab has worked so hard to get the carousel back to its former glory and the kids, too, documenting it."

"Our family has always supported the endeavors of our community. It's our duty and our pleasure."

Spoken like a true grande dame, Abbie thought.

"And besides," Millie added, her eyes twinkling, "now Sister will have no excuse not to have a big party for Beau's birthday. And you'll never believe . . . Bethanne brought Mary Lou Henderson by earlier this mornin'. Her daughter's getting married in the spring and when she saw the gazebo and the ballroom, she just begged me to let them have the weddin' here. I just didn't have the heart to say no."

"And that's okay with you?" Abbie couldn't imagine how Bethanne had pulled that off.

"Why, of course. The Henderson family has been friends with our family for generations. I was happy to oblige. Especially now that I have a little pocket money to spruce things up a bit." She smiled happily. "I'm so glad I didn't let Marnie sell off all the silver like she wanted."

Revisionist history had found a home with Millie.

"And the most wonderful thing. Celeste called to say she's coming down at the end of summer. We're just delighted. Excuse me." Millie floated away. "Ivy, that epergne ought to go over there on the round table."

Stabbed by an unexpected but familiar pang of wistfulness, Abbie wandered out to the patio where another group was busy setting tables and carrying trays of food. She was still an outsider. Of course she was.

Everyone had pulled together to make this all happen. They'd worked all spring for this night. For their town. For their future. And suddenly it was moving too fast, and Abbie wasn't ready for it to be over.

After this weekend, they would settle back into their lives and all move forward together. A community. But where would that leave her?

Millie had once said that Beau and Marnie were home at last, where they belonged. Everyone should have somewhere they belonged.

Abbie had had a wonderful time here, come to love the people, but did she belong? How did you know when to settle down? For her parents, it had never happened and she doubted that they would ever retire to one place. They were happy traveling. They had each other.

Home is where the heart is might work fine for her parents, but Abbie wanted a stationary home—brick and mortar, clapboard, hell, it didn't matter. She wanted a zip code where her mail would come. Have it delivered to her own mailbox and actually be there to receive it.

And the same friends year after year. She could imagine herself growing old, drinking lattes at Penny's, maybe letting things with Cab take their course, grow into love or settle into a platonic friendship, best friends. She could make new friends, document Ervina's life.

She touched her nautical star. Beau promised it would lead her home, but to where? For the first time in weeks, panic seized her and didn't let go.

People began to arrive a little after four: kids, parents, grandparents, friends, townspeople, summer people with their children, who played freely with the kids from the center, people staying at the inn, even a few people who had heard about the weekend and had driven in from other towns.

Some wandered down to the beach, others *oohed* and *aah*ed over the ballroom. Old friends reconnected. The mood was festive. Millie presided over it all, and wherever Millie was, Bethanne was nearby. They were both very pleased with themselves.

The only ones who weren't happy were Joe and Dani.

They both had been groomed and cleaned until they practically sparkled. Ervina, dressed in an even more elaborate attire than what she'd worn for the interview, held each one by the hand.

"Hey, what's the matter?" Abbie asked. "Your film is about to have its world' premiere."

Normally this would have sent them into giggles, but tonight they just nodded together and sighed as if they were one person.

Abbie looked at Ervina for an answer.

"Their auntie is back from Afghanistan and she's offered to take them in permanently."

"Don't wanna go," Joe said. "She be like uncle."

"Mr. Know-It-All don't know nothin'." Ervina gave him a gentle shake. "Ervina talked to her and she sounds real nice," she said to Abbie. "Their mother's sister. She's been overseas for the last few years. Had no idea of the situation here." Ervina pulled Joe close. "She's got a nice place, and I wouldn't be surprised if you gonna get a dog."

"Uncle beated our dog and it ran away."

Ervina sighed. "Didn't Ervina tell you she ain't never gonna give you up to somebody who don't love you good? You just wait and see."

"I'm sure she'll be nice," Abbie said, hoping that was true.

"We wanna stay here," Joe said and buried his head in Ervina's long skirt.

The lights flickered on the veranda, and everyone made their way to the ballroom.

"It's time. Come on, you two, and help me introduce our video."

She hurried them inside.

When everyone finally took their seats or found a place to stand at the back, Millie, who was dressed in an extravagant hostess gown, walked slowly to the front of the room. "Good evenin'. My family is so happy to be able to welcome you to-night for this lovely movie. And after the film we invite you to join us in the garden for some of Silas Cook's famous bar-becue."

She nodded at Abbie who stepped forward and thanked her for her support and gracious invitation. Millie smiled and nodded and was escorted to the center of the front row by the mayor himself.

Abbie introduced all the children who had worked on the film and announced the premiere of *Stargazey Carousel—An Oral History*.

"As with any film, we had way more material than we had time for. Additional pictures and the full interviews can be seen at StargazeyCarousel.com. And now . . . lights, please."

The lights went out. There was some hooting and squealing. Carousel music filled the air, the screen lit up; the title grew to fill the space, which earned some applause and more noise from the kids. After that, no one said a word. Bits of carousel shots were interspersed with snippets of the interviews. Some of the shots were a little wobbly and there was some good-natured gibing among the children, but the wobbles only made it more endearing.

When Momo's face came on the screen, Jenny shouted out, "That's my gramma!"

After that, each kid identified his or her parent with a shout.

The film culminated with the mermaid being taken out of the crate and hung on the wall and Ervina saying "Come to the Stargazey carousel," making the invitation sound like a divine summons.

The video was a success, and everyone applauded enthusi-astically as Abbie had each child and interviewee stand. When Joe and Dani stood with Ervina, people jumped to their feet.

And there's one more person who we owe a special thanks to," Abbie said.

"Mr. Cab," Pauli shouted.

"That's right," Hadley called out. "He brought this town back."

"Amen."

"Mr. Cab," the children squealed.

Whistles from Jerome and Otis. A fist pump from Sarah and a grin wide enough to light the room. And Abbie knew in that moment that Sarah would never desert the Point. She talked a big game, but her roots, her love, were tied to the people here.

"We owe it all to Cab Reynolds."

"Here, here."

"Here's to young Cab."

Applause broke out again. Cab appeared from the back of the room and took a bow straight out of the circus. He straightened up, and his eyes met Abbie's.

"To Mr. Cab," Abbie said.

Chairs scraped, fabric rustled, and Cab and Abbie were surrounded by people hugging, pumping hands, slapping backs. Gradually people moved out of doors, and Cab and Abbie were left alone.

"Big night. Congratulations," said Cab. He looked tired. His cheeks were hollow, and his eyes were bruised from lack of sleep, but he looked happy.

"Same to you. It was a little rough around the edges but ready to be seen by friends and family and a few sympathetic visitors. How about you? Ready for tomorrow?"

He smiled mysteriously. "It's going okay."

"I hope it's going better than okay. Everyone is expecting a ride tomorrow."

He grinned. "Including you?"

"Absolutely including me."

"Then why wait?"

"You're going to open the carousel tonight?"

"No. But I'm considering giving you a sneak preview."

"Now?"

"Why not? Everybody is stuffing their faces with barbecue and homemade lemonade. They won't miss us for a while."

"Okay. Let me just tell someone I'm leaving."

"There's Beau and Ervina coming across the lawn. We'll tell them." He took her hand and pulled her outside. "I'm taking Abbie for a ride on the carousel. We'll be back."

"Take your time," Beau said.

"Do you want to come?" Abbie asked. "After all, you were a big part of the restoration."

Beau smiled. "No, thank you. I have something I want to show Ervina upstairs."

Cab took Abbie's hand. "All right. See you later. Save us some barbecue."

"Cabot?"

"Yeah, Beau?"

"I'd take her to sit under Neptune's tail if I were you." He smiled, his shock of white hair riding tall over his forehead, then he and Ervina walked into the house. Moses shot out of the shrubbery and raced after them.

"I wonder what Beau's going to show her?"

Abbie thought she knew, but it wasn't her business to speculate. "What was that about Neptune's tail?"

I know I'm taking a chance here," Cab said as he unlocked the door to the carousel. "But close your eyes."

"I won't run, promise," she said, blushing slightly as she remembered her first reaction to Midnight Lady. She'd grown to love the carousel over the last few weeks.

He guided her through the door and stopped there. She could smell the fresh paint, but the room was completely dark.

"Don't peek."

"I won't." She put her hands over her eyes to seal the deal.

She felt him move away. She didn't peek. She knew what to expect this time around and she was excited. She heard the click of the lights. Spots danced on the inside of her lids, their heat wrapped around her.

A bell rang. *Ding.* It rang again. *Ding. Ding.*

The calliope music startled her.

"Open them." Cab was standing beside her again.

She opened her eyes, but she couldn't take it all in. Couldn't move, couldn't speak as the most magnificent cavalcade circled before her. It was amazing.

"Come on," Cab yelled over the music. He grabbed her hand, pulled her toward the carousel, and together they jumped to the platform as it whirled past them.

They stood there, feet braced, holding hands as the walls of the building whirred past in a blur of yellow, red, green, and blue.

She turned to look at him. He was smiling; proud, exultant, king of the mountain. Peter Pan, he might be, but he was also warm, generous, passionate, someone you could count on. And standing there with the lights swirling about them, she knew that she loved him. She loved him. No sadness, no guilt, no regret overwhelmed her, just the warm colorful lights, the rousing music, and Cab.

"Look where we're standing."

She looked around. "Where?"

He gestured to a chariot: Neptune, the sea god's face on the prow, his cheeks puffed out as he blew up an ocean storm. And behind the chariot his curved green tail formed a canopy over a red bench. A ride for the less adventurous, the old, the young; a ride for lovers.

She climbed in and Cab climbed in after her.

The chariot scooped them up, and they fell laughing onto the seat. Lights whirled past them in streaks of color; the tinny calliope music surrounded them, released after a decade of silence, to fill the air with a tune that seemed to sing, free at last, free at last.

Cab's arm stretched across the back of the seat; Abbie relaxed against the cushion. The mighty Neptune led the way, trident in the air. The fanciful tail of a mythological sea creature curved over their heads, creating a private cocoon where lovers sat close, made plans, and spoke secrets that no one else could hear. No wonder this had been the favorite ride for lovers, young and old.

Abbie looked over at Cab, strong and warm beside her. He was smiling, happy, triumphant, but he was looking at her. She sighed and didn't move away when his arm slid down the seat back to her shoulders.

The lights blurred, the music faded; Abbie settled close to her companion and wondered if this was like being home.

Chapter 29

The sun was bright, the day was warm, and the parking lot was beginning to fill up with people. There was still an hour before the carousel opened for business, but Abbie was too excited to wait for the three Crispins.

It was just like being a kid, she thought, as she waved to Hadley, who stood on the front porch of his store, broom in hand and tossing candy to everyone who passed by.

People wandered up and down the main street carrying cardboard cups of coffee compliments of Flora's Tea Shoppe and sampling Penny's miniature icebox cookies. A couple stopped to look at the painting in the Gaillard Gallery window. A trio of women emerged from Sweetgrass carrying colorful shopping bags.

Abbie made her way to the center, past a table with bags of pink and blue cotton candy, a cart roasting peanuts, a lemonade stand, sodas chilling in big tubs of ice, and on the grass verge at the pier's entrance, an impromptu farmers' market.

The carousel was still closed, but Otis and Jerome and several other men were in position to raise the new storm windows to reveal the restored carousel.

Abbie climbed the steps to the community center and slipped

inside. Almost everyone was there, ready to go en masse to the carousel. They were a motley crew, tall and short, skinny and chubby, dark and light, girl and boy.

"Would you look at the little angels," Sarah said. "It won't last, but it's nice to dream."

"Oh, come on," Abbie said. "They hardly use their fists instead of words anymore." She thought about it. "Well, not as much. And definitely less head cuffing."

A crowd was gathering around the carousel. The door to the center opened, and Jerome stuck his head in the door. "Y'all ready?"

"Ready when you are," Abbie told him.

All the kids made a beeline for the door and crowded around Jerome.

"Hey, let's have a little order here."

After a mad second of changing places, they managed to put themselves into two relatively straight lines.

"All right. Heads up, stomachs in—"

"Aw, we don't have no stomachs, Jerome."

"Joe does."

Joe grinned and arched back to show his nonexistent tummy.

"Then here we go." Jerome opened the door, calliope music filled the air. The children marched down the steps to the carousel, and a thrill ran through Abbie.

"Come on, I'm not missing The Third's grand gesture." Sarah followed the children out.

"I wouldn't miss it for the world," Abbie said and shut the door behind them.

The crowd parted to make a lane for the little parade, then closed in behind them to surround the carousel. Just inside the entrance, the kids broke rank and ran to choose a figure to ride. Jerome and some of the older kids helped the little ones up and buckled them in.

When they were all seated, Cab clanged the bell. *Ding*. The platform jerked.

Abbie held her breath.

He clanged the bell again. *Ding. Ding.* The carousel began to turn. With a shrug, Jerome jumped on Midnight Lady's back, his grin wide, and Abbie wondered if he, like Cab, was riding over the beach to parts unknown—to his future.

She looked over to Cab, who looked so happy that it almost hurt her to watch. And the carousel turned. Horses, Neptune, the lion, the sea horse passed before her in a swirling cavalcade.

When the ride was over, the children tumbled off and were swallowed up by their friends and family while others took their places.

Cab turned the running of the carousel over to Otis and came to meet Abbie.

"Your assistant?" she asked.

"For a while. He's underemployed, and I need to get some paying employment, myself, so I can afford this thing."

They walked through the crowd, stopping for Cab to be congratulated again and again. They stopped for lemonade.

"Think we can get away for a nice quiet dinner tonight?" he asked.

"That sounds good, but we better play it by ear. Now that all these people are here, it might be hard to get them to leave."

"That's another reason I hired an assistant."

"Miss Abbie! Miss Abbie!" Ahead, Dani and Joe were running toward her, pulling a woman between them. It wasn't Ervina. She was tall and young with her hair pulled severely back in a bun at the nape of her neck. And though she wasn't in uniform, her carriage alone told Abbie this had to be their auntie who was taking them away.

Her throat caught. She'd miss them. Of course, she might be going away soon, too.

"Miss Abbie, Miss Abbie." Dani and Joe stopped in front of her, their faces smeared with ketchup, mustard, and cotton candy.

"We don't have to go away," Dani said.

"We're going to her 'partment to pack her things and then we all three gonna live here. In a nice house."

"Auntie says we can still come to the center when school starts."

"That's wonderful," Abbie told them, then took the hand their aunt offered her.

"My name's Lisa. Their mama is my sister. I had no idea how things were. I've been on my second tour of duty. I just got back two weeks ago, so I have some things to settle. But I'll be looking for a place here where we all can live. They love the center so much, I don't have the heart to uproot them. They've had it hard enough as it is."

"What are we gonna do next, Miss Abbie?"

"What are we gonna do next, Miz Abbie?"

Lisa laughed. "It'll take some getting used to having everything in stereo."

Kyle popped up behind them. "What story are we gonna tell next?" And suddenly she and Cab were surrounded by children, all wanting to know what the next project was going to be.

Sarah was standing a bit off. She shrugged as if to say, *Don't look at me.*

But it didn't matter. They were expecting her to stay, Abbie realized. It hadn't entered their minds that she, too, would be leaving when Sarah did and someone else would take over the center. Someone appointed by the county or the state most likely.

"Can I use the digit camera first?" Joe asked. He tugged on her shorts. "Can I? Can I be first?"

She looked down at them and couldn't speak. Marnie and Millie had offered her free room and board. Bethanne needed help with her new wedding venture. Beau didn't say much, but she knew he would be happy to have her. He'd made her the nautical star.

"Yeah, what are we gonna do next?" asked a much deeper voice. Cab came to stand by her side. "I think we might have a story to tell."

They all wanted her to stay. Hell, she wanted to stay. She looked out at the festivities, beyond them to the pier where Beau was probably carving another mysterious figure. And beyond to the brilliant sea.

There was a whole world out there waiting. But not for her. She knew she couldn't change the world; she didn't want to. But she did want to make her little bit of it an okay place to live.

She touched her nautical star. She'd been home these last two months and she hadn't even realized it. She had found her way home.

She looked at Cab and smiled down at the children surrounding her. "Well, let's see, what kind of story would you like to tell?"

BOOKS BY SHELLEY NOBLE

STARGAZEY POINT
A Novel

Available in Paperback and eBook

Devastated by tragedy during her last project, documentarian Abbie Sinclair seeks refuge with three octogenarian siblings, who live in edge-of-the-world Stargazey Point. Once a popular South Carolina family beach resort, the beaches have eroded, businesses have closed, and skyrocketing taxes are driving the locals away. Stargazey Point, like Abbie Sinclair, is fighting to survive. Abbie thinks she has nothing left to give, but slowly she's drawn into the lives of the people around her: the Crispin siblings, each with his or her own secret fear; Cab Reynolds, who left his work as an industrial architect to refurbish his uncle's antique carousel in hopes of breathing new life into his childhood sanctuary; Ervina, an old Gullah wisewoman, who can guide Abbie to a new life and her true self, if only she'd let her; and a motley crew of children whom Abbie can't ignore.

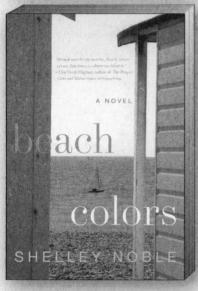

BEACH COLORS
A Novel

Available in Paperback and eBook

While renowned designer Margaux Sullivan was presenting her highly praised collection during New York City's Fashion Week, her husband was cleaning out their bank account. Suddenly broke, betrayed, and humiliated, Margaux has nowhere else to turn to but home: the small coastal town of Crescent Cove, Connecticut, where she once knew love, joy, and family before she put them behind her on the climb to fame. When she's stopped for speeding by local interim police chief Nick Prescott, Margaux barely remembers the "townie" boy who worshipped her from afar every summer. But Nick is all grown up now, a college professor who gave up his career to care for his orphaned nephew, Connor. Though still vulnerable, Margaux is soon rediscovering the beauty of the shore through young Connor's eyes . . . and, thanks to Nick, finding a forgotten place in her heart that wants to love again.

Visit HarperCollins.com for more information about your favorite HarperCollins books and authors.

Available wherever books are sold.